Cynthia [illegible] Mid-Glamorg[illegible] nd in Porthcaw[illegible] provides the setting fo[illegible] novels. She has been a teacher and a journalist, contributing articles to a variety of magazines and newspapers and also interviews for radio. She is at present working on a new novel.

Also by Cynthia S. Roberts

The Running Tide
Upon Stormy Downs
A Wind From the Sea

A Seagull Crying

Cynthia S. Roberts

KNIGHT

First published in 1989
by HEADLINE BOOK PUBLISHING PLC

First published in paperback in 1990
by HEADLINE BOOK PUBLISHING PLC

This edition published 2000 by
Knight an imprint of Caxton Publishing Group

10 9 8 7 6 5 4 3 2 1

ISBN 1 84067 267 6

Typeset by
Colset Private Limited, Singapore

Printed and bound in Great Britain by
J. H. Haynes & Co. Ltd., Sparkford, Somerset

Caxton Publishing Group
20 Bloomsbury Street
London
WC1B 3QA

To my dear aunts,
Adele, Ceinwen, Emma, Mary, Peggy and Stella,
with deep affection.

Chapter One

Spring came unexpectedly to the shores of Wales. The sun grew suddenly warm. Throughout the long winter, it had been pale and without heat, as if it, too, had been cased in ice, with rivers, ponds and frozen earth.

Now, with the melting of the snows, came a resurgence of life, a quickening of blood and sap. Trees were downy with buds, as softly furred as the animals which stirred within their hollow depths. In the high branches, nesting birds scolded with shrill voices, or sang with such fragile sweetness that their spun-glass notes seemed to quiver and splinter upon the air.

Joe Priday, pierced by some shard of memory, paused in his labours at the anvil of his small forge, the steady clanging of iron upon iron slowly dying. Hearing the thrush's fluid song, so haunting in its purity, he felt such a violence of pain for what was over and lost that, for a moment, he was unable to continue. Tasting the saltiness of sweat crusting his lips, he wiped a leathery palm across his mouth.

It was just such a spring when his wife had first come to him, and now all that remained of that warm and loving flesh he had shared was his daughter, Ruth. Seventeen years on, and it seemed but yesterday. Priday's dark eyes grew blurred from the sweat which ran down the springing black curls at his hairline, splashing in droplets from nose and jaw. He sniffed, shaking his head irritably to rid himself of them, hearing them hiss and spit upon the white-hot metal he worked.

For all his forty years and more, Joe Priday was a fine figure of a man, handsome and well-muscled through toil, flesh stretched firm upon his massive frame. There were few men who would have chosen to offend him, and those either strangers or fools, although, like many another of his kind, he was a gentle-natured soul. If there was a darker, more violent, side to his nature, then none had ever seen it. Perhaps it had been subdued, and shaped as carefully as the iron he so skilfully wrought, or, like Priday himself, had been hammered and cooled by circumstance. Yet those who knew him best were aware of some restless energy trapped within him, but lying dormant like the spent ashes of a fire, seemingly quiescent and without life until a raked ember burns bright with unexpected flame, swift and devouring.

Priday shouted to his apprentice to 'Look to the fire!' The boy obediently raised the mighty bellows of leather and wood, crying out involuntarily with the effort of prising the handles apart, then forcing them together again. As he pumped, his breath was expelled, rhythmic and fierce, as if the bellows sucked air, not from the humid smithy, but from his own raw lungs. The apprentice's face glowed, warm and incandescent as the fire, as Priday plunged the hot iron into water, hearing it sizzle, then send up a veil of vapour to hang suspended.

The lad, who was some twelve or thirteen years of age, watched with open admiration, the contours of his young face childishly unformed yet giving firm promise of the man he would one day become. His gaze set fast upon Priday's face, moved to the blacksmith's dexterous hands, his expression so filled with eager devotion and vicarious pride that the smith could not resist a smile. Priday was put, so absurdly, in mind of a puppy, trembling hopefully for a pat or kind word from its master, that his good humour was immediately restored. Smiling and indulgent, he allowed the apprentice to take over his task, which the boy did with joyful alacrity.

Priday, glancing out from the small stone smithy with its roof of turf, its open front screened by the gates of scrolled iron he had fashioned, saw his daughter, Ruth, passing upon the narrow, dusty way, and his face softened to tenderness. He could hardly, even now, believe that this child was truly his, and not some changeling, so gentle and ethereal was her beauty.

She was, he thought, all sunshine and light, like springtime itself, as young, and filled with the innocence and wonder of growing things. She set him in mind of lambs, and wild daffodils, and the soft yellow downiness of newly hatched chicks. Oh, but she was such a sweet and gentle thing, filled with compassion and tenderness, and loved by all. A glowing, golden girl. His throat was thickened with pride and love as he acknowledged the swift smile and wave of her hand as she led her small donkey to the great pool, fondling its soft ears, soothing and coaxing it over the rough stones of the track. His Ruth was more than a memory of what was past, she was a promise of happiness present, and to come. She was all of his life.

He turned abruptly to the apprentice, labouring at the anvil, his blows striking upon the metal with the clean resonant lightness of a bell.

'Well done, Tim, my boy!' he praised warmly.

The boy's face, already polished red as a burn from heat and exertion, glowed brighter than the fire with happiness. It was spring. The sun shone. There was nothing in all the world he would have exchanged for that one rare moment in a perfect day.

* * *

Joshua Stradling, the young parish constable to the three small hamlets of Newton, Nottage and Port, was feeling equally euphoric as he rode his splendid grey mare from the courthouse at Pyle. Upon the instruction of the justice, Robert Knight, he had been seeking information in that dusty crypt below the courthouse which held the brittle remains of long-dead cases. The work had proved tedious and unrewarding, and he had been glad to emerge from its depressing dullness into the clear sunlight of a spring day.

Vestiges of snow still clung upon the softly enfolding hills about, and lay drifted against tussocks of coarse grass and dry-stone walls. Elsewhere upon the way its crispness had been eaten into holes by the sun's heat, distance lending them the curiously blind and vacant look of empty sockets. Nearer, beneath the mare's hooves, the quickly melting snow was already an oleaginous, brown mess, muddied and cold, its spray flung in icy droplets darkening the mare's forelegs and breast. She was a high-bred, arrogant creature, with her gleaming hide, arched neck and graceful delicacy of movement; a sight to gladden the most jaundiced eyes. There was no doubting that she complemented her rider perfectly, for he shared that same unselfconscious elegance, the natural arrogance of those who need not strive to make impression upon others, secure in their acceptance of life, and themselves. There was a unity between rider and mount, a shared rhythm of movement and understanding, intuitive and complete.

Joshua Stradling, despite his mere two and twenty years, possessed a quality of calm authority, reinforced by his strength and stature. He was a little over six feet three inches in height, strong-boned and broad-shouldered, most splendidly arrayed in his constable's uniform and the singularly impressive helmet, designed by the parish vestrymen. His corn-coloured hair grew thickly beneath it, and his blue eyes were keenly observant in the clean-featured face, his fairness of skin stirred to warmth and colour by exposure to wind and weather.

There were many young gentlewomen within the three hamlets and, indeed, in the Vale of Glamorgan beyond, whose innocent dreams were invaded and made captive by his presence. There were others, too, of humbler, more earthy, stock, whose imaginings were distinctly less idealistic and more carnal. Their minds were set upon 'bundling', that curious courtship ritual of being stitched ceremoniously into a chastity bag before sharing the bed of a suitor. Whether it was a test of abstinence and will power, or merely of ingenuity, none could say. It was an old custom, and amongst the poorer classes a common prelude to wedding. Yet, if Joshua was aware of the yearnings of his admirers, whether tender or lascivious, he gave neither encouragement nor sign. His affection was for Rebecca de Breos of Southerndown Court, whom he had loved as cocklemaid and, now, as heiress to Sir Matthew de Breos. She had always been to him a woman of quality, and would remain so, whatever her situation in life. It was of Rebecca, with her vivid, dark beauty and intelligent, blue eyes, that he was thinking now as he rode homewards towards his cottage in Newton village. The pleasure of their betrothal was warm within him, and the possibility of their wedding in the summer of the year.

Joshua's world was filled with such bright happiness that he sometimes felt, superstitiously, that it was too perfect a joy to last, that some payment must be exacted, some debt to God or fate, crippling in its sacrifice; even, perhaps, death itself. He knew that his friend and former tutor Dr Peate would have cast scorn upon both him and the idea, declaring that such puerile nonsense was the province of conjurors and their credulous followers, not God-fearing folk. It was but the primitive fear of the pagan, naught but superstition and cant, owing nothing to belief and intellect.

Joshua, approaching the tiny, stone-built church of St Mary Magdalene at Maudlam with its squat embattlemented tower, felt a sense of calmness steal over him, as surely as if he had entered within. It was so solid and serene a place, its old stone permeated, perhaps, by the devotions of those who had gone before; a small bright beacon of faith, set high upon an eminence, and below, the wind-drifted dunes, mile upon mile, flowing in golden waves as restless and changing as the ocean beyond. Held fast in the pale softness of sand lay the pellucid, blue waters of Kenfig Pool, a sapphire set into gold, taking its depth of colour from the sky above, the sun shimmering now across its surface, touching it with points of light reflected in the darker waters of the sea beyond.

The cry that broke the silence was savage and wild, more animal than human. Some creature caught in a trap, Joshua wondered uneasily, or the eerie call of the curlew, possessed by the restless soul of one drowned? The mare stumbled and would have halted, ears pricked back in terror, eyes wild, but Joshua, with a firm rein and reassuring word, steadied her. Again the cry came, desolate, and filled with such an agony of despair that Joshua felt the soft hairs at the nape of his neck prickling and rising in alarm as urgent as the mare's. Yet, at once, he set her resolutely upon the nearest track through the dunes and towards the sound. The going was hard and progress slow, for the mare's hooves could get no purchase upon the fine sand, sinking in its shifting grains, scarce able to breast its awkward slopes.

A SEAGULL CRYING

Upon the peak of the highest dune, bounded by tufted spears of marram grass, Joshua gazed over ridge upon ridge of smaller dunes, and to the gullies and grassy plains between. It was then that he saw with concern a dwarfed, unrecognisable figure, struggling along a path through a cleft in the dunes. It stumbled and wove its way, seemingly without purpose or direction. Someone sick, perhaps, or bearing some burden; he could not be sure, for distance defeated him. He turned the grey towards the lone figure, feeling bewildered and strangely apprehensive. For a time other sandhills obscured it from view, and then, suddenly, unexpectedly, Joshua was on the pathway behind it, calling out urgently.

The figure stopped and turned, disturbed by his cry, and Joshua was, for a moment, unable to summon his senses to rein the mare forward, so strangely terrifying was the scene. The man's face was twisted with such anguish that it was scarce recognisable as human. There was a wild despair about him, and although he had turned, Joshua could not be sure that the man was aware of his presence. In his broad arms the man clutched an obscene bundle of bloodied rags, filthy and sand-smeared. It was only when Joshua had leapt from the saddle and stood face to face with him that he saw, with sickness and horror, that what the man held was the body of a girl, face bludgeoned so viciously that no features were discernible, recognisable as mortal only by the naked flesh of one awkwardly splayed arm. Joshua could not tell whether she lived, yet the very lifelessness of her limp body and the unnatural twist of her neck told him that she did not. Pitiful and frail as she was, cradled in the man's thick, brawny arms, she was not as pitiful as he. His strong-boned face seemed to have dissolved and grown forlorn in grief, the tears coursing silent and unchecked from eyes dark with bewilderment.

Joshua moved towards him gently, hands extended to relieve him of his burden, but the man instinctively moved back, closing his arms more protectively about her, stroking the fall of pale hair, matted and crusted with a darkness of blood.

'No!' His voice rang out, raw with anguish. 'No! None shall touch her, save me!'

There was a wildness in the man's eyes and manner which frightened Joshua, for he realised that shock and hurt had all but crazed him.

'Please,' Joshua's voice was calm, but filled with real compassion, 'I beg you, sir, to let me see if she lives. I would bring help for her, a doctor, to tend her wounds.'

The man looked at him, unseeing, and Joshua thought he had not understood, for he pressed his face hard to the girl's bloodied bodice, rocking her helplessly, crying aloud in his grief. Yet, as Joshua touched a hand upon his arm, he nodded, and thrust her towards him. Joshua, seeing for the first time the cruelty of the injuries inflicted upon her, and her youth and frailness, felt the surge of sickness rise to his throat, sour as gall, but forced himself to reach out and feel for the pulses at her neck and wrists. Her flesh was clammy and icily cold, and when he removed his hands, it was to see them reddened with the stickiness of her blood, but, by an effort of will, he neither recoiled nor changed expression, saying evenly, 'I think, sir, that there is, perhaps, some vestige of life, some trace.'

In truth, he had felt no pulse, and believed her already dead, but could not take upon himself the burden of this stranger's grief, nor rob him of hope, fearful for his sanity.

'She is your child, sir? Some other member of your family?' he probed, with little stomach for his task.

'Ruth, my . . .' The words caught and thickened in his

throat, and he shook his head helplessly, unable to speak further.

'If you will let me hold her, sir, for a moment only,' Joshua urged, 'until you climb upon my mare?'

The man looked at him confusedly, not seeming to comprehend.

'I will lift her into your arms,' explained Joshua quietly, 'that you may let her rest against you, to give her comfort and support. Then I will lead the mare homeward. It will be quicker and less painful so.'

The man looked hard into Joshua's eyes, as if seeking some reassurance of what he should do. Then, silently, he relinquished her to the constable's gently outstretched arms and swung himself into the saddle upon the grey. Almost at once, a sigh escaped him and a tremor seized his whole body, as if possessed of some fierce ague, his jaw clenched tight, limbs held rigid as he strove to subdue it, to bring it 'neath control.

The mare fidgeted restlessly, feeling the tremors invading her own limbs, and looked to Joshua for aid, but he could offer her none, for his arms were held fast about the girl. When it seemed certain that the terrified mare would rear up or bolt, Joshua's firm commands and quietly reassuring tone soothed her, and she subsided, calm but still trembling as her rider, too, curbed his inner terrors and grew stilled. His broad face was ravaged by unbearable hurt, but there was no longer a wildness in his gaze, simply an exhausted realisation of what had occurred. The horror which had come upon him and his child acknowledged, living must begin again. He held out his arms to take her, cradling her now with tenderness and compassion, once more Ruth's comforter, as of old.

Joshua took the mare's reins and, slowly and steadily, drew her upon the sandy way, feeling an ache in his soul for the now quiet, bewildered man, his shirt front and worn leather apron, with the exposed flesh of his face and arms, as reddened with blood as if his own wounds wept as rawly as those of the girl pressed to him.

'Where, sir, must I lead the mare?' Joshua's voice sounded thin and unnatural in his own ears as he eased the grey carefully up the shifting sands of the dune, concentration and effort burning in every muscle, stiffening him with pain. 'I do not know from whence you come,' he confessed, 'or where you would return.'

Joe Priday raised his head swiftly, the tenderness with which he had watched over Ruth still softening his dark eyes.

'To Maudlam, sir.' His tone was firmer, more confident. 'It is our home, Ruth would wish it so. There are friends who will care for her with love, you understand? Whatever befalls.'

Was it an acknowledgement, Joshua wondered, that her return might be in death?

'I understand,' he said, seeing above them now the small church with its crenellated tower and softly encircling walls, comforting and secure as the strong arms which already held Ruth. But he would never understand the violence and tragedy of life and death, their nearness, one to the other. The swift ending of joy in sorrow, as now.

Silently he led the grey with her burden along the small stony track to the hamlet. Hearing the sound of the mare's hoofbeats, Priday's apprentice came hurrying on to the wayside beside the forge, tongs clutched in hand, blinking rapidly in the strong sunlight.

The tongs cluttered, unheeded, to the ground as the boy started forward, a cry torn from his throat. Shock and confusion halted him a few yards distant from Joshua, face frozen in disbelief. Sweat and dirt had blurred the fiery redness of his skin, and he suddenly looked the child he was; vulnerable and uncertain. 'Mr Priday!' He took a hesitant step forward, willing himself to act like the man his master would have him be, strong, dependable. Yet when he tried to speak, he was ashamed to hear his own voice cracking, high-pitched, the words unintelligible. Joshua, still holding the reins, took a step towards the boy and gripped his shoulder firmly, in comfort.

'Best be about your business, lad, and tend to the smithy,' Priday said tonelessly. 'There will be work to do.'

The boy nodded and stooped to retrieve the fallen tongs. As he straightened up, his eyes met Joshua's in helpless appeal, his moist underlip trembling, face puckering like a forsaken child's as he struggled to fend off tears. His return to the forge was slow, dispirited, his young shoulders bowed 'neath the burden of his inadequacy.

'You are a good, dependable lad, Tim.' Priday called out. 'An honest workman. I trust to you.'

The boy's harsh sobs reached them before the louder rhythmic clang of iron upon the anvil drowned out all else. Yet the blacksmith's words, spoken kindly in the midst of intolerable grief, told Joshua more of the man than all the questioning he might be forced to undertake.

By the time they had reached Priday's small, stone-built cottage, beyond the church, a straggling band of villagers had gathered behind them. Concern, and perhaps awkwardness in the presence of the unknown constable with his fine horse and uniform of authority, had rendered them silent and fearful. As Joshua halted the mare, they hung back, expressions sullen and suspicious, unsure of themselves, and him. Yet, when Priday made to hand his daughter's blood-stained body down to the constable, they surged forward instinctively to aid him, exclaiming in horror at her broken flesh, questioning, comforting, arguing, or bitterly swearing vengeance. Not a few of them wept, or turned aside, unable to bear the tragedy of it and of Joe Priday's hurt. It seemed to Joshua that when the blacksmith descended from the saddle, he had somehow grown smaller, and less in command of himself, as if diminished by a weight of reality and grief. Or, perhaps, he thought compassionately, here amidst his own people, there was no further need to dissemble or arm himself with spurious courage.

Ruth, as her father had promised, was home. Within moments, it seemed to Joshua, the girl was laid tenderly upon her bed while, unobtrusively and without comment, gifts and help were brought. They came shyly from young and old alike, offerings of warm blankets, salves, stone hot-water jars to heat the bed, home-brewed cordials and receipts, victuals to tempt the blacksmith's appetite, small treasures and comforts. That Maudlam was a small hamlet, Joshua was aware, and many were poor and lacking work, but what little they had, they were eager to share. It was a visible sign of their caring, and Joshua, observing the poverty of their clothing, and the poor inadequacy of the hovels which sheltered so many, could not help but be moved by their selflessness.

'It seems, sir, that you do not lack for true friends,' Joshua said warmly, when the blacksmith had been, with difficulty, persuaded to rest in a chair at his daughter's bedside, and to take a draught of the cognac which Joshua kept in a pewter flask within his saddle bag. 'Is there one who would ride swiftly to Newton to summon a physician?'

Priday said quietly, after some thought, 'If you would

send Tim, my apprentice, sir. It might ease his mind and let him feel of service. He will do no good at the forge, for he has no heart for work, of that I am sure. He will run to John Harries at the farm, and beg him to lend his mare. She is a docile creature, I know, for I shod her only yesterday, and she is quick and reliable.'

Joshua, unable to procure paper and quill, for none within the house could read or write, schooled the apprentice carefully in the message he must take to the physician's house, and set him anxiously upon his way to beg use of the farmer's mare. He would not catechise Joe Priday too mercilessly upon the events which led to his finding of his daughter, so brutally beaten, and left so callously for dead. Had Ruth, he wondered, been the innocent victim of some lunatic assault, frenzied, but without reason? Worse, had she been bludgeoned near to death, her body first forcibly violated, innocence destroyed? It was not a question to pose to Joe Priday, already sickened with shock and grief. Dr Mansel would confide to Joshua whatever damning evidence he might find, in the absence of any witness to the crime. The victim herself could tell them nothing.

He sighed heavily, meeting Priday's tired, apprehensive gaze as the blacksmith glanced up enquiringly from his vigil at Ruth's bedside. How do you comfort a man, Joshua wondered, whose life lies in ruins about him? Where are the words? How do you ask, dispassionately, if there is one who seeks to do her harm? A man capable of such savagery? How do you question whether she still clings to life, or is already dead? Murdered by person or persons unknown?

'If you will be . . . If you will stay here until Dr Mansel comes,' he amended, 'I will go and search for the attacker.'

'There are those who would go with you.' Priday's

voice was low, almost inaudible. 'But it is wiser that you go alone, sir.'

'Yes,' agreed Joshua soberly, 'for there is here a violence of feeling, of natural revulsion and a thirst for revenge. I know, for I feel it within myself, and cannot swear that I will have strength enough to control it.'

Priday said quietly 'But one alone, even should you stumble upon him unawares, will be easier to control than many, Constable. Should the wrong man be found, those who accuse him would be incensed beyond reason or halting. An innocent death would add guilt to bloodshed.' He shook his head helplessly. 'Remorse and regret would be too heavy to bear. I do not know if I have the courage to bear what I already must.'

'You are a good man, sir, and wise,' admitted Joshua sincerely.

'No,' Priday answered with honesty, 'for if I found the man who wrought this . . . vileness, and knew him guilty, I would kill him with my bare hands, and rejoice at his suffering. That is nearly as great a tragedy, that his cruelty provokes an answering cruelty in me.'

Joshua stayed silent.

'There are few men hereabouts with the means or opportunity to possess a mount,' confessed Priday. 'That is your answer, that upon foot, they would be a greater hindrance, giving noisy warning of their approach, trampling and obliterating any footprints or tracks which might aid your searching.'

'I thank you, sir, for your advice, and will act upon it.' Joshua gripped Priday's arm warmly. 'It is better that I act upon it without delay, else he will escape and find a hiding place.'

'There is no place on earth far enough, or secure enough, for him to escape my retribution,' said Priday simply, his very quietness giving the words a chilling certainty. 'No, he will not escape.'

Joshua said uneasily, 'I will do all I can to bring him to justice, I swear, but the tracks will now be more difficult to follow, for once upon grass or the highway . . . Had I gone at once –' He broke off awkwardly.

'Had you gone at once,' finished Priday, 'then Ruth would undoubtedly have died.' He rose, looked steadily into Joshua's eyes, then put a huge, gentle hand upon the constable's shoulder. 'I thank you, sir, for giving her a chance of life.' The pressure of his hand increased. 'You did what needed to be done, when shock and despair had all but robbed me of my reason and action. Yes, I thank you for that.' He glanced towards his daughter, his face ravaged with such naked hurt and love that Joshua felt the swift pricking of tears behind his lashes, and was forced to turn away to control them, and himself, lest Priday see the full depth of his pity. It would not do if he believed that Joshua thought her already dead, or settled so deep into unconsciousness from injury and loss of blood that he held no hope of her recovery.

Joshua hesitated, then moved very quietly to the door, murmuring to Priday that he would return as soon as he was able. His words, he knew, went unheard by the blacksmith, and his leaving unnoticed.

Priday stood at Ruth's bedside unmoving. The torn and ragged fusion of bone and blood which lay before him was part of his flesh, for ever. He felt its pain within himself. Its death would be his own. He prayed for her soundlessly, knowing that the mercy he begged for was not only for Ruth, but for himself.

Chapter Two

Joshua returned dispiritedly through the small hamlet, seeing the older cottagers gathered in troubled, anxious groups, or watching him covertly from their doorways. Yet now, he felt sure, there was no hostility or suspicion in their gazes, they were with him in his quest for Ruth's assailant as surely as if they rode beside him upon the way. There were children, too, wide-eyed and darkly watchful, naked limbs and feet smeared with the dirt of living, clothing unkempt over wiry bodies. The sight of a uniformed constable upon a fine horse had brought into their lives an excitement they would long remember, Joshua thought. He saluted them gravely, and they returned his salute with equal gravity, or with shyness, or occasional exuberance, depending upon mood or the nearness of their elders. There was little enough to bring them cheer or amusement in that poor, isolated place, he thought regretfully as he urged the mare past the churchyard walls and across the highway to the dunes. Yet, even as the thought surfaced, he chided himself. To a child, the moment was all. The restlessness and yearning came later, in manhood, when he searched in vain for something he could not even name and did not always recognise when he came upon it.

Joshua, glancing ahead and seeing Priday's young apprentice about to enter the highway upon John Harries's mare, called out an urgent summons. Startled, the lad hesitated, then dismounted to await the constable's coming, barely able to hide his restless impatience to be away.

'The message, sir . . . you bade me deliver . . .'

'I will not long hinder you, but there are questions I must ask, things I could not bring myself to ask of Mr Priday, you understand?'

'Yes, sir. 'Tis more fitting you speak to me, for he has more grief upon him than he can bear. He is a strict master, but honest and fair in all his dealings. What is it you would know? I will answer as truthfully as I am able . . . as he would, sir.'

'Good lad, Tim,' Joshua approved. 'For you know Mr Priday and Ruth better than any other.' The boy flushed with pleasure and nodded, lips trembling and eyes bright with unshed tears, as Joshua added, 'And your help may lead me sooner to the wretch I seek.'

Tim answered those questions the constable had hesitated to put to Priday and others besides. Ruth, he assured him, was a gentle, unassuming girl, as tenderhearted as she was pretty, and none could wish to do her harm. There was not a man, woman or child in Maudlam who would speak a harsh word of her, much less raise a hand to harm her. The trusty, earnest young face, fiercely proud with conviction, grew suddenly bleak with the remembrance of what she had borne.

'What caused her father to search for her when he did?' Joshua demanded. 'There was some cry, some noise, which alerted him, perhaps? Anything you recall? Think carefully.'

The apprentice's ingenuous face creased with the effort of remembering.

'No, sir, there was nothing. Had there been, I daresay the noise of the anvil would have drowned it.'

'What then?' Joshua fought to suppress the unfair irritation in his voice.

'The donkey, sir . . . Yes, it would have been the donkey. Ruth . . .' he faltered over the name, 'she might have returned unnoticed, passed the forge unseen, were she alone. But that donkey, sir,' he smiled ruefully, shaking his head, 'that donkey is a knowing beast, stubborn and indulged by all. He would not have returned past the forge, his duties done, without some bribe or sweetmeat from Mr Priday or me. It is his habit, you see. He would have honked incessantly, and refused to budge, were it not forthcoming.'

'And that was what first alerted Mr Priday, you think? The donkey's absence?'

Tim hesitated. 'Yes, sir, I dare say it would be that. I cannot rightly say, for I had been sent upon an errand, and returned to find the forge deserted. 'Tis all I can think of to account for it.'

'He has returned, then, this donkey?'

'No, sir. In all the haste and trouble, I fear he was forgot.' Shame and pity made him hang his head. 'I should have remembered him, sir. If he has come to harm, it is my doing.'

'No,' Joshua sought to calm him. 'If he has wandered, then have no fear, I will find him and bring him back.'

'He would not wander, sir. He would return of his own accord, unless someone has harmed him, for he knows every inch of these ways, and is loved and recognised by all. I had best search for him.'

'No!' Joshua's response was sharper than he intended. 'Your duty is to ride to Newton and summon Dr Mansel.'

The boy made no argument and went at once as bidden, yet Joshua glimpsed the stubbornness of his jaw and the soft shimmer of tears before he turned abruptly and set his foot into the stirrup of his borrowed mount.

'His name?' Joshua cried out to appease him. 'The donkey's name, that I may call him to me?'

The boy halted, hesitating and biting his underlip, until Joshua supposed that the animal had been given no name; then he blurted, 'Ruth called him Lucky, sir, claiming that was what he was, for he had suffered ill-treatment and neglect, and now had shelter and care from those who loved him.'

Without another word spoken between them, the apprentice had climbed into the saddle and reined the horse towards Newton. Joshua damned the solicitude which had made him ask, and the pity and remorse which would ride beside the boy upon the lonely way.

Joshua, retracing his mare's distinctive tracks through the clefts and gullies of the sand-swirled dunes, paused upon a summit to gaze about him to the sedge-fringed pool and the restless sea beyond. He felt an answering restlessness within himself, his earlier mood of quiet goodwill shattered as violently as Ruth's soft flesh. Joe Priday's face, haunted and ravaged by hurt, was vivid in his mind, and even after he closed his eyes, the image of it stayed branded upon the darkness as if seared there by the red-hot iron within the forge.

What manner of man was it, he wondered helplessly, who would wreak deliberate havoc upon the body and life of so gentle a girl? Ruth was scarcely more than a child, foot not yet firm upon the threshold of womanhood. He felt a shiver of disquiet rise, cold, within him. Whosoever had violated her, Joshua thought with pity, had destroyed not only flesh, but spirit. Even should she survive, her life would never again be innocent of hurt. All she had known of men was Joe Priday's warm, protective love. It had taught her to trust and offer unquestioning friendship in return.

'Dear God!' Joshua felt the mare stiffen and tremble beneath him as he spoke the words aloud. Remorsefully, he stretched out a comforting hand to soothe her neck, steadying her with gentle words before setting her upon the narrow way to the poolside.

In the hollow of the dunes, where he had first come upon Joe Priday, he reined the mare in and dismounted, allowing her to crop unhindered on the salt-washed turf. The blacksmith's shoe prints had been driven hard into the sand, forced deep by the weight of his burden. If it had been Rebecca, beaten and so close to death, borne within his own arms, Joshua knew his cries, like Priday's, would have split the air, desolate and wild as the howling of a wounded beast, his lust for vengeance no less savage and bloody.

The knowledge stirred him into urgent action, his morbid introspection ended. If Priday happened upon Ruth's assailant first, then it would be her attacker whose life would be ended, swiftly and without mercy. Joshua would have admitted honestly that this outcome would have distressed him not at all, despite the justice's oft-repeated avowal of the sanctity of the law. No, it was the inevitable outcome for Joe Priday which would grieve him: the blacksmith's trial and incarceration. The punishment would be severe. At the very least he could expect a flogging, then transportation in irons to Botany Bay. At worst, Priday would face death upon the gallows. Should Ruth die, the blacksmith would count his own life of little worth. Yet, should she survive, then cruel indeed would be the added burden of her father's exile or death.

Resolutely Joshua willed himself to set about his task, although he feared that the trail would now have grown cold, the tracks of little real value. Who could tell how long Ruth had lain there, helpless, before her father was troubled enough to leave his smithy and seek her out? Whoever her attacker might be, whether on foot or a passing horseman who had watched and planned, then followed her relentlessly, he must, by now, feel himself to be secure. Once upon that highway with the snow dissolved, there would be few traces. If mounted, he might have already returned to Pyle, or one of the inns at Newton, and taken a hired coach, disembarking at any of the succeeding staging inns, mingling unobserved with the guests, or travelling as passenger on any number of successive coaches. Such a tangled web, Joshua knew, would be impossible to unravel. He would check the livery stables against the return of a mount by some stranger; but no man intent upon crime would be foolish enough to have disclosed his true name or destination. Even if the culprit were careless, or the attack upon Ruth impulsive rather than premeditated, Joshua knew it would avail him nothing. At best, he might elicit a description of the villain from the owner of the livery stables, or from one of the grooms or ostlers at the inns. Experience had shown him that even that would prove diverse and contradictory, for memory was fickle, and what was unknown was oft cheerfully invented in an effort to oblige.

Joshua had now reached the fringes of Kenfig Pool, with its coarse, thorny scrub and twisted roots of stunted willows. It was a daunting task, for the vast expanse of fresh water was fed by underground streams erupting from icy caverns beneath the waste of dunes, and was more than two miles in circumference. Moreover, its edges were marshy and unpredictable, much of it unexplored by those who came to water their beasts. Such excursions had worn small inlets and cleared tracks in places by frequent use, the hooves of sheep and cattle trampling a way made filthy by their ordure and droppings of fleece and briar. Elsewhere around the pool's rim, the sedge grew thickly impenetrable, the rushy clumps sharp-pointed, stems crusted with little brown excrescences of flowers. At one of the watering places, then, or at the sheep-dipping pond, Ruth's assailant must have come upon her, for, with the donkey to lead, she would have chosen a well-tramped, easy path.

It worried Joshua that there had been no sighting of the beast from his vantage point upon the summits of the dunes. Had the poor animal been beaten as cruelly as she, and fled in terror deep into the heart of the acres of dunes? If so, it could surely be tracked and found. All who dwelt hereabouts would know it and hold it in affection as Priday's apprentice boy had claimed. Had it been abused and left callously to die, like Ruth herself, its carcase hidden by the press of tangled scrub, a prey to scavenging birds or predatory foxes? If so, no birds circled above to mark its grave. Yet, had Ruth's assailant been on foot, and used the donkey to make good his escape, then, sooner or later, Joshua reasoned, he must chance upon its tracks and follow them to an end. If it were so, then there was more danger to the villain than swift arrest by the constable. He would be set upon, murderously, by all the villagers of Maudlam, Kenfig and beyond. The donkey would undoubtedly bear Ruth's tormentor, not to safety as he hoped, but to death. A strange, unlikely Nemesis, but apposite, and solving many of his problems, Joshua thought.

After much fruitless searching among raking thickets of bramble and blackthorn which pierced even the protection of his riding boots and left him irritable and scored with briars, Joshua began to despair of finding anything of relevance or aid. The ground upon which he stood sucked and oozed beneath his boot soles, a viscous slime of mud and greenish scum beyond a small inlet. It had been so ploughed and churned by the trampling hooves of flocks and herds that it had become a useless quagmire, yielding nothing but the stench of animal excrement which coated the leather uppers of his boots with an evil-smelling and glutinous film. Yet he was unaware of it or, indeed, anything save the sight of the sedge before him flattened and ripped as by the weight of fallen bodies, or fierce struggle.

Joshua fell to his knees, unheeding of the marshy land, groping in the dank slime for some evidence, although he knew not what he sought. Deep in the sedge, and held fast in its white roots, his fingers closed upon a thick metal object, some tool or agricultural implement, he thought. He withdrew it tentatively to examine it, and gave an involuntary cry, part anguished, part triumphant. Its original use was no longer of concern to him, for the part which lay above the water-line was thick with dark blood crudely congealing, its stickiness harbouring, unmistakably, human hairs. He felt sickness souring his throat, and all but hurled the grisly object away in a rage of fury and disgust, for the hair sticking to the clotted blood was the pale, bleached gold of Ruth's.

He wrapped the iron carefully in his silk kerchief and strode unsteadily to where his mare was tethered, hampered as much by horror as by the stubborn sucking of the marsh at his boots. Then, with a word of reassurance to the grey, he placed the iron object within his saddlebag and retraced his steps. A careful and thorough search nearby uncovered the wooden buckets which the donkey must have borne, the straw rope which joined them still fastened firm. At least, Joshua supposed them to be the same, reasoning that they were too new and serviceable to have been abandoned deliberately, for the villagers were poor and, of necessity, frugal. He discovered, too, scraps of bloodied cloth, torn, he felt sure, from the sprigged cotton of Ruth's bodice, one with a button of shell still stitched upon the fabric. Finally he picked up a fragment of dark grey broadcloth, raggedly torn from some outdoor garment and trapped upon a barb of blackthorn. Whether the twig had been blown there in some gale, or dropped from the fleece of a wandering ewe, he had no way of knowing, but it was all he could find of human presence. He bore it carefully, with all else, to the mare, and having emptied the coins from the leather pouch within his coat into his pocket, he placed his finds within the pouch, secured the drawstring, and set it into his saddlebag. Then, leading the mare along a small pathway to the water's edge, he allowed her to drink freely while he explored the terrain all about. He saw no sign of recent human footprints, or of any iron-shod mount, save his own. Even after he remounted, and traversed the greater part of the pool and carefully inspected the drifted sands between the dunes, where an attacker might most readily have escaped, Joshua found nothing save for the old trampled hoofprints of herds and flocks and the marks of their drovers and herdsmen. There was no fresh trail. Had Ruth's assailant carefully retraced his steps that way, then, hoping that his footprints would be lost among so many others? Joshua thought not, although he could not be sure, for the man's tracks would surely be evident since, in his fever to be away, he could not pause for long enough to disguise them as he ought. The edges of the pool, then? Had he been wily enough to ride his mount, or the donkey even, through the shallows, eliminating all obvious tracks? Or had he guided it through the small drifts of snow then remaining, reasoning that as it melted so would all evidence of his flight?

Joshua had approached a small grassy plain now, surface cropped close by sea gales and foraging sheep, and dotted with straggling bushes of browned gorse, sulphurous heads defiantly ablaze, thorny stems hunched against the wind. The mare stumbled, and halted, and Joshua was all but hurled over her head, so deep had he been in thought. Dismounting to see what had disturbed her so, he saw almost beneath her hooves a rock of rough limestone, its craggy surface viscous with blood and coarse grey hairs. The fur of some animal, he thought. There was no mistaking the soft hoofprints upon the small drifts of melting snow, nor the droppings and blood which stained and darkened the grass at his feet. The donkey had been wounded, and badly, the strangely blurred and awkward pattern of its hooves, wherever they could be traced upon the spongy turf, speaking clearly of a leg lamed and useless, and the irregular patterns of blood of other wounds to its belaboured hide.

The donkey had kept to its way despite the hurled stones which marked its halting, awkward progress. Upon the highway the dripped blood ceased, and Joshua could find no more. Of one thing he was sure, the animal had escaped alone, and was incapable of being ridden. It seemed to have been spirited away; vanished without trace, like its oppressor.

Joshua remounted pensively and turned the mare towards Maudlam and Joe Priday's cottage. He had accomplished little enough by his endeavours. He prayed that Dr Mansel's would yield kinder results. If Ruth Priday died, then no stranger, be he friend or foe, would be welcome here, or safe from revenge.

As Joshua reined the grey across the highway to take the narrow track to Maudlam, the early spring sunlight lit upon the church of St Mary the Magdalene set high upon its rocky mound. For a moment it seemed to him that a fire burned within, its flames licking the windows to molten gold, lending their stained glass incandescence. Like those mean cottages and hovels which surrounded it, its walls, embattled tower, and even the winged roof of slate had been limewashed white, so that in the glowing light, the whole church coruscated and shone, as if alive. It lay with wings outspread like some wounded bird forced to earth and unable to take flight, plumage stained with red, and gleaming iridescence.

How strange, Joshua thought, men's continuing need to build a special place, holy and set apart; an oasis of the Spirit, a place of purity and order, refuge, perhaps, from the squalor in which they lived. A church built upon a hill. A Calvary. A sign of what they, too, must endure, and to what they might aspire. Well, he reflected, with unusual irony, perhaps their poverty and deprivation would make the promise of heaven the sweeter, for, in all conscience, they had little enough to give praise for upon this arid earth.

His arrival at Joe Priday's cottage was amidst a surging, cheerful throng of noisy urchins, running barefoot alongside the mare, dancing expertly out of range of her glancing hooves. Another small group stood guard over a small cabriolet, the wheeled and hooded one-horse chaise which Joshua recognised from the distinctive, skewbald mare, as belonging to Dr Obadiah Mansel.

The portly physician emerged at that precise moment to stand upon the doorstep, his pale gooseberry eyes screwed against the sunlight. He was immaculately, indeed, incongruously, attired for this poor place in an Albert frock coat, shirt front and collar agleam with starch, trousers pressed to perfection. Yet, as always, any hint of sartorial stiffness and formality was softened by his warmth of manner. With his plump cheeks and corolla of fine, wispy hair circling his pink pate like dandelion floss, Joshua thought, amused, he looked less like a Home Office pathologist than a good-natured friar.

'You have seen . . . examined Ruth?' Joshua heard the tenseness in his own voice.

'Ah, Stradling.' Mansel blinked rapidly, a frown of concentration forcing his pale, bushy eyebrows together as he sought to draw Joshua into focus. 'Yes! Yes! But it is better that we speak within the house.'

Joshua surrendered his mare to a willing cottager who tethered her to an iron ring set into Priday's wall, pausing only to cast indiscriminate clouts at any guttersnipe who ventured too near the doctor's carriage.

Joshua followed Mansel into the dark, ill-furnished room at the rear of the cottage and stood waiting awkwardly. He had no doubt that he had been brought within to be told of Ruth Priday's death in privacy, and felt a great weariness as he asked, 'She is dead then? Ruth is dead?'

'What?' Mansel seemed to have scarce heard him, so deep was he in thought. 'No! No!' he exclaimed testily. 'She is alive, barely. I confess, Stradling, that there is something in this affair which troubles me deeply, apart from the violence of her injuries.' He relapsed into silence, face grave, seemingly oblivious to Joshua's presence.

'You think she will recover, sir?' Joshua prompted when the silence had grown oppressive, with Mansel showing no inclination to speak.

Mansel hesitated. 'I do not know the true extent of her injuries, save those which are visible and can be treated. There is something deeper, more puzzling . . . I cannot be sure.' He spoke quietly, hesitantly, as if trying to clarify it in his own mind. 'No, I cannot be sure.'

'The shock, sir, and perhaps the delay in finding her?' ventured Joshua.

'Yes, that certainly, and loss of blood causing weakness, coma.' His pale, opaque eyes looked searchingly into Joshua's, as if he were making up his mind whether to confide what troubled him. 'I admit, Constable, that the head injuries which she has suffered are severe and extensive, a depression of the bone, a blood clot, perhaps, but experience, instinct, still tell me –' He broke off, confused. Then, 'Damn it, Stradling!' he blurted. 'I have seen enough of it in the past, in my own wife even, to recognise the symptoms. It is my belief that the girl was deliberately drugged that she might set up no resistance to her attacker.'

'But how, sir? When?' Joshua asked stupidly.

'That, sir, is your province rather than mine,' declared Mansel with the barest glimmer of humour, 'and I thank God for it, for I have more than enough to occupy my mind. I have told you that it is what I suspect only. I have no proof, you understand. I would not have it bruited about. I tell you in confidence, knowing it to be secure in your keeping.'

'You may count upon my discretion.'

Mansel placed a reassuring hand upon Joshua's shoulder, saying with great warmth, 'You have proved it in all our past dealings. I have good cause to value your integrity, and, indeed, your friendship.' His hand fell awkwardly away, and, as if aware that he had revealed too much of himself, he declared brusquely, 'I will return, bringing my partner, Dr Burrell, with me. I am not averse to seeking a second opinion, although I fear it will but serve to strengthen and substantiate my own.'

He smiled uncertainly, his deceptively mild eyes shrewd. 'You do not recognise this strange humility, Stradling? You have seen me as arrogant, opinionated, relentlessly sure of my surgical skills and conclusions?' He held up a hand as Joshua made to deny it. 'No, I beg you, allow me to continue. You have seen me conduct a post mortem. My conclusions must be firm, my confidence and belief in myself absolute, else all I do is valueless. If I am coldly incisive in my approach to the dead, it is because there is no other way to do the work. I must remain so in thought, as in action, to survive.'

Joshua said quietly, but with conviction, 'I have never thought you other than humane, sir. I do not confuse you with the work you do, although I respect your skill and dedication, as I respect you.'

Dr Mansel sniffed, and blinked, colour flooding his plump cheeks. 'Well, I had best return to seek out Dr Burrell,' he said awkwardly. 'There was something more you wished to say, Stradling?'

'To ask, sir: there were other injuries besides the obvious wounds?' He could not phrase the words he needed to ask, for they seemed, in some way, to brutalise Ruth's innocence.

'Yes, I believe that she was savagely assaulted, that her attacker had carnal knowledge of her. That is what you require to know?'

'Yes.' Joshua's voice was low. 'That is what I required to know. You have not told her father?'

'No.' Mansel shrugged helplessly. 'It would serve no purpose save to increase his anguish of mind. It might well be that she will not survive. There is time enough, if it must be spoken.'

Joshua said hesitantly, 'Dr Mansel, I know that Joe Priday is a proud and honest man, but . . .' he glanced around the comfortlessly bleak room with its simple furnishings, 'he is poor, as are all in this hamlet, for there are few hereabouts who can afford the indulgence of a mount, or even to pay for the repair of their few tools. If you will allow me the privilege of . . . answering your fee, without his knowledge, sir.'

'There is no fee, Stradling.' Mansel retrieved his leather box from a wheel-backed chair beside the window, and with it his high silk hat. 'There is no fee,' he repeated sharply. 'Dr Burrell, in his own time, devotes his skill and energies to providing medical aid to the indigent.'

Joshua was unsure what response was expected of him, so was relieved when Dr Mansel continued, 'It is a duty he has taken upon himself, an obligation. His work among the cholera victims, and his long incarceration in that . . . foul prison, have given him an insight into the lives and needs of the poor. He counts himself one of them. His work is a need, an exorcism. It drives away the spectre of the past.'

'But you, sir?' Joshua blurted clumsily.

'Have I not more to exorcise?' Mansel had secured his box beneath his elbow and was awkwardly fingering the brim of his elegant silk hat, staring at it intently. When he looked up, his eyes were unreadable. 'I make reparation to Burrell in the only way I know,' Mansel said tonelessly. 'It was my wife's viciousness and lying which saw him unjustly imprisoned, and my own apathy which kept him there. I was a credulous fool, Stradling. I do not deny it.'

'Yet you expiate it, if there is need, as Burrell would wish,' Joshua said with conviction.

'It is a debt hard to repay, Stradling. He was imprisoned for longer than the whole of your lifetime,' Mansel reminded him soberly.

'But now Burrell has an opportunity to practise medicine again, through your kindness, sir. He is able to begin a new life.'

'Yet the old intrudes. We cannot go back, Stradling; that is our tragedy. We cannot go back,' he repeated forlornly. 'I do not think John Burrell will stay long.

There is a restlessness in him. A need. I fear he will be always searching, always moving on.' His eyes met Joshua's bleakly. 'I cannot move on, Stradling; there is no escaping.'

Mansel set his silk hat upon his head, the wispy circlet of hair softy curling as a child's beneath its brim, his plump cheeks and soft, full underlip giving him the faintly absurd look of a child who has dressed up in an adult's formal clothes. Yet, somehow, he appeared to Joshua dignified and admirable rather than comic.

At the door, the physician turned, teeth biting anxiously at his lip, before admitting, 'I recall, a long time ago, telling Madeleine that "Old sins cast long shadows". I did not know then, Stradling, that their shadows can be cast from the grave itself, and beyond. The darkness is as lonely and inescapable as death.'

Joshua glanced towards the bare stairway of boards which led to the bedroom above, where Ruth lay, and where Joe Priday waited silently. 'Yet the work you do sometimes defeats death, sir,' he gently reminded to comfort him.

Mansel nodded. 'For a time,' he agreed. 'A brief time.'

Chapter Three

Joshua's farewell to Joe Priday brought him as little comfort as had his search at Kenfig Pool, for, despite Dr Mansel's ministrations, Ruth remained deeply unconscious. When Joshua had entered the small bedroom, the blacksmith's strong-boned body had seemed to dominate the room, the only living flesh within it. Yet his stillness had been as absolute as Ruth's: the quietness of one who waits despairingly for the return of a child from that abyss which separates the living from the dead. How eagerly would Priday have entered there in her stead, Joshua thought compassionately, and yet it is the one journey all must undertake alone. Not even those who share the pangs of one's birth, or the love that creates us, can share in it.

Priday had looked up and taken Joshua's hand in his huge, grainy fists, saying, 'I believe there is a change in her, sir, some ease.' His eyes had searched Joshua's face anxiously, willing him to respond, but Joshua saw only the inert body upon the bed, skin as pallid as the bandages which now concealed the crusted wounds and blood.

'Perhaps you are best placed to see the change,' he said carefully, 'for you have watched her constantly, sitting beside her, and aware of all.'

Priday's hands had dropped to his side, defeat suddenly rendering him old and uncertain. 'I do not know,' he admitted helplessly, 'I cannot reason any more, or believe in what I see. I think perhaps this is all a nightmare, a dream from which I shall awaken with a cry, God willing, and weep my relief that all is as it was. Yet I know in my heart that I have not even that comfort. I could not know such pain in sleep, or even in death, as that which possesses me now.' His massive fist crashed into his palm and a cry broke from him, terrible in its anguish, and yet the figure upon the bed remained silent and unmoved, remote, even from such grief.

'I will return tomorrow with others to aid me in my search, I promise. I will not rest until Ruth's attacker is caught, that no other will suffer such hurt.' The words faltered and died away, lost in the thickening of Joshua's throat.

Priday had returned to his vigil at Ruth's bedside and did not look up. 'I thank you for your kindness, sir. I am not good with words, but Ruth is clever. Clever and kind. She will thank you when she is able.'

'Yes, when she is able,' said Joshua gently, not knowing if he sought to comfort first Priday or himself.

As Joshua rode back to Newton village, his mind was firmly set upon the task which lay before him: the capture of Ruth Priday's brutal attacker. His first commitment must be to inform the justice, Robert Knight, of what had occurred, and to seek his consent to pay any who might help him in his search. The vestrymen, who apportioned funds from the parish rate, were frugal to the point of parsimony. Indeed, they could be as grudging in their charity as in their ladling out of gruel to paupers; rendering both thin and unpalatable. Still, even they could scarcely cavil at a demand for aid to track down so ruthless and craven a villain. Should they be disinclined, then Joshua did not doubt Robert Knight's rhetoric and powers of persuasion. He smiled involuntarily, then returned with the stubborn persistence of a cur gnawing upon a bone to his rumination as, unmindful of the countryside which lay about him, he allowed the reliable mare her head. The acres of pale, sandy dunes, softened with marram grass, like the silvery sea beyond and the flung coast of Swansea Bay, went as unnoticed as the lengthening shadows. In his mind were pictures of what had occurred that day, cameos hard-etched upon stone, faces anguished and bloody, raw with loss. He could have wished it otherwise.

Illtyd Cleat, the young hunchback and hayward to the cottagers' flocks upon the common lands, was in a more sanguine mood as he rode out upon his piebald pony, Faith. There was a warmth in the sun today, he thought, feeling it soft upon his cheek; an ending of winter and a beginning of spring. There would be new-born lambs to tend upon the salt-washed turf that bounded the sea, and on the high, wind-swept rockiness of Stormy Downs. He must be vigilant and upon his guard, for there were predators from beyond the three hamlets who would be tempted to thieve; human carrion every whit as cruel and devious as foxes or scavenging birds. It was not only nature which stayed bloody in tooth and claw.

He urged the pony up the steepness of Dan-y-Graig Hill. About him the bare trunks of trees showed ribbed and darkly cleft as rock, slender twigs barely swollen with buds. Yet there was a stark beauty in such simplicity, Illtyd thought, an austerity which had no need of ornament, as if by a process of slow excoriation the real essence was revealed, the sap that fed the flower, the bone that shaped the flesh. Straight and perfect, or bent and twisted as his own? He would not dwell upon that, for deeper yet must lie the core of a man, his mind and soul, and if he did not believe it, then there was no comfort, in living or in death.

Once upon the bleak, wind-scarred heights of Stormy Downs, he felt no misgivings. He loved every inch of this wild, unwelcoming place, feeling an affinity with its strange and crippled landscape. Thorn bushes hunched against the salt-ridden gales from the sea, barbs holding wisps of torn fleece like pale, ethereal blossom. Decaying ferns, red as the foxes they sheltered. Outcrops of pitted, grey limestone, eroded into hollow-eyed shapes, primitive as gargoyles. Hidden gullies. Overgrown quarries. Marshes which oozed and sucked beneath a pony's hooves, bubbling with the coldness of underground streams and caverns. A place for a man who sometimes felt the need for solitude among creatures whose violence and savagery were neither personal nor unjust, merely the price of survival.

The frightened, despairing cry of a sheep came from a coppice close by, and Illtyd was immediately alert, urging the piebald towards it, instantly protective. The pony moved forward obediently, sure-footed and unafraid, and the hayward, hand touching the saddlebag beside him, was grateful to Joshua for the gift of this sturdy mount, for without it and the tools of his trade, his life would have been as bleak as the land about him.

Illtyd did not know what he would find. A ewe, perhaps, with a new-born lamb, too weakened to fend off a predatory fox or bird? A sheep wedged in some gulley and in peril of starving, or trapped upon some quarry ledge? Wounded, or with a broken limb?

As the gaunt trees thickened about him, Illtyd dismounted, securing the pony to a stout branch and, taking rope and crowbar from his saddlebag, he followed the thin, despairing sound. In a small clearing beside a rough-hewn woodcutter's hut, he saw the poor beast, its body trapped fast in a wooden paling, wedged so securely that it could not extricate itself, despite its frantic struggling. Its eyes were wild with fear, thin limbs scrabbling so fiercely upon the stony ground that its hooves were worn and ragged. Its struggles increased as Illtyd strove to set it free, levering away the spars of wood to ease its bloodied sides. Then, in an instant, it stood, trembling and confused, barely able to stand before crying its anger and relief aloud, and bounding, tail flying, through the trees and out of sight. Illtyd, smiling and triumphant, felt the weariness in his arms and awkward, useless back, and steadied himself upon the paling before moving forward to the woodcutter's hut to rest upon the bench of rough, split wood beside the door.

Even as he moved, a swift and furious rush of sound at his head made him pause and instinctively leap aside from danger. It was like no other sound he had ever heard; louder than the flight of a bird, fiercer than a wind. Quivering and vibrating still, an arrow lodged itself in the wood of the hut, shaft aflame. Illtyd felt a sick shock of fear as legs and brain refused to act. With a conscious effort of will he forced himself to turn and seek his attacker. About him the naked trunks of trees, barely touched by sunlight, seemed grey and coldly menacing, their budding branches swollen to gnarled and twisted limbs.

'Show yourself!' he cried angrily. 'Face me like a man! Tell me what you want of me!'

His voice drifted back to him, raw with rising fear.

The tethered pony, hearing his distress, whinnied her terror, rearing up, hooves raking the air. Without thought for himself, Illtyd ran to Faith, stumbling over tree roots and snaking bramble, breath sobbing as he went lest she be hurt or driven away. Seeing that she was unharmed, without pause he swung himself into the saddle, thrusting his rope and crowbar away as he rode. Yet, even as he urged the piebald out of the trees and into the sunlight, the air beside him whirred with the piercing shrillness of a broken string, and a flaming brand thudded to earth at the pony's heels. Illtyd drove his mount on relentlessly, knowing that this was no cottager set upon some childish prank, but a stranger. Moreover, a stranger violently intent upon remaining so.

Knowing that there could be no help from the constable and reluctant to place his stepfather, Jeremiah, in danger by seeking his aid, Illtyd drove the pony harder than was his wont, fearful for Faith's safety. So it was that with both of them atremble and in a rare lather and sweat, Illtyd scarcely took breath until they had negotiated the archway into the Crown Inn and the pony's hooves were striking sparks from the cobblestones, then stilled.

Ossie, the walnut-skinned ostler, paused in his labours to hurry out of the stable and grasp the piebald's reins, soothing her until her agitated trembling ceased.

'Had I known the fierceness of your thirst for ale, Illtyd,' Ossie rebuked cheerfully, 'I would have rolled a hogshead to the arch!'

Then, seeing Illtyd's pallor and fatigue, he took his friend's arm and helped him dismount, signalling to a stable lad to rub down his mount. 'We will go to my stable loft,' he said firmly, 'for it is more private there, and you shall tell me what on God's good earth ails you, for I swear you look as bloodless as if you had seen a ghost!'

'No ghost, Ossie,' said Illtyd quietly, 'or if it is so, then a phantom that shoots arrows aflame.'

Ossie, who had been supporting the hayward, half leading, half carrying him up the stone staircase to his room, stood rigid upon the topmost step, hand extended towards the latch, a look of comical disbelief upon his face. 'You actually saw this creature?'

Illtyd's weathered skin, drained of all colour, had taken on a sallow look. 'No, but –'

'Thank God!' cried Ossie fervently, before Illtyd could explain. 'There is much talk in the inns of some strange being upon the Downs, resurrected, they vow, from the dead, although,' colour flamed into his cheeks as he disclaimed, hurriedly, 'I hold it as superstition and fancy. Most like to be the ramblings of some drunkard in his cups!' He turned aside to lift the latch, ushering Illtyd into his arid, cheerless room, settling him upon a wooden bench, busying himself with a jug of ale and some pint pots which he wiped absently upon the hem of his shirt before setting them upon the bare table. 'No, 'tis my belief,' he continued, 'that our "ghostly archer", hearing the old tales, has raised himself, not from the dead, but the living, for some purpose of his own.'

Illtyd nodded. The coursing of the ale through his veins and Ossie's concern had warmed and steadied him, and the experience, although bitter, now seemed to have an edge of humour for the telling.

'I confess to you, Ossie,' he said, setting his empty ale pot upon the table before him, 'that I flew from there like a bat out of Hades, never pausing to inspect arrows or archer! Indeed, had I ridden straight through him, I should not have known, since my eyes were closed tighter than a miser's purse!'

They laughed companionably, before Ossie refilled their jars with ale, demanding, 'What will you do about it? I know Joshua is absent, for I saddled his mare for him but an hour since. You will not raise a party to search for this . . . person?'

Illtyd studied his ale as if he might find an answer within. 'No,' he said finally, 'for what would it accomplish, save to make me look foolish . . . and a craven, which I readily admit! What would I charge him with before the justice? Robert Knight would think me unhinged, dispatch me to the asylum for lunatics at Briton Ferry! Besides, we would never discover the true purpose of this mad archer's frolics. No, I will tell it to Joshua upon his return, and no other.'

'Yes. You are wise to do so,' agreed Ossie, 'for it must be settled, and soon, so that you may be about your lawful business upon the Downs. You do not think it is the work of a thief? A sheep or cattle stealer?'

'I do not,' declared Illtyd emphatically, 'for he would simply have herded them with his fellows and been off upon his way, either by boat from one of the creeks, or secretly by cart or on foot upon some ill-used byway. He would scarce have paused to bludgeon me, much less warn me off with fiery arrows!'

He began to laugh, quietly at first, then with real enjoyment, his mirth so infectious that Ossie could not but join in his merriment, and they sat there laughing and wiping their eyes until their ribs ached and they could laugh no more.

'Well,' said Illtyd, when calm and reason were restored, 'I had best be on my way to the common lands. I thank you, my friend, for your hospitality.' He held out his hand, and Ossie took it in his horny, work-grimed fist.

' 'Tis a poor enough place,' Ossie said, smiling, and gazing about him at the rough straw bed and few crude sticks of furniture.

'Redeemed by its warmth and that of its owner.' Illtyd's response was sincere, for he knew that every penny Ossie earned was lavished upon those poor and winded creatures saved from the cruelty of livery and coach stables when age or blindness sapped their use.

Ossie, although absurdly pleased, was saved the embarrassment of replying by a commotion from the yard which had the two men running to the loft's single, breath-misted window which Ossie wiped with his palm. There was such a commotion below as had rarely been seen or heard; a frenzied clattering of hooves and scraping of cart wheels upon the rough cobblestones, overlaid by cursing and shrieking and such a bustling about and clanking of pails and shouted orders that the inn might have erupted into battle.

'Dear heavens!' cried Ossie. ' 'Tis Rowden the miller, else I am mistaken, and his cart afire and blazing like corn stubble.'

As Illtyd made to accompany him, Ossie pushed him firmly upon the bench, declaring, 'You have seen quite enough action for one day, my friend. Wait here, upon my return, for my stable yard is heaving like an anthill and I will not have it!'

When he had gone, Illtyd ventured to the window, seeing Ossie, squat and bow-legged, rushing about with zeal and authority, restoring order to unseemly chaos. He seemed to be everywhere at once, comforting and settling the miller, uncoupling the terrified horse, directing the stable lads and potmen into lines from which the water-filled buckets flowed as freely as the water from the well beside the inn door. Finally, with the fat and hirsute miller settled upon Tom Butler the landlord's arm and led, unprotesting, into the inn for refreshment, the lads dispatched about their business, and the blackened remnants of the cart smoking and hissing, Ossie returned to the loft. His face was smoke-grimed and his eyes watery and pink-rimmed, but he seemed as jaunty as ever.

'What happened?' asked Illtyd, alert with curiosity. 'Was Rowden the miller hurt, or his horse?'

Ossie's smudged face broke into a gap-toothed smile as he wiped his hand across his mouth, gratefully accepting the overflowing ale pot which Illtyd offered.

' 'Tis a story of woe and tragedy worse than the Old Testament,' declared Ossie, grinning, 'I can scarce restrain my tears . . . of laughter,' he added wickedly. 'It seems that the unfortunate miller was bringing some empty flour sacks and straw leavings to his friend, Ezra the Box, at his coffin shop. Do not ask me for what purpose, I did not dare to enquire. Having wined and dined not wisely, but too well, Rowden responded to a call of nature by leaping from the cart and rushing for the shelter of the nearest copse to ease his discomfort, leaving the horse unattended. As he strove to retrieve his breeches Rowden swore that he heard a fierce noise, "as of a mighty, rushing wind", or so he vowed, straight-faced, followed by a ball of fire! The landlord asked him who brewed his ale, for in truth it was stronger than any he could lay his hands upon.'

'A coincidence, you think?' demanded Illtyd, intrigued. 'This adventure of his? Or inspired, perhaps, by the gossip at the inns?'

'He was almost persuaded so by the jibes of the potmen and stable lads. Their cavorting and posturing all but sent me into convulsions through laughing.'

'But you were not convinced?' Illtyd's eyes were shrewd and enquiring.

'Oh yes, I was convinced!' Ossie unwrapped the piece of sacking still clutched within his hand, spreading it upon the table top. There was no mistaking the fire-blackened arrowhead of iron, nor the charred remnants of cloth upon what remained of the shaft. Its brittleness dwindled into charcoal dust, even as Illtyd reached out a hand and touched it.

* * *

As evening fell, and Joshua dispiritedly rode his grey under the stone archway to the Crown Inn at Newton and into the stable yard, weariness and self-doubt seemed to have seeped so deeply into flesh and bone that he could scarce summon the energy to dismount.

Ossie, hearing the sound of the mare's shoes clattering upon the cobblestones, came hurrying from the stable, the ready smile of welcome dying upon his weathered face as he observed Joshua's exhaustion and dishevelment. That this was no moment for his usual jocular exchange with the constable was plain, for he had watched his friend ride out sartorially elegant and in rare good humour, only to return so wretchedly travel-worn, clothing disfigured with marsh filth.

'I fear the day has not proved to your liking,' he ventured tentatively, grasping the mare's reins in his horny palms. 'Will you not take a jar of ale within the Crown? It would serve to ease away the day's bleakness and your own.'

'No, Ossie, I thank you.' Joshua glanced down wrily at his mire-stained doeskin breeches and boots. 'I am barely fitted to serve as a scarecrow, much less parade myself in company.'

'Not company, Joshua, friends,' Ossie reminded him gently, his creased face warm with concern.

'Indeed, friend ostler, it is as well to be reminded of one's privileges as well as one's manners, for I come close to forgetting both.' He gave a tired smile. 'If you will deliver my horse to a stable lad, and invite me to sup ale with you in your loft, then I would appreciate your company and advice above all other.'

Ossie nodded, pleased, his mouth widening into its familiar gap-toothed smile before he cried out to a willing stable lad to see the grey warmly rubbed down and bedded.

Once secure in Ossie's stark loft and refreshed with good ale, Joshua's mind was greatly eased by an unburdening of the unexpected and tragic events of the day. Ossie was a patient and intuitive listener, asking no questions until all was revealed to him, then saying, with face gravely concerned, 'Such viciousness and depravity are hard to fathom, Joshua, as is the mind of one so grossly obscene. There is some madness in the creature who committed such an act, an evil. I have seen it but once in an animal, a gelding which came into my hands. A beautiful thing. A joy and delight to the eye, but flawed. Neither kindness nor firmness could check it. It was some viciousness born in the blood, a taint which could never be subdued, or bred out.'

'And what became of it?' Joshua asked quietly.

'It was a grief to me then, and it grieves me now to think upon it, but I knew it to be a rogue bent upon destruction, and nothing would stay it.' He looked at Joshua steadily, his eyes dark with remembered pain. 'I set a bullet into his brain.' His voice faltered and died away. 'It was better so,' he continued tonelessly when he was able. 'It would have destroyed itself, and others with it, do you see. There was some blood lust beyond control.'

'You have regretted it since, Ossie,' Joshua murmured compassionately, moved by the ostler's distress.

'No, I have not regretted the act, for there was no other way. Oh, but I have regretted the need for it, and grieved long and bitterly since. But the guilt fell neither upon the animal nor me, we were not culpable for what was within us. We did what we were impelled to do. You understand, my friend, what I am trying to say, in my awkward, stumbling way?'

Joshua gripped the ostler's shoulder reassuringly, saying simply, 'You fear, Ossie, that such a task might well devolve upon me?'

Ossie nodded but did not speak.

'Then I thank you for the warning. I shall hold myself ready, lest the need arise.'

'You will never be ready,' said Ossie with cold conviction, 'but you will do what has to be done, of that I am sure. Should you falter, then memory of that child's wounds and violation will give you strength. You would not see such tragedy forced upon another such innocent.'

'You are a good man, Ossie, and wise.' Joshua's voice was warm with sincerity.

'No. I am ill-educated, and not a scholar like you,' the ostler disclaimed, 'and life is a rough old school for learning. Yet, perhaps, one learns more of oneself from cruel experience than from the books of others, however clever they be. I have learnt that men and animals are little different, one from the other. Saving your good company, I would as soon devote myself to my horses.' He smiled delightedly at Joshua's spontaneous laughter, adding, 'Perhaps it is because I am ruler of my own small kingdom, and none can argue, harangue me, or take me to task.'

'A consummation devoutly to be wished!' declared Joshua fervently, rising to take his leave. 'I could wish the justice as appreciative! At least the three hamlets provide no immediate trouble.' He hesitated at the expression upon Ossie's creased, leathery face. 'Well, Ossie?' he asked sharply. 'There is something I should know?'

Ossie's face was shadowed in the light of the candle-lantern, part averted, so that Joshua could not see his expression, but his voice was strangely muffled as he fought to control it.

'Something, or someone . . .'

'You talk in riddles,' exclaimed Joshua in vexation. 'Speak plainly! I have neither the time nor inclination for childish guessing games! There is trouble?'

'Of a kind.'

Joshua saw quite clearly now by the lantern glow that the ostler was struggling helplessly to control his mirth. 'Well, what is it, man?' cried Joshua. 'Tell me! I am scarce in a mood to linger idly!'

'Nor was Rowden the miller.' Ossie erupted into such fierce gales of laughter that he was powerless to continue, growing more bent and awkward as he hugged his stomach and aching ribs, vainly seeking ease. He straightened with some difficulty, still wiping the tears from his grainy cheeks with his fists.

Joshua, his impatience growing, demanded, 'Miller? There is something amiss with Rowden the miller?'

'More his cart.' Ossie's lips twitched despite all his efforts to compose himself. 'Some . . . phantom, which shoots fiery arrows, attempted to set light to Rowden's cart, and worse! But you had best seek out Illtyd. He is within the Crown, and will tell you all. The inn is so agog with news of it that I'll warrant none will even notice you, much less your scarecrow breeches!'

Joshua followed him down the stone steps from the loft and into the yard. To his credit, he did not question whether Ossie were drunk, or had merely taken leave of his senses, but demanded innocently, 'So, apart from this troublesome . . . apparition, it has been quiet here?'

'As the grave,' called back Ossie, admirably straight-faced.

Chapter Four

Upon the morrow, after a restless night mazed with confused dreams, Joshua arose early from his cramped bed under the eaves and donned his workaday uniform for his meeting with the justice. He made a bundle of his soiled garments of yesterday and, securing it beneath his arm, descended the steep staircase, his boots scraping fitfully upon the worn stone. He set the bundle upon a three-legged stool beside the smouldering turf fire where, he knew, his cleaning woman would inevitably see it and deliver it to the washerwoman for purification. His doeskin breeches were in a sorry state from the slime of the marsh, and he regretted the additional labour which would be needed to set them to rights.

He delved anxiously into his pocket and set an extra three pence upon the pile of grimed clothing, knowing that it would be useless to pen apology, for few of the cottagers could read or write. He consoled himself with the knowledge that to the widow who toiled at her wooden wash trough in the open air, such bounty would be a godsend – the difference between poverty and destitution; incarceration within the poorhouse. No, she would not willingly forgo the backbreak, nor grudge the hard gathered lye of fern ash and bleach of urine. Neither would she spare herself in her stiffening, ironing, and goffering of the frills upon his elegant shirt. She would rather count it a privilege to return a garment of such rare quality to pristine perfection.

He sighed. How hard was the life of such people! It was surely a soul-destroying occupation to remove the filth and the sweat of others by the violence of one's own. He remembered his visit to the widow's cottage, a poor, decaying hovel, her one room, for living, foetid with dampness and the overpowering heat of the driftwood fire. Above it hung, suspended, a steaming kettle upon a chain, and a trivet held heavy flatware irons cooling, or sizzling with globs of spittle as she tested them for heat. All about, beams and surfaces were cobwebbed with wet clothing, and the earthen floor treacherous with baskets of garments neatly ironed. He had felt barely able to breathe in that dankly misted atmosphere, stifled by its suffocating heat and moisture.

He smiled wrily. How great had been the change in him since coming here to the three hamlets. Once, in his life of sheltered indulgence upon the prosperous farm in the Vale, he would have accepted such tasks and sacrifice without thought or demur. Now, he was a cottager like the rest, and prey to their fears and deprivation, while Rebecca, whom he loved so dearly, had reversed her role as dramatically as he. Poor cocklemaid to gentlewoman; gentleman to peasant. Yet would not such knowledge as they had gleaned of poverty and plenty bind them more closely in whatever the future held? Would it not bring understanding and compassion to all their tasks, and their dealings with others, whether their estate be high or low? He could not doubt it. He thanked God for Rebecca's love, and for the satisfaction of his work as constable; a privilege long-sought, and not attained without some hurt and grief to others, and to himself. He could only pray that he had the strength of mind and purpose, with the knowledge needed, to bring Ruth's assailant to account. Ossie, with his natural earthy wisdom, was right. Came the hour; Came the man. He must strive to be that man.

He wrenched aside the bolt of the heavy back door and walked out into the bailey. For all the elegance of its name, it was little more than an arid square of compacted dirt which housed the rack and pinion well and the privy midden. Some previous tenant of an artistic and humorous bent had edged the pathway with cockle shells, and, in early summer, a few wind-scattered marigolds, their stems pale and attenuated, struggled restlessly from the soil. As Joshua sluiced himself at the well, the morning air chill upon his flesh, he thought how absurd and pitiful the decoration seemed, yet somehow touching, like a cheap necklace about the throat of some poor harlot, seeking to hide the ravages of time.

He dried himself upon a piece of washed sackcloth, feeling it roughly abrasive against his flesh. The early morning breeze and the iciness of the well water had shocked him into life and sharpened his appetite, and he made a hearty breakfast upon cold bacon from his father's farm, with ale and oaten cakes, before donning his helmet and setting off for the Crown.

Then, with a word of cheer for Ossie who had saddled his mare and smilingly delivered to him the arrowhead reclaimed from the miller's cart, he rode out under the arch. Ossie's voice, grainy and filled with wry humour followed him as he went: 'Best ask the vestry for a suit of armour, sir, or carry a pail or two of water upon your way, for it is as well to be prepared.'

Joshua was smiling as he rode past the inn and the village green which skirted the little Norman church of St John the Baptist, its crenellated stone towers precisely incised as a child's toy against the clear-washed blue of the sky. The few clouds were soft and vaporous as steam from a kettle, thinly transparent as if they had been stretched to the limit and might soon dissolve away. A breeze ruffled the mare's mane and the few attenuated shrubs and withered flower heads which had survived the winter gales in the small cottage gardens. Here and there an occasional scrawny hen scratched optimistically at the bleak earth between gnarled cabbage stalks, lean as their scaly legs, and a brindled dog barked menacingly as they passed by upon the Clevis Hill, straining and rattling at its restrictive chain, until a chamber pot of slops from an upper window silenced it.

Ossie was right, thought Joshua, as he rode on past the cattle-filled meadows and up the steepness of Dan-y-Graig Hill. It is best to be prepared. But how did one prepare oneself against what was, at worst, a ghostly apparition, at best a fire-crazed archer and madman? And how would he explain it to the justice? Before the death of Robert Knight's nephew, he would simply have offered him the few facts he knew, not doubting that the justice's dry, pedantic wit would have surfaced, sharp and scathing, and a solution found. Joshua had long enjoyed their verbal battles and the justice's swift irony, but now he showed neither spirit nor humour, bogged down in a slough of self-pity and apathy. Small comfort to Robert Knight that his deliberate shooting down of his own nephew had saved Elizabeth Crandle's life; an innocent girl, abducted and held to ransom, and whose life would certainly have been forfeit at his nephew's hand.

Was this, then, the tragedy of killing that which was loved but flawed, of which Ossie spoke so fiercely? How much more excoriating to destroy one's own flesh and blood. Would the news of Ruth's attacker serve to reopen that old wound, so slow in healing? Well, it must be told, and Illtyd's and Rowden's misadventures. Joshua worked at Robert Knight's direction, despite a certain degree of latitude and independence, and owed him the courtesy of a report upon all matters affecting the three hamlets. He was, after all, not only justice, but rector, and held the inherited lordships of two great manors. There was nothing, whether secular, fiscal or spiritual, which did not intimately concern him. However, in his present mood, Joshua thought wrily, it might have been less unnerving to face the fiery archer.

He rode through the familiar griffon-topped pillars of Tythegston Court with little enthusiasm and, upon surrendering his mount to a waiting groom, tugged at the brass bell pull set into the door. It was opened almost immediately by the justice's elderly manservant, Leyshon, an austere, forbidding old fellow with rotting teeth, his spine held stiffly erect by a wooden splint. His rigidity of stance and movement fostered the impression that he was aloof and unbending, regarding all about him with an air of pained condescension. Yet Joshua was a great favourite with the old man, and knew him to be a loyal and devoted servant.

Leyshon greeted Joshua warmly, taking his helmet and placing it upon a hall chair before escorting him to his master's library.

'The justice is well?' asked Joshua quietly.

'There is no change in him, sir.' Leyshon's voice was low and troubled. 'It grieves me to see him thus.'

Joshua nodded agreement, saying awkwardly, 'Perhaps time will make alteration.'

'No, sir,' said Leyshon. 'I know the justice better than any other upon the earth. What he needs, sir, is something to be enthusiastic about, something which compels his whole attention to the exclusion of all else.'

'Is it not true of us all?' muttered Joshua as Leyshon entered to announce the visitor's presence.

The justice was seated at his desk and, as he glanced

up, Joshua thought his normally plump and amiable face had thinned and grown melancholy. Hè motioned Joshua to a chair, without speaking, his fingers drumming rhythmically upon a document set before him, as if he were insistently tapping at some melody which occupied his mind against his will, and he strove to be rid of it.

Joshua waited for him to speak, but since he did not attempt to do so, said quietly, 'I have come to seek your advice, sir.'

'Advice?' the justice echoed in puzzlement.

'A young woman has been viciously assaulted at Maudlam, sir, and lies near to death.'

'Then what advice do you seek? You must do what is necessary. Gather men for a search party, question, evaluate, seek until you find the culprit. It is, after all, what your work as constable demands. It ill becomes you to be hesitant and dilatory in such a matter, Stradling! I trust that you are not finding your duties too onerous – beyond your capabilities?' His voice was cold.

'No, sir. I sought your advice merely upon the question of payment by the vestrymen.'

'Then do not concern yourself with such trivialities. They will do as I instruct, as, I am sure, will you. I will not delay you, for it is plainly imperative that you need to be about your business.' His hand reached dismissively towards the bell pull to summon Leyshon.

'There was another matter, sir,' interjected Joshua quickly.

'Well?' There was no doubting his irritation, for his fingers had resumed their discordant drumming and his tone was sharp.

'It seems, sir, there is some phantom upon Stormy Downs.'

Robert Knight regarded him with cold distaste. 'A phantom, you say? Superstition and nonsense, sir! I had thought better of you than to countenance such puerile ramblings, Stradling!' His voice was contemptuous, but the drumming of his fingers gradually died away as he asked, 'You come to me in my role as priest, then, rather than justice?'

Joshua unwound the handkerchief from his breeches pocket and threw the arrowhead upon the desk where it clattered, and was still. 'And this, sir?'

The justice inclined his head towards the offending metal, then, with his first show of interest, let his hand slide towards it until it lay exposed upon his fleshy palm.

'An arrowhead, Stradling? How do you come by it?'

'From Rowden the miller's cart, sir, which it set aflame.'

Joshua repeated the story of Illtyd's escape, and of Rowden's unfortunate retreat from the copse, in some dishevelment, and of his pursuit by the demon archer, culminating in his spectacular arrival at the Crown with his cart ablaze.

The slightest of smiles touched the corners of the justice's mouth, and his lacklustre eyes grew fractionally brighter and more alert.

'The arrowhead is solid enough,' he ventured.

'As, no doubt, is the archer!' Joshua exclaimed. 'I cannot help but wonder, sir, what he is at such pains to hide.'

The justice inspected the arrowhead more closely, first setting it down upon the desk, then clipping a pair of eyeglasses over his ears. His protuberant eyes, much magnified behind the lenses, were intently assessing.

'A vicious enough weapon,' he pronounced, 'and certainly unusual. Rather an excessive way of dealing with an honest tradesman and a hayward, would you not say,

Stradling?' A flicker of amusement touched his brown eyes.

'It depends, sir, upon the value of what he hopes to conceal.'

'Or whom he wishes to conceal,' supplemented the justice. 'An escaped convict, perhaps, or someone abducted and held to ransom.'

'Perhaps,' Joshua conceded, 'although I think it more likely that it is a thief or smuggler we are dealing with.'

'Not I,' corrected the justice, 'you, Stradling. I give you carte blanche to deal with him in your own way. You may hire as many stout helpers as you need from among the cottagers, and use their services to seek the assailant of the young woman at . . . Maudlam, you said?'

'Yes, sir. Ruth Priday, the only child of the blacksmith and farrier.'

'You think it possible that her attacker and this alleged fiery phantom,' he spoke the words with a grimace of disgust, 'that they might be one and the same?'

It was a premise which had not occurred to Joshua. 'I think it unlikely, sir,' he answered carefully. 'The cruelty inflicted upon the girl was frenzied and murderous. Dr Mansel cannot be sure, even now, that she will survive. As for the . . . well, the so-called fiery archer, I think his arrows were meant to frighten off rather than wound, for his aim was absurdly poor.'

'Or absurdly good, Stradling,' chided Robert Knight, 'if such was his intention. It does not always do to leap to the obvious conclusion. One must learn to be as devious as he.'

A strangely immoral stricture from the lips of a clergyman, Joshua thought amused, but Robert Knight continued gravely, unsmiling, 'You will, of course, keep me informed as to what transpires, both here and at Maudlam.' He removed his eyeglasses and replaced them in the shagreen case, carefully closing it and putting them away, and with them, Joshua felt, all further interest in the matters. 'If that is all . . .' Robert Knight rose dismissively to his feet.

Joshua felt a sense of disappointment, a stirring of regret, for failing to do or say anything which would have aroused the justice from his morbidity. He bowed formally to Robert Knight, and made to take his leave.

'A moment, Stradling!'

Joshua turned obediently.

'This cart of Rowden's,' the justice asked sharply, 'it was destroyed completely?'

'Yes, sir.'

'Hmmm. Yes, yes, I see.' He nodded, plump, blue-grained jowls quivering with the affirmation. He stood for a moment, fingertips pressed tightly together, mouth pursed. 'A fire-cart,' he declared.

Joshua stood there bewildered, unsure of what to reply.

'A fire-cart!' repeated the justice triumphantly. 'Of course. Come, Stradling!' he ordered testily. 'Pull yourself together, man, else you will give the impression of being either deaf or simple-minded. We shall build a fire-cart, or perhaps three; one each for Newton, Nottage and Port. I shall give the order to Daniel the cartwright at Nottage as soon as I have planned the design. There will need to be casks of water always stored upon them, in case of some conflagration where there is no well. They can be manned by volunteers. An alarm would have to be given. What do you say, Stradling, church bells, or beacons perhaps?' He was looking at Joshua expectantly, eyes alive with anticipation, once more purposeful and in control.

Joshua thought of all the reasons why it would not be feasible: the able-bodied men would be at their work, only the ancients and senile would be there to command; the carts would be too cumbersome and slow to deal with roofs of thatch; how would they procure the horses? The bells would be heard in Newton alone, elsewhere their peals perhaps muffled by the wind. Bonfires upon low-lying fields could not be seen!

He looked at the justice, the arguments for rejection already upon his lips. Leyshon's words came back to him as clearly as if he stood beside them in the room, 'All he needs is something to be enthusiastic about . . .'

Joshua smiled, declaring firmly, 'I believe, sir, that it would be a master stroke, a bold original plan and one which the people of the three hamlets would support and welcome wholeheartedly.'

'Yes,' confirmed the justice with pride, 'I felt sure that you would agree. You will excuse me, Stradling.' He strode to the bell cord and tugged it imperiously. 'There is much to occupy me. I must begin at once.'

Joshua rode back to Newton cheered by the justice's wholehearted involvement in his scheme to build fire appliances for the three hamlets, although he was less sanguine about the results. The justice's enthusiasms were swift and absorbing, but the means of their practical accomplishment concerned him not a jot. He simply left such tedious detail to others. Joshua, recalling the spectacular failure of Robert Knight's life-saving rocket which had been fired from the shore, only to be hurled back by the wind, and his life-saving craft which proved incapable of being launched at all in heavy seas, hoped that caution would temper optimism. Yet there was no doubting the justice's good intentions. Joshua smiled indulgently, thinking that should an epitaph ever be required for Robert Knight's tomb, then 'He meant well' could properly be engraved in letters of gold.

When skirting Clevis Hill to return to his cottage, he

was surprised to see Ossie at the archway to the Crown, urgently beckoning him within. Joshua reined in the mare and dismounted, following the ostler into the cobbled yard.

'Ossie, there is something amiss?' asked the constable, puzzled by the ostler's furtive glances about him and his air of ill-suppressed excitement.

'No, naught amiss,' declared Ossie, 'but I have something of rare interest to show you. Something which you might find rewarding.' He beckoned Joshua into the darkness of an empty stall, having first called out to a stable boy to take the reins of the grey.

'You mean here? In the stall?' asked Joshua, looking about him in bewilderment, and believing that Ossie might, once again, have rescued some ill-treated bag of bones from a rapacious coach proprietor or horse dealer, aware of his generosity of heart and purse.

Ossie beckoned him closer, his face in the dappled light aglow with self-importance. Joshua was painfully aware of the overpowering stench of horse sweat, leather and the pungent odour of animal dung and urine that permeated the place as Ossie, with a satisfied smile, unbuttoned his shirt and produced a hand-lettered play bill which he handed to him solemnly, after making an abortive attempt to smooth out the creases upon the backside of his none-too-clean breeches. Joshua regarded it in puzzlement.

'You wish me to read it to you?' he asked at length, for he was aware that Ossie was unable to read.

'No!' cried Ossie in vexation. 'Look at the picture, man!'

Joshua regarded it in silence, still seeking enlightenment.

'Can you not see what it is?' Ossie's voice was rough with frustration at Joshua's wilful blindness.

'I see that it is a programme of sorts and advertises a one-day fair and circus upon the green,' admitted Joshua, 'and that they make a return visit. A band of players of rare skill, with unusual talents.'

'Yes. Yes!' said Ossie in exasperation. 'But the picture, Joshua, the drawing! Does it not interest you, give you pause for thought?'

Joshua studied it carefully. 'There is a dancing bear,' he said helplessly, 'and a juggler, and beside it . . .' His face cleared in delighted recognition. 'Ossie! You are, without doubt, an inspiration, a genius!'

'No doubt,' said Ossie complacently, but could not resist adding tartly, 'which is why, unlike you, sir, I devote my energies to ailing horses rather than people! But you will see that they intend to give a performance tomorrow afternoon, or so the circus master informed me. It will include "The Magnificent Marvo", pictured –'

'Cleverly shooting arrows to encompass his blindfolded accomplice, set against a target,' Joshua finished triumphantly.

'It seems,' Ossie informed him nonchalantly, 'that they arrived in the area yesterday, and have been encamped upon the far side of Stormy Downs, for they are first to appear at Pyle.'

'I shall search them out upon the instant,' declared Joshua, 'and, should your guess prove correct, learn the real truth of it!'

'Could you not leave it for a while?' begged Ossie wistfully. 'They have hired the town crier to publish it abroad for them, and there would be many from the three hamlets, especially the children, sad and disappointed . . . Surely a day or so would not gainsay?'

Joshua looked doubtful, but finally acquiesced.

'It is the finale which I particularly yearn to see!'

declared Ossie wickedly. 'It is then that he lets fly a fiercely blazing arrow!'

Joshua left the grey in Ossie's care, promising to return and claim her as soon as he had ascertained that no urgent message awaited him at his cottage, nor villager with some tale of woe which would command his immediate intervention.

To his relief, no one awaited him, and those few tradesmen and villagers he had encountered upon the way merely exchanged civilities with the grave courtesy to which he had grown accustomed.

He had scarcely removed his helmet and banked up the fire with turf to keep it smouldering gently until his return, when he was disturbed by the rare and unexpected sound of a carriage drawing up at his door. From the exceptional clamour of horses and harness, the rumbling of its wheels and the confusion of activity and voices, it was undoubtedly a coach which attended him. For a moment he almost believed that it might be Rebecca, arriving unheralded with her chaperone, the redoubtable Mrs Louisa Crandle, but he knew that the good lady would never countenance such a bizarre breach of social observance. He did, indeed, open the door upon the elegant sight of the smaller de Breos equipage, the family crest emblazoned upon its side, the liveried coachman in the familiar colours of plum and gold already extracting the steps that the occupant might conveniently disembark. From his supernumerary's perch upon the box, Edwards, the old coachman, his well-splinted leg stiffly mummified before him, raised his venerable tricorne to bid Joshua a smiling 'Good-day, sir.' But it was to the occupant of the carriage that Joshua looked to glimpse with the opening of the door, the diminutive, stooped figure of his old tutor, Dr Handel Peate, descending. Joshua hurried to support the frail old gentleman's elbow, guiding him towards his cottage, bidding him enter.

'I regret, sir,' declared Dr Peate, disengaging himself firmly, 'that this is but the most fleeting of visits, and beg you will excuse me, for I must return immediately to Tythegston Court where my friend and fellow clergyman Mr Robert Knight, and my luncheon, await me.'

There was no mistaking Dr Peate's frostiness of manner, nor the aloofness upon his normally amenable features.

'If I have offended you in some way, sir,' Joshua began uncertainly, 'then I regret it profoundly.'

'Not at all, sir,' replied Dr Peate stiffly. 'It is merely age and accompanying infirmity which discountenance me,' he paused, 'also the inconvenience of a long and tedious journey which, in the event, has proved unnecessary.'

'Unnecessary?' echoed Joshua, bewildered.

'Certainly,' declared Dr Peate, motioning to the young coachman who was standing by that he required him to return to his seat upon the coach. 'Age, Stradling,' he adjured severely, 'has not totally dulled my memory, although it seems that your own suffers regrettable lapses, despite your comparative youth.'

'Indeed, Dr Peate, I confess that I do not quite comprehend,' admitted Joshua, at a loss.

'Do you not, sir? Have you forgotten that it was upon *your* written persuasion that I abrogated my duties as tutor to Miss de Breos and Miss Crandle?' he demanded coldly. 'I came in order to lend spiritual support and aid to my colleague, Robert Knight, whom you so impertinently described as being dispirited, apathetic, and in dire need of consolation. I own that I have never seen him in more ebullient spirits! Indeed, so absorbed was he with plans and excitements that he scarce took breath to greet me. Now, sir, if you will kindly permit me . . .'

He climbed stiffly upon the carriage step, frail body rigid with hurt pride, as Joshua blandly observed, 'Then I am sure, sir, that you rejoice as wholeheartedly as I in the justice's return to humour.'

Dr Peate turned his head sharply to declare, 'Indeed!' Then, despite his efforts to remain injured, a smile softened the corners of his mouth. 'It all comes of that ridiculous tale of yours, Stradling, of the so-called phantom, some fiery archer resurrected, I am to believe, from the dead! Stuff and fiddlesticks, sir! I could have hoped my past tutoring might have convinced you that phenomena, miracles, do not occur.'

'Save, perhaps, to the justice, sir?' Joshua asked innocently.

Dr Peate kept his face carefully averted, but Joshua observed the tell-tale shaking of his shoulders and the gratifying sound of Edwards's chuckling upon the box.

Chapter Five

Joshua was still smiling at his verbal exchange with Dr Peate as he rode out, once more, upon his grey. He planned to interrogate Rowden the miller at his stone-built flour mill. It was, of necessity, a bleak, isolated dwelling and workplace, set upon the high point of Stormy Downs, where the winds from the sea could best serve its skeletal sails and the vast stone grinding wheels within. He would need, too, to search for some clue to the archer's motive in striving to terrify Illtyd and the miller out of their lives and, in Rowden's case, well-nigh out of his breeches! Joshua smiled involuntarily. He'd vow that the miller, despite his massive bulk and lethargy, had never moved swifter in all his life and, no doubt, that indulged, moth-eaten cob between the shafts.

He was convinced that Ossie was right, and the fiery archer was 'The Magnificent Marvo' of travelling circus fame. Perhaps 'fame', Joshua reflected, amused, was a modest exaggeration; indeed, hyperbole on a par with the leaflet Ossie so prized, although unable to decipher it. Painstakingly hand-lettered as it was, Ossie would no doubt be commanded to return it when the circus came upon the morrow. It would be as prized by the circus owner, who had paid some scribe handsomely to letter and illustrate it, as by the folk of the three hamlets. Small matter that few, if any, could read its words. It was a thing of curiosity and worth; a promise of rare delights to come.

Joshua urged the mare along the stony, ill-made track to Rowden's mill, hearing the rush and swoop of the sails like the wingbeats of some monstrously soaring bird. He would not tarry overlong upon his task, for he, too, had promise of delights to come. He was to ride directly to Southerndown Court to take luncheon with Rebecca and her grandfather; an engagement of longstanding, and one he was loath to forgo, despite the urgency of the commissions which awaited him.

He dismounted before the mill and tethered his mare upon an iron ring set into the earth, that it might crop safely upon the wind-ruffled grass.

Rowden came from within the mill upon hearing the mare's hooves striking the stones, a smile upon his broad, good-natured face. Joshua greeted him courteously and with warmth, thinking that, covered as the miller was in a grey misting of flour, he seemed well-equipped to challenge the archer as a wraith. Yet he was surely the brawniest, most hirsute apparition, and the most solid ever seen. Every small crevice, wrinkle, thread or hair, whether upon clothing or flesh, was ghostly bleached. Eyebrows, hair, lips, even his sailcloth apron and shoes were veiled and made gauzy with flour, so that when Rowden smiled, even his teeth seemed to fade and disappear into the overall whiteness.

'You have heard, then, of my . . . adventure of yesterday?' he asked expressively, broad hands scattering a cloud of flour as he wiped them fruitlessly upon his apron.

'Indeed,' agreed Joshua, 'it is the talk of the three hamlets, with every man offering a wilder, less plausible explanation than his neighbour! You have some notion of your own, perhaps? Some theory?'

'I'll wager that our phantom archer is no more a spectre than that old Welsh cob of mine!' declared Rowden, emphatically. 'Although I can testify, to my cost, he moves swifter and to better purpose!'

'Save, perhaps, for his hurried flight with the cart yesterday?' prompted Joshua slyly.

'Our flight,' corrected Rowden without rancour, 'for I'll swear, Constable, we escaped swifter than bats out of hell! Yet I cannot believe that the man, for flesh and blood he undoubtedly was, had murderous intent. With hindsight,' he started to laugh immoderately, 'if you will forgive the coarse reference to my rawness, sir, I feel he meant me no real harm.'

Joshua joined in the miller's spontaneous laughter, declaring that no apology was needed, save for his cart, since its loss must cost him dear.

'Even that,' declared Rowden, with cheerful optimism, 'has its wry humour, for I have already secured the use of another.'

'How so?'

Rowden motioned Joshua towards the side of the millhouse, where a funeral cart, complete with mourning trappings, lay upended, surrounded by sacks of flour.

'You have borrowed it from Ezra the Box?' asked Joshua, amazed, for the little undertaker's parsimony was well known.

'No, sir, not borrowed, hired, and at the burial rate, which will all but ruin me, I do not doubt! Still, beggars cannot be choosers.'

Joshua smiled despite himself at the undertaker's cunning and business acumen.

'What's more, sir,' offered Rowden, 'it is my duty to remove the drapings and pay for them to be laundered and later restored, and should any death occur, then I am to return the cart upon the instant, and to pay the full day's hiring fee, and deliver it to Ezra's door.'

'Then I trust,' declared Joshua solemnly, 'that you will not drive it, unthinkingly, powdered as you are, or I'll vow that Ezra will have many another corpse upon his hands, for the sight of you would frighten the boldest cottager into an early grave!'

'It would grieve me to bolster Ezra's fortunes, sir,' jested Rowden good-humouredly, 'for I doubt not that he would charge me extra for transporting them to his door!'

'You can tell me nothing of note about the fiery archer, then? No description or observation which might serve to identify him?'

Rowden thought for a moment and shook his head, then his whole plump body trembled with mirth beneath the sacking apron.

'I fancy,' he said, 'that he had a better view of my backside than I of his face, Constable! That I did not stop to play the hero, I confess without shame. If he had some reason for wanting me gone, something to hide, then I did not think it politic to enquire – no more did my cob! There is value in knowing when discretion is the better part of valour.'

Joshua smilingly agreed.

'I regret, sir, that I cannot help you further,' said the miller, 'but at least the cob and I arrived at the Crown Inn in a blaze of glory that will not easily be forgotten. One must take one's immortality as it is offered,' he winked knowingly, 'and one's refreshments, too. I'll own that the ale I was freely afforded by sympathisers was enough to have extinguished the fire upon my cart twice over.'

'It is an ill wind,' said Joshua, untying his mare to take his leave.

'As I have come to know,' countered Rowden, surveying his windmill's whirling sails. 'With that archer's speed, and Ezra's business sense, what could I not achieve?'

'Friends with genuine respect for your unfailing kindness and good humour,' answered Joshua truthfully.

Rowden's cheeks grew warm with colour which glowed through their dusting of flour at Joshua's unexpected praise. He could barely hide his pleasure as he fidgeted, stamping his broad feet to release a cloud of flour, before saluting and turning to re-enter the mill.

Joshua, after leaving the miller to his insalubrious craft, returned to a task of his own, the search for clues as to what had stirred the 'fiery archer' into such bizarre activity. He was convinced that Ossie was right, and that the Magnificent Marvo was safely ensconced at Pyle, preparing to dazzle the cottagers with his unique show of pyrotechnic archery. Joshua felt a grin tug the corners of his mouth. It was no good. Despite the destruction of Rowden's cart, and Illtyd's and the miller's frenzied flights to the Crown, he could not take the creature seriously. It was all too absurd! Most likely it was but a thoughtless prank upon the part of the archer, disturbed while practising his fiery tricks. A stupid joke which had gone awry with the burning of Rowden's cart, and might have ended in tragedy. No doubt the culprit had fled, in terror as great as his victims' own, his laughter turned to distress. It had been the whim of a moment, no more; swiftly passing as the sound of his arrow shafts, and as impossible to stay. Well, tomorrow would bring the offender to his entertainment upon the village green, and there would be opportunity to question him. It would be too cruel to deny the villagers of the three hamlets their rare and glorious venture into The Arts, and such officiousness would scarcely endear their constable to them, or secure their future co-operation.

Joshua dismounted from his mare and briefly scanned the many copses, thickets and boulder-strewn fields abutting the wayside and, aware that his search had been desultory and fruitless, set out again upon his way. He would return by the Clevis Hill so that he might call upon Dr Mansel and enquire as to Ruth's condition, for Joshua had no doubts that either Mansel or Dr Burrell would have returned, at night, to be at her bedside. Joshua felt a fleeting prick of guilt at his own eagerness to be away and with Rebecca as he turned the mare through the imposing iron gateway to Obadiah Mansel's house.

Lily, the tiny, shrew-like maidservant, with raw-skinned nostrils and a nervous, darting walk, opened the door to admit him to the hall, sniffing, and saying awkwardly, 'Dr Mansel and Dr Burrell are not here, sir. They are gone out, visiting the sick.' Her pinched face brightened delightedly as she recalled what she had been instructed to say. 'You may wait in the libree, sir.'

Joshua declined, observing, 'No. I thank you. It is of no great importance. I shall return at a time more convenient.'

'Oh, sir! I had all but forgot!' Her childish face grew stricken. 'Mrs Pritchard would nigh on murder me for it! There is a note I was to give you from Dr Mansel.'

She retrieved it from the silver salver with a gadrooned edge set upon the hall table. Joshua scanned the note hurriedly, fearful that it might confide that Ruth Priday was already dead.

'Stradling,

Should you call in my absence to enquire about the child at Maudlam, I regret to inform you that her condition remains grave, but unchanged. She has not returned to consciousness, and it might be some days before we can ascertain whether she will recover, and, if so, to what extent. There is no possibility of your questioning her. Please return at the earliest convenient opportunity. There is an aspect of this affair I would discuss with you.

Your obedient servant, sir,
Obadiah Mansel.'

Joshua thoughtfully folded the message and placed it within his pocket, offering a word of thanks to the little maidservant, who scurried importantly before him to attend to the door. Once upon the doorstep, Joshua set his handsome helmet securely upon his head before bending to say, 'I beg that you will inform Dr Mansel that I shall return as soon as I am able. Oh, and Lily?'

'Sir?' Her narrow, pinched face was ugly with concern lest she had somehow offended him.

'Should Mrs Pritchard attempt to murder you, or even box your ears, then the full weight and panoply of the law will descend upon her. I give you my solemn word. Never doubt it!' Joshua gave her the full radiance of his smile, and a broad, conspiratorial wink.

'Oh, sir . . . Oh, sir . . .' Lily muttered, colouring in confusion as, delighted and embarrassed, she closed the door and made swift her escape to the kitchen.

Mrs Pritchard, the austere chatelaine who ruled over the household staff, looked up and regarded Lily sternly, chiding her for her over-hasty entrance, then declared tartly, 'I hope, miss, that you remembered the instructions I gave you, and behaved circumspectly, for once, and with the required dignity.'

As Lily sniffed and wriggled uncomfortably, Mrs Pritchard continued, 'For heaven's sake, child, take time to wipe your nose! You scurry and fidget about so that it makes me giddy just to watch you! You did not forget to give the constable Dr Mansel's note?'

'No, ma'am.'

'Constable Stradling is a gentleman, Lily, and would expect to be treated with good manners, courtesy and respect.'

'Oh, I know, ma'am,' confided Lily in a rare burst of loquacity and enthusiasm. 'You would have been ever so proud of me. I did everything you told me to. I copied you exactly, Mrs Pritchard. No one would have known I wasn't a proper lady.'

'Indeed,' said Mrs Pritchard, trying to suppress a smile. 'I am flattered, Lily, that you take me as your example.' Her dour expression grew indulgent. 'I must see that I live up to your good opinion.'

'Yes, ma'am,' agreed Lily innocently. 'Mr Stradling's too.'

Joshua returned to his cottage overlooking the village green to prepare himself for his visit to Southerndown Court. He was grateful that Ruth still clung stubbornly to life, despite the violence of her injuries, for he had feared that shock and horror might have broken her will to survive. Did she recall any, or all, of it, he wondered, in that dark, solitary place, that limbo bordering upon hell which now possessed her? That place which neither love nor hatred could penetrate? And when she awoke to reluctant life, would reality, he wondered, be too painful for her to bear? There was no doubting that for Joe Priday, Ruth's return to living would bring the only thing on earth he truly sought. He believed that his daughter's recovery would be an end to grief. Yet might it not be a beginning of a greater hurt, the realisation that Ruth had been lost to him more surely than in death? Dead, she would have been preserved in memory as the child he knew, time deepening affection, softening loss. What could soften for her, or for Priday, the sudden loss of innocence and trust? The inevitable change?

Joshua washed himself in the icy well water in the yard, and dressed himself in his gentleman's finery with less enthusiasm than was his wont. Had Ruth's assault become a murder, he knew that he would have remained, without thought, to seek the offender out. Rebecca and Sir Matthew, appreciating the exigencies and demands of his work, would have understood. More, they would have respected his commitment to the task. If Dr Mansel were to be believed, then a visit to Maudlam would avail Joshua nothing, for Ruth was unable to speak. Yet he could not shake off a feeling of guilt, a sense of betrayal which dimmed his pleasure in the meeting ahead. It was several weeks since he had shared Rebecca's company, and letters were a poor enough substitute for her warm and loving flesh and her joyousness in living. His work as constable possessed him, often to the exclusion of all else, and he sometimes regretted his neglect of those he loved for those so fiercely dependent upon him.

No, for a few hours, he would put aside the problems and trials which awaited him. He was resolved upon it, for he would come back refreshed, and with a new perspective upon what troubled him, and the energy to act with resolution. Accordingly, he rode out upon the grey, as promised, with the picture of Rebecca's lively, intelligent face and her remarkable blue eyes clear in his mind. Why, then, did it blur and fade, and the ravaged, bloodstained face of Ruth Priday overlay it, so that they became one and the same? Confused. Indissoluble.

As the mare's hoofbeats measured out the miles with a steady, rhythmic pace, Joshua's mind began to relax. The sound was gently soporific, regular and comforting as a heartbeat. Soon they had reached the hunchbacked dipping bridge crouched over the Ewenny river, its clearness swirling and sucking over stones and roots of trees that clung precariously to grassy banks, gnarled feet seeking the waters.

Joshua reined in the mare and led her to the river's edge and on to the flat bedrock, where she might drink in safety. As he did so, an iridescent kingfisher flashed from the far bank, swift and luminous, soft body colourful as a peacock's throat.

A wisp of memory stirred, soft as the breeze that ruffled the waters at his feet. Rebecca at the justice's table, shoulders bared, the shot silk of her gown a subtly changing richness of blues and greens, the sapphires at throat and wrist no finer or more lucent in the candlelight than her clear, bright eyes.

He led the grey back to the bank, remounted, and took the highway that skirted the gull-strewn estuary, the mud flats far below dotted with damp, green islands and grazing cattle, with, beyond, the yellow crescent of the bay, the dunes, and the foam-topped waves reflecting the sky.

Of his love for Rebecca and its promise to endure, he had no doubts, nor of her affection in return. It was, he thought, as firm and constant as the sea and the land; the tides of birth, and life, and death.

Beyond the river estuary, the land now began to rise and change, the steep hillsides boulder-strewn and clothed with brittle, long dead ferns, their brown barely softened by the curling silver fronds of new growth. Amidst the rocky outcrops and dry-stone walls, sheep grazed upon the salt-washed turf. As his mare cantered by, they paused in their eating, lips raised disdainfully over yellowed teeth, protuberant eyes pained and puzzled, like dowagers mutely deploring the unseemly antics of the young. Their own young tumbled and leapt beside them, awkward upon new legs, their cries as plaintive and lost as those of the estuary gulls.

As Joshua reined the grey through the wide, imposing

gateway of Southerndown Court, he saw, far below him, the sea, its calm surface reflecting the blue of the sky, its transparent ripples edged with milky foam. Then he glimpsed the soft, amber-gold of wet sand, and the scarred rocks, before the curve of the carriageway hid all from view.

He had barely delivered the grey which was prancing skittishly, head tossing, to the care of a young groom when the great door was flung open beneath the porte-cochere, as, regardless of footman, groom or propriety, a young woman impulsively descended the steps. In a flurry of excited movement and cries, rose-pink skirts and petticoats were twitched above matching slippers as her feet sped across the gravel, then her arms were about Joshua's neck, and her soft lips upon his cheek, dark hair tumbling about him.

'Oh, Joshua! Joshua!' she exclaimed, when she could at length take breath. 'How pleased I am to see you!'

'And I, you, ma'am,' returned Joshua, smilingly disengaging her arms and linking his arm within hers. His eyes were warm with amusement. 'I have a notion, Mistress de Breos, that I am uncommonly susceptible to the allure of high-stepping fillies.'

'Then, sir,' she replied with mock severity as she led him up the steps, 'it speaks more for their persistence and unwillingness to be broken than your strength of character.'

'Indeed,' he agreed as he laughingly escorted her within, 'I shamelessly confess to the weakness, and cannot even swear to change.'

'Then I forgive you, sir, and gladly,' she observed, smiling indulgently, 'for I could not bear to live with a paragon. Besides, I will give you something to live up to.'

Joshua would have been satisfied merely to have remained in Rebecca's company, believing, like many another before and since, that his beloved's sweet presence was all of food and drink that he required. Yet he consumed his luncheon with the keenest enjoyment, for he dined too often alone, and upon cold, unappetising fare. The food at Southerndown Court was excellent, 'perfectly complementing,' he declared gallantly, 'the supreme elegance of the party and the conversation.'

There were six present in all for, in addition to the host and the betrothed pair, Mrs Crandle and Elizabeth had been invited to dine, and to Joshua's surprise and pleasure, Dr Handel Peate. He had believed his mentor, whose scholarship and humour now enlivened lessons for Rebecca and Elizabeth, to be dining at Tythegston Court. When partaking of a little pre-prandial refreshment with the gentlemen in Sir Matthew's library, Dr Peate had swiftly disabused him of the notion.

'It is by the charitable offer of Sir Matthew that I dine at all, sir!' he declared with some asperity. 'So engrossed was Robert Knight in his plans for that wretched fire appliance that he barely remembered to extend a civil word, much less his invitation to break bread. I freely admit, sir, that even dry bread would have been as welcome a sight to me as those ravens which fed Elijah!'

'Then I may hope to offer you something more appetising and substantial,' declared Sir Matthew, amused.

'To my shame,' confessed Dr Peate, smiling in response, 'old age and bachelorhood have made me pernickety and set in my ways. I am set firm as a fly in amber, fossilised. I am quite unable to mortify the flesh as I ought. I do not mind owning, since the ladies are absent, that all too frequently it is my stomach which mortifies *me*, by rebelling most audibly. It is vexatious and humiliating!' Amidst laughter, he continued, 'I fear I can never now aspire to becoming a saint or martyr.'

'I do not think I would altogether be comfortable in the company of a saint or martyr,' offered Sir Matthew as consolation. 'He would remind me too painfully of my own sins and omissions! No, your friendship and honesty are much to be preferred. Besides, a martyr would not as easily be inclined to humour, nor to appreciate the delectable feast prepared. Shall we not add to our pleasure by joining the ladies?'

'Certainly,' declared Dr Peate wickedly, 'for, although I am a bachelor, I am almost as susceptible to the charms of the fairer sex as to the allure of dining.'

It was, as Joshua had intimated, a congenial, well-matched gathering, with Sir Matthew an attentive host, anticipating his guests' every need and skilfully drawing them into discussion, then guiding it, unremarked, into safe channels.

Joshua was acutely aware that but for Sir Matthew's charming ease of manner and his understanding of those about him, the savage currents of past events might well have been a danger. Elizabeth and her mother owed their present home and good fortune to Rebecca's compassion and to her grandfather's generosity. It was not easy for a gentlewoman of birth and breeding like Louisa Crandle gracefully to accept such charity, even when offered so sensitively, and with genuine affection. How much harder then, Joshua thought, to accept that it was he, in his role as constable, who had pursued her son, Creighton, to his death, and had sent her husband to be immured in that vile prison? Through Sir Matthew's intervention, Hugo Crandle had mercifully been removed to a private refuge for those disordered in mind, although Louisa Crandle would not, even now, admit that he was insane, even if circumstances and time had forced her to believe that he had been thief and smuggler, and her only son a murderer without pity or redemption.

Joshua, glancing at Louisa Crandle's smiling, animated face amid the gracious elegance of crystal and silver set upon pristine napery, and softened with epergnes of fruit and flowers, thought how bitter it was that the sins of the dead so often were inherited by the living. It was those who survived who redeemed their debts, and made payment, like Elizabeth and Mrs Crandle, Joe Priday and Ruth.

Sir Matthew, turning to address Dr Peate, glimpsed the naked pain upon Joshua's face, raw as skinned flesh. What was it, the old man wondered compassionately, that had such power to wound the young man so? Some memory, deep and unhealed, too new, perhaps, to scar? Well, there would be many such hurts inflicted by duty, lacerating, exposing nerve, as Sir Matthew could testify, and age would not subdue them. Joshua had made his choice and would learn to live with it, as he himself had done. Of one thing Sir Matthew was sure, young Stradling, too, was a survivor. He had the will and integrity, and there was no doubting his courage. Yes, he would survive, but at what price?

Sir Matthew, looking up, and seeing the quick smile of affection and understanding exchanged between Rebecca and Joshua, thought how like Emma, his dead wife, his granddaughter was, with her warm tenderness and joy in living. Grief caught his throat with the pain of loss so savage that he all but cried aloud. Then the blurred sounds and the faces of those around him steadied and grew clear as he chided himself, she would not have me grieve for the past, for it would be a betrayal of all that was between us, and what now exists in Rebecca, the present and living flesh.

He turned to Mrs Crandle, his face composed, smiling, listening attentively as she spoke, murmuring response with the grace of long habit. Only his friend, Dr Peate, noticed the tightness in Sir Matthew's voice and the barely noticeable tremor in his hands, reading into them those signs of age which he now divined so often and with such impotent fury in himself, First and second childhood, he thought wrily, how alike and yet how different they were. Alike in feebleness, dependence, and the awkwardness of limbs and speech. Yet they were different in that what was endearingly helpless in a babe was judged crassness and perversity in the old. No, he could not welcome the failing of the senses, the slow disintegration of reasoning, and memory, and flesh.

'Do you not think, Sir Matthew,' he asked unexpectedly, and with a resurgence of his old, dry humour, 'that there is much to be said for Oriental custom? Reverence for the aged, ancestor worship, even?'

'Certainly,' declared Sir Matthew, straightfaced, 'it shows an unusual degree of acuity and civilisation, and has more to commend it than the habit of the Esquimaux. I believe they remove their ancients by sledge to some wild, forsaken place and abandon them to the elements!'

There was a rush of appreciative laughter, amused comment and sly suggestions before Sir Matthew turned to Mrs Crandle, saying gently, 'I believe, ma'am, that the future and the young are our hope and consolation. Captain Devereaux will soon return from his voyage to Valparaiso. You have, I am sure, the preparations for his wedding to Elizabeth well in hand?'

Elizabeth's gentle, intelligent face grew animated as the plans for her quiet wedding to the young sea captain were discussed, and she spoke with warm gratitude and pleasure of Sir Matthew's kindness in granting them the Dower House in which to make their home.

'My dear,' he said with sincerity, 'I look upon you as part of my family. I would have it no other way, and am only grateful that you will remain near at hand. I am sure that your marriage to Captain Devereaux will bring us all the keenest of happiness, for he is an admirable young gentleman in every way, and justly deserving of such a loyal and loving partner.'

If Mrs Crandle's thoughts were of her husband, she gave no sign. She accepted most gracefully the generous chorus of good will and affection which greeted Sir Matthew's words, for she knew them to be but the truth. Elizabeth was indeed all Sir Matthew praised, and more, and she loved her daughter dearly. Yet, as is the perverse way of nature and the world, in the deepest recesses of her heart, Louisa Crandle's love was not for Elizabeth, the gentle, sacrificial lamb, but for a wild, untamable fox, cruel and devoid of pity, hair bright as the blood he so heedlessly shed. Elizabeth had always accepted that she was loved less, as she accepted her mother's tears and weakness, and her father's disgrace; reversing the roles of caring, becoming parent rather than child, protecting, sheltering, loving them for what they were and not for what they might have been.

It was, Sir Matthew thought, Elizabeth's greatest strength, this loyal, clear-sighted affection, without conditions or demands. It was something young Roland Devereaux would learn to value in the years ahead.

The general mood of pleasure and post-prandial satisfaction spilled over into talk of Illtyd and his affairs, in particular his grotesque encounter with the fiery archer, which occasioned not a little affectionate hilarity, with increasingly bizarre guesses as to its probable explanation. Joshua related, too, the burning of Rowden's cart, carefully expurgating the miller's true reason for entering the copse lest Mrs Crandle's delicate sensibilities be offended, although he had no doubt that Rebecca and Elizabeth would have been vastly amused. He deliberately refrained from mention of the vicious attack upon Ruth Priday, for it would have served no purpose other than to alarm and depress the ladies, and to remind them cruelly of events past and best forgotten. Yet he resolved to discuss the affair later with Sir Matthew and Dr Peate, for he valued their opinions greatly. They shared the merit of having sharp, incisive minds and dispassionate judgement. With their long experience of life and people, their conclusions would serve him well.

The talk turned, inevitably, to news of Jeremiah Fleet and his new bride, Sophie, and all their many acquaintances in the three hamlets, including Rebecca's good friend Rosa, and Cavan, her ebullient Irish groom, newly recovered from a highwayman's bullet.

'I believe,' declared Sir Matthew, his glance resting affectionately in turn upon Elizabeth and Rebecca, 'that since we are gathered together in such quiet harmony of spirit, and with Elizabeth's marriage to Captain Roland Devereaux so soon to be celebrated, it is an occasion for warm celebration.'

He motioned to a footman to fill the glasses of the guests, then raised his own glass with the barest tremor of his hands which, Joshua saw with pity, were liver-freckled with age, the skin wrinkled and hanging loose, as though the bones beneath were already freed of flesh, sere as a skeleton.

'I give you a toast, my friends. To the persuasive power of love, and the fulfilment of marriage.'

All eyes turned upon Elizabeth, who blushed and responded prettily, as befitted a bride-to-be. Joshua's gaze was turned questioningly upon Rebecca's face. She gazed back at him steadfastly, her extraordinary blue eyes dark-lashed, their expression veiled and unreadable, as he raised his glass, and drank.

Chapter Six

It was after the civilised and elegant meal was ended, with some natural reluctance upon the part of the guests, that Joshua's host quietly bade him, 'Attend me in the library, sir, when time allows, for I would have private discussion with you.'

It was a summons which Joshua, with some disquiet, obeyed. Dr Peate obligingly engaged the ladies in some discussion of a determinedly frivolous and inconsequential nature, and Joshua excused himself from their presence, their delighted laughter following him upon his way.

Sir Matthew greeted Joshua pleasantly and motioned him to a chair before seating himself. Joshua thought, not for the first time, how well the serene and ordered atmosphere of the library became the old gentleman. They seemed to have matured together, sharing the same warmth and dignity; the rightness which cannot be deliberately created, for it derives from all that is best of the past, whether in flesh and blood or other men's words.

Sir Matthew was watching Joshua intently, his fine intelligent eyes alert and questioning in the strong-boned face. 'I have asked you here, sir, because I was aware that you seemed pensive and withdrawn. If it is some problem of a personal nature which so occupies your mind, then I beg you will discount my concern. Yet, if it is something which might be lessened or clarified by the telling of it, then it will be my privilege to listen.' he smiled understandingly. 'I will not say advise, for advice, unsolicited, is an imposition and impertinence.'

'It is a matter of my work, sir,' confessed Joshua, 'and a matter which I was unwilling to discuss before Mrs Crandle, Rebecca and Elizabeth, for there are aspects of the affair which do not easily bear repeating, they are so cruelly degrading.'

Sir Matthew listened intently and in silence while Joshua recounted what had befallen Ruth, sparing no detail.

'It is barely credible that any man could behave in so vicious and depraved a fashion.' Sir Matthew's voice was inexpressibly tired, his face drawn with pity. 'There are times when one despairs of one's fellow men, Joshua! Beasts of the field and wild animals would not behave with the same savagery to others of their kind. It is past comprehension! That is the only opinion I am able to give.' He shook his head in perplexity. 'As to what devilry stirs such evil into life, or what demon possesses the soul of such a man –' He broke off helplessly.

'My difficulty,' confessed Joshua, 'is that in every other case which has bedevilled me, I have been able to think myself into the villain's mind, to recognise the catalyst which prompted such violence, whether greed, revenge, or self-preservation, terror of discovery.'

'I fear,' said Sir Matthew, after deliberation, 'that terror of discovery might well be the motive. If the girl's assailant were known to her, might he not choose to kill her? Should she recover and disclose his identity, her father's wrath and the vengeance of those who knew and loved her would be bloody indeed, and who could fail to understand it? If it were a daughter of mine, or my grandchild, so violated and defiled . . .' He checked himself before saying with awkward abruptness, 'I speak, not as a justice, but as a man like Priday, and cannot regret that I have the same feelings as those who have been wronged. Unless a magistrate recognises the despair of the victim, and the grief of those whose lives are ripped asunder, he cannot truly judge the crime or the criminal.'

'It is a hard task, Sir Matthew, to be human and impartial,' ventured Joshua compassionately.

'Not merely hard, but impossible,' the old gentleman admitted wrily. 'It is the law which must remain impartial, inviolate. That is the only absolute. All I can hope to do is to administer it with humanity and with honesty. That is the strength and the failing of our judicial system, that those who sit in judgement are themselves as human and fallible as those who err, and I have often thought, there, but for the grace of God . . . Who knows what crimes poverty and despair might drive me to commit?'

'Yet never such a crime as that upon Ruth, however bleak your circumstances or future,' declared Joshua with conviction.

'No, never that. What could it profit me to maim or to kill someone as poor and even more defenceless than I? My anger would be for those in authority, the profligate and uncaring. Lust may be more easily satisfied, even among the poor, unless . . .' He paused, uncertainly.

'Unless, sir?'

'Unless he is a man hopelessly flawed, one embittered and corrupt, who cannot bear to see innocence and good in others, and so seeks to destroy it violently. There are such creatures, Joshua, and they are the most difficult to bring to justice, for such perversity is hidden behind a mask of respectability, bland and impenetrable. Their very normality is their shield.' He looked at Joshua steadily. 'There is a possibility, too, that the man you seek is a man of substance, reputable, his position within the community placing him seemingly above suspicion. It is not unknown, and I admit it with shame, for putative gentlemen to behave differently towards women whom they consider to be of a lower class of society, treating them as beneath contempt. They set no value upon chastity, or the emotions of others, ruled only by their need for self-indulgence. I pray that it is not such a man whom you seek, Joshua, for the way to him will be barred by many who depend upon his charity or patronage to survive. Droit du Seigneur! Those enshrined rights of lordship linger still, I fear, despite all efforts to end such heresy.'

'I do not know where to begin,' said Joshua wretchedly, 'for the girl can offer no help, and the villagers would not shelter a man so depraved, of that, I am sure. No, not even one in authority over them, for their horror and rage were apparent.'

'You spoke of Dr Mansel's wish to discuss the affair with you, did you not? There was mention of some opiate?'

'Yes, Mansel's own wife was dependent upon laudanum, and her craving for it led her to disaster and death.'

'Then if his suspicion that Ruth had been persuaded to partake of a similar substance proves correct, or that an opiate was forcibly administered, you have a starting point. From there, your task must be to isolate and question all those who have special knowledge of such substances – apothecaries, doctors, conjurors, all those who sell laudanum and such noxious remedies freely. The real tragedy is that the lives of the poor are as arid as the hovels in which they are forced to live. They are offered neither comfort nor hope of change. It is small wonder if they seek escape in drunkenness and drug-induced sleep. Oblivion is kinder than reality. Physicians readily prescribe drink to numb the wounds of the body, yet we curse those who seek to ease such hurts of mind and spirit.' Sir Matthew sighed despairingly. 'The rich are the worst of hypocrites, Joshua, and I must number myself among them. Those excesses we berate in others as sins, we indulge in without remorse, counting them virtues, and proof of our worldly success. Drunkenness, gaming, lechery even, are considered proof of manliness in the upper echelons, degeneracy in the poor.'

'I believe, sir,' said Joshua with sincerity, 'that you have always discharged your duties as landowner and justice with the greatest compassion, and are much respected as an honest man.'

'Then I had best live up to my reputation,' said Sir Matthew with a dry smile, 'and confess that I now require a favour of you.'

'Then I shall gladly grant it, sir, if it is within my power to do so.'

'Yes, it is within your power.' The old gentleman hesitated, before confessing, 'I admit I scarce know how to begin.'

Joshua waited, giving him no help, until Sir Matthew broke the silence by exclaiming vexedly, 'Damn it, sir! I would have you persuade Rebecca that it is time you were wed; that I am neither ancient, crippled, nor yet deprived of my few remaining faculties.'

Joshua's astonishment could not stem the mirth which bubbled within him at this unexpected outburst. He broke into laughter, apologising even as he did so, yet seeing Sir Matthew succumb to the same unquenchable humour at the absurdity of it.

When they had regained composure, Joshua asked with mock gravity, 'Am I to assume, sir, that there is some reluctance upon the young lady's part? That there is some impediment of which I am unaware?'

'*I* am the impediment,' declared Sir Matthew irrepressibly, 'and not you, sir. Upon that score you may be reassured.'

'Then, if you will forgive me, Sir Matthew, I admit that I am relieved to hear it,' countered Joshua smiling, 'for if I were the cause, then the future would seem bleak indeed! But what would you have me do?'

'I cannot convince Rebecca that it would be my greatest joy to see her wed, that I would have her immediate future settled above all else.'

Joshua asked carefully, 'You have spoken of this to her, sir? Used the exact words which you now address to me? Forgive me, but perhaps you have not set it out plainly enough.'

'If I were to set it out more plainly, sir,' declared Sir Matthew, with wry humour, 'then I fancy she would take leave upon the instant, feeling her presence intolerable to me!'

Joshua's lips twitched as he shook his head in denial, saying firmly, 'I think you need have no fear upon that account. Rebecca's love for you, as your own for her, could never be in doubt. That is the sole reason for the delay.' He broke off in embarrassment, before explaining, 'She believes that she owes you her obedience, sir, as a return for your kindness to her, and to others, like Mrs Crandle and Elizabeth.'

'Obedience is scarcely the word to use,' corrected Sir Matthew, good-humouredly, 'for in this, as in all else, she remains stubbornly adamant. I feel it is a trait she might well have inherited from me.' He chuckled conspiratorially. 'Perhaps, Joshua, your powers of persuasion might eclipse mine, else what advantage has love, or loving?'

Joshua did not think it seemly to reply.

Sir Matthew had turned aside, and Joshua studied him

as he poured two measures of brandy from the decanter upon his desk, the hand which offered the glass trembling almost imperceptibly. Sir Matthew looked suddenly old and uncertain, his spare, fleshless frame scarce appearing strong enough to bear the weight of all that troubled him, as he confessed, 'I could wish for Rebecca the freedom of her own home, and family, untrammelled by care while she is able, as I would hope to see my great-grandchildren grow, unhindered by early shadows of what must inevitably come – the cares and responsibilities of their inheritance.'

'Then we are united, sir, in the same desire.'

Sir Matthew nodded, satisfied. 'Then I am content, Joshua, to leave Rebecca to your care, knowing that you love her as dearly as I, and would never see her hurt or her spirit broken.'

He rested a hand briefly upon Joshua's shoulder, almost as if it were a benediction he offered, and Joshua fancied he glimpsed the softness of tears before Sir Matthew pulled away quickly, saying with forced lightness, 'I think, my boy, that since we are so plainly in accord, we might appropriately refresh ourselves for the battles ahead, for battles there will most assuredly be!' He smiled, adding, 'Rebecca is a de Breos born,' and there was no mistaking his extreme satisfaction.

They drank in companionable silence for a time, sharing the warmth of those in perfect accord, before Sir Matthew set down his glass, his elegant features grown grave.

'This young woman of whom you spoke – Ruth Priday; if there is anything which she might need, I would count it a privilege to help.'

'No, sir. I thank you on her behalf and that of her father, but assure you that Dr Mansel's care is all-embracing.'

Sir Matthew nodded his understanding, his eyes serious. 'I hope, Joshua, that the child is well guarded. If her assailant knows where she lives . . .' He left the sentence unfinished.

'For the moment, Sir Matthew, I am sure that her father will remain at her side, unwilling to leave her. It is not yet known whether she will live.'

'But later?' Sir Matthew insisted. 'If she should survive?'

'I shall see that she is well guarded, and never left alone,' Joshua promised.

Long after Joshua had left him, Sir Matthew sat, immersed in thought, secure in the enclosed comfort of the room he loved best in all the house, breathing in its familiar mellowness. He savoured the masculine odour of leather, wax and tobacco, and the pervasive mustiness of pages dank with age. They mingled with the smells of sealing wax and ink, and that strange, inseparable fusion of stone, mortar and heavy fabrics permeated with dust and wood smoke – familiar, comforting. Yet his spirit was heavy.

I shall miss Rebecca, he thought bleakly, I shall miss the child more than she can ever know. It will be harder, now, than before I knew her. Then, remembering Priday's all-consuming grief with a feeling of shame, he sternly roused himself. I have so much, and he has so little, he thought, and yet, today, we are one flesh, one hurt. If it were always so, would not pity serve to make the world a better place? Or would there be too much pain to bear? Dr Peate would doubtless turn his thoughts to One who already knew, but Joe Priday and he were human and fallible, and could not be consoled.

Joshua, upon leaving the library, had hoped to go at once to be with Rebecca, for time was pressing and the journey to Newton better made before darkness fell.

However, he was immediately waylaid by Dr Peate, whose evident pleasure in his old pupil's company it would have been churlish indeed to rebuff. He seemed to Joshua even more stooped and frail, skin drawn and mottled and fine as parchment upon his contracted frame. Yet, despite the thinning of his features and the sparseness of his baby-fine hair, his eyes were sharply observant. They were, Joshua thought, the only things about him untouched by age.

'Well, Stradling,' exclaimed Dr Peate, grasping Joshua's hand and shaking it excessively, 'I am indeed delighted to have stumbled upon you again so fortuitously.'

Joshua did not seek to challenge this polite fiction, for they were both aware that Dr Peate had impatiently awaited him.

'It is my duty, sir, to offer you my most sincere and abject apologies,' declared Dr Peate, without preamble. 'I behaved, this morning, with extreme petulance and boorishness.' Seeing that Joshua was plainly mystified, the good gentleman continued in explanation, 'My concern for my friend Robert Knight was real enough, yet overshadowed, I fear, by my overweening conceit and arrogance.'

'I am sure, sir, that you do yourself an injustice,' protested Joshua.

But Dr Peate waved him aside, declaring firmly, as if he were an unruly pupil, 'No, sir, do not interrupt! Pray allow my confession, for it is said to be good for the soul. The truth is that when my presence proved unnecessary, and my words of solace were denied, I felt my friendship to be spurned. You understand?'

'Yes, sir.' Joshua's voice was gentle. 'No man likes to see his good intentions rejected.'

'Yes, that is the crux of it, Stradling! I valued my own

stupid pride above Robert Knight's recovery. I take no joy in the admission.'

'Perhaps, like Mr Knight, the comfort and forgiveness you so freely offer to others might be extended to your own . . . frailties, sir?'

Dr Peate smiled. 'Indeed, Stradling,' he observed drily, 'it is of some small consolation to me, in my declining years, to recognise some latent spark of intelligence in those whom I laboured so sedulously to instruct.' He hesitated, then added with evident warmth, 'It pleases me more that you show understanding and compassion, for they cannot be taught.' He placed a frail hand upon Joshua's arm. 'I regret that when you spurned my advice to enter Jesus College as a student I made my anger and disappointment plain. The virtues and talents I discerned in you then will not be wasted in the work you choose as constable.'

Joshua, pleased beyond measure by this handsome testimonial, thanked his old tutor sincerely before confessing, 'There are times, sir, when I feel bewildered and painfully inadequate for my task.'

'If you claimed otherwise, then I would certainly judge you to be so,' rebuked Dr Peate briskly. 'It is a wise man who strives for perfection, Joshua, but a fool and a charlatan who would claim to have found it, for it has been achieved only once, and that vicariously.'

'Yet it was ever your contention, sir, that a man's aim must exceed his grasp, else what is a life worth?' Joshua quoted with affected innocence to Dr Peate's unconcealed amusement.

'I am flattered, Joshua, that you recall my borrowed words, and trust that you duly profited from them. No doubt they inspired you to set your sights upon Miss de Breos! I will detain you no longer, for my apology is made.'

'And accepted,' declared Joshua magnanimously as Dr Peate returned his bow with elegant formality.

'As to what a life is worth,' Dr Peate seemed to be reflecting aloud, 'that is a question which Robert Knight must one day resolve, with God's help, for I could give him none.'

As Joshua made to deny it, the old gentleman murmured bleakly, 'I went to him, not as a fellow priest, seeking to philosophise, but as a friend who cares.' His intelligent eyes looked steadily into Joshua's. 'Strange that I should use those words, a friend who cares. I fancy that is what Robert Knight has lost.' As Joshua remained silent, Dr Peate continued, his voice unusually troubled, 'There are many whose lives are aimless, undirected, lacking faith, but to have known faith and to have lost it is a crueller burden to bear. It is enough to break a man.'

Shoulders stooped, he went upon his way, so deep in contemplation that he was no longer aware of Joshua's presence nor that he had left him standing there. Dr Peate had spoken with such depth of feeling, Joshua thought, that it seemed almost as if he shared that same rawness of loss.

Feeling uncomfortably saddened, Joshua made his way to the music room where he knew that Rebecca awaited him. He was determined upon resolving the question of their proposed marriage, and in setting a date for the ceremony, as he had promised Sir Matthew. He had not, however, reckoned upon the quiet tenacity of Mrs Crandle in her role as chaperone. He could not pretend that she was wilfully obstructive. Indeed, she was the very model of self-effacement, curiously intent upon her needlework, all faded prettiness and decorum in her lace-frilled cap. She scarce made sound or movement, so determined was she to remain invisible, and had she been able to dispense with her needle, there is no doubting that she would have done so, and stitched with her fingers! The result, of course, was that Joshua was able to make only the most banal and stilted of conversation, his gaze returning unwillingly to Mrs Crandle, like a rabbit fascinated by a stoat. In fact, so motionless was the good lady upon occasion that Joshua had to glance at her to ensure that she had not wilfully stopped breathing.

It was with relief that he heard Rebecca declare that it was high time that he was upon his journey if he hoped to make Newton before nightfall. She would escort him to the pathway, she informed Mrs Crandle, her status as Joshua's betrothed affording her that small privilege. Mrs Crandle looked confused but did not demur, for to have done so would undoubtedly have cast aspersions upon her charge's virtuous intent and, no doubt, upon Joshua's honour. She did, however, caution Rebecca that the spring air still held a winter chill, and that it would be wise to linger as little as possible out of doors, to wrap herself warmly, and to avoid the unpleasant draughts and dampness of the shrubbery. Indeed, so positive were her strictures upon the matter that she emphasised her concern by involuntarily stabbing herself with her crewel needle, a calamity which, to his shame, troubled Joshua not a whit.

'Now, Joshua,' began Rebecca, when his horse had been saddled and returned to him, and they were safely hidden from view of the house by the thickness of the shrubbery laurels, 'perhaps you will deign to tell me what ails you. I have no doubt that something does, for you have been as scratchy as a lovesick rooster, and as civil.'

'Ah, there, ma'am, you have the nub of it!' said Joshua, laughing, and securing his mare to a branch that she might crop upon the grass unhindered. 'I am indeed lovesick, and if it has made me uncivil, then it is because I would have you beside me, always, as a wife. You understand?'

'I understand.'

A small breeze had stirred the darkness of her hair and blown a strand of it across the softness of her mouth, and Joshua gently brushed it from her lips with his fingertips. Unable to resist the nearness of her, he took her into his arms and kissed her long and deeply, and with the greatest satisfaction.

'You see, Rebecca, my love,' he declared when she was released and her dark-lashed blue eyes intent upon him, 'these few shared kisses are not enough. Love cannot stand still. It must either grow and reach completion or, like all else, wither and die away. I would not have that!'

'Why, Joshua,' she said, trying to control the amusement that obstinately curved the corners of her mouth, 'you are a true romantic. There is a poetry in likening love to a flower, is there not? I swear I have never heard you speak with such . . . elegance before.' The candid blue eyes regarded him mischievously. 'Your interview with Grandfather fared well, I hope? Of late he has been importuning me constantly with pleas for an early wedding.'

'Indeed?' said Joshua, affecting indifference.

'Indeed,' she echoed.

'And your conclusion, ma'am?'

'That it was quite unnecessary, sir. I had already decided upon that course, but wished you to be the first to hear of it. June, do you think? Since you are so incurably romantic, sir, and it is the month of warm, scented nights and roses . . .?'

'It is you who are my only rose, my dear love,' he exclaimed, taking her into his arms and holding her closely imprisoned against his breast before whispering, 'and a devious, conniving, altogether too clever little minx, whom I firmly intend to leave wilting at the altar!'

* * *

When Joshua arrived at the base of Clevis Hill at Newton after his visit to Southerndown Court, the spring warmth of the day had faded with the light. The way back had seemed infinitely longer to him, and more forlorn, lacking as it did the bright promise of being with Rebecca. As he rode, he felt the chill of the early evening mist settling upon him, its dampness transparently veiling the skin of his face and forming drops upon his hair and lashes. He had shaken his head irritably to disperse them but, monotonous and insistent as the mare's hoofbeats, they had returned to bedevil him.

At the dipping bridge over the Ewenny, the river mist had thickened into fog, its opaque greyness fusing water and stone into a swirling, all-enveloping cloud, thick and acrid as wood smoke. The mare, moving blindly, had stumbled and, in her fury to recover herself, had all but thrown Joshua over the shallow stone parapet and into the river below. He had steadied her until her trembling ceased, then dismounted, and led her across, reluctant, but trusting to his command. He had made his way by touch alone, one hand firm upon her bridle, the other tracing the rough stone curve of the parapet, while with awkward shuffling steps, his boots had scraped the base of the wall, guiding her past those treacherous holes through which the sheep were thrown for dipping. It was with relief that he had remounted upon the other side, the river fog clearing to show the silver-stemmed beechwoods upon the way, pale as the mist, and set about with the cries and wingbeats of returning birds, their dark shapes flung like tossed leaves against the sky.

When the mare had finally emerged upon the highway to the three hamlets, Joshua was still undecided as to whether to ride directly to the Crown Inn, that Ossie might stable her, or first to call upon Dr Mansel. Dusk was, he thought, an unconscionably awkward time to go calling, and yet it was the hour when the physician was most likely, as all good folk, to be taking his ease. If Mansel were already at dinner, for many still favoured the old formal regimen for dining, then the servant had merely to inform Joshua, and he would ride discreetly away, leaving the household undisturbed. Mansel's note had seemed urgent enough to warrant an intrusion, and there was no denying that news of Ruth would be welcome. No, welcome was too sanguine a word, for should she have died, then a hue and cry must immediately be called to hunt down her murderer. With passions running high, none would be safe. Her father and the villagers of Maudlam would be driven to near insanity by grief and a thirst for revenge. Innocent people, in fear for their lives, might easily be mistaken for the guilty, terror and desperation lending them a savagery as bloody as their aggressors.

His mind seething with conflict, Joshua dismounted uneasily on Clevis Hill and, bidding the mare stand, struggled to unlatch the vast wrought-iron gates to Mansel's house, hearing them creak and grind upon their hinges as he dragged them open and secured them fast. Then, remounting the grey, he rode her towards the lighted windows of the house, her hooves raking the crushed stones of the carriageway, and echoing the forlorn drag of the ebbing tide upon the shingle of the bay beyond.

It was a manservant who came in answer to Joshua's insistent tugging upon the bell. He peered out, part blinded by the darkness without, the oil lamp in his hands casting strange shadows upon the walls, and distorting his features grotesquely in its light. Joshua's enquiry about Dr Mansel brought the physician himself hurrying from the library to bid Joshua enter. Joshua, with a muttered apology, followed him within, suiting his long paces to the physician's light, nervous ones, so strangely at variance with Mansel's assured plumpness.

'You have come in answer to my note?'

Without benefit of reply, Mansel motioned Joshua to a chair and proceeded to pour two measures of cognac from the decanter upon the vast partners' desk before him. There were oil lamps set in wrought-iron brackets upon the walls, and large moderator lamps, suspended by thick chains from the ceiling above, and casting a glow upon the gleaming pinkness of Mansel's bare scalp, the soft wisps of white hair surrounding it, fine as thistledown.

'Well.' He straightened up, dismissing Joshua's explanation with a wave of his plump hands and handing him a well-filled glass. 'You had best drink this, sir, before we begin,' he commanded. 'I will brook no polite refusal,' he declared as Joshua demurred. 'I prescribe it as a physician and friend. I have eyes in my head, sir, and it is plain that you are in dire need of it.'

Fatigue had deepened the lines of Joshua's face, and dampness clung to his clothing, but the fiery warmth of the liquid sent blood surging through his veins and drew colour into his cold flesh. Mansel watched Joshua drink before tasting his own, the look of concern in his opaque gooseberry coloured eyes turning to approval as Joshua's vitality returned.

Mansel said abruptly. 'Burrell has driven the gig to Maudlam, and has not yet returned.'

'Ruth Priday survives, then?' blurted Joshua. 'And her condition, sir?'

Obadiah Mansel regarded him assessingly, biting the flesh of his lower lip before saying, as if he had not heard, 'Burrell agrees with me that some noxious draught was administered by her attacker, who then took carnal knowledge of the girl.'

'But she is still living, sir, and like to recover?' Joshua persisted anxiously.

'She has regained consciousness, certainly,' admitted Mansel cautiously, 'but I await John Burrell's return.'

'When may I question her? I had planned to ride out at first light.' In his eagerness, Joshua had carelessly spilled some liquid from his glass, and was dabbing at it ineffectually with his linen kerchief. He looked up to see Mansel's eyes upon him, their expression unreadable. 'Well, sir?' Joshua was aware of anxiety sharpening his tone.

'She is unable to speak a word, Stradling. I do not know if she can see, or even understand.'

'But if it is shock, sir, which renders her speechless, then she must recover, surely?' Joshua was unashamedly pleading for a reassurance Mansel was powerless to give.

'Shock, or some injury to the brain.' The physician's voice was curiously lifeless, although his eyes were quick with compassion. 'I cannot tell what affects her so grieviously, Stradling, nor can I say with certainty that she will recover.' His helplessness seemed as deep as Joshua's own.

'Time is said to be a great healer, sir.' Joshua could have wished unspoken those facile words, so thoughtlessly uttered.

There was no bitterness in Mansel's voice as he replied quietly, 'Then I pray you are right, Stradling, for I am painfully aware of my own sad failure and limitations, and grieve that it is so.'

Chapter Seven

After a restless sleep, made miserable by grotesque, disordered dreams, Joshua awakened feeling unusually depressed. His gentleman's clothing of the previous day was neatly arranged upon the wooden butler beside his bed, and he recalled, shamefacedly, how in the darkness he had let out a cry of alarm as the flickering candlelight had lent it spurious life. Instinctively he had reached for his pistol, and the coldness of metal upon his flesh had shocked him into wakefulness. He smiled, despite himself, at the thought of how nearly he had taken aim at the intruder. Appearing at Southerndown Court in finery as riddled with holes as a sieve would have demanded swift explanation and a convincing tongue if he were not to be made a laughing stock. Unlike the aristocracy and the landed gentry, a village constable could not take refuge in eccentricity. It was a privilege reserved for gentlemen.

Yet, even as he washed himself at the jug and bowl of icy water upon his washstand, Joshua was aware that beyond his amusement lay disquiet. As he dressed himself in his everyday uniform, he could not suppress the knowledge that, without thought or volition, he had been primed to shoot, as effortlessly as his own gun. Past experience had changed him inexorably. It was his own flesh which would lie shattered, or another's. Kill, or be killed. Joe Priday had been right. Violence in others bred violence within oneself. Joshua could justify his own swift defensiveness and aggression as necessary, not only for his own survival, but for the protection of the innocents like Ruth, who depended upon him. I am two people, he thought, as diverse as the two lives I lead; the elegant gentleman and the bucolic constable.

His glance went instinctively to the wooden butler. A curious dichotomy. One day, when Sir Matthew was dead and Rebecca the inheritor of Southerndown Court, his future would be decided. Indeed, it was predetermined by circumstance and promise. His constable's uniform would be set aside, and he must reluctantly take on the mantle of a gentleman of property. For the moment, his immediate concern must be to be about his business as constable; to bring to account Ruth's assailant and the Fiery Archer. On a personal level, a time for his marriage to Rebecca had finally been set. His love for Rebecca was a vital, ever-growing emotion. It enriched every moment of his day, giving purpose and meaning to all he did. Without her, he would be bereft; denied feeling and the will to exist. If, in the years ahead, there were regrets for what had been lost to him, then he must learn to endure it. His choice was Rebecca. There could be no other. He must make himself and others believe that there was nothing upon the whole earth that he would alter, or mourn. His play-acting would convince all – save Rebecca. She saw past the outer carapace to what was beneath, tender and vulnerable. For her, there was no dichotomy; no confusion. She knew the hidden Joshua better than he knew himself.

When he had eaten an unpalatable breakfast of boiled cold bacon, marble-veined with yellowed fat, and barley cakes with butter, which only served to settle his mind upon Southerndown Court and the contrast with yesterday's bounty, he refreshed himself copiously upon hot, sweet tea. The tea, and its elegant teapoy, were an extravagance of his mother who was convinced that, 'Life in that unspeakable hovel in which you choose to dwell, Joshua, will serve to sap you of all strength and vitality. You will take some flux, or ague, if you so neglect yourself.' His laughing denial had prompted the tart comment, 'You will accept my advice and my gifts gracefully, sir, and now! It will give me less pleasure to lay flowers upon your early grave.'

'Even should it give you the opportunity to declare, "I told him so, repeatedly"? ' he had asked her with sly innocence.

'Doubly so,' she had responded, a smile enlivening her delicate prettiness, 'for I would mourn not only an obstinate son, but wasted victuals and breath!'

'You had best do as she asks, first as last, Joshua,' his brother Aled had urged with mock seriousness, 'else she will be forced to buy herself a mourning gown and bonnet, and the jet and hair-brooches to go with them. With Father berating her for extravagance, and Mama declaiming that black ill becomes her complexion, I shall be living in Bedlam!'

'You will miss me sorely, brother?'

'Unconsolably,' Aled had declared, 'for you serve to deflect attention from my own peccadilloes. Constant carping would undoubtedly send me to an early grave, then we would both be undone!'

'Mama would not be best pleased,' Joshua had replied gravely, 'for that would prolong her mourning.'

'You are a pair of idle, prattling infants, with neither sense nor appreciation for all that is done for you,' Mrs Stradling had exclaimed, vexation struggling against affectionate indulgence. 'I cannot think where either of you has sprung from! You are as little like your dear papa as . . .' she glanced helplessly about her, 'as that tom cat to a bull!'

She had finished triumphantly, her triumph turning to bewilderment, then pique, as their gusts of irreverent laughter drowned all else, save their helpless mirth. Charlotte Stradling had, notwithstanding, had her way.

Joshua smiled, remembering, and after emptying the tea leaves from the pot upon the earth beside the privy midden, returned indoors to place it upon the hearth, beside the kettle, and with it the tea caddy and a crock of spice cakes, that his cleaning woman might avail herself of them. The simple fare, which his mother so deplored, was luxury beyond achieving to the cottagers of the three hamlets. It was but a small gesture, he was aware, but would be accepted gratefully and not abused. He had learnt to treat the people here with the warmth and dignity they deserved, and returned to him. He had become so familiar with their ways of thought and speech that he could almost believe that he was a villager born. He banked up the fire with a mixture of peat and fern, fashioned into roughly-shaped fuel, and, donning his helmet and taking his pistol, quit the cottage. He could only hope that his knowledge of the people, and their acceptance of him, would serve him well in the task ahead.

At the Crown Inn, Ossie came forward with Joshua's mare ready saddled, his gnarled fist of a face aglow with pleasure at the constable's coming.

'I can scarce hold myself in check for the fun we shall have this afternoon upon the green,' he blurted, his crooked smile showing the gaps in his teeth. ' 'Twill be a spectacle of the greatest magnitude, Joshua,' he declared excitedly, 'for it's rumoured that the circus folk have appeared before crowned heads.'

'Crowned with what,' demanded Joshua sceptically, 'chamber pots? Bay laurel? Credulity?' Upon seeing the ostler's face grow uncertain, and his pleasure fade, Joshua felt immediate remorse at his discourtesy.

'Forgive me, my friend,' he said, laying a hand in apology upon Ossie's bent shoulders, 'my anger is with myself and not you, that I am helpless to aid Ruth Priday or her father. I beg you will forgive me, although I do not justly deserve it.'

He told the ostler of Dr Mansel's fears and conclusions, and saw Ossie's expression grow as troubled as his own.

'Where will you begin,' Ossie asked soberly, 'for there is so little of use to act upon?'

Joshua shook his head. 'The doctors, apothecaries and wise men - the conjurors - must be questioned, of course, but I fear that what they have to relate will be of little help. Those who have something to hide will scarcely confide in me, lest they incriminate themselves, and those who are blameless will know nothing.'

Ossie looked at him consideringly, as if choosing his words with care, before speaking them aloud. 'I have heard that the gypsies are encamped near Nottage,' he confided, 'the true Romanies. I tell you, not because I suspect them of ill-doing, but to make you aware, because every man's hand will be turned against them. Perhaps they will have need of your vigilance and protection. I recollect that they have helped you, willingly and to good purpose, in the past.'

'Yes, that is so,' Joshua admitted, 'and I owe them the protection and aid I would render any in need of it. But I see by your expression, Ossie, that there is something more.'

'For too long I was an outcast myself,' confessed Ossie, 'blamed for every ill that occurred, and forced to redeem myself and make amends for sins I did not commit.'

'So you have sympathy with them?'

'More. I know that such senseless violence is not a

crime they would readily accept, or perpetrate. The vengeance of their tribe is rough and merciless to those who break their code, for they must learn to live in amity with those about them, to ensure their survival as a race.'

'I will see that none harms them, or denies them water and safe grazing, if it is within my power. I shall speak on their behalf, have no fear.'

'That donkey of which you spoke . . .' Ossie began awkwardly, breaking off in hesitation.

'You have seen it? It has been brought to you at the inn?'

'No,' Ossie disclaimed, 'for I would have told you at once, for I know my duty.'

To Joshua's muttered apology at the rebuke, Ossie simply nodded, continuing, 'Had I, or the Romanies, seen a donkey beaten and ill-used, we would have removed it to safety, judging that its owner deserved its loss, you understand? I would rather believe that it had come into their hands than into the clutches of some horse dealer, ruthless and uncaring of their flesh and needs. But tread carefully, Joshua, for your uniform and authority will make them, and you, vulnerable.'

Joshua thanked him warmly, and, putting a foot to the mare's stirrup, swung himself into the saddle, bending to say, 'I shall return to witness the fiery archer's act, I do assure you.'

As the grey cantered out beneath the archway, Joshua ducked his head to hear Ossie's hoarsely uttered shout, smothered by swift laughter, 'Have a care for your breeches, then! I'll warrant that Rowden will! Should Ezra's funeral cart go up in flames, then there will be all hell to pay!'

'As many who have made use of it will testify, were they able!' called back Joshua, his good humour gratefully restored.

Joshua halted the mare briefly upon the cobblestones beside the village green, undecided as to whether first to ride to Maudlam, or to turn the mare towards the Rhyl at Nottage, where the gypsy encampment was most likely to be. The undulating land there was fertile, its shallow valley providing shelter from wind and weather, and good grazing for the Romanies' donkeys, ponies and mules. The small pool, fed by an underground stream, was clear and accessible, providing safe drinking water for owners and beasts alike. His most urgent task, he decided, was to return to Joe Priday's house, and thence to the scene of the crime, in the vain hope that some new evidence had been uncovered by accident. Perhaps Ruth's condition had improved dramatically overnight, despite Dr Mansel's gloomy prognosis, and she might be able to tell him something of value to aid his search. Certainly he could, with profit, make enquiries of apothecaries, physicians, even conjurors, those so-called wise men with their legendary powers of healing, inherited, it was claimed, from sorcerers and wizards long dead. If Ruth's attacker had been wounded in the struggle, or was troubled in mind, might he not confide in them and demand their help? They would harbour knowledge, too, of opiates or herbs. Yet such wise men would not be easy to find. Few would divulge their names, or where these miracle workers might live, for the peasantry held them in awe and guarded their solitude jealously, lest they wreak revenge. But in the hunt for Ruth's attacker, Joshua felt sure none would prevaricate or bar his way.

Accordingly, he rode out once again through the farmlands bordering Nottage and the sea, and over the sand-swirled dunes to Kenfig and on to Maudlam. Seeing the smoke curling in grey wisps through the chimney of Priday's forge, and the wrought-iron gates flung open upon their hinges, he dismounted and tethered his mare without. The apprentice lad, Tim, came hurrying out, face raw-burned with heat, eyes screwed against the change of light, and Joshua heard the hiss and splutter of hot metal he had set into water beside the anvil. Joshua had forgotten how young and vulnerable the boy was; big-boned, yet awkwardly gangling as a young colt, unsure of the power of its limbs, or how best to control them.

'Constable, sir,' his feet fidgeted nervously upon the stony pathway, 'you ride to Mr Priday's house?'

'Yes.' Joshua smiled encouragement. 'There is some message you would have me take him?'

'No, sir.' Tim's face grew redder still, and he blinked rapidly, wiping away the sweat which glistened upon his skin and lashes. 'Something for Ruth' was all of his mumbled explanation that was audible to Joshua before the boy disappeared into the forge, to return with his hands held stiffly behind his back, shielding whatever he held from view. Then, after a long silence, standing stiffly and with increasing tenseness, he defiantly thrust a small bunch of marsh violets ringed with their own dark, heart-shaped leaves into Joshua's hand, blurting, 'Ruth is fond of them, and sometimes gathers a posy to wear upon her dress.'

'It is a kind gesture, and one which she will appreciate, of that I am sure.' Joshua was painfully moved by the boy's thoughtfulness.

The lad shuffled uneasily and looked down at his feet, as if trying to stare them into obedience. 'I have asked about Ruth, sir, and would not intrude again, you understand?' His head was still bowed. 'Mr Priday said she is unable to speak, or understand . . . that nothing stirs her. I thought might not the smell of violets, the scent . . . remind her of better times . . .' His voice broke uncertainly. 'It was but a thought, sir.'

'I will see that the flowers are placed in Ruth's hands, Tim, where she can feel their petals, and drink in their fragrance,' promised Joshua, and Tim raised his head and nodded, eyes bright.

'The donkey, sir, Lucky, you have found him, or have news?'

'I fear not. But I will widen my search to include the villages beyond, and ask the fishermen and farmhands upon the shore at Sker to keep watch for him.'

'I fear, sir, he is dead.' The tears which glistened unshed for Ruth fell now in earnest. 'I took a lantern last night and searched for him along the pool and over the dunes, until dawn, and saw no signs of him.' He sniffed and turned away, shaking his head irritably to disperse his tears, ashamed to wipe his eyes lest Joshua see his hurt and think him childish and unmanly. 'There are many to care for Ruth, but he is but a beast, and of no account to any but Mr Priday, Ruth and me.' His voice was muffled. 'But I would like to know that he is safe, or even that he is dead, for that would be an end to it, and there would be no more hurt.'

No more hurt, for animal or boy, thought Joshua compassionately, and knew that he could not promise that it would be so. 'You are busy, Tim?' he asked, seeking to divert the lad from his melancholy. 'I am sure that Mr Priday values your help.'

'No, sir, the few small jobs of repairing broken tools for those who labour upon the farms or in their own vegetable plots, which I was told to do, are ended. I work upon beaten iron for practice only. There is little trade hereabouts for smiths and farriers. We are a poor village, hidden from view, and too far from the highway. Few villagers own a horse. They could not afford to feed or care for it,' he said simply, without rancour. 'It is all they can do to feed themselves.'

'I will speak to the ostler at the Crown Inn at Newton, and at the inn itself,' promised Joshua quietly. 'There are horses aplenty upon the stages, and upon the farms. He is a good man, and honest, and the blacksmith at Nottage, Ben Clatworthy, is overburdened with work, and would be grateful to relinquish some to another.'

Tim's bland, ingenuous face was alight with new hope and gratitude. 'It would be a godsend to Mr Priday, sir, for he has struggled hard to survive. I do not think he will mind the telling of it. It would be a balm to him in his trouble, I know,' His rough-skinned hand reached out to Joshua's hesitantly, then gripped it firmly, as if it were a bargain they sealed. 'I will work until I drop, sir, if need be, and promise that none will fault my work, or my application. You may depend on me.'

'As I will work to find Ruth's assailant, and the donkey, Lucky,' said Joshua kindly as, remounting his mare and clutching the posy of marsh violets, he took his leave.

As he rode, the warm sweet smell of the fragile-stemmed flowers came to him, elusive and haunting, stirring some half-forgotten memory. He could not recollect whether they spoke to him of life or of death.

As Joshua rode apprehensively towards Joe Priday's mean, ill-furnished cottage, he could not help but dwell upon the harsh contrast between the lives of the poor and those possessed of vast inherited wealth and lands. There were too many such landowners to whom labourers and tenants were little more than serfs; mere chattels, to be bought and sold, possessed of neither feelings nor human dignity. It was a sad reflection upon mankind, he thought, that a man's worth was so often judged upon the value of what he possessed rather than what he contributed to life. The pauper, cruelly reviled and hounded in life, was, even in death, denied identity, and buried with neither cross nor markings upon his earthen grave. If there was a certainty of life and glory in the hereafter, Joshua mused wrily, then a small sample of it upon earth might have lent strength to their labours, and to them.

He dismounted before Priday's bleak dwelling, securing his mare, reluctant to enter within, Tim's posy of violets clutched awkwardly in his hand. The rich man in his castle. The poor man at his gate. The words sprang unbidden to his mind. Dear God, he thought, how little we have learnt. How slow and halting our progress. If the measure of a civilisation lies in the care of its weakest members, we have little enough to commend us. And yet, he hesitated, the scent of the gentle apprentice's violets made fragrant in the warmth of his hand, for every man of evil who preys upon the innocence of those like Ruth, there are a hundred like Tim who care. For every physician who puts wealth and privilege before the needs of the indigent sick, there are others, like Dr Burrell, whose mission is to heal. For every landowner who battens upon the flesh of those who labour, there are those like Sir Matthew and, God willing, one day, Rebecca and me, who share their fears and hopes, and strive to make their lives kinder.

Determinedly Joshua placed his fingers upon the latch and quietly entered Joe Priday's house. There was neither bell nor knocker to forewarn the blacksmith of his coming. There had never been need, for all were welcome, all were friends. All were trusted – until now, and the coming of an alien violence to Ruth. Whoever was to blame for Ruth's broken flesh had destroyed more than a life, or a family. He had destroyed a community.

At East Lodge, the home of Louisa Crandle and her daughter, Elizabeth, upon Sir Matthew's estate at Southerndown Court, there was a scene of quite unprecedented confusion and disorder. Yet Louisa Crandle, that most correct and meticulously proper of gentlewomen, could not have been more delighted. The object of her pleasure was Elizabeth, who, clad discreetly in her bodice and petticoats, was being pintucked and gathered into her wedding gown by a plumply perspiring dressmaker. The highly waxed surfaces of the small drawing room, and every chair and stool, were obscured beneath unfinished nightgowns, undergarments, day dresses, formal gowns, and all the essential accoutrements of a modestly planned trousseau, for, at Elizabeth's expressed wish, it was to be a simple wedding. To the uninitiated, such as the poor cottagers of the three hamlets, as indeed to Elizabeth herself, it would have appeared to have already taken on an undeniable extravagance and luxury. But to Louisa Crandle, archetypal arbiter of taste and fashion, it seemed austere to the point of deprivation.

Their circumstances were absurdly reduced since their unmerited 'misfortune', but Sir Matthew, with characteristic generosity and discretion, had granted Elizabeth and young Captain Devereaux the tenancy of the Dower House, bidding her alter and furnish it to her own satisfaction, selecting from the furniture within the storerooms of the Court any pieces which she admired or needed for her comfort. Sensitive to her independence of spirit, he did not offer to pay directly for fabrics and refurbishing, fearing that Devereaux might feel such a gift an intrusion, or his own position usurped. Instead, the old gentleman, confiding to Elizabeth that he loved her as dearly as a granddaughter, begged to be allowed, in that capacity, the privilege of settling upon her a modest sum which would give her the advantage of purchasing those small necessities which should be every woman's right, without in any way challenging Captain

Devereaux's role as provider. So it was agreed, to Sir Matthew's delight, to Elizabeth's warm gratitude and to Mrs Crandle's entire satisfaction, for his modest gift proved handsome enough to make her daughter a considerable heiress in her own right.

But now, all the sordid financial transactions resolved, Mrs Crandle stood watching Elizabeth with justifiable pride as the wedding gown of rich, ivory coloured silk took elegant shape around her. Elizabeth was, perhaps, just a shade too slender, Louisa Crandle decided, yet there was an undoubted dignity about her, a natural grace and serenity which seemed to be less a purely physical attribute than some emanation from within. Her daughter's features were pleasing, certainly, being regular and fine-formed, but with no dominant beauty of eye or lips or bone to startle or surprise. There was a soft velvetness about her, in texture as in depth of colour, permeating through the warm creaminess of her skin into the tawny darkness of her hair, and the clear brown of her perceptive eyes. If Rebecca de Breos, with the arresting, exotic beauty of her blue-black hair and remarkably vivid blue eyes, was evocative of summer in all its brilliant colour, heat and vitality, then Elizabeth was autumn, subdued but no less appealing, the brown richness of beech leaves and the mellowness of fruit, warmed and ripened by the sun. Yes, Louisa Crandle was sensible to her good fortune in having a daughter who was amenable, good-natured, and eager to please. Her own Titian-red hair was irreparably faded now, sucked of colour by time and circumstance; like her life, a pale reflection of what had been. Without its contrast, she was aware that her magnolia-like skin seemed merely drained of colour, her pale-lashed eyes lacking definition. Nonetheless, it would have been a joy if Elizabeth had inherited Creighton's vividness of colour, all bright flame and burning intensity. Creighton, her son, fiery and unpredictable as the sun, and without him, coldness and the lonely dark . . .

She glanced up to see Elizabeth's eyes upon her, disturbed and questioning, and felt again the old guilt that she could never love this grave, self-contained child who was her daughter as passionately and uncritically as she had loved her wilful son, and tears came readily to her eyes. The dressmaker, sensitive to the emotional nature of the occasion and the inclination of gentlewomen to swoon, detatched the vinaigrette from the chatelaine at her waist and, with admirable presence of mind, waved it beneath Mrs Crandle's nose and cleared a chair that she might recompose herself. Since Louisa Crandle felt that such a display of sentiment was allowed, indeed expected of her, she fluttered and trembled most convincingly, commanding the attention of both the dressmaker and her little apprentice seamstress, although she had a disturbingly intuitive feeling that Elizabeth was unconvinced.

Elizabeth had been thinking, not of her mother, but of Roland Devereaux, Captain of *The Stormy Venturer*, who was at that very hour returning upon the ship he commanded to wed her. She could see so clearly his tall, broad-shouldered leanness, skin warmed and tanned by salt-winds and weather, and deepening the blue of his clear eyes and the fair thick-clustered hair. Her hand went involuntarily to the small heart-shaped locket of gold at her throat, engraved with the message, 'In your Keeping'. Indeed, her own heart was truly in Roland Devereaux's care, for she loved him deeply and without reserve, grateful for his gentleness and the warm protectiveness that marked his every gesture towards her. Had he but known it, she had loved him before she had ever set eyes upon him, from her childhood, when Mary, his sister, had spoken of him and his travels, eyes aglow and filled with the excitement of his adventures. How eagerly Elizabeth had looked forward to the letters he had sent, more eagerly, she sometimes thought, than Mary herself. Perhaps the picture she had formed of him was born of childish idealism, romantic and high-flown, yet the reality had not disappointed her, for Roland was all that her childhood imagination had created, and more. Elizabeth loved him with a depth and passion which few suspected, so reserved and gentle were her manner and her speech.

Elizabeth would not dwell upon that hideous cruelty of fate which had brought Mary Devereaux trustingly to her door in her absence, and Mary's violent, senseless death at Creighton's hands. She had believed that her brother had killed not only the dearest, gentlest friend she ever knew, but all fond remembrance of the past, and hope of what might have been. Yet, unbelievably, Captain Devereaux had greeted her with a warmth and generosity she had no right to expect, thanking her, gravely, for those kindnesses which she had shown to Mary, and laying no blame upon her for the tragedy, rather begging that they might meet again in gentler times with the past no longer dividing them. And so it had proved. Elizabeth Crandle, who had loved Roland Devereaux vicariously, and with a child's innocence, knew without doubt that the love she felt for him now was a woman's love, deep, complex, and filled with a vitality and passion that touched soul and emotions as surely as flesh. It was undying and inevitable, and she thanked God devoutly that He had given her this one perfect gift, more precious to her than her own life: the joy of becoming part of Devereaux, in knowledge and blood.

As she looked up from the pleasure of her gentle reverie, reluctant to be forced back to practical realities,

Elizabeth saw with concern that her mother had suffered some crisis of nerves and was being clumsily revived and ministered to by the plump dressmaker and her seamstress. Forgetting her unfinished gown, and filled with shame and guilt at her preoccupation, she rushed to her mother's side, pricked as fiercely by pins as conscience. To her surprise her mother's face was ugly with real tears and, despite Elizabeth's suspicion that Mrs Crandle was revelling in the attention, and her role, she could not doubt that some remembrance had stirred within her pain and deep emotion. Soon they were held in each other's arms, weeping and smiling in turn, comforting themselves as best they could, to the immense pleasure of the romantically-minded dressmaker, who, abristle with pins as a hedgehog, whispered to her awed apprentice, ' 'Tis always so, my dear, with the well-bred ladies of quality. They have a sensitivity which we common folk do lack. It is born in the blood. There is no doubting it, for it is a simple fact!'

Mrs Crandle, weeping contritely, clung to Elizabeth, crying vexedly, 'Oh, I am sorry, my dear . . . forgive me. I am truly sorry . . .'

And Elizabeth answered gently, 'Hush, Mama! Do not distress yourself further, I beg of you, for there is nothing in all the world to be sorry about.'

Her mother's voice grew anguished, imploring. 'He was a special boy, was he not? In spite of all, Elizabeth, he was special, and he loved me?'

Elizabeth, whose hatred of her brother, rank and corrosive, burned within her, said quietly, 'Yes, he loved you, Mama, of that I am sure. And yes, Creighton was ever different, high-spirited, and handsome too. You must not regret that to you, he was special.'

If the dressmaker thought Elizabeth's manner was cold and preoccupied as she helped release her from her wedding gown, then she put it down to the natural stresses of the occasion and Miss Crandle's concern for her mother, poor lady. She could not know that Elizabeth's thoughts were elsewhere, with that poor bewildered creature who had fathered her and given her love and comfort in her growing days. Her grief was not for his helplessness, for his lack of understanding protected him from pain and bitter regret. No, her grief was because her mother had not once spoken of him. To Louisa Crandle, her son Creighton would always be vital and alive. It was her husband who was dead.

Chapter Eight

Joshua followed Joe Priday up the bare stone staircase to Ruth's small bedroom under the eaves, the blacksmith's murmured warning, 'Have a care for your head, sir!' making him bend low to guard his head from the lintel. Once within, he adjured himself, it would be wiser to keep to the centre of the room, where the exposed roof timbers sloped to a peak. Elsewhere, his six feet three inch frame would be awkwardly bent, and his head in some danger of assault from the massive oak beams.

In the dim light from the single low-set window, he glimpsed Ruth's bloodless face, swollen and disfigured by bruising. The rough bandages which swathed her head merged into the whiteness of pillow, so that all that seemed visible were the large pale eyes fixed, not upon him, but some distant place, remote and unreachable.

'Ruth, my love, I have brought the constable to see you. You remember that he . . . he brought you safely home?'

The face upon the pillow remained void, expressionless, the eyes wide but unseeing. Joshua was painfully aware of his clumsy awkwardness as he stood at the bottom of Ruth's iron-framed bed, the bunch of brittle-stemmed violets clutched in his over-large hand. Already they were wilting, minute heart-shaped leaves curled inwards, purple heads crushed. Yet the scent of them grew even stronger, insistently filling the room with its strangely evocative odour. He looked towards Priday helplessly, and the blacksmith took them into his roughened grasp, and moved to the head of the bed, setting the violets into Ruth's unresisting hands and, with great gentleness, lifting them towards her face that she might breathe in their fragrance.

'Tim picked them for you,' Joshua's voice sounded unusually loud and harsh in the silence of the room, 'to remind you of kinder times.'

Ruth's expression did not change, and there was no movement of lips or hands, but to Joshua's pity, a tear gathered in the corner of her eye. He watched, raw with sadness, as it trembled, then spilled, coursing in a single, hesitant runnel to touch the edge of her mouth and fall from her chin.

Joshua was unable to speak, incapable of movement, as Priday went to her, sitting awkwardly upon the bed, cradling her silently to him, her head upon his breast, soothing her, crooning in a low, monotonous voice as to a troubled babe. Quietly, without bidding, Joshua moved across the bare floorboards and out from the room, conscious that he was an intruder upon Priday's hurt and a moment that was not meant for sharing. His riding boots struck the stone steps as he descended, their lingering echoes bleakly monotonous, invasive as a knell.

Once below, he did not know what to do to occupy himself. Should he wait for Priday to descend, or take himself off to question the doctors and apothecaries in the villages nearby? Or should he ask among the villagers and drovers, lest one of them had visited the pool and stumbled unwittingly upon some new evidence or clue? Then there were the gypsies to be seen, and warned. A man must be paid to stand on permanent guard over Ruth and Joe Priday's house, lest the attacker return. He must extract the names of the conjurors and wise men hereabouts, and seek their advice and knowledge.

It was Priday himself who resolved Joshua's dilemma for him, as he strode into the room, massive form filling the doorway from the staircase, huge hands extended, clasping Joshua's hands in his horny palms.

'I am sorry,' Joshua said helplessly, 'I am sorry indeed to have caused Ruth distress.'

'There is no cause in all the world for regret.' Priday's brawny arm was clasped firm about Joshua's back, his ruddy, shining face alive with real joy, although the wetness of tears lay untouched upon his polished cheeks. 'It is the first sign of understanding she has given, whether of pleasure or pain. It is little enough to rejoice in, yet I welcome it with gratitude, for it gives me hope. It is a small miracle, and wrought by Tim's kindness. Given kindness and love enough, may she not survive?'

There was such an intensity of pleading in Priday's voice that Joshua answered, despite his own doubts, 'Yes, how could she not respond?'

'You will tell Tim, sir? Put it down to his goodwill. It was an act which does him credit.'

'I will tell him,' promised Joshua, 'you may depend upon it.'

'As I depend on you to bring the man who wrought this vileness to judgement,' declared Priday, 'although whatever punishment is meted out to him, it is the judgement of God he must ultimately face, as must we all. Then, even I might spare him pity.'

Afterwards Joshua did what Priday had bidden him and, with good grace, halted the mare at the forge to deliver the blacksmith's message. If Joshua had anticipated some show of joy, or indeed emotion of any kind from the lad, then it was not forthcoming. Tim's expression was almost as bland and unreadable as Ruth's had been. He listened in silence, gaze level and unwavering, and nodded his understanding.

'I thank you for your courtesy in bringing me the message, sir,' he said with quiet dignity, 'for I wondered afterwards whether it was childishness, a foolish impulse which would make Mr Priday irritated and think the less of me, for my mother berates me often for my slow and stupid ways, and I am mocked for my awkwardness by others. I fear my body is too big for my years,' he confessed gravely, 'and I cannot rightly make it do what I would have it do, save for my hands at the anvil. Perhaps when I am a man like Mr Priday, I will grow to better fit my flesh, and others will not think ill of me, and grow abusive.'

'I think you already have the makings of a good and honest man,' declared Joshua, setting his boot into the stirrup, 'and those who think ill of you jeer, not at you, but at their own inadequacy. You must learn to stand aloof, and pity them.' He settled himself into his saddle and, with a touch of a hand to his helmet in salute, rode away, calling back, 'Mr Priday bade me tell you he values your aid.'

If the words were not strictly Priday's, but his own, Joshua felt no regret at speaking them, for Tim's smile sprang fiercer than the fire within the forge, and burned as bright.

As Joshua turned the corner which hid the forge from view, he saw, advancing from the track below the church from the main highway, two of the stable boys from the Crown Inn. Each was mounted upon a small pony and led by the bridle alongside him a carriage horse, head tossing, and prancing upon the way. The stable lads acknowledged Joshua respectfully as he rode by. Joshua smiled in return. Ossie had done what Joshua had promised, but generously and of his own volition. It would gladden young Tim's heart even more than his own.

As the grey settled into a steady rhythm and stride, Joshua glanced back at the great pool, its surface not blue and clear as before, but dulled and monotonous as the overcast sky, its surface plucked with angry, grey ripples. If it were an omen I sought, he reflected, turning away, I would think like the most superstitious of peasants that it boded ill for me. Small wonder if, from fear and credulity, the cottagers spend their few pence upon charms from soothsayer and conjuror. It is not advice or reason they are buying, but hope, and who is to blame them? His glance turned briefly to the whitewashed church, secure upon its hill, and he sighed. The church should be their spiritual panacea, their refuge and strength. Where had it failed? Perhaps because it sought to bind them too firmly in fear and blind obedience, when what they sought was a gospel of love. There were too many priests whose parishes were in the gift of the families to which they belonged. They inherited them as surely as their elder brothers inherited the land, or a regiment of the line. One could be schooled from infancy to administer an estate, or to respect the history of a great regiment, but could one be taught as easily to honour God? Surely the priesthood was not a career, but a calling – a vocation even? What conviction could such clergymen offer to inspire the needy? They knew nothing of them, and were reluctant to learn. True, there were good men like Dr Peate and Robert Knight, with some compassion and understanding of deprivation, but often their pedantry alienated them from those whose need was for a simple faith.

Was there, he wondered, a clergyman at Maudlam, or did he live in one of the larger neighbouring villages? It seemed strange that no one had spoken of him, or sought his spiritual comfort. Joshua was tempted to return and beg news of him, or seek him out. Tomorrow, and tomorrow, and tomorrow, he thought helplessly, urging the grey forward. And even then, would there be a solution?

For the moment, his immediate quest must be to capture and detain the fiery archer, if he existed! Even so small a victory would divert the justice temporarily. He would take Cavan Doonan with him, for the big Irishman's fists were worth any ten others in conflict, and he was a lively and agreeable companion to ride beside. Yes, he would go at once to his friend's cottage at Newton. The archer might have already returned to Stormy Downs in order to attend to whatever villainy drew him there, since he was to appear with the circus upon Newton Green within a few hours. Even should he be absent, then they might find evidence of crime.

As Joshua approached Nottage village, he reined in the mare, debating whether to veer off towards the Rhyl and warn the gypsies of Ruth's tragedy, and the cruel backlash of revenge it might bring. No, it was unlikely that the men of Maudlam would venture so far afield, for as Tim had reminded him, they must needs come on foot, and their poverty forced them to remain steadfastly at their toil. He reined the grey resolutely towards Newton.

'Dear heaven!' he exclaimed aloud, smiling involuntarily. 'Should we capture the fiery archer, Ossie's wrath will be harder to quell!'

Rosa Doonan was busily engaged upon sanding and sweeping out the stone-flagged floor of the small cot near the village green at Newton. Despite the simplicity of her cheap cotton dress and the mob-cap which concealed her hair and slipped unbecomingly low upon her forehead, there was no mistaking that her figure was comely, her features delicate and well formed, and that she was quite astoundingly pretty. Now she was also exceedingly vexed, a condition which only served to heighten the colour in her palely transparent skin and give life to the fine blue eyes with their corn coloured lashes, which were quite indecently thick and silky. She did not feel at all pretty. In fact, as she protested to her recently acquired spouse who was the cause of her unusual vexation, chivvying him from place to place with her broom, 'I declare, Cavan, I sometimes think you get underfoot just to provoke me! Why do you not take a walk in the fresh air, or aid Jeremiah Fleet with his fishing? I swear that I did not expect this of married life, that I should be for ever sweating and damp, trussed like a boiled pudding in a net!'

Cavan lumbered to his feet, a great clumsy ox of a fellow, awkward and slow of movement, but with his unlovely face wreathed in self-conscious smiles beneath the shock of red hair.

'Why, Rosa, my love,' he said, 'you are more appetising and appealing than any pudding set upon a fire!' He slipped behind her and put his brawny arms about her waist, kissing the nape of her neck tenderly and hugging her to him. 'I vow I could devour you, my love, to the very last crumb!'

She rounded upon him furiously, striking at him with her broom and declaring, unfairly, ' 'Tis all you think about, Cavan Doonan, kissing, and filling that great belly of yours!' She burst into tears, cap slipping awry, and could not be pacified despite his efforts to soothe her, saying, between sobs, to his utter bewilderment, 'I do not want to be like a pudding! You great Irish donkey! Cannot you see that I want to be like I was before we were wed?'

'Without me, do you mean?' His eyes were so

comically hurt and incredulous that Rosa began to laugh against her will as she pushed him upon a chair and sat upon his knee, casting her broom away and, with it, the ugly mob-cap. She cradled him to her, fondling his thick red mane, her own corn coloured hair falling softly about him.

'No. I would never be without you, Cavan!' she exclaimed, kissing him fervently, and immediately contrite, remembering with pain how she had believed him dead from the highwayman's bullet as, newly wed, they returned from Ireland upon the coach. She placed her soft cheek against his. 'You are all of my life, and my dear love. Without you, I would have nothing. I am a stupid, wilful girl, and I do not deserve to have the bravest and truest husband in all of the three hamlets. No! In all of the world!' she amended generously.

Cavan, puzzled by this swift change in mood, and his fortunes, wrinkled his massive forehead briefly, then gave up the struggle to understand. For the moment, it was enough to kiss away the tears from her pretty eyelids, marvelling at his good fortune in having for his own the most beautiful, tempestuous and loving wife in all of the earth. He knew that he was a clumsy, cloddish oaf of a fellow, with no pretensions as to position or learning. It was a miracle to him that such a paragon as Rosa had ever deigned to look at him, much less accept his ugly work-grimed hand – well, soon he would be back at his toil at the quarry face, recovered from his wound, and would work for her until he dropped, if need be, to buy her those pretty things which she richly deserved.

An urgent knocking upon the door interrupted their pleasant reconciliation as, reluctantly, Cavan set Rosa down from his knee and moved to open the door.

'Joshua!' There was no mistaking the Irishman's real pleasure as he clasped the constable warmly about the arm with his massive hand and drew him inside, calling, 'Rosa, Rosa, my dear, see who has come to visit us.'

Rosa, aware of her faded gown and dishevelment and the traces of dried tears upon her cheeks, grew flushed and apologetic, declaring as she smoothed her hair, 'I fear, sir, that you find me at a disadvantage, ill-prepared for visitors, even one as welcome as you.'

Joshua said sincerely, 'You could never be at a disadvantage, ma'am, for I have never seen you less than beautiful.'

For a brief moment there flashed vividly upon his mind the picture of her pale, stricken face as he had once seen her at the justice's house, eyes empty of all but hurt, Cavan's blood crusted and dark upon the grey bodice of her silky gown.

'A pretty speech!' applauded Doonan, laughing. 'And have you no fine compliments about my accomplishments?'

'Indeed, it is for that very reason I am come,' Joshua responded, straightfaced, 'to court your help in battle, for I would rather have your great fists with me than a full score of others!'

Rosa and Doonan listened incredulously, and with not a little amusement, as Joshua related the story of the fiery archer, and his plans for the creature's capture.

'Well,' declared Doonan philosophically, 'if he is not a phantom, then my fists might indeed serve you well. And if he is, then my legs will doubtless serve me better, for I warrant I will move faster than any flaming arrow!'

When Joshua had seen Doonan mounted upon the horse which he had hired from the stables at the Crown, and was himself ensconced in his saddle upon the grey, Rosa watched them ride off, still exchanging nonsense, and filled with a feverish excitement to be away.

Cavan was naught but a silly, impetuous, great boy

who had never outgrown his urge to prove himself the bravest and the best, Rosa thought indulgently. Like those awkward, knock-kneed lambs chasing each other unsteadily to the top of the hillock, noisily bleating their triumph, but never knowing why they did it, or what it proved. She shook her head resignedly and returned indoors. Was this what marriage was, she wondered, a continuation of childhood? The need to prove? She only knew that Cavan was hard to live with, but harder to live without. There was nothing he had need to prove to her. She already knew. There was no man in all the world his equal.

The two friends could hardly have made a more unlikely contrast as they rode out together, first clearing the Clevis Hill, skirting the great pool at the foot of Newton Downs, and then urging their mounts up the fierce gradient of Dan-y-Graig Hill. Joshua, upon the grey, was, despite his height and the breadth of his shoulders and well-muscled body, all unselfconscious elegance. He was indubitably a gentleman. Like the mare, it was there in the breeding; instantly recognisable and incontrovertible; some distinction of bone and blood which governed movement and manners and set him apart. Doonan was his antithesis in every particular. A huge, shambling, ungainly creature, clumsy as a dancing bear, and as close to nature. His temper was as fiery as his hair, and he was rashly impetuous, known for his drunken brawling and the might of his massive fists, raw-fleshed as hams. Yet he was a mass of strange contradictions: outwardly volatile and bellicose: inwardly, as Rosa had found, bewildered and tenderly protective, as swift to sentimental fears as fury. To Joshua he had proved a loyal ally and dependable friend, whose courage he had grown to respect. Perhaps the truth was that his powerful body and the potential for violence contained within it, and the huge fists, conditioned strangers' expectations of him. As ever, he was willing to oblige them. Those, like Rosa and Joshua, whose belief in him demanded better, were seldom disappointed for he had no cause to prove his strength or latent violence.

Now, as he rode beside Joshua, urging on his chestnut mount, there was a force and vitality in man and beast, a richness of shared colour which made laughter bubble within Joshua, a feeling of rare goodwill. He was reminded of the glossily polished horse chestnut fruits of his childhood, soaked in vinegar and then baked until hard, to thread with string and play at the village game of 'conkers', battering and splintering all that dared to oppose them. Yes, there was much of that in Doonan, and few who could stand against him.

As if he had read Joshua's thoughts, the Irishman said, 'I shall give that phantom a run for his money, Joshua, I promise you! He'll be out of that thicket faster than a flushed partridge, and with feathers flying!' Doonan's face was aflame with the certainty of it.

'Make sure, then, that the feathers do not fly at the end of an arrow – his!' cautioned Joshua, smiling. 'For should you flee, your backside would make a wider target than your horse's!'

'Indeed,' said Doonan, with a burst of humour, 'he would be sore pressed to choose between it and the larger emptiness of your head!' and laughing immoderately at his own joke, he urged his horse fearlessly into the copse, with Joshua, more sedately, following.

There was one small impediment of which Joshua and Doonan were unaware. At the moment when they were riding into the trees and towards the woodcutter's hut, the circus, such as it was, was wending its way through Nottage and thence along the broad highway towards Newton and the Crown, upon some whim of its owner.

Despite the change in the weather, the takings at Pyle had been disappointing, for money was hard-earned and not to be squandered upon entertainment. There was a Puritanical streak in these people, thought the circus owner disgustedly, they believed that the pleasures of self-indulgence were reserved exclusively for the rich and the sinful, as were the ever-burning fires in the bleak hereafter. He supposed that since the peasantry had experienced a foretaste of hell in their living, they were determined not to repeat the process for eternity. The rich, as always, must take heed for themselves!

He had persuaded those who travelled with him that it would be as well to journey to Newton by way of Nottage, for it was from there that much of the money would come. The rich, agricultural hamlet was peopled with well-to-do farmers and, although parsimonious in their everyday dealings, they often vied with each other in displaying evidence of their prosperity. They were duty bound to see that their wives and families were better dressed, had finer carriages, and were denied none of the amusements which might be enjoyed by their neighbours. To do so would be to declare their own incompetence, and publish it abroad as loudly as if they had hired the town crier to proclaim it.

So the raggle-taggle procession made its way, with the crier with handbell and tricorne walking ahead of them, proclaiming that the spectacle which was to unfold before them upon the village green at Newton had dazzled and confounded the very highest in all the land. They had appeared in lands which lay beyond the seas, been applauded and cheered in royal courts. Crowned heads were bowed before them . . . For one penny, all this magnificence would be the villagers, part of their heritage and memory for ever, with but an additional half-penny for each of the amazing and quite incredible sideshows. How could they dare to miss the revelation of a lifetime?

The villagers were politely interested but inclined to be sceptical, for if the performers were used to hobnobbing with the mighty, what had reduced them to appearing in Newton? Still, the pleas of the children were so loud and pathetic that the owner had high hopes that they would be persuaded.

He rallied his motley company behind him, motioning them forward, surrounded, as they always were, by the barefooted urchins of the village, ragged-breeched and open-mouthed, bellies as empty as their pockets. He was not a hard man, but weighed down with the responsibilities of providing for all who travelled with him. The winter had been long and the pickings meagre, and sometimes they could have scarce survived save for the work they sought upon the farms and the poor food that was the payment for their labours. The donkeys and mules were thin and pot-bellied, rib cages stark beneath their scarecrow hides, their carts worn and ill-fashioned. Their drivers fared little better. Abrahams looked about him disconsolately. God knows, they were a strange and unprepossessing crew, with few talents and fewer illusions, save that one which served to goad them, every one. They were artistes and, as such, deserved to survive. They would not join the ranks of paupers and ordinary men, they had their creative pride: the dwarfs and tumblers, clowns and jugglers, the fire-eaters, the fat lady, the pedlar, the fiery archer . . . He hesitated briefly, eyes searching the straggling caravan. Damnation! Where was he? Well, he had better show his face at the village green, else it would be the worse for him.

The circus owner brushed aside a runny-nosed sweeping boy who was attempting to clamber over the wheel and on to his cart, giving him a clout over the ear to ease his frustration. So much for the royal courts of Europe, he thought, dispiritedly. Then he rallied his flagging spirits. There would be ale at the inn overlooking the green, and when the people came to view the show, they would be entranced and uplifted by the grand illusion of colour and beauty. Yes, that was what it was all about, illusion, and creating it. The greater the poverty, the greater the artistry needed to dispel it. His troupe were artistes indeed. His was a rare privilege which outweighed the tawdry responsibilities. He would do well to remember it.

Chapter Nine

The village green which skirted the grey walls of the church of St John the Baptist seemed, with the stones of the church itself, to have absorbed a calm dignity over the years. Ossie, who never tired of gazing at the scene of rare tranquillity, framed 'neath the archway of the Crown, thought of it as his own private oasis; a refuge of greenness and peace where his tired body and mind might find deep refreshment. It could have changed little since Norman times, save that within the churchyard walls the anonymous green sward had given way to turned earth and monument, the graves of those remembered briefly until rain and salt-laden winds had erased their names, returning them to the anonymity from whence they had sprung. It was this feeling of timelessness which the ostler loved, the certainty that the same sky, trees and stone had witnessed the changing of time and seasons and the perishability of flesh while itself remaining constant.

But now, as Ossie surveyed it from the cobbles of the yard, it was with an uncharacteristically jaundiced eye, his normally placid disposition choleric. The green was a heaving, surging anthill of life. Yet the incessant movement appeared strangely disorganised, chaotic almost, as if people, animals and carts moved like crazed automatons, wound by some giant hand, then inexplicably jerking awry. Ossie's disgust at this invasion of his sacred place was mixed with a guilty excitement and exhilaration at the prospect of becoming a part of this spectacle, and of Joshua's pursuit of the phantom, albeit vicariously. There was no sign of the fiery archer, as far as Ossie could see, although, he rebuked himself solemnly, the creature was hardly likely to be easily identified in that milling throng. It was scarcely to be expected that he would be advertising himself by waving a burning quiver aloft, any more than the fire-eaters would be breathing flame free of charge. Ossie's weathered brown face creased into a smile. There was no doubting that their thirsts would give Tom Butler a good day, just so long as they kept their tricks for the green, and did not set fire to the Crown!

Rosa Doonan, with her sanding and sweeping completed, settled herself upon a three-legged stool at the fireside, pondering upon what she should take for her next household task. In truth, there was little to be done, for the tiny cot was already shiny and neat as a new pin from a pedlar's tray. With Cavan absent upon his mission with Joshua, she could take pause to look about her to better purpose. Much as she loved her husband, there was no denying that his massive presence dwarfed the inadequate rooms, and his clumsiness, although sometimes endearing, was more often a threat to the few surviving treasures among their wedding gifts. She thrust the poker disconsolately into the driftwood upon the fire, staring into the leaping flames which she had stirred into life. As a child in her mother's lodging house in Port, she had gazed into other fires, seeing with a child's eyes the goblins and witches, dragons and strange, unearthly shapes born of her imagination. Now, all she could picture beyond the quick crackle of sparks and that bright glow which died into white-hot ash was

Cavan's broad face as he had turned in the saddle to wave to her, skin flushed, restless eyes softening with naked affection. A burning arm of driftwood spurted into flame, to fall with a crash upon the hearth beneath. As she stretched out her hand to lift it, feeling the heat savage her flesh and her fingertips burn sharply as she threw it back, The Fiery Archer . . . the words sprang unbidden to her mind, and for the first time Joshua's and Cavan's quest became reality, and not a humorous, light-hearted escapade. Rosa shivered involuntarily, distracted briefly by the sound of the town crier in the street nearby.

She rushed at once to the door, for his presence too often presaged some calamity, and always news which could not be ignored. Rosa, like many of those in the three hamlets, could neither read nor write. Apart from the daily newspaper readings upon the village green, given at the justice's behest and delivered by a scholar vestryman, the crier was their main source of news. Since the payment for his services often amounted to a full shilling, his efforts were not called upon frivolously, or by the poor, only those in authority.

It was with relief and a sense of her own foolishness that she heard tell of the circus upon the village green. And the town crier, a wizened ancient in livery inherited from previous incumbents of broader girth and greater height, seeing Rosa's smile, forgot the ache in his limbs and the heaviness of the hand bell, repeating the words he had been coached into uttering with new-found vigour. And if he looked shrunken and absurd in his ill-fitting clothes, movements stilted as those playthings so beloved of the gentry, the clockwork monkeys which bowed and gaped and closed their simian mouths obediently, then no matter. Today he did, after all, perform the same function for the poor, working for their amusement and delight. There was too little to gladden them in their lives. Better a harbinger of joy than a bird of death. He smiled, meeting Rosa's bright eyes. He could not know how nearly his thoughts reflected her own.

When the town crier had gone, first raising his tricorne to reveal the shining pink pate set about with hair like wisps of discarded sheep fleece, and bowing grandiloquently, Rosa returned within. She was still smiling as she took her last glimpse of him, heading for the Crown, lean shanks bird-like 'neath his breeches, opulent cuffs covering all but his fingertips. He was, inevitably, followed by a band of ragamuffins, wet-nosed and posturing, scrapping over which one was to carry his hand bell, that he might share for one heady moment the glory of such a calling.

Rosa stood in the living room of the cottage, looking restlessly about her. She knew that Cavan would not be pleased should she visit the circus upon the green unattended, for, despite their poverty, the good folk of the three hamlets were more rigid than the gentry in their adherence to the laws of society and what was proper. As a newly-wed and mistress of her own house, it would ill become her to flout convention. Besides, there was much to be done at home had she but the enthusiasm. Now, where should she make a start? Perhaps upon the cooking utensils. She could clean them with straw and a handful of wood ash, a dirty and time-consuming occupation, and one which she considered unnecessary since her own pans were so new, and each one shone fit to use as a looking glass! She might scour her fireside irons with brick dust, or whiten her doorstep or hearth with softstone if she chose. 'No!' she exclaimed aloud. 'I do not choose! I shall go where I please, as Cavan does! It pleases me to go to the circus!'

So, fetching some water from the well in the yard, and

filling a kettle to suspend over the fire from the iron rod and hook, she divested herself of her workaday cotton and fetched one of her prettiest gowns from the bedroom, and with it her lace-trimmed petticoat and the dainty shoes made by the cordwainer for her wedding day. Using a ball of precious soap, a gift from Rebecca, she washed herself from head to toe, then set about making herself into an elegant lady of fashion. She would call upon Bella, the wife of Tom Butler's son, Reuben, at the Crown. She too was newly wed, although delivered of an infant but three months after the wedding. Rosa knew that the child was sickly, and a wet nurse had been called upon to feed him. Bella would be much cheered by a visit to the circus, and who could fault two married ladies of virtuous character – saving Bella's small lapse – for keeping each other company at such a modest and public distraction upon the green? It is said that the devil makes use of the most unlikely advocates. Rosa, with her pale-skinned innocence, silken hair and delicate beauty convinced herself and Bella Butler with consummate ease.

The circus owner, Job Abrahams, had often been heard to declare that his name suited him a rare treat, since it needed the patience of Job and the foresight of a prophet to manage his affairs. He was a large florid-faced man with deep-set shoe-button eyes set into fleshy pouches. When he smiled, which was seldom, his eyes seemed to disappear altogether, as if to make way for the excessively large mouth crowded with ivory-coloured teeth. As he surveyed the scene before him, upon Newton Green, his teeth were much in evidence as he picked at them with a grubby fingernail, mentally thanking whatever saints protected itinerant circus owners for their intercession. The booths were already erected, the stalls of sweetmeats and trinkets set up, the few scurvy animals ready for display, their small cages draped with rough cloths to protect them from the prying eyes of those ruffians unable, or unwilling, to pay.

There were few enough animals, in all conscience, and those there were, mangy and ill-disposed: a couple of curs which leapt through paper hoops, or walked upon their hind legs and danced to a fiddler's tune; the grey parrot which screeched and cursed at the name of Bonaparte, lying stiffly upon its back and 'dying' for Wellington, claws patriotically clutching the union flag; the piebald pony upon which the dancer (Job's wife) rode bareback - both of them, he conceded, unremarkable and well past their first flush. The monkey was intelligent enough, but inclined to be sickly, although its lassitude and dullness of eye sometimes merited extra sympathy. It was a grief to him that the parrot was a dull-coloured grey, and not a bright-hued creature, and to compound the injury, he had been told by the landlord at the Crown that there was a bigger and better seafarer's parrot within, whose language was fit to blister a barnacle. A born performer, the landlord had insisted, and, no, he would not sell him, not for love nor money.

Job Abrahams sniffed. It was certain that the fat woman was fatter than most, some disorder of the liver or bowels, perhaps, made her so, although he fancied that the bleak winter had thinned her somewhat, as it had them all. There were the dwarfs, of course, and the tumblers, clowns and jugglers, who were colourful enough, and the strong man, and the bare-knuckled fighter who would challenge all comers. There were the side shows of skittles, toss the horseshoe, and games of chance - although, he smiled, not too much chance. And the fortune-teller was a great draw with the village maidens, and told them all that they most dearly wished to hear.

Oh, but he regretted that the man with the chained, dancing bear was no longer with them, having taken his leave the previous year. Some accident, it was said, with the animal which, goaded beyond endurance, had turned on him and cruelly savaged him. Now he could scarce leave his house, always refusing, for some reason, to exhibit himself at the circuses as 'The Ugliest Man on Earth', although Abrahams had tried to persuade him. Yes, he reflected, it was a pity about the bear.

Cavan Doonan, although warned by Joshua of the archer's prowess and of the dangers of hasty or impetuous action, urged his mount into the copse and towards the woodcutter's hut with his usual recklessness. His near fatal shooting by a highwayman, some months earlier, which should have proved a salutary lesson, had done nothing to cool his rashness, and neither did Joshua's commands or entreaties. Joshua did not know if it was courage or sheer pig-headedness which drove the Irishman on, but his own predilection was for quietness and caution and the value of surprise. Doonan, it must be said, reasoned otherwise, convincing himself that Illtyd and Rowden the miller had tried that tactic and, consequently, they were the ones surprised, Rowden, perhaps, more than the hayward! The humour of it twitched his mouth into a smile, and soon he was laughing so uproariously that his companion suspected that he had taken leave of the little sense he possessed.

As Doonan charged through the copse, blundering as noisily as any wild boar, Joshua braced himself to hear, at any moment, the whine and thud of an arrow as it embedded itself into a tree trunk or, worse, flesh, for unless the archer were deaf, he must be prepared for their coming.

As the trees thinned and they came to the clearing, the

woodcutter's hut might have been thought empty, were it not for the mule and cart tethered to a nearby branch. The fallen leaves, heaped and rotting upon the earth, were partly decayed and had softened their approach despite Doonan's excesses, and Joshua could only hope that the archer was within the hut, for if he were hidden within the trees, they would have no shelter from his onslaught. Now, even Doonan seemed to have recognised the need for caution for, despite his awkward weight, he dismounted almost silently, tying up his mare and gently creeping forward. Joshua did likewise, quietly slipping his pistol from its holder upon the mare and edging forward with the weapon gripped reassuringly in his hand.

There was no sound from within the hut, and no smoke arose from its crude chimney, and yet there was an almost unbearable sense of menace in the quiet scene, with its long-abandoned logs, their surfaces crusted with roughly peeling bark and green cushions of moss or sprouting fungi, fleshy and obscene as growths. Yet, above all, it was the dankness of the leaves underfoot and the silence which affected Joshua most, for although a weak sun shone above, it seemed only to deepen the darkness of the woods about them, with no sounds of birdsong or the rustle of small foraging creatures to speak of life. Joshua felt the beating of his heart within his rib cage and in the pulses of his throat so fiercely that he half expected the noise to explode through his flesh, but all was strangely, unnervingly silent.

Doonan's great fist was all but upon the latch when the fearful, hideous cry of the mule violated the air, startling them almost to flight. Doonan surged forward instinctively and flung open the door upon the small, terrified figure of a man, a yew bow clutched in his shaking hand as he vainly tried to extract an arrow from the quiver hanging at his waist. Before he could act, Doonan was upon him, holding him up by the breast of his coat in one mighty hand, while snapping the bow across his brawny knee as easily as a dry twig. The archer was not fiery now, but pathetic and cowed, eyes bulging startled from his head, throat uttering noises no less fearful than the mule's as Doonan's grip inexorably tightened and choked him. At Joshua's command, the Irishman released his prisoner, saying contemptuously as he set him down, 'A fine, brave gentleman we have here! What has put out your fire, little man? I swear you would be ill equipped to light a candle!'

The archer who, upon inspection, was even older and more diminutive than he had first appeared, reacted so violently that Joshua was fearful for the poor wretch's teeth, so fiercely were they clenched.

'I see, sir, that you have a rushlight candle set nearby,' Joshua wrinkled his nose disgustedly, 'and from the almighty stench have been dripping rags in rancid fish oil and skimmings of hog fat to set around your arrows. And the object of so strange an enterprise?'

'Answer him!' commanded Doonan, fastening upon the archer's sleeve and so confusing him that he could not utter a word, and the sounds, when he tried, were less than a whimper.

'I think,' said Joshua, who had been glancing inquisitively around the small, bleak hut, 'that we might already have found the answer.' He strode to where the dirt-grimed floorboards had been hastily replaced, their surfaces cleared of the dust which covered all else. 'And here, if I am not mistaken, it lies.'

Swinging the archer aloft by the neck of his coat, Doonan carried him writhing to where Joshua stood, delivering him to the constable's care. His massive hands tore impatiently at the floorboards, ripping them aside and tossing them noisily into the corners of the hut; then he knelt forward to peer into the darkness beneath. Joshua would have retrieved the lighted rush candle to assist him, but Doonan could not wait, plunging an arm into the tunnelled earth.

It was with a cry of astonishment that he brought out his first trophy, a caudle cup of silver, wrapped in a cloth. The vessel was tarnished by damp and disuse, but when rubbed upon the backside of Doonan's breeches, there could be no doubt that it bore the unmistakably engraved crest of the justice, Mr Robert Knight. The oath Doonan uttered was no less incredulous than Joshua's more pious exclamation of 'Saints and Ministers of Grace preserve us!' He rounded upon Doonan in his bewilderment, 'I do not understand,' he declared. 'Robert Knight has said nothing of this to me!' But Doonan had already returned to his task, the impressive mound of silver cups and objects of virtu growing beside him.

The little archer, deprived of his bow, though not of his wits, was by now attempting to escape, until Doonan, awakened to his flight, scrambled up to lay him low, descending upon him with such brute force that the archer's breath was noisily expelled from his body. The poor wretch was vainly gulping air, mouth agape like a stranded fish, and struggling up when Doonan's boot returned him implacably to the floor.

'There was a robbery at the Great House, at Tythegston,' continued the Irishman, as if their conversation had not been interrupted, 'some months before you came to the three hamlets as constable, Joshua. I recall it well, for the justice was angered and deeply distressed, and spoke of it in a sermon, declaring that he would offer a most substantial reward for its return.' His broad face flushed with expectation as his eyes sought the constable's questioningly.

Joshua shook his head.

'Well,' said the Irishman, philosophically, 'better a state of grace than riches, although the rector seemed hard enough to convince!' His mighty bellow of laughter all but shattered the remaining floorboards of the hut. He bent down and heaved the archer to his feet, commanding, 'Tell the constable how you robbed the justice, you miserable little toad!'

The archer, who was plainly terrified, managed to blurt out, 'It was the man with the dancing bear . . .'

'Bear?' Doonan was nonplussed.

'Last year, the bear at the circus.' He paused and wetted his lips before continuing in a high-pitched nervous voice, 'We were coming over the hill from the main highway from Bridgend, the two of us . . . well, and the bear. The bear trainer was with me upon my cart, and the bear in his cage on wheels. We were on our own, do you see, for the others had gone before.'

'Get on with it!' cried Doonan in exasperation, tightening his grip upon the man's coat front.

'Well, the bear owner, Hoddle was his name, he said it was a likely place to get food and drink, for a bear sometimes is as good as a shilling in your pocket in house or inn . . .' He broke off, then feeling Doonan's grip tightening again, continued hurriedly, 'The household servants came out in high excitement at the treat we offered. One of them, an aged fellow with rotten teeth and a stiff back, sent me to get some titbits for the beast from the kitchen with one of the kitchen maids, but not before she had let fall that the owner was absent upon some visit, and would not return before next day.'

'So while she was returning with the sweetmeats, and the rest were intent upon the bear's antics, you robbed the house?' prompted Joshua in disgust.

The man nodded. 'I had taken my mule and cart with me to the stable yard, under pretext of watering the poor animal, saying we had travelled far.'

'Too far!' said Doonan with feeling. 'But why did you not take the valuables with you, then? When you left the place?'

The archer said dully, 'We would have done. Hoddle knew of this woodcutter's hut, for when he was a child, his father, a ferreter, had oft brought him here. So we hid the . . . things beneath the floorboards, intending to retrieve them when our performance at Newton was ended. The bear man, Hoddle, moved from circus to circus, place to place, working alone, and tied to no man, dependent upon no one.'

'Save the bear!' exclaimed Doonan. 'And I'll be damned if he did not prove a better friend than most!'

'No, indeed, sir!' disclaimed the archer earnestly. 'For it was then that things went awry. The bear turned upon him and savaged him most fiercely, and since then Hoddle has been an invalid, scarce able to leave his house, and I have been constantly upon other roads with Abrahams' circus, unable to return until this day.'

'I fear you should have confided in the fortune-teller and palmist,' said Joshua unfeelingly, 'for you clearly did not choose auspiciously.'

Doonan asked unexpectedly as he prodded the archer towards the doorway of the hut, 'And the bear? What of the bear?'

'Sold. To some gentleman in a great house, who gave him a compound in which to roam freely, with food aplenty. It is said that he lives like a lord, although he is captive.'

'Poetic justice!' declared Joshua drily amused. 'Although I fancy your resting place will be the same, I fear the hospitality will not match it.'

'Nor your welcome at the justice's,' declared Doonan, 'for without the bear you have little to commend you.'

'Save the justice's silver,' reminded Joshua, smiling as Doonan set the archer unceremoniously upon the mule cart and loaded the valuables behind him.

'A word,' said Joshua to the archer as he and Doonan mounted and urged their captive disconsolately before them. 'Do not try to flee, for I am armed and will not hesitate to shoot you. You understand?'

The archer nodded miserably.

'And another, as vital to your wellbeing. It would be as well to avoid describing the exact circumstances of the robbery, neither involving the bear nor the justice's servants, if you value your hide.'

Doonan, riding beside Joshua, adjured with admirable gravity, 'I trust, Constable, that you do not aim to pervert the course of justice?'

'Indeed, no!' declared Joshua. 'The law is designed to protect fools and innocents from corruption, is it not? Those like the justice's manservant, Leyshon, and the bear.'

'Exactly,' said Doonan, chuckling, 'although I would not like to judge which is which!'

Chapter Ten

Rosa, quite immodestly pleased with her reflection in the hand glass which lay upon the scrubbed pine table in the bedroom, made her elegant way downstairs and into the kitchen. There she carefully removed the lid of a pretty, ornamental teapot which had been a wedding gift from Joshua, and removed a shilling from their savings and placed it in the purse within her reticule. She was a frugal, sensible girl, notwithstanding her deceptively ethereal beauty, and since Cavan's shooting had set aside a portion of the money paid to her by the quarrymen who, respecting his bravery, had made up his losses from their own poor wages. If she hesitated at the door, then returned to the teapot, it was not through guilt or shame, but to take into her possession another shilling and a sixpence. The teapot stayed but an ornament, for tea was a luxury which they could ill afford, a rare occasional treat. Well, it was all the better for being so, like today's excursion.

In her pretty gown of blue, and her matching bonnet which her mother-in-law had ordered stitched for her in Ireland, she looked as delicately slender and pretty as a wild harebell, her sparkling eyes the same vividly arresting blue. As she stepped out lightly to the Crown to call on Bella, there was not a woman, young or old, upon her way who did not envy her such youth and loveliness, nor a man who did not feel his heart stirred by her passing. It was, thought Tom Butler, glimpsing her from the window of the Crown, as if all of springtime and sunshine walked with her, and he turned away, unable to name the sadness of loss within him.

Bella, walking beside Rosa across the highway and on to the village green, was feeling less sanguine than her friend, although she was grateful for the diversion being offered her, and the clean freshness of the springtime air. Reuben, her husband, was away upon a voyage these few months, a crewman upon Captain Devereaux's ship, *The Stormy Venturer*. He had yearned to join the ship's company, stirred by the thought of adventure and the tales which the captain told so vividly of foreign ports and exotic unknown places, the companionship and, to be fair, the trials and hardships of a life at sea. She had not had the heart to dissuade him, even had she been able to do so, for she was wise enough to know that such an opportunity might never come again. Reuben was a warm-hearted man, strong and impetuous, filled with wild dreams. He would be a hard man to hold, and her instinct had been to bind him to her with the coming child, but her mind had urged her to bid him go. It was the surest way to make certain of his return, for he was a loyal and devoted son to the Butlers, and would one day show the same qualities in his love for her and the boy, Joseph. Dear God, she missed Reuben sorely, and the babe was puny enough, mewling always like a sick kitten, despite the services of a good wet nurse who had milk enough to spare. She stumbled upon a clod of grass and Rosa's arm came out to steady her.

'You are all right, Bella?' she asked anxiously. 'You are pale and tired looking enough since the child's birth. You are sure the excursion will not tax you too much?'

Bella's face was indeed drained of the colour which normally gave warmth to her cheeks, and her skin had a sallow, waxen look which heightened the bruised darkness about her eyes.

'No, I shall enjoy the outing, Rosa. It is a rare treat to have your company.'

Rosa's hand tightened reassuringly upon her friend's arm. 'Today will bring the roses to your cheeks,' she promised, smiling.

Bella smiled in return. There will be roses and loving aplenty when Reuben returns, she thought. It must be soon now, very soon. The brightness of its certainty glowed within her, warm and comforting as a candle flame in the dark. Then the baby and she and all the world would surely be set to rights again.

Jeremiah Fleet, his early-morning fishing ended and his catch delivered to his eager customers in the three hamlets, had changed, at his wife's behest, into his special occasion finery. He wore the coat and trousers of grey, stitched for their recent wedding by the tailor in Newton village, a small, industrious mole of a man with damp, pinched nose, eyes puckered and grown dim in working by lamp and candlelight. He seldom ventured into the daylight, preferring the cool darkness of his own abode. But had he ventured abroad that day, there is no doubting that he would have gained more satisfaction from the sartorial elegance of Jeremiah Fleet than from the stalls, sideshows and animal extravaganzas set out for public delectation.

Sophie, her arm proudly and securely thrust through her husband's, thought that he was the most elegant and distinguished of men, with his arrogant bearing and the thickly abundant grey hair and beard which so perfectly complemented the paler greyness of his keen eyes. There was about him, she thought, the look of a visionary, an Old Testament prophet. Not, of course, that she could read of such things, like Illtyd, her son and Jeremiah's dearly loved stepson, who was a scholar, but she had seen pictures in the family Bible in Daniel the cart-wright's house, and there was no denying the resemblance. In fact, if it were not near sacrilege, she would have eagerly confessed that when the sun lit up the stained glass windows of the parish church, illuminating the good Saint John with heavenly light, she was so forcibly reminded of Jeremiah that it was sometimes near impossible for her to attend to the rector's sermon, so turned were her thoughts to carnal, fleshly, less spiritual things. Still, she supposed it was all right, for they were wed in the eyes of God, and to love someone so devotedly could surely not be a mortal sin? Oh, how lucky she was, and how dearly she loved Jeremiah! He was the love she had hungered for through all the lean years, the light of her flesh and spirit, and they were truly one being, fused and inseparable. 'As long as ye both shall live . . .' The words of the rector returned to her clearly, and with a pleasure as intense as pain, 'And after,' she wanted to cry, 'oh, and after, please God . . .' She squeezed Jeremiah's arm and he turned to look at her, eyes questioning and filled with affection.

'What shall we see, Sophie?' he asked. 'Have you a mind for the fire-eaters, or the fortune-teller, or the strong man?'

'Shall we just stroll, my dear?' she asked. 'For I confess I am relishing the sights and sounds, and even the smells of the place! Besides,' she added, her voice so low that he had to bend his head to hear her above the cacophony of circus cries and the warm, surging excitement of the crowd, 'I admit that I see little virtue, or use, in eating fire! As for my fortune, I have no need for greater wealth than I now possess, in you. The strong man could not hold a candle to you, Jeremiah.' His face was so close that she dropped an impulsive kiss upon his weathered cheek.

Jeremiah was flushed with an exhilaration which seemed to curl the very toes within his new, lovingly polished boots, but he chided gently, 'Remember, Sophie my love, that you are a married woman of a certain age and dignity. Such displays are best kept for the intimacy of the bedroom.'

'Indeed,' agreed Sophie, unabashed, 'but I confess that I can scarce discipline myself, for you are head and shoulders above all others in every way. I must be for ever touching you, my dear, for I can scarce believe that you are real, or my good fortune.'

Jeremiah thought for a moment, gazing about him as if seeking inspiration for a suitable reply. 'I declare, Sophie,' he said, self-consciously, 'that no other man here wears a shirt so well starched and ironed as mine. Your industry is an example to all.'

He stood bewildered as her shoulders in her pretty dove-coloured cotton gown began to shake with laughter. She laughed so long, and with such enjoyment, that she had to wipe her eyes upon the lace-edged handkerchief which she kept only for show.

'Oh, Jeremiah!' she said, beginning to laugh again. 'What am I to do with you?'

He looked at her in puzzlement. Perhaps it was her age, or being a woman, that brought on these strange emotional outbursts, for he could recollect nothing he had said to amuse or vex her. He took her arm authoritatively. 'We will buy you some trinkets and sweetmeats,' he declared, guiding her towards the crowded stalls, 'for I do not mind telling you that I cannot countenance the sideshows with performing dogs and other animals. It is as degrading to us as to them, for we are all God's creatures, every one.'

Sophie pressed hard upon his hand to show that she was in agreement.

'We will not bother with the fat woman, my dear, for she is not a patch on you . . .'

Sophie tried so hard to still the laughter that was again rising within her that the effort made her feel quite physically sick, and she had to turn away briefly, hoping that her coal-scuttle bonnet would hide any remaining traces of ill-subdued mirth. She took his arm again and hurried beside him, trying to adjust her small steps to his swift pace.

'Oh, Jeremiah,' she exclaimed breathlessly when he had finally halted and she could trust herself to speak without betraying amusement, 'do not ever change, I beg of you. You are the dearest, funniest and kindest man in all the three hamlets. A man above all others, and I love you dearly!'

'Nonsense, my dear!' he said, flattered and pleased that his small compliment had delighted her so. 'I am no different from any other man.'

Emily Randall, in her coach loft above the stables of the Crown, had been sedulously engaged upon her fine stitching for the seamstress in Newton village. It was tedious, exact work, hard upon the eyesight, and needing all her concentration and skill for a meagre recompense. Yet she performed her task with neither impatience nor rancour. On the contrary, Emily sang pleasantly as she sewed, gratified for the rare opportunity such work afforded her to retain her independence. It had been but a few brief months since she had been an in-pauper at the workhouse at Bridgend, deprived of all rights and human dignity – a charge, as she was constantly reminded, upon the parish and its people. Yet those same people of the three hamlets had shown altogether more generosity of spirit than the cold charity of those in authority, and it was to Joshua and to them that she owed her good fortune.

But today, Emily's thoughts were not upon the past, for the music and gaiety of the crowd had lured her from her solitude. She stood alone beneath the budding branches of the sycamore tree which overhung the churchyard wall, a smile of genuine pleasure upon her lips. She was a serene, gentle-featured woman of some forty-five years or more, slim and elegant in her gown and bonnet of pale amber-coloured silk which complemented the deeper brown of her eyes and the soft wings of hair which curved gracefully over her temples, to edge the high-boned cheeks. There was a quality of repose about Emily Randall which those about her found restful, a calmness reflected in her quiet voice and the natural fluid grace which flowed through every movement, making the smallest gesture beautiful. Emily returned the greetings of her new-found friends with warmth and courtesy, glad to be part of the relaxed and happy throng.

Hannah, the cartwright's wife, from Nottage, passed by, her hand upon her husband Daniel's arm, and he, thought Emily amused, with a face which would not have shamed a thundercloud, so dark and overcast his expression. He was clearly not enjoying himself, and there under sufferance, but he greeted Emily with his customary kindness, for he was, by nature, a mild-mannered man. Civilities over, he grew restive, grumbling, to Hannah's vexation, ' 'Tis like a gathering of maggots upon dead flesh!' Then, catching sight of Jeremiah, he made his excuses and hurried after him to persuade him to seek sanctuary at the Crown.

'Indeed!' exclaimed Hannah, half cross, half amused, 'I do not know why I prevailed upon him to bring me! He provides less company than Jemima, my old sow, and 'tis certain he is worse tempered!' With a smile and a hasty apology, she followed him, righting her coal-scuttle bonnet which had been pushed askew by a careless elbow.

Emily gazed after her, taking in the incredible colour and joyousness of the scene, for there was a festive, holy-day atmosphere in the air; a carefree surging of excitement and anticipation. The women, children and few men who were not about their daily work were dressed in their good Sunday clothes – at least, the few who could afford such decadent luxury, for most of the cottagers owned but the one set of clothing, and that poor and ill-made. Often, it was handed down from others who had outgrown them, or inherited from the ungrudging dead, now more suitably attired in their shrouds.

Emily wondered if, in surveying his resplendent congregation at the parish church of a Sunday, the rector ever reflected upon the back-breaking labour which had gone into the preening of his fine-feathered flock. From her days in the foetid steaming dampness of the poorhouse laundry, she might have told him, and that while the rich bemoaned the irritating scarcity of starch for their ruffles and flounces, by reason of the potato famine in Ireland, there were those who starved for want of simple nourishment.

No, she rebuked herself sternly, I will not spoil this perfect day with resentment or regret, for such emotions are profitless, serving only to sour and corrupt. It was, she conceded, an admonition she might well have delivered to any of her pupils in her days as a governness.

Smiling, she fingered the soft, amber silk of her gown, charitably sent by Joshua's mother, with others no less extravagant and fine, to await her arrival from the poorhouse. It was absurdly inappropriate, she knew, for such an outing as this, but she was aware that it suited her colouring admirably. A few deft stitches with her needle, and it became her 'as to the manor born'. Well, perhaps more 'as from the poorhouse removed', she thought, unable to stifle a smile.

She glanced anxiously about the green, hoping that she might catch a glimpse of John Burrell, but there was no sign of his lean, cadaverous figure, and she felt sure that he would have come to seek her out. It was not his medical duties as partner to Dr Mansel which kept him occupied, she suspected. There were too few prosperous landlords, yeomen and merchants in the three hamlets able to command his services. As for the poorer villagers, whom he would willingly have treated without charge, pride made them scorn his charity. Besides, they put their faith in conjurors and wise men . . . men sharing their own roots and ills. No, it was more likely that he was visiting the aged out-paupers and sick at the request of Walter Bevan, the parish overseer to the poor, an earnest, sallow-faced young man who cared for those dependent upon him with the same selfless zeal as Ossie lavished upon his ailing beasts. Strange, Emily thought, that three men of such disparate talents and birth should share the same passion for the outcasts and abused in society. Was it born in them, or had the cruelties and deprivation in their own lives made them fiercely aware of the hurts of others?

She had grown to understand John Burrell through the letters which Jeremiah Fleet had begged her to pen for him, after the old fisherman had been delivered by the doctor from a fever. She had shared, through Burrell's vivid pen, the anguish and fears of the cholera sufferers he tended, the squalor of his surroundings and the excoriating rawness laid bare. She oft times felt he had knowingly exchanged his former prison for a harsher, crueller place. John Burrell had not even known Emily's name, or that she was Jeremiah's amanuensis, and it was better so, for he wrote as man to man, with nothing hidden or softened in the telling of it. Sometimes, as she had read his words aloud to Jeremiah, her cheeks were wet with tears of impotence and pity for the unknown dead, and Jeremiah, too, was moved to unmanly grief. Yet, for Burrell, she felt sure, the unburdening of himself and the crystallising of his fears were a relief, the cleansing of a deep and suppurating sore that healing might begin.

The core of the corruption lay, Emily knew, in his committal to prison for a killing in which he had played no part. Almost a quarter of a century of corrosive, devouring bitterness had eaten into him, she thought, exposing nerve and raw flesh. Yet, might not even that be soothed and healed by the love of someone who understood? A woman such as she, who could give him the devotion and care he had so long been denied, and would demand nothing in return, save to be with him? Someone who could accept that his love and energies would always be offered first to others, and would never reproach him for it, nor seek to change his ways? That she loved him, Emily had no doubt, but of his feelings for her she was unsure. Would personal commitment imprison him anew, limiting him, shackling his freedom to do what was needed for his own salvation? She would accept him on any terms, without conditions of her own, even should it lead to public contempt and rejection. Yet what had she to offer him, save love? She had neither youth nor beauty, money nor breeding.

Emily glanced above her at some movement in the tree. A small, inquisitive wren was pecking at a newly opened bud, the cleanly cut calyx drifting to earth like the creamy-pink wings of some dismembered butterfly. The silvery leaves beneath were pleated, gently unfolding fans, breaking free of all that had imprisoned them.

An omen, Emily thought, a good omen, for sure. And I? I am the wren, small, drably brown, insignificant, yet able to release something of beauty and worth in others by my poor efforts.

Emily's smile, although gentle, was so warmly embracing that a pretty, fresh-cheeked woman, bearing a child in her arms, stopped beside her, an answering smile upon her own lips. Another infant was clutching at her skirts, unsteady on his plump legs, thumb thrust into his mouth, fingers curled protectively about his button of a nose. He surveyed Emily gravely, all dark eyes and curiosity, before burying his head in his mother's skirt, shyness provoking the urge to be invisible. The cloth of his dress was bundled tight in the fist of his sister, a child of three or four years, with the same dark hair, pert and inquisitive as a starling, and as quick and darting in her movements as she tugged at her brother to prise him from his mother's gown, for all the world, Emily thought, amused, like a determined bird tugging at a plump, recalcitrant worm. But he would not be budged, burrowing more deeply, and grizzling softly with tiredness and excitement, and his urgency to be away.

'You have your hands full, Mistress Crocutt!' said Emily, smiling.

'Indeed,' agreed the young widow, shifting the baby more comfortably upon her hip bone, and wiping the dribbles from his chin with the cloth in her hand. 'Yet were I to answer all their demands upon my purse, we would starve until Michaelmas, for they are determined to miss nothing!'

Emily was about to offer her assistance to shepherd the children upon her way, asking as she glanced about her, 'Dafydd is not with you today?' She was fond of the grave, intelligent boy who, at barely nine years of age, was sole breadwinner for the family since his father's violent death at the hands of the wreckers. 'He is at work upon the farm, perhaps?'

To Emily's surprise, the enquiry brought a flow of blood to Eira Crocutt's face, colour adding warmth and animation to the broad, pretty cheeks. She bent her head, briefly, to the child's skirts, to hide her confusion.

'No, Dafydd is here, and Haulwen, too. Our neighbour, James Ploughman, tends the farm for an hour. The children are with Elwyn . . .' again colour flooded her skin, 'with Mr Morris, that is.'

Before Emily could make reply, Elwyn Morris was beside them, bowing stiffly to Emily, then lifting the grizzling child from his mother's skirts, settling him comfortably within his strong arm. It was the most natural thing in the world to do, but there was a proprietary air in his manner, and in his smile at Eira Crocutt, which Emily barely had time to record before Haulwen hurled herself towards her, crying out a welcome, her arms clasped affectionately about Emily's waist, and kissing her with exuberant enthusiasm. There was a real affection between Emily and the child, for it was to Emily's poor loft that her father had delivered her when, as a destitute ex-pauper, he had braved the murderous wrath of the wreckers to give evidence before the justice of Jem Crocutt's death. Haulwen was as restless and outgoing as a puppy, all affectionate kisses and awkward limbs, boisterous, and as sensitive to rebuff. Yet it had not always been so.

Emily felt the burn of tears behind her eyes as she recalled the silent, stiff-faced child, seated upon the makeshift donkey cart, eyes naked with terror as the poor contraption rounded the archway to the cobbled yard of the Crown. Haulwen's skin had been grimed with the dust of that harsh journey from the hilltop farm, dried tears leaving runnels of pink flesh. Her dark hair hung matted and filthy, her thin figure huddled deep into her father's threadbare coat, as if its familiarity might give her the shelter and protection so long denied.

As they had approached, the child had stumbled from her awkward perch, hampered by the ugly garment, its too-long sleeves flapping uselessly as she flung her arms about the neck of the moth-eaten donkey whose fierce bones all but pierced its fleshless hide. She had dared them to touch the beast or drive it away, her face rigid with mistrust, until Ossie had gathered the outcasts into his care. Even now, Emily could feel again the child's frail bones as she had clung to her, wetting the bodice of her gown with long-held-back tears, as Emily soothed and gave clumsy comfort, her tears mingling with the child's own.

Emily smiled now, and held Haulwen gently at arm's length, her eyes meeting Dafydd's as, grave-faced, he bowed to her formally in greeting, saying, 'Good-day to you, Mistress Randall. I hope, ma'am, that you fare well.'

'I do, sir, and thank you for your kind concern.' She delved into her reticule and, opening the drawstring purse, brought out a sixpence, declaring with equal gravity as she handed it to him, 'I should be grateful if you would take charge of this small offering, since you are the gentleman of your house, and use it to entertain and give pleasure to your brothers and sister, and to Haulwen.'

Dafydd thanked her civilly, clutching the sixpence tight as Haulwen and his sister, Marged, now relieved of her role as nursemaid, ran to inspect the treasure and exclaim over it, already arguing about how it could best be used.

'The fire-eaters and the fat woman!' declared Haulwen lustily.

'The monkey with the red jacket,' cried Marged, clapping her hands in joyous anticipation, 'and sweetmeats, and a ribbon, and a wooden clown upon a stick, who swings and jumps!'

Eira Crocutt, face pink and happy, strove to shush them and restore order, the babe in her arms yelling to add to the cacophony of noise and excitement.

'It is a generous gift, ma'am,' said Elwyn Morris quietly, his clear, intelligent eyes intent upon Emily as he settled the wriggling child more securely in his arms. He smiled wrily. 'The workmaster, Mr Littlepage, would claim such profligacy to be evidence of thriftlessness and moral weakness, I do not doubt.'

For a moment the extravagant sounds and sights about them died away, and they were back in that wretched, arid place.

'I have learnt, Elwyn, that thriftlessness is most destructive when it stems from wasted time and emotions, for unlike money, they can never be replaced.'

Elwyn Morris's voice was low and compassionate. 'It is a hard lesson to have learnt, ma'am, and in a harsh climate.'

'Yet its very harshness brings greater joy to today, and every other, in its freedom. So even the . . . experience . . . of the poorhouse and Mr Littlepage might be salutary, if we allow it to be so.'

'It is not one which I would wish upon another,' exclaimed Morris fervently, 'be he friend or enemy!'

'No, but for us it is past.' She touched him gently upon the arm which encircled the infant, now fallen suddenly to sleep, cheek roundly curved, eyelids transparently blue-veined. She drew his gaze with hers to the other children's eager, impatient faces as they strove to curb their fierce longing to be caught up in the heat of the crowd and the promise of the circus. 'It is past, Elwyn, and will not return, just as this day and childhood will never come again.'

'Indeed, I thank you for reminding me, ma'am.'

His affectionate gaze encompassed Eira Crocutt, Haulwen and Dafydd, the infants in his arms and the widow's, and Marged who had shyly reached up to take his free hand, and was clutching it as if she would never set it free.

'My father is a hero, Mistress Randall,' declared Haulwen proudly. 'He is to be given a medal and reward for saving the horse-drawn tramway . . . or something,' she added uncertainly.

'I doubt that it will bring the joy of your sixpence, Emily,' said Elwyn Morris, smiling, 'or so shining and brave a memory!'

Chapter Eleven

Job Abrahams nodded in approval at the scene around him. His florid face shone with heat and sweat, the reddened skin upon his cheeks so stretched with grins of self-congratulation that they seemed in danger of bursting apart like over-ripe plums. He was not a musical man, as he would have been swift to admit, but the sounds of the crowds' delight, the familiar, rhythmic harmony of performers and animals, and the tunefulness of pennies and ha'pennies falling into the big wooden buckets uplifted his soul. It was all down to organisation, of course. Method. There was no doubting that he had flair, it would be foolish to deny it. His shiny, deep-set eyes disappeared briefly into his cheek pouches as he smiled benignly upon Rosa and Bella, prettily passing by. Bella, who was a sociable, inoffensive girl, smiled back politely, but Rosa bestowed upon him a glance of such withering frostiness for his presumption that it all but extinguished the bright glow from the takings, as well as his smile. 'Hoity-toity, ma'am!' he muttered, and, 'Pride goeth before a fall!'

He sniffed, and set about his work of seeing that all was well, clumsily weaving about amidst the stalls and sideshows, chivvying, encouraging, even insulting the crowds into parting with their pence. As they did so, his rancour vanished. Yes, it promised to be a good day. None of the artistes had thrown a temperament; the sun shone; the animals had neither savaged their patrons nor refused to perform; there had been no accidents with the fire-eaters; the bare-knuckled fighter had won all his bouts; no one had bested the strong man . . . but the fiery archer's enclosure remained empty, bereft of his presence, and the crowds were growing vocal and restive.

Hell and damnation! Abrahams thought as he made extravagant apologies. What had become of the fool? Drunk, most likely, and sleeping it off in some ditch! It was the basest ingratitude! Biting the hand that fed him! But for Abrahams' circus he would be penniless and unknown! He had a mind to fire him . . . Fire him! Job Abrahams, who was not without a sense of humour on a good day, could not help but be amused at his own wit, and promptly related the gem to the stiltwalker who all but fell to the ground with most satisfying appreciation.

Now, if I could just get my hands upon one really good act, to draw the crowds, Abrahams thought, I could make my fortune! A cannon, perhaps? That was it! Firing a man from a cannon. Heaven knows, there must be cannon aplenty, lying useless and unwanted from the wars with the French. He could dress someone up as Bonaparte! Yes. Bill him as the 'Flying Corsican'. His keen eye fell assessingly upon the fat woman. No, perhaps not. He turned to look at his wife, balancing precariously upon the piebald pony to the barest ripple of restrained applause from the crowd, and a chorus of lewd and insulting suggestions as to how she might improve her act. Dear Heavens! If she got any unsteadier he might be forced to use her as cannon fodder! The idea quite restored Job Abrahams' good humour.

Joshua and Doonan accompanied their prisoner, whom the Irishman had rudely and appropriately rechristened 'The Most Miserable Marvo', towards Tythegston

Court, the house of the justice. It was an odd procession with the mule honking, cantankerously refusing to budge so often that, finally, Doonan had been forced to dismount and drag the obstinate creature onwards, securing his own horse to the rear of the cart. Joshua, on his splendid grey, rode guard, keeping an equally judicious eye upon the prisoner and Robert Knight's silver, not, he would have acknowledged wrily, that the poor wretch seemed likely to leap off the cart and flee, despite its constant stopping and starting, for he was a pale, nervous fellow with little stamina, and Doonan's battle with the mule had so inflamed his temper that their captive seemed more disposed to creep under the coarse sacking for safety with his recovered haul.

At the griffon-topped gateway to the Court, the recalcitrant mule refused to move at all, despite Doonan's muttered imprecations, entreaties and brute strength. A battle of wills of the Titans, Joshua thought, amused, and would not have been prepared to wager upon the outcome, so evenly were the antagonists matched for strength and obstinacy. Doonan and the mule surveyed each other critically. Doonan tugged, and the mule dug in its hooves. He tugged harder, and the mule dug in its hooves harder. Doonan made the mistake of relaxing his grip upon the reins, and in a moment the mule had bared its teeth, lips curling with contempt, and in one brilliant manoeuvre simultaneously kicked up its heels and fastened its jaw upon the Irishman's arm, hurling him into the pathway while upending cart, silver and occupant into the dust.

'Damn! Blast! And hell fire!' yelled Doonan, staggering to his feet, his face so suffused with rage that it all but matched the fiery redness of his hair. So incensed was he that he seemed to have actually swollen in his rage, eyes bulging and inflamed, the muscles in his neck stiff as cords. The mule meanwhile sat triumphantly upon the ground, its ugly, rasping cry so absurdly like manic laughter that Joshua could not but laugh with it, snorting and spluttering as helplessly, and quite incapable of rescuing Marvo as he lay stunned amidst the justice's treasures, the wheels of the overturned cart still furiously revolving beside him. Indeed, Joshua could not be sure which were the more demented, the wheels of the cart or the prisoner's eyes.

With a roar to silence the mule's, Doonan leapt towards it, the throbbing of his nipped arm lending him fury.

'I will not be beaten! You miserable, fly-blown, moth-eaten fiend!' He let flow a vitriolic tide of oaths and curses, his great hand fastening upon the bridle. 'I will subdue you . . . you . . . you devil incarnate!'

'It seems,' came the rector's controlled and imperturbable voice from behind him, 'as if my arrival is fortuitous, since you appear to be engaged in deadly combat with my avowed adversary.'

Doonan let slip the bridle and stood shamed and mortified.

'I cannot but applaud your vehemence,' said Robert Knight, protuberant brown eyes amused, lips twitching, 'although perhaps a little excessive, would you not say, Constable?'

Before Joshua could control himself sufficiently to make coherent reply, the justice continued tartly, 'Meanwhile, Stradling, perhaps you will explain this charade, this debacle. My coach stands waiting to convey me to the travelling circus upon the green. I confess I had not anticipated such an ill-timed performance upon my own doorstep. Perhaps you would be wise to consider most seriously whether you have missed your vocation!'

The mule erupted into such an outrage of noise that even Robert Knight could not fail to join in the hilarity for it sounded so exactly as if the beast were vastly amused. 'You will remove this . . . contraption,' he declared, 'and that mule with it.'

As Joshua dismounted from his mare to oblige, for Doonan made no move to do so, the rector squeezed with audible difficulty through the gap between the pillar and the cart, his eyes alighting incredulously upon the dazed prisoner and the sack of spilled valuables.

'My silver!' he exclaimed in comical astonishment. 'I declare, Stradling, you have found my stolen silver! I can scarce believe it! I had thought it all lost to me, for ever.' He surveyed the abashed prisoner belligerently. 'What part does this puny wretch play in it? Is he the culprit?' The rector hauled the man unceremoniously to his feet by gripping his none-too-clean shirt front, commanding, 'Explain yourself, sir!'

'It was all down to the dancing bear, your reverence, sir! I swear it!' blurted the snivelling captive.

Robert Knight looked to Joshua for enlightenment. 'Is the villain deranged, or merely impertinent, Stradling? What is his part in this affair? Who is he?'

'The fiery archer, sir. The phantom of the Downs.'

The rector stared at the cowed, shivering creature in disbelief. 'This is he? The creature who so terrorised Rowden and the hayward? Who held the population of Newton, Nottage and Port in thrall?'

'Assisted by the mule, sir,' said Doonan straightfaced.

Robert Knight's shadowed jowls began to twitch and tremble as he bade the Irishman remove his prisoner to the kitchens for refreshment before escorting him to the cell at the Crown. Then, gravity sufficiently restored, he called out to his coachman and groom to help right the cart, water and feed the mule, and convey the silver within.

'You will ride alongside my coach to Newton, Stradling,' he instructed, 'and explain this peculiar affair as we go. I do not doubt that it will tax even your fertile imagination and Thespian flair!'

'Yes, sir,' said Joshua, remounting the grey.

'There is, of course, the matter of the reward,' reminded the rector.

'I have explained to Doonan that he cannot claim it, sir, since he rode as my aide.'

'Indeed.' The rector considered for a moment, tapping his fingertips together and biting his lower lip to aid his concentration. 'Yet a modest gift or small honorarium would not go amiss, I feel, to recompense him for his . . . aggravation from the mule. I shall instruct Tom Butler at the Crown to furnish him with a month's supply of free ale. A good suggestion, do you agree?'

Joshua nodded, thinking that it might prove less costly if the rector merely handed him the recovered silver. 'A gracious thought, sir, which will, doubtless, be appreciated.'

'Perhaps,' said Robert Knight, determined to be magnanimous, 'I was a little harsh on you earlier, Stradling. I do not doubt that you have the makings of a better constable than a clown.'

Joshua was left to reflect upon the compliment, if compliment it was, while the justice climbed into his carriage and the mule and cart were righted. The cart proved no obstacle, with the aid of the coachman, groom and several willing stable boys, but the mule remained vocal and obstinate, responding to neither threats nor bribes.

In great vexation the justice descended from the carriage and, motioning all aside, took the beast's bridle.

'Get up, this instant!' he commanded. 'Or 'twill be the worse for you!'

The mule struggled awkwardly to its feet and, with a final subdued honk of defiance at the rector, submitted itself to be led away.

'All it needs,' said the rector, 'is calmness, consistency and a superior intellect. One must always demonstrate one's unchallengeable supremacy. It is a lesson you might do well to emulate, Constable.'

'And modesty?' Joshua was tempted to ask innocently, but sensibly refrained.

Robert Knight, secure in his role as mule trainer, returned to his seat in the coach. As it drew alongside Joshua, and the constable made ready to ride beside him and begin explanation, the rector said gruffly, 'A fair day's work, Stradling. Yes, a tolerable outcome . . .'

The Reverend Robert Knight was not given to hyperbole.

Job Abrahams was not an overtly religious man, yet, in his own way, he was devout. The uncertainties of his calling and the rigours of his travelling life precluded him from regular attendance at church, indeed from any attendance at all save at those offices recording birth, marriage, and death. The first and last being inescapable, and the other being the means of perpetuating them. In his closeness with nature, however, he saw the permanence and grandeur lacking in his life. True, there was an inevitability in the changing of the seasons which somehow echoed his own moving on, and that greater journey from being born to dying. He would not admit to 'extinction', even in his own mind, for if trees and flowers were so gloriously resurrected, it would surely have been wasted effort on the Creator's part to let flesh dwindle into dust. He looked about him now, thanking whoever had created him for at least one perfect day; for sunshine and laughter, and the ability to please, for the maidens in their pretty dresses, the promise of good food and ale at the close of the day, and for putting into the hearts and pockets of these people the desire and pennies to support his dreams. Job Abrahams was that rarest of creatures, a happy man.

The same benign spirit seemed to permeate the jostling crowds. Emily found herself being swept along physically and emotionally in the excited fervour of the onlookers; the jocular, skylarking sailors and their innocently flirting girls; the wide-eyed infants, sated with tricks and sweetmeats, their mothers harassed and pleased, indulgent and scolding; the runny-nosed urchins and the sweeping boys sneaked from their labours. She waved cheerfully to Rosa and Bella who were being jostled and swept, laughing, towards the booth of the Strong Man, leopard-skinned over a suitably modest undercovering which had become grubbily moth-holed into quite startling lewdness. Rosa was evidently amused and fascinated by the spectacle as he flexed his arm muscles and struck ridiculously unlikely poses, but Bella . . . Emily caught a glimpse of the girl's pale-fleshed face before she was diverted by the bodies about her to the fire-eaters at the edges of the green. The spectacle gave her no pleasure, for she saw not the warm, exultant leaping of the flames, but Bella's face, raw with such a confusion of pain and naked sadness that Emily felt her eyes pricked with vicarious tears. The child had never recovered fully, she thought, from the birth of the babe in the absence of Reuben. She was a kindly, sweet-natured girl and Emily and all at the Crown were fond of her. Yet the joyousness seemed to have been extinguished within her.

Emily turned away, troubled. She would talk to John Burrell, and beg him to find some excuse to observe both mother and child during his visits to the Crown. He would do it circumspectly and without giving cause for alarm, she felt sure.

Suddenly, Emily felt inexplicably tired and dispirited. Dropping her halfpenny into the beaver hat which Job Abrahams held before her, she tarried only long enough to buy Ossie a small paper cone of sweetmeats from a pedlar with a tray and returned to the Crown. Ossie greeted her unexpected fairing with quite disproportionate delight which all but restored Emily's composure. She had no doubt that much would be sacrificed to his ailing horses, a treat to raise their spirits. It was in such sharing that Ossie's true pleasure lay. How eagerly she would have shared all with John Burrell, she thought, if he did but ask it.

Rosa was so filled with exhilaration at the wealth of diversions offered that she scarce had time to reflect upon Bella's growing quietness and lack of response to her excited chattering. She was already delving into her reticule for the coins which would enable them both to view the activities of the strong-muscled giant before them, and his would-be challengers.

Bella felt peculiarly detached and light-headed, as though her mind and limbs belonged to another, and all she saw and experienced was through the eyes of a stranger. Since the babe's birth, and it had been long and difficult, for the child had been lying awkwardly within her, and the midwife brutish and incapable, Bella had felt this deep sadness well up within her. It was, she thought, like a spring of despair which would rise and bubble through the surface, then gradually disappear, only to reappear elsewhere, its force and violence greater. The Butlers were kindness itself to her, for she was a foundling with no known family of her own, and they treated her as if she were theirs. Phoebe Butler had assured her that it was the loss of blood and the rigours of motherhood that rendered her weak and exhausted, and it was but to be expected. Yet Bella was not wholly convinced. She missed Reuben sorely, but this terror and sense of desolation and abandonment could not be solely on account of his absence. As for the child, Joseph, Phoebe and Tom Butler were besotted with him, kissing him extravagantly and picking him up upon the instant he whimpered, which he did constantly, by day and night, his thin wailing pitiful, piercing her mind with a needle's sharpness, for nothing would console him.

'It will come all right. You may be sure of it,' Phoebe Butler declared. 'It grieves you because you love him so, he is part of you.' Yet, was he? The awful tragedy was that she could feel nothing for him at all, and dare not confess it, for she would be branded unnatural, cruel. No, she felt nothing for him, or those around her, for there was some barrier which set her apart from others; a membrane which could not be pierced or broken apart, separating her now, even, from remembering the comfort of Reuben's coming. She was aware that Rosa had spoken, but could not recall what she had asked.

'Are you not coming within?' Rosa repeated patiently. 'It promises the greatest of amusement. I will pay for you, Bella, for I have money enough, and to spare.' Rosa was, by nature, a kind-hearted girl, but so absorbed in the enjoyment of the moment that her friend's listlessness went unobserved.

'I will sit awhile,' said Bella, grateful to excuse herself. 'It will please me to watch the crowd. But go within, Rosa, I beg of you. It would grieve me to spoil your pleasure.'

'If you are sure . . .' Rosa needed no second bidding and was all too soon swallowed up in the surge of bodies and sound.

When Bella finally arose, she moved aimlessly,

allowing herself to be drifted, then swirled and eddied as by a river current, a leaf, weightless and torn from the branch which succoured and protected her, like that child torn from her own bruised flesh.

Unable to stop of her own volition, so trapped was she by the bodies of others, she looked up to see what had stilled their motion. A monkey, clothed in a little red jacket, a minute cap like an upturned flowerpot upon its head, was leaping towards her, rattling a tin cup, but hampered by a chain fastened by a nail to a cart edge. Its skinny hands, so human in shape, stretched towards her as if in recognition, cup and coins falling to the floor. The monkey man jerked it back, irritably, to his side, wrenching at it with such force that the chain bit cruelly into its neck, causing it to scream and lose its balance, but still he pulled it relentlessly towards him, his hand uplifted to strike.

'No! Stop! Stop, I say!' Bella's voice screamed out despairingly as she tried to push herself through the barrier of flesh towards the cowed and whimpering animal. The man's hand was stayed, and the monkey stretched its small paws towards her in mute appeal, the wizened face piteous under the ludicrous hat, its eyes so filled with pain and despair that it was her child she saw, calling to her; for their faces and bodies were one, wasted and inseparable. There was a harsh screaming filling her ears and head, and the very blood and nerves within her, but she did not know that it was her own. She knew nothing, save that the crowd parted about her and fell back as she ran, half blinded by tears, her throat constricted with pity, across the green sward and into Ossie's protective arms at the archway to the Crown.

' 'Tis some fever of child birth, to be sure,' declared Phoebe Butler to her husband when a shivering Bella was tucked in her bed with a candle aglow beside her, and a warmed brick, set into flannel, at her feet. 'You will go, this very instant, Tom, and buy that monkey, poor creature.'

'What shall I offer for it?' asked Tom Butler, awkward and distressed, for he loved Bella as dearly as if she were his own daughter, and grieved to see her so changed.

'Whatever it costs!' declared Phoebe. 'Every penny we own, if need be, five pounds or fifty! Money makes no matter. I tell you truly, Tom, I am afeared for the girl's mind. Women are prone to strange fancies before and after a birth. From what I can make out, she has some notion that if that animal is harmed, then so will the child be.'

Tom's open, honest face was shocked and he could not hide his bewilderment, but without another word he did as he was bid, taking every penny he could spare, and some besides which he could not.

When he returned, there was no need to ask the outcome, it was there, in his eyes and the slow dragging of his footsteps upon the stone-flagged floor. He looked at Phoebe and uttered no word, but simply shook his head. Despite all his pleading, and the generosity of the price he offered, the monkey man would not sell, declaring stubbornly that the creature, although puny and feeble, was as gold in his pocket to him. It would buy comfort for him now, and security in his old age, for some people were amused by its pretty tricks and antics, and others moved to generosity through pity although, for his own part, he had not much looks upon the animal, for it was nought but a bag of skin and hair which grizzled incessantly.

Tom Butler confessed that there was nothing more to be done, for he had offered to add to the exchange the talking parrot which sat upon the bar, and which he cherished as dearly as any friend. 'Yes,' he said to Phoebe, 'I would have given him away, though, I confess, with a heavy heart, my dear, to ease poor Bella's troubled mind.'

Phoebe moved to where he sat and kissed him warmly upon his roughened cheek. His arms held tightly to her waist as he rested his face against the rounded plumpness of her breast. She stroked his bowed head, feeling the coarse hair, so like their son Reuben's, springing harsh beneath her fingertips.

'It will be all right when Reuben comes,' she said helplessly. 'It will be all right, I am sure.'

Tom Butler was not a superstitious man, nor a fanciful one, but a coldness pierced him through, as though a splinter of ice were pressed deep into his heart, and he knew that, with its melting, his own life blood must flow.

Rosa, having dutifully paid her entrance fee into the Strong Man's theatre, a primitive arena of carts and waggons enclosing a patch of green sward abutting the churchyard wall, was less than satisfied. She found herself hemmed in by heaving, sweating male bodies, reeking stalely of chewing tobacco and ale. She could scarce see above their broadly wedged shoulders and bobbing heads, and they paid no heed to pretty dress or fragility. Indeed, they stepped upon her delicate shoes with their great, clumsy boots, and seemed to crush and press upon her, merely for the amusement of it, pressing their flesh so close and insultingly that she began to feel fear rising within her. The more she struggled and fought to free herself from the mass, and make for the open air, the harder and more cruelly she was imprisoned. She was gasping now with terror, fearing that she would be trampled underfoot, aware only of the shouts and fierce cries about her as she struggled blindly to stay upon her feet.

She was scarce able to breathe, her bonnet was knocked askew, and her reticule wrenched from her hand so violently that the cord had cut into her wrist with the rawness of a burn. She was sobbing hopelessly now, and without check, her whole body trembling with fear, but although she called out, no one paused to come to her aid. Rosa realised, too late, how wilful and conceited she had been, and how foolish her indiscretion. The men surrounding her had paid their dues and were absorbed in the action before them. In imagination, they were the real challengers of the Strong Man; trading lift for lift, grunt for grunt, strength for greater strength. If they were aware that there was a woman in their midst, it was cast aside in the fury of the action before them. And when all was over, Rosa realised numbly, they would treat her with even less respect, believing that a woman who came alone to such a violent spectacle was deserving of their rough handling.

Rigid now with fear, the tears coursing unchecked down her cheeks, she was dimly aware of renewed cheering and screams of prurient, mocking laughter, and felt herself lifted bodily into the air and passed, almost fainting with terror, over the shoulders of the crowd, handled crudely by coarse, rough hands, until she was passed to, and imprisoned in, the brawny, hard-muscled arms of the Strong Man. His hands were about her waist, hard-boned and unyielding, the veins upon them dark as whip cord. The more she struggled to be free, the more relentless grew his grip as, to lewd jests and salacious laughter all about, he swung her aloft, petticoats disordered.

I shall die of shame and humiliation, Rosa thought, too pained and dispirited to make resistance, and she prayed that she might do so at once, that she would no more see their hideous, leering faces, with their lascivious grins.

So near to swooning was she, that she closed her eyes, shutting out the rare sight of Cavan, her husband, leaping over the carts, then bellowing and charging through the onlookers like an enraged bull, intent upon slaughter.

The Strong Man, viewing this demented giant's approach and seeking to escape, let Rosa fall to the floor, careless of all but his own bodily safety. He was strong, certainly, and his muscles well-exercised, but he was neither pugilist nor hero, and could not stand against this monster with the wild eyes and flailing fists. To the exhilaration of the crowd, the Irishman, with a toss of his red head and a fierce unearthly cry, grasped the Strong Man by his leopard-skinned chest and held him aloft as roughly as he had held Rosa. Doonan's face was ruddy with effort, eyes starting from his head, thick neck bulging and sinewed as, with a mighty effort, he crashed his victim to the ground. Dazed and miserable, the Strong Man struggled awkwardly into a sitting position, only to be jerked to his feet again, and downed by a blow from Doonan's massive fist. The crowd went mad with ecstasy, shouting and applauding at this unexpected sideshow, and fell into such a frenzy of cheering and stamping that all other attractions were forsaken as the entire population of the green converged upon the scene.

Job Abrahams was there first, and would have offered the victor a purse for his winning, or the offer of a permanent booth, but the Irishman's contemptuous gaze made him falter and turn aside. Without a word, Doonan lifted Rosa into his arms, and the crowd parted before him as he made his way through the entrance and out on to the green.

When they were safely without the arena, Rosa, choked with shame and regret, and smarting with humiliation, struggled free, then rounded inexplicably upon her deliverer, first boxing his ears soundly, then falling gratefully upon his broad chest, weeping.

'Now, Rosa my love, do not take on so,' said Cavan stolidly, and with clumsy fingers adjusted her bonnet which had fallen askew and was dangling by its ribbons from her slender neck. He touched her cheek with gentleness. 'It is too rough a place for the likes of you. You are as pretty as a butterfly, and as fragile and easy to bruise.' He offered her his vast arm. 'Come, my dearest, let us step out, and hold your head proud, for you are head and shoulders above all others in beauty and goodness.'

The justice, who had stepped from his coach in time to witness Rosa's rescue, turned to Joshua who stood beside him.

'It seems,' he said drily, 'that Mr Doonan has more success with the ladies than with mules!'

'Indeed,' agreed Joshua, amused. 'Perhaps it is all a matter of tactics, and he should change his approach. Although I fear he would have as little success in bullying Rosa as in wooing the mule!'

Chapter Twelve

Robert Knight clipped his eyeglasses over his fleshy ears and peered myopically about him, his large protuberant eyes deceptively mild behind his lenses. Yet Joshua knew that there was no detail of the scene of merriment and frenzied activity before them which escaped his notice.

'I could wish my sermons even half so well attended and enjoyed, Stradling,' he said good-humouredly. 'Bread and circuses . . .'

'Indeed, sir. An apt quotation,' returned Joshua, smiling, 'for today's work began with the miller and ended here – without the fiery archer!' As soon as the words had left his mouth, he regretted them, for he felt sure that the justice would seize upon them to promote his favourite crusade – the need for fire-carts.

The justice swiftly fulfilled his expectations. 'A conflagration here,' he declared sombrely, 'would be a disaster of the greatest magnitude, Stradling, or at the Mabsant bonfires, should they ever blaze out of control.'

Joshua nodded, saying urbanely, 'I think I had best seek out the circus owner, sir, for he will have no knowledge of the archer's capture, and will doubtless be incommoded. I beg that you will excuse me.'

'I will walk with you,' said the justice, 'that we might continue our conversation.'

They fell into step, an absurdly differing pair: Joshua

athletic, strong-boned and well over six feet three inches in height; the justice short, rotund and singularly unathletic. Their conversation, to Joshua's relief, progressed sporadically, defeated by the noise and the need for each to acknowledge the courtesies of the villagers.

Joshua paused to ask one of the augustes where they might find the circus owner, and he replied that Job Abrahams would most likely be counting his money, for it was his favourite occupation! He dwelt in the small Romany caravan yonder. The clown's painted, lugubrious expression remained grotesquely unaltered during his speech and Joshua, upon leaving him, looked back with a feeling of awkwardness and unease, but the justice's wide mouth twitched as he remarked with seeming innocence, 'Not as rewarding an occupation as your own, Constable, would you say?'

Joshua's lips twitched in turn as he replied, 'Yet needing the same skills and much the same trappings.'

'Indeed, how so?' demanded the justice, puzzled.

'First, a recognisable uniform.' As the justice nodded, Joshua paused and considered for a moment before adding, 'Then, curiosity, a spirit of adventure, of course . . . and the nerve to make a fool of oneself, and not to mind laughter.'

'Well said,' applauded the justice, chuckling so delightedly that his loose jowls trembled, and his plumply rounded belly with them. He clasped a hand upon Joshua's arm, saying good-humouredly, 'You have forgotten the most obvious thing, Stradling.' In answer to Joshua's look of enquiry, 'The face! The expression . . . fixed, unalterable. I fear your own gives too much away. It is altogether too intelligent, expressive, and honest –'

He was interrupted by a most violent noise and commotion from the rear of the caravan towards which they were heading in search of Job Abrahams. There was the jarring sound of the wrenching of the door and wood splintering, punctuated by the harsh, terrified braying of a donkey. Then came a fury of oaths, curses and shouts, interspersed with clashing staves and a shrill, anguished screaming.

Joshua ran swiftly towards the fracas, followed by a plodding and somewhat slower justice who arrived breathlessly panting to a scene of extraordinary confusion. Two brutish looking ruffians were furiously setting about the circus owner with cudgel and stave, beating him viciously and without mercy, while a third was thudding blows upon the caravan, shattering wood amidst cries of terror from the donkey. The poor beast, like its master, was vainly trying to escape the fury of an attacker who was gripping the bridle with one hand while belabouring it ceaselessly with the other. The screams came from the circus owner's wife, who was huddled in the gaping hole of the caravan doorway, for the door had been crudely torn from its hinges, offering her neither protection nor shelter from the scene of violence.

Joshua ran forward instinctively, wrenched a stave from the wretch who was belabouring the donkey and, after felling him to the ground, turned remorselessly upon the other offenders. To his credit, the justice, equally incensed and careless of his own safety, followed suit, raining blows upon one of Job Abrahams's assailants with his clenched fists, and receiving a mighty stave blow across his shoulders for his temerity. This only served to enrage him the more as, with most unclerical ferocity, he delivered first a blow, then a kick, to the villain's soft underbelly which not only forced the air from his body, but sent him crashing to his knees, thence to keel forward upon his face. With scant pause for self-congratulation, the justice sank, with the agility of long practice, to his knees beside the brute, then sat hard upon him.

Joshua, glancing up briefly from his battling, permitted himself a brief smile, which widened considerably when he saw that Jeremiah and Daniel had joined in the struggle and were dealing out punishment with conspicuous lack of concern for either their opponents or their own Sunday finery. Ossie, too, had come running from the Crown to make sure that the donkey had suffered no broken bones or contusions. Had the poor beast been gravely wounded, there is no doubt that Ossie's vengeance would have been swift and salutary, creating not only work for the bone-setter of the parish, but also for Ezra the Box.

In the event, the donkey proved in better condition than its tormentor, and certainly less crippled by the weight of its experience than Robert Knight's victim by the weight upon him! When Job Abrahams had been helped to his feet, bloodied but able to support himself, trembling, against the donkey's side, and his wife's screaming had turned to vituperation against their attackers, then to sobs of relief, Joshua and his supporters took stock. The justice, who had inadvertently forgotten to remove his eye-glasses bent, groaning audibly, to pluck them from the ground. One of the lenses had been trampled underfoot. He poked out the glass fragments with a sniff and clipped the frame over his fleshy ears, the better to survey the villains. Joshua was hard-pressed not to laugh, for he presented a most formidable sight. One protuberant, brown eye stared, accusingly, and much magnified, from behind its lens, the other through the empty frame, giving him a wild-eyed, demented look, curiously lopsided and menacing, as he demanded of the routed villains, 'Well, and what is the meaning of this disgraceful fracas, this vicious and disorderly attack?'

The offenders, held firm in the grip of Jeremiah,

Daniel, Joshua and Ossie, kept their heads well bowed, mumbling inaudibly, each waiting for the others to speak.

'Come, come,' demanded the justice testily, 'explain yourselves! My patience grows thin. You, man!' He indicated the cowed and broken wretch whose coat cloth was held in Jeremiah's strong fist. The man babbled incoherently, and Jeremiah's grip tightened upon his collar, jerking his head up to face the justice's fearsome eyes.

'Well?' demanded Robert Knight implacably. 'Was it robbery? Or sheer, bloody violence?'

'Neither.' The fellow had twisted himself free of Jeremiah's hand, and, terrified though he appeared, addressed the justice with conviction. 'That man, Abrahams,' he pointed to the bloodied figure aside the donkey, 'I have seen him before, I swear, and near to the Great Pool. Let him deny it, if he can!'

Abrahams stared at him mutely, too horrified to make reply.

'Who else but a stranger would have beaten Ruth so? A stranger who knows the Pool from earlier times. Look at him! See how he cringes! Guilt is there in his face, for all to see!'

'Abrahams?' The justice's voice was curt.

'It was but to seek water for my animals, as before.'

'He lies. He is a vicious ruthless blackguard, or worse. A near-murderer, who beat an innocent maid near to death for his own filthy needs.' He glanced defiantly at his companions. 'We have travelled on foot from Maudlam, sir, to see Ruth Priday avenged. We are not rabble, sir, but honest men, with wives and children of our own. As God is my judge, I will swear that there is not a man among us who would not kill him in cold blood for what he has done, and hang for it, if needs be!'

There was a chorus of angry assent from his

companions, with ferocious oaths and muttering against the circus owner, who stood, white-faced and shivering uncontrollably, so terrified that he could scarce find the words to claim his innocence. When he could speak, his voice was strangely cracked and hoarse and he gazed about him, dazed and uncomprehending, as though trying to rouse himself from some hideously recurring dream.

'No, you are mistaken. It is some other you seek. I swear to God, I am innocent. I know nothing of this!' He stared at his wife in mute appeal, scarce able to credit the charge, his plump face a mask of shock and bewilderment.

She ran to stand beside him, crying in outrage, 'They are liars! It is some ploy to hide their true intentions!' She faced the justice, rounding upon him furiously. 'Will you believe such filthy scum? They are come to steal.' Her face crumpled and grew ugly as she cried despairingly, 'Let them take what they will, then go upon their way. He is a fine man, and truthful. Do not let them rob him of his good name, sir! I beg of you most humbly.'

There was no doubting her sincerity, or belief that a wrong was being done, and the justice and the rest were silenced by the force and vehemence of her defence. Even Abrahams's accuser looked chastened and unsure. Then, before Joshua or the justice could resolve the situation, Mistress Abrahams whispered something to her cringing husband, thrusting him away, hard. Then, bending to pick up a cudgel from the ground, she waved it aloft, defying anyone to pass as he stumbled behind the donkey and caravan, as though numbed or bereft of his senses. Even as the justice ran forward to calm her and force her to surrender her weapon, Abrahams had reached the churchyard gate and was fleeing along the path, past the astonished verger at the porch and into the church, breath rasping drily in his throat as he flung himself, weeping, upon the altar steps. He lay there, body shuddering, aware only of despair and the coldness of stone seeping into flesh. His sobs echoed back hollowly from stone walls, the empty pews and the high-arched saddle-back roof.

Job Abrahams had never felt so alone. He raised his face towards the altar and the spring light which seeped through the windows above it in shafts of pale gold, thin and restlessly moving as strands of moonlight.

'Oh, God!' he prayed aloud to the light, or whatever dwelt within it, or had created it. 'Help me! Help me . . .'

The verger hurried up the aisle as best he was able, for he was old, and his feet twisted and awkward in movement. He knew not who the intruder was, or why he had entered the church, simply that the fury of the man's flight past him boded ill. Besides, had he not been set to guard the door from vandals by the rector himself? It would vex him sorely if it were to be discovered that he had failed in his duties.

His hand fell fiercely upon the miscreant's shoulder and, despite his frailty, he would have dragged the creature to his feet, but a firm, unmistakable voice from the open doorway commanded, 'No! Leave him, Verger. I would speak with him alone. I thank you for your vigilance.'

Robert Knight put his hand reassuringly upon the old man's bent shoulders as he moved awkwardly by, head bowed with the weight of his failure to protect the church.

The rector still wore the broken-lensed eyeglasses, but he was unaware of them, or their incongruity, for he was once more a person of authority, in command. This was no ordinary place, but God's house, and he its temporal keeper. He appealed to Job Abrahams with calmness and dignity, first bowing to the altar, then commanding, in a voice which brooked no argument, 'Arise, sir, and come with me.'

Meekly, Abrahams struggled to his feet and followed the rector to a pew, where he sat resting his head for a moment upon the coolness of wood, trying to regain his composure.

'You have been accused of a grave crime,' Robert Knight said, without preamble, holding up his hand to silence Abrahams as he made to protest his innocence. 'I know that you deny your guilt, but I must caution you, most strongly, to surrender yourself to the constable, and the process of law. It is your duty.'

'No!' said Job Abrahams, firmly and distinctly.

'No?' the rector was incredulous. His jowls sagged, and his whole body grew slack with disbelief.

'No,' repeated Abrahams, with conviction. 'I will not be tried for a crime I did not commit!'

It was difficult to judge whether he or the rector was the more astonished at this outburst.

'Of course you will surrender yourself!' declared the justice sharply. 'It is your only course, man! Take a grip upon yourself!' His normally pallid face was unbecomingly flushed and he blinked angrily in the face of such obtuseness and defiance. 'I will summon the constable to escort you.'

'I will not be moved!' Job Abrahams's former despair had given way to a cold, rock-like certainty, firm and immovable as the grey walls about him. His florid face, puffed and swollen with weeping, was ridiculous, with its over-wide mouth, the small eyes all but swallowed up in pouched fleshiness. Yet there was something heroic in his stubbornness. The justice, however, was unimpressed.

'The full panoply of the law will serve you if you are innocent!' Robert Knight declared sententiously, knowing, even as he spoke, that it sounded pompous. Flustered, he removed his spectacles, and absent-mindedly started polishing the single lens, declaring, 'The law will not convict an innocent man!'

'No!' Job Abrahams's voice was stronger now, more assured. 'The law is . . . that rabble, those outside, who have already convicted me! Without trial, or with, it is one and the same. They have already found me guilty!'

'Rubbish! Stuff and nonsense!' declared the justice, his usual acuity deserting him in the face of this rebellion. He mumbled inaudibly before pronouncing, 'It is my privilege, sir, to uphold the law!' then repeated sternly, 'The law will not convict an innocent man. You have my word upon it as rector and justice.'

For a moment he thought he had won, for Abrahams was plainly wavering. The justice followed his gaze to the beams of light, the altar, then the crucifix nailed upon the wall, strangely, brightly radiant in the truckled light, as though pierced by the beams of a lantern.

'There was another law, another land,' said Abrahams unexpectedly. 'It could not save Him, or His innocence.' He did not know whence the recollection came, nor even why he had said it.

'You cannot stay here. It would not be proper! There is nowhere to sleep, no food, no comforts.'

'I ask only the comfort and shelter of the church,' insisted Abrahams stubbornly, 'sanctuary from those men without the walls.' He looked at Robert Knight calmly now, his eyes unwavering. 'I claim sanctuary. Here, in the house of God.'

The rector nodded and made his way, heavy with defeat, to the church door, and then out to the crowd, surging upon the pathway beyond. Dear God!

he thought. What am I to say? What to do?

His voice, when he spoke, was assured, inflexible, brooking no defiance. 'The man within has claimed sanctuary,' he said. 'Let no hand be raised against him, and let no man violate such sanctuary, lest he violate the house of God, and God Himself.'

The crowd dropped back, startled, their cries and excitement hushed, then they returned, uneasily, to the promised gaiety beyond. Yet already the stalls were being dismantled upon Mistress Abrahams's command as, dry-eyed and palely authoritative, she stood watch. Then, when all was completed, she climbed resolutely upon her broken wagon and, looking to neither right nor left, gave the signal to be off, the donkey plodding stiffly upon its way at the tug upon its reins. She was watched by Job Abrahams's attackers, their silenced captors, and the folk of the three hamlets, and the puzzled urchins and sweepers of the place. No one attempted to halt the poor procession, nor rail at it, nor cheer. The faces about were as sombre as the performers' own.

Tom Butler, watching from the doorstep of the Crown, saw the leaving of the circus and was grieved, not for custom lost to him, but a greater loss he knew must come. The man upon the cart, with the monkey chained beside him, nodded in passing, and Tom Butler saw that the creature lay curled upon a nest of filthy rags, hat askew, and fast asleep. Yet he saw its troubled eyes and tiny paws outstretched towards him as clearly as if he held it in his arms.

The premature and hasty exodus of the circus, its bewildered performers set upon their shabby carts with their ill-kempt animals fastened beside them or stumbling, reluctantly, behind, had left the village green with a sad and forsaken look.

The sweeping boys from the Crown and Ancient

Briton had been despatched by the landlords to restore order, their numbers augmented by those runny-nosed ragamuffins and guttersnipes whom the bright promise of a halfpenny or crust had seduced.

There were a few ancients intent upon scooping up the animals' ordure for their gardens, or as a bleach for their laundry, and the usual stray curs scavenging and sniping amidst the hummocks of tufted grass; otherwise there remained only Joshua, the justice, Abrahams's accusers and those who guarded them. The women and children had been the first to leave, the shawled babes rigid as chrysalises in their checked cocoons, those infants able to walk or cling to a mother's skirt grizzling from weariness and a surfeit of sweetmeats, or because their adventure had been so abruptly ended. Their menfolk eagerly embraced the refuge of inn or tavern, grateful to refresh themselves upon ale and the spice of male company. Yet, wherever they travelled and whomsoever they met, the gossip was of one thing – the sheer effrontery of that villain who had actually claimed sanctuary within their own parish church, and the curious dilemma it posed for Robert Knight, rector and justice.

Robert Knight was well aware of this dichotomy and the conflict of his roles. That Job Abrahams should face the full discipline of the law, he did not doubt. Nor could he doubt that, morally, he could not disregard the fugitive's plea for sanctuary. He was in little doubt, either, of the wretch's guilt, for he looked a shifty-eyed, unprepossessing creature, full of avarice and cupidity. Yet it was not his place to judge . . . Yes, of course it was, as justice . . . No, that was God's prerogative . . . his duty, as a priest, must be paramount! Still, he must give his parishioners the full protection of the law . . .

Confused and upset, he turned to Joshua with curt irritability. 'Glean whatever you can from these miserable reprobates, Stradling. Learn the full story. I leave it to your intelligence and judgement as to whether they deserve to stand trial for their sins, their excessively violent behaviour. It will be a test of your initiative!'

'Yes, sir.' Joshua approached the task with little enthusiasm, knowing that Robert Knight's ambivalence would cause him to pour scorn upon any decision his constable made. 'And the –' Joshua broke off awkwardly. 'He who has taken sanctuary in the church, sir? What would you have me do with him?'

The justice's protuberant brown eyes regarded Joshua with vexation from behind his unbalanced spectacles. 'Do, sir?' he thundered. 'Do you expect me to do your work for you? Are you incapable? Have you no shred of acumen or self-reliance? It was for these very qualities the vestry appointed you as constable! Take whatever action is appropriate, that is your answer!'

He turned to Daniel and Jeremiah whose holy-day finery was ludicrously disarrayed by their battle with the men they now held as cowed prisoners in their unrelenting grips. His gaze softened fractionally as he confessed, 'I thank you both for your public-spirited defence of those threatened by physical violence! I am glad, sirs, that I may rely upon some members of society for prompt and salutary action when need arises.'

Rebuked, Joshua strove to hide a smile.

The justice turned upon the offenders, declaring scathingly, 'Violence is the refuge of scoundrels, blackguards! Whatever the provocation, it solves nothing. Nothing!' He paused momentarily, losing the thread of his diatribe, and Joshua knew that his thoughts were not on Abrahams's and the men's predicament, but his own. 'Well,' he finished lamely, 'I leave this small matter with you, Stradling. You will, of course, make a full report to me upon the matter. I will return to my coach, for more urgent, spiritual matters demand my immediate and total attention. You understand?'

'Perfectly, sir,' said Joshua with such bland innocence that Robert Knight looked at him sharply, hesitated, then made his way to his carriage, back rigid with disapproval of the whole sorry affair. As he mounted the step to the coach, he turned, saying irascibly, 'Stradling, you had best pay one or two well-muscled cottagers to keep guard upon the church door. I will not have it violated by brutes such as those, seeking retribution, you understand? Anyone caught invading the sanctuary will be swiftly dealt with! A spell upon the treadmill, in a house of correction, will be but a prelude to transportation to the colonies. You have my oath upon it!'

Joshua watched him signal to the coachman and ride away in a rumble and creak of wheels, muffled, clopping hooves and jingling harness, his rotund figure bouncing over the rough grass, fleshy jowls atremble. With a word to Jeremiah and Daniel to watch over the subdued prisoners until he could question them further, the constable entered the church.

There was no sign of Abrahams, and Joshua was fearful that the poor wretch might have become deranged by the gravity of his circumstances and abandoned himself to grief, or even fled. Then, he thought with pity, I shall need to set up a hue and cry, should his guilt in the matter be questioned.

He walked down the long, flagstoned aisle, peering into the pews lest Abrahams had taken refuge there, or collapsed in terror and fallen to the floor. Joshua saw and heard nothing save the empty clatter of his boot soles striking upon the flags. He saw no sign of the man in the bell tower, and hurried, apprehensively, to the newly built vestry aside the pulpit, drawing the curtain noisily across its brass rail.

Abrahams, composure mildly restored, was seated upon the rector's velvet cushioned chair, feet upon a table, a bottle of Communion wine at his elbow, and a glass of it raised comfortingly to his lips. By his flushed cheeks and the gleaming of his eyes, Joshua was sure that he had already imbibed well. Joshua's breath was exhaled in a gasp of outrage at such blatant temerity.

'I hope, sir, that you are well provided for,' he said with rough sarcasm, 'and in need of nothing?'

Abrahams's small eyes disappeared into their pouches as his smile consumed his face. ' 'Tis kind of you to ask, sir,' he said ingenuously, pulling a half-sovereign from the purse in his pocket. 'If you would step to the Crown and beg the landlord send me whatever victuals he can provide, a straw mattress and a firkin, I should be greatly obliged to you – and take a jug of ale for your kindness.'

To Joshua's credit, he went wordlessly and did as he was bid.

Chapter Thirteen

While Joshua's mind and wits were concentrated upon securing food, clothing and the barest necessities to ensure Job Abrahams's physical comfort within the church, the Reverend Robert Knight's moral dilemma was less easily solved. As a Christian, and one who therefore professed to love his neighbour as himself, he could scarcely reject Abrahams's plea for sanctuary in God's own house. Even less could he order the fugitive to be forcibly removed to stand trial before the courts. Indeed, that very Sunday he had preached a most moving and salutary sermon upon the story of the good Samaritan, declaring, with passionate conviction, that it was man's inescapable duty to aid the afflicted and destitute. A denial of those in need was a denial of Christ Himself.

It was true that he knew where his duty lay, with God rather than Mammon. He simply wished that the practical accomplishment of such ideals was not so squalid and disheartening. How would Abrahams perform those practical needs which all flesh was, unfortunately, heir to, and where? Not in his new vestry, he hoped! Yet it was unthinkable that the creature should wash, shave, perform his bodily functions within the body of the church itself. Even the thought was an obscenity. Yet where was the man to go? Where eat and sleep? The bell tower was too small, and within view of the congregation. Heaven knows, his sermons were ill-attended to enough, without further distraction. True, the bells were cracked and useless, but he could scarce banish the poor wretch to the 'embattlemented tower', for the floor of it was in as sorry a state of repair as the bells, and Abrahams was a stout man, more than usually restless and weighty. It would not do to have him descending unheralded through the roof, or even shuffling about noisily overhead, for the cottagers were easily distracted. Worse, they might set upon the culprit and do him some injury, believing his accusers' taunts that he had all but murdered a poor innocent girl that he might satisfy his lustful purpose.

No! There was only one thing for it, Robert Knight resolved. He would transfer his burden to broader shoulders and a mind better fitted to solve the moral and ethical dilemma of sanctuary. The bishop! Yes, the Bishop of Llandaff. Who better equipped to advise and guide him upon the firm path of righteousness? It would prove his own humility – that as a mere parish priest, although perfectly able to settle the question in his own mind, and to act upon it, he sought wiser counsel. He was prepared to abase himself, to surrender himself to higher authority. He would demonstrate that he was neither too vain nor too hidebound to take advice. Surely the bishop would be flattered that a subordinate set such a value upon his opinion. Besides, it never went amiss to draw attention to the rigours and difficulties of one's calling – and, hence, to oneself. Yes, it was decided. He would go to Hawick House in Chepstow on the morrow, taking a small gift as a token of his esteem and respect. Nothing ostentatious, for the bishop prided himself upon being a simple man. A brace or two of pheasants; some good French brandy; a bottle of claret from his cellar, or perhaps some port.

His spirits remarkably lightened, the rector took the

keys to his wine cellar and, with Leyshon preceding him cautiously with the lantern, descended the steps. For the moment the nightmare of his nephew's violent death, and his part in it, receded. If it were instantly replaced by another problem, then no matter. Leyshon, attentive to his master's every request, selected a cobwebbed bottle from its dusty catacombs, presenting it with due reverence for inspection as he held the lantern aloft. Robert Knight nodded, satisfied. Perhaps, he thought, with a glimmer of hope bright as the splintering light beams, the bishop might be prevailed upon to give his opinion on the virtues of fire-carts? He smiled. After all, fire was the devil's avowed instrument – sinners' eternal damnation and torture. The topic should be easy enough to insinuate into a civilised and erudite conversation between two men of the cloth.

Leyshon, clumsily lighting Robert Knight's way upwards, and moving with difficulty because of his awkwardly deformed spine, saw his master's shadow loom up starkly menacing in the lantern's glow. The skin of his face shone pale as the wet flesh of a drowned man, save for the shadowed jowls and the coarse black hair, his one surviving lens feverishly glittered like the eye of some brooding Cyclops. But Robert Knight struck no terror into the old servant who had tended him devotedly from birth, and knew him to be the gentlest and most amiable of men, save in the pursuit of those inflicting savagery and violence upon others. Leyshon knew that in wreaking pain and death upon his nephew, his master had wrought a greater pain within himself, and a crueller kind of death: survival. Leyshon had prayed hard and devoutly over the months; not for God's forgiveness for Robert Knight, he had no doubt of that. No, he had prayed that his master might forgive himself, as freely and generously as he forgave others. Could it be that his prayers were at last being answered?

If the good folk of the three hamlets were agog with excited speculation about Job Abrahams's guilt, or innocence, and their rector's best course of action, then the mood at Southerndown Court was agreeably tranquil. The talk between Rebecca, Elizabeth and Mistress Louisa Crandle was centred upon the joyfully awaited nuptials of the two young gentlewomen and their respective bridegrooms. Rebecca, as her birth and position in society decreed, was to have a wedding celebration of quite exceptional pomp and circumstance, a distinction she would gratefully have surrendered had she not owed obedience to her grandfather's wishes. It would have pleased her to have wed Joshua at a simple, intimate marriage service at Newton parish church, with a modest meal afterwards at the Crown Inn, in the company of Sir Matthew, Joshua's parents, and a few of their dearest friends. Yet she knew that such a decision would not only grieve her grandfather, but bitterly disappoint all the tenants and those employed upon the estate, and others as far afield as Newton, Nottage and Port. There was, as Rebecca was painfully aware, little enough to celebrate or anticipate with joy in the lives of the frugal, hard-working cottagers. The privileged security of her present existence had not erased those memories of the physical hardship and discomforts of her life as a shellfish gatherer, rather served to sharpen them. She had but to close her eyes to relive the bitterness of that wind from the sea, its cutting edge lacerating exposed skin, or the bleak iciness of rock pools which flayed and chafed her legs and hands to whipped flesh, raw as a burn, raw as the tears which dropped, scalding, upon her cheeks as though they fell into open wounds. Yet the greatest wounds had been the ever present fear of sickness, hunger, and the poorhouse. Strangely, there had been no fear of death itself for, to many, it brought a peace and promise they had never known in life. No, Rebecca thought, it would be insensitive and mean-minded to deny them the small pleasure of seeing their constable so splendidly wed, and a part in the festivities.

Louisa Crandle had no such plebeian concerns to trouble her single-mindedness. She was intent upon making Rebecca's wedding celebrations memorable, and a credit to Sir Matthew's elevated role in the strict social hierarchy. If it also elevated her own, then it was not an accident to cause her too much distress. However, to her credit, it must be said that she was truly fond of Rebecca, despite her aggravating tendency towards headstrong and unladylike ways, which Mrs Crandle was gracious enough to pardon on the grounds of the known eccentricity of the highborn. Indeed, such pure-blooded aberrations, she convinced herself, might even be proof of Rebecca's refinement and sensitivity, like that charming nursery tale of the Princess and the Pea. In any event, the de Breos – Stradling nuptials would be as elegant, distinguished and unforgettable as any ever seen in the Vale and beyond, she was determined upon it. The etiquette demanded would be followed to the letter; the style would be dignified, understated even, as befitted such an ancient and honourable family. Yet there would be delicate touches of refinement, élan, to prove that those of breeding might occasionally create rules of their own, for they were the innovators and arbiters in matters of taste. Yes, she would see that all was impeccably planned and conducted – the reception, the flowers, the refreshments, the invitations, of course, the conveyances, the servants, the musicians . . . although Joshua's supporter, his brother Aled, would doubtless take charge of the victuals and entertainment for the rude hoi polloi in the hamlets and those upon the estate. It was not in her province to provide diversions for the lower orders, and yet Rebecca was adamant that they should not be excluded.

Louisa Crandle turned her attention for the hundredth time to arranging and rearranging the seating plans for the two hundred guests who were to be accommodated in the Great Hall, and to the disposition of chambers for those who would be granted hospitality overnight. No! No! It simply would not do. She tutted audibly, to the delight of Rebecca and Elizabeth who exchanged indulgently amused glances as, with a sigh of vexation, Mrs Crandle hurried from the drawing room.

Impatience had made her mother almost pretty again, Elizabeth thought, forcing pinkness into the pale ivory skin, bringing animation to her clear blue eyes, the only physical feature which remained young, unchanged. Since Creighton's death, all her former liveliness had been drained, as if it had been leached away with his blood . . . The red of her hair, bright as burnished copper, had faded and dulled, even her brows and lashes had grown sparse and colourless, as though the loss of her son's blazing glory had dimmed all colour and vitality in her. Elizabeth, aware that Rebecca had spoken to her while she was immersed in her thoughts, looked up from her embroidery enquiringly.

'I said your mama is in quite a taking!' exclaimed Rebecca. 'I hope that we have not overburdened her with preparations; there are so many details to plan and consider. I swear, Elizabeth, that I am exhausted already, with all that pinning and stitching, selecting and rejecting, and I have but to stand still and be ministered to. I have a mind to leap into a carriage and take myself to Joshua's cottage, bidding him take me as I am!'

Elizabeth smiled, setting down her embroidery frame. 'And if you did, then he would simply bundle you back without ceremony, or return you, with Ossie, in the gaol-coach, your reputation as tattered and bloodied as that needlework which vexes you so!'

'Indeed,' declared Rebecca, tossing her dark head, eyes alight with mischief, 'were I to be given the choice, Elizabeth, I would sooner take a turn upon the treadmill at a house of correction than sew another stitch, for I am as ill fitted for the polite arts as a . . . giraffe to pianoforte!'

'It is true,' said Elizabeth, straightfaced. 'Now that you bring it to my attention, I see a similarity.' Elizabeth's soft mouth curved irresistibly, and her dark eyes were warm with humour as the two friends broke into companionable laughter. 'You need have no fear on Mama's account, Rebecca,' she began when she had regained her composure, 'the wedding preparations have given her a new lease upon life, they absorb her utterly. I fear, though, that the quietness and simplicity of my own wedding is a sadness to her.'

'You are set, then, upon a marriage service here, at the private chapel? You will not reconsider?'

'No.' Elizabeth's gentle face was gravely intent. 'I would have it no other way, could not . . . The circumstances . . .' She broke off, and Rebecca was grieved to see that her companion's eyes were soft with unshed tears. She hesitated, and would have risen to comfort her, but Elizabeth abruptly turned her head, defiantly shaking away all traces of her hurt, saying, 'Devereaux has no family, and there is the closeness of Mary's death. I have no other blood relation, save my father, and he . . .' her voice grew firmer, 'even if he were able to attend, then he would not know me. It is better so. To have him here would grieve my mother as deeply as it grieves me to see him absent, in flesh and in mind.'

Rebecca nodded, saying awkwardly, 'Devereaux would probably like it better thus, Elizabeth, for I sometimes feel that the relentlessness of the affair sweeps me along like a tide, swift and inescapable, bearing me away, and distancing me even from Joshua, whom I love.'

Elizabeth said quietly, 'I cannot believe that you mean that. You say it from kindness, to comfort me. But I have no need of comfort, Rebecca, truly. Devereaux, even in absence, is here with me. I do not believe that we can ever be separated in spirit. I am as much a part of his flesh as if we were already one, indissoluble, indivisible . . .' She faltered, flushing deeply. 'I beg you not to mock me, Rebecca, for such a romantic conceit. It is gauche, perhaps, and childishly sentimental . . .'

'I do not think you sentimental,' said Rebecca, arising and kneeling beside her to embrace her with affection. 'I think you to be loyal and loving, as no other I know, to your parents, Mary and Devereaux, too. You deserve the greatest of joy and happiness.'

There was a sadness in Elizabeth's face, and a dark shadowing of her brown eyes as she confessed, gripping Rebecca's hand tightly with her own, 'I sometimes think, Rebecca, that God has given me this one perfect thing, Devereaux's love, in exchange for all the horror and sadness that has gone before. I could not confide it to any but you, for Dr Peate would think it irreverent and foolish, and my mother would not choose to be reminded of the past, for she will not accept my father's existence, even now. I feel that until Devereaux came to care for me, and protect me, I was but half alive, a poor, bewildered thing, seeking to give help to those who depended upon me, yet knowing no help for myself, or reason for living.' A soft wing of dark hair had fallen across her cheek and Elizabeth soothed it back gently with her fingertips, and said, smiling, 'I shall look forward to your marriage, Rebecca, for then I shall be an elderly married lady, discreet and respectable, and fitted to tell you, unblushingly, of the beauty of being joined in flesh as deeply as in spirit.'

'You have no reservations?' asked Rebecca, anxiously. 'No doubts. No fears that . . . all will not be as it ought?'

'How could it not be,' demanded Elizabeth, 'since I am to marry the finest, dearest, bravest, most handsome man in all of the world?'

'Indeed!' declared Rebecca, with mock indignation, 'I fancy, ma'am, that you are mistaken. That honour, most assuredly, belongs to me!'

Joshua would, no doubt, have been elated to learn that his bride-to-be, Miss Rebecca de Breos, held him to be the very paragon of men in every particular. Yet he was sensible to the fact that not everyone regarded him with the same loving and uncritical devotion. Job Abrahams, now that his initial terror had abated, was growing uncommonly demanding. Indeed, were it not for the sanctity of his surroundings, Joshua might well have taken him by the scruff of the neck and kicked him bodily into the graveyard, to the accompaniment of most unclerical oaths, a solution which might have eased his aggravation, but undoubtedly displeased Robert Knight. Tom Butler at the Crown had been incredibly accommodating to the fugitive, for he was by nature a generous, warm-hearted man, well suited to his occupation as landlord of an inn. He treated Abrahams as if he were a welcome guest within his own walls, providing water for washing, a chamber pot, those toilet articles necessary for a man to retain his self-respect and dignity, enough ale to keep him jovial, but not obstreperous, and the same victuals and cooked meals enjoyed by his wife and himself. In addition, from sheer kindness of disposition, he supplied, free of charge, a stable lad to empty the inevitable slops, and a sweeper boy to brush out the detritus of living. Butler resolutely refused to take sides in the argument as to Abrahams's guilt, declaring that it was for God and Robert Knight to judge. If the lines between the two were a little blurred in his mind, then it was entirely due to the force of the good rector's sermons and, perhaps, a confusion more excusable than the good rector's own.

However, the more Tom Butler strove to make the interloper's stay agreeable, the more carping and ungrateful Abrahams grew, the fiercer his demands, the more ridiculous his complaints and the wilder his abuse of the poor unfortunates who served him. Joshua's patience grew thin as Abrahams grew proportionately fatter, nourished by the excellent victuals from the Crown. It was with relief and added determination that Joshua set out upon the grey to find the circus and the truth of the matter. Ossie, bringing him the saddled mare, asked, screwing up his clenched fist of a face assessingly, 'Your lodger fares well, Joshua?'

'None better!' said Joshua abruptly. 'I swear he would survive and flourish in a desert, were he so minded.'

Ossie smiled, revealing the gaps in his teeth, and shifted his hold on the bridle, venturing, ' 'Tis certain he has found a cosy little nest.'

'Yes, like a damn great cuckoo!' exclaimed Joshua irritably. 'And I the one foolish enough to succour and protect him.'

'They have a habit of edging out all about them, or so I have heard,' said Ossie with commendable gravity. 'Take care that he does not land *you* in the mire, sir.'

'Your warning comes too late,' declared Joshua. 'He has already done so, with a vengeance!' He gathered up the reins securely. 'I am surprised that you do not offer me advice,' he said, with unusual asperity, 'You are usually so free with your texts and homilies. Surely you have some pearl of wisdom to offer?'

Ossie strove to suppress a grin. ' 'Tis a dirty bird which fouls its own nest,' he suggested, turning aside.

'Excellent!' cried out Joshua, reining the grey towards the archway. 'That will certainly stand me in good stead. Perhaps you will tell me what in hell it means, that I may act upon it!'

Ossie ran beside him, stable boots striking the cobbles with the mare's hooves, almost too helpless with mirth to loose hold of the bridle.

'I only quote the words, not write them!' he declared, striking the horse's rump affectionately in parting. 'You are the scholar. I had hopes that you might tell me!'

Joshua's verbal exchanges with Ossie had, as always, put him in a kinder humour, for the ostler possessed that rare talent of knowing how best to calm fears, or irritation, in humans as in beasts, with a few careful words. He possessed a sensitivity and knowledge which belied his lack of schooling and humble occupation, and Joshua greatly admired the hard-working ostler, and was pleased to call him a friend.

Yet now even Ossie's intelligence could not serve to help, for the constable was plagued by a dilemma which he alone could solve. It was not merely the vexed problem of Abrahams's claim to sanctuary which bedevilled him, but whether the circus owner was guilty of Ruth's assault. The justice, not unnaturally, seemed more concerned with the moral and ethical effects of the suspect's occupation of his church. Indeed, Robert Knight's disquiet at the situation seemed to grow proportionately as

Abrahams's anguish decreased. Joshua's patient questioning of the apothecaries and doctors at Pyle and at Kenfig village had elicited nothing of use to him in his investigation, and he now had the uneasy knowledge that there were those at Maudlam who had declared themselves ready to take Abrahams by force, if need be, and who would have no compunction in killing him.

At the justice's behest, and to the annoyance of the vestrymen, a stout labourer had been employed to keep a watch upon the church, and give warning should vandals seek to abduct the circus owner by force. Joe Priday's house was similarly guarded, although it was a foolhardy man who would have braved the blacksmith's wrath, Joshua privately thought. Yet there already seemed to have been some relaxation of the initial anger and horror which had surged with the discovery of Ruth's hurt, an acceptance, perhaps, that the culprit had been secured within the church, and that his arrest and punishment must, inevitably, come.

Joshua was not convinced. It was true that the wretch was infuriating, brash, and altogether ill-mannered and unappreciative, but there seemed to be no real evil in him. Joshua was not puerile enough to believe that every criminal could be readily identified by his sinister features, or his air of menace. If it were so, then his work would demand neither effort nor intellect. Yet, surely, if Abrahams were guilty of such heinous violence as the assault upon Ruth, he would be fearful enough of the consequences to make excuse for his actions, or to show remorse? Even a consummate actor could not appear so carefree, or so absurdly pleased with his petty victories over those who reluctantly served him. There would be terror at the threat of the gallows which could not be hid, and some inevitable plea to the rector for absolution. Job Abrahams was not a fool, but undeniably shrewd.

Shrewd enough, then, to have considered all of the arguments which Joshua now put to himself, and to have anticipated them?

Joshua sighed, and turned the mare towards the smithy at Nottage, his anxieties unresolved. As he passed by the forge, Ben Clatworthy the blacksmith looked up from his labours at the anvil, where he had been intent upon shoeing Illtyd's piebald, Faith. Clatworthy's face was drenched in sweat, and droplets glistened like oil upon his black hair, and upon the naked arms, brawny and seared with small burned crescents of flesh. Joshua nodded and shouted a greeting, which Clatworthy and his apprentice echoed, while Illtyd raised a hand in salute, the piebald fidgeting and tossing its head nervously amidst the hiss of steam, the acrid, pungent smell of charred hoof sizzlingly released.

Almost against his will, Joshua found himself reining in the grey and dismounting at the Rhyl, beside the gypsy encampment. He could not say what impulse had prompted him to travel there, for he had meant to ride directly to Maudlam. There seemed little call for him to warn the Romanies of the ill-feeling of the men at Maudlam, for many believed Abrahams to be guilty, and the rest were prepared to defer judgement until his impending arrest. In his conversations with Dr Mansel and Dr Burrell, Joshua had tentatively broached the possibility of taking Ruth to the church at Newton to identify her alleged attacker, by glancing, perhaps, through a window, unseen by him. The response had been swift and unequivocal. Such action could not be entertained. The girl showed little progress and was devoid of speech. Her only reaction was one of terror to every man, save those she recognised, and trusted. Should she be faced with her attacker, even if she were recovered enough to undertake the journey by coach, then collapse and mental disorder might follow, without hope of recovery. Joshua knew that it was a risk he was not prepared to take, even should the justice countenance it. There was less chance of persuading Abrahams to forgo his sanctuary within the church, and even should he be forcibly removed, then his life, innocent or guilty, would certainly be forfeit.

There was a fierce outbreak of barking and rattling of chains as the lean curs of the encampment strained menacingly at their leashes as Joshua advanced, leading the grey, who eyed them nervously, neck rigidly arched. There was added clamour from the rasping cries of the donkeys and mules, and the fidgeting of the ponies, tethered to their iron rods; but the greatest outcry came from the inquisitive, barefoot children. They swarmed about him noisily, showing neither shyness nor restraint, until a harsh voice bade them 'Go! Leave him be!' At once, like a darkening swarm of bees, they gathered and were gone, and Joshua was left in peace, smiling at his deliverer.

The leader of the band of Romanies was a dark, hirsute man of below middle age, hard-muscled and with a natural dignity and grace of movement. Joshua extended a hand, and it was clasped firmly in greeting. Despite the differences in their appearances, for Joshua was as fair-complexioned as the gypsy was dark, and the taller by several inches, there was an undeniable similarity in the two men, that purposeful manner and self-reliance which comes with authority. They had been allies upon occasion in the past, yet, should custom and duty decree, each knew that he might as easily be facing a declared enemy. They faced each other respectfully enough, yet not without a certain wariness and reserve.

Joshua was vaguely aware of some change, a growing quietness. Fighting a sense of unease, he glanced covertly about him, to see that, like the children, the women who had been busily engaged upon their tasks of cleaning, scouring and tending the huge cauldrons chained upon the rough triangle of sticks above the fires had silently crept away. If the leader of the gypsies had made some sign of dismissal, then Joshua was unmindful of it. He was mindful, however, that the men of the encampment had drawn together in a stealthy circle, close enough to overhear what was said, effectively sealing off any chance of escape.

Joshua purposefully quietened his mare with a firm grip on the bridle and a muttered word of command, before saying, his voice deliberately loud and unhurried, 'I have come here as a friend who respects your ways and traditions in order to seek your help.'

There was a murmuring from the ring of men, and a shuffling of feet, but the Romany leader's face showed no change of expression as he waited for Joshua to continue.

'A young woman, a girl, has been cruelly set upon and beaten at Maudlam.'

'That is none of our doing!' The voice from the crowd was angry, shrill with resentment.

'No, I am convinced of it.' Joshua's denial was firm. 'I come merely to warn you of the anger hereabouts, and to beg your assistance, if you will give it.'

The discussion and disagreement grew steadily more insistent, until their leader motioned them, swiftly, into silence. His eyes upon Joshua were shrewdly assessing.

'It has been rumoured that the offender has already been taken, and is within the church at Newton.'

'I do not believe that he is the guilty man, but his life is painfully at risk. The one who is to blame goes free, unknown, and so unpunished.'

Joshua and the Romany were regarding each other

steadily, as if locked in some unexplained contest of will. As the silence lengthened and deepened, Joshua, feeling increasingly oppressed, was almost persuaded to mount his mare and drive a pathway through the hostile barrier of bodies. Caution halted his flight, but it was with relief that he saw the gypsy nod and turn away with a shouted command. Swiftly the atmosphere of hostility changed, and Joshua was left wondering uneasily if he had imagined it, or if it had been spawned by his own fear, emanating, not from those about him, but within himself.

'We will do what we can to aid you.'

It was a solemn pact, and Joshua thanked him gratefully.

'I can tell you nothing of the man you seek,' continued the Romany quietly, 'and if he had been one of our people, he would have been dealt with, at once, swiftly and without mercy, since he showed none. His punishment would have equalled his crime, in cruelty, for that is the penalty demanded by our own law. Violence brings dishonour upon our whole race, and hatred and revenge upon those who are innocent. There is more than one victim of such a crime.'

'Indeed,' agreed Joshua soberly, 'for I have seen its effect upon the girl's father, and others who love her.'

There was an unexpected commotion behind him, and he turned with instinctive speed, arm raised to defend himself. Shamefacedly he stared, then let his arm drop foolishly to his side, a smile of delight and incredulity upon his lips.

'The donkey?'

'As you say, the donkey. We have tended him with herbs and remedies long familiar to us, and proven. His wounded leg yields slowly to treatment, although he remains sensitive of using it. I have no doubt that, given time, it will heal.'

'The young woman who was assaulted,' Joshua began awkwardly, 'the donkey is hers, and much loved, although she is unable yet to speak, or tend it.'

The gypsy nodded his understanding. 'This man, this creature who wrought such savagery upon her, belaboured the animal with equal violence, leaving it all but dead. There is a madness in such brutality, a venom which must be halted lest its poison spreads. You will return the beast to its owner?'

'I will pay you, fairly, for your labours and help.'

'You may pay for our labour, as custom demands. Our help we give freely, where it is needed.'

Joshua reached within his pocket and brought out a leather pouch containing two gold sovereigns, a fortune, and thought the money well spent as he put it into the Romany's hand, thanking all those around him with warmth and sincerity. Then he mounted his grey and took the bridle of the bewildered donkey in his hand.

'I will travel slowly,' he said, 'and with care for the animal's injuries.'

'Once, a long time ago,' the Romany said, 'I left a carved horse of ash wood without your cottage, as evidence of my good faith.'

Joshua drew the same carving from his pocket, allowing the mare's reins to lie loose, and held it towards the Romany, who shook his head.

'It is a sign of good faith. Return it to me, should you need my help. I will understand, and come.'

Joshua smiled and, with the donkey puzzled but unresisting at the mare's side, set out for Joe Priday's house.

Chapter Fourteen

At Newton, it was with much relief and lightening of spirits that the coachman and guard upon the company stage cleared the archway to the Crown Inn and the cobbled yard. The journey had been tedious, and their limbs were stiff and uncomfortable from their enforced vigil upon the box. Here, they and their passengers would be assured of warm, clean beds, good victuals, and a quiet rest. Under Ossie's watchful eyes, the leaders and wheelers would be unharnessed and cared for as devotedly as the guests within Tom Butler's inn. Too often, the horses on the cheap company stages were blind or ill-used, run by those who financed the companies until they died in harness. It grieved the ostler that, in life, they were underfed and ill-used; in death, their lean carcases sold to the soap and glue makers or the leather tanneries for what little they might fetch. More often, they lay where they fell, their rotting flesh a lure for stray curs and carrion, or those of the poor who were hungry enough, and desperate enough, to scavenge for food.

But within the Crown Inn, no such gross and unpalatable truths impinged upon the contentment of the guests who, well rested and well victualled, were thankfully supping their ale. The travel was tedious, despite the diversions of games and *Patterson's Roads*, those amiable guide and puzzle books which served to while away the long hours. Yet it could not cushion them against the unbearable cold any more than the straw heaped upon their feet. As the limbs and brain grew numbed with iciness and boredom, so the flesh grew bruised and the bones aching and jarred by the continuous bumping over pothole and cart rut. The air within the coach grew stale, foetid with human sweat and the stench of unwashed bodies, and the mingling of lotions, orris powder, and the lingering odour of ill-digested meals and ale upon the way. Often the parcels the passengers clutched upon their knees or hung about their persons stank from keeping: over-ripe cheeses, dead game grown high and maggot-ridden, salmon and crabs, farm butter turned unappetisingly rancid. Over all hung the odour of horse flesh and animal excreta and, very often, their own, for inns were far apart and the coachmen were afeared to halt too long or too often, on account of highwaymen. Only the rich, with carriages of their own, were afforded the refinement of travellers' chamber pots of silver, or even the luxury of soap, since it was so grievously taxed. It was no wonder that Tom Butler's inn offered a very haven of delight upon the way.

He seemed, to weary travellers, to be the archetypal inn-keeper, jovial, welcoming, agreeably hospitable. His rotundity bore testimony to the superiority of his meals; his well-scrubbed features and spotless clothes a tribute to the cleanliness and order of the place, and to his wife's good house-keeping. It would have been hard for any stranger visiting to know how grieved he was, or how filled with unease and pain.

Both he and Phoebe, his good wife, were sick at heart, and had been so since Bella had given birth to the child, Joseph. Unlike the poorer of the cottagers who were expected to give birth unaided, often in a crowded, one-roomed hovel, with neither privacy nor creature comforts, their daughter-in-law had been watched over lovingly through all the days when she was carrying the babe. Why, Phoebe would scarce let her lift a finger, lest she overtire herself or cause the child injury. 'Twas well known to the womenfolk that any shock or sudden fright could cause a hare-lip or some such deformity, just as a craving for some foodstuff, if denied, would set a birth mark upon the child in that very shape. It was strange that their grandchild had been born with a caul across his face, that veil-like membrane which promised good fortune, for it meant that the lad need never be afeared to die of drowning. Tom Butler shook his head regretfully. Aye, that was the crux of the matter. It reminded Bella too starkly of Reuben's absence and the perils he faced upon the sea. Oh, but he would be glad when his son returned, for he was sorely missed. It was no life for a married man with a newborn son, this adventuring across the seas. It was neither natural nor just to gallivant so. Yet who could blame a young man for finding the lure of unknown lands and faraway places more insistent than a place at his own hearth? A seat in the chimney corner was a last refuge for old men whose dreams were dead, and whose eyes too dimmed to see those lost horizons. Perhaps it was as well that Reuben had gone while his limbs and yearnings were strong enough to carry him wherever he wished to travel. Regret was a bitter companion. 'Too late. Too late . . .' – how often had the words sprung to his own mind, and the cry, 'If only . . .'?

He turned at the sound of Phoebe's steps upon the stone-flagged floor of their small kitchen, and was grieved to see the tears coursing silently down the plump, high-coloured cheeks, her mouth softly slack, hair disordered beneath the lace-edged cap. He hurried to her side and she buried her face in his shirt front, weeping openly now, and noisily, shaking her head as if in pain. He hugged her to him, large hands clumsily patting, soothing with helpless words. Then he lifted her chin that he might look into her tear-filled eyes, fearful of what he might see there.

'The babe . . . Joseph?' His voice was thin with alarm.

She shook her head, brushing her cheeks roughly with her palm. 'No, the child sleeps comfortably, at last. I see a change in him, Tom. A better grain, thank God. No, it is Bella I weep for, so changed, and without hope, without even strength enough to open her eyes to see the babe. I do not think she will survive until Reuben's coming. You had best search for Dr Burrell, and beg that the rector comes, for I fear it will be a coffin christening . . .'

She sank heavily into a chair and, laying her head upon the scrubbed wood of the table, covered her face with her hands as if, in blotting it out, she might deny the reality of what she had seen. Then she wept unashamedly. Tom's hand hovered restlessly above her hunched shoulders, then fell, defeated, to his side. Without a word he walked out to the stables. Ossie would saddle a horse for him, that he might ride out at once. He would trust no other. Could not.

Rebecca, seated at her lessons in the shabby schoolroom which had been refuge to so many generations of de Breos children, felt a warm kinship and affection for all those who had gone before. She thought of them as a pageant, a constantly changing procession of the known and unknown, yet linked always through living blood and flesh. Some were as dear and familiar to her as Grandfather and her own father, Edward; others remote and austere. Their faces, frozen in hauteur, stared from within the frames of their portraits in the long gallery, elegantly costumed and bewigged. Yet, for all their aristocratic reserve, long ago they, too, had spun the vast globe with eager, questing hands, and struggled with Latin verbs; wept for some broken toy or childish dream. One day, God willing, her own children and Joshua's, fair and straight-limbed, or dark as she, would sit at this self-same desk, secure in the warm fusion of past and present, enfolded always in the security she had been denied.

Rebecca's life at Southerndown Court had been a joy and revelation to her. Although her father's efforts to instruct and educate her as a gentlewoman had been sporadic and limited by the altered circumstances in which he found himself, she had proved intelligent and eager to learn. Her mother's early death and the threat of penury had demoralised him, for his privileged upbringing had rendered him quite unsuited to earning a living. The burden of supporting them both had therefore fallen upon Rebecca, who, although a mere child, was more practical and sensitive to their plight than he. So she had become provider, gathering shellfish from the shore, seeking buyers from among the cottagers and tradesfolk. At first, she had boiled and delivered them by hand, awkwardly clumsy with the heavy woven frails, half lifting, half dragging them from the rock pools and bays up the long, back-breaking way from the sea shore. Then with a milkmaid's yoke pressing hard upon her thin shoulders, she had set the boiled cockles into buckets, the weight of them spread more evenly, although her skin was all too often rubbed to raw flesh beneath their burden.

She had become a familiar sight to the folk of Newton village, her childish figure, undaunted by season or weather, trudging out over burrows and highway under a burden which would have defeated many a grown man. The cottagers, who were, by nature, frugal and hard working, admired her for her industry, and would have taken her into their hearts, and poor homes, but for the cold gracelessness of her father who made no effort to hide the fact that he despised them as inferiors, vulgar and ill-educated, and quite unworthy of his attention. The villagers, who were proudly independent and spirited, counted his spurning of them no great loss, save, perhaps, to him, but as their contempt for his uselessness and dependence upon the child grew stronger, so did their admiration for her. When Rebecca's industry and thrift allowed her to purchase a shaggy Welsh cob, and equip it with panniers, their pleasure was as real as her own, and when, much later, it was joined by a battered cart which the wheelwright in Nottage had painstakingly repaired and set to rights, their respect for her strengthened.

Her father, however, denied her mother's presence and warm comfort, and growing increasingly sick and conscious of the deficiencies in his life, withdrew into himself. He could find no kinship with the strange, independent child, so unlike the sheltered gentlewomen of his acquaintance. He deplored the crudeness of her work, the continual stench of boiled shellfish, her absences, the labour which demeaned and degraded her. Most of all, he resented seeing her dressed like a common labourer, her hands chapped raw and ugly by the bitterness of tide and wind, and the pitiful, beggarly return it brought them. His efforts to educate her grew less. What would it profit her to learn the rules and mores of a society to which she could never hope to aspire? She was a lady by birth and a drudge by occupation, and it was kinder to let her remain so. She could never, now, hope to escape that treadmill of poverty and work which, once begun, was endlessly grinding. Conscious that he alone was to blame for their misfortunes, his irritation was none the less with her, and not himself. So, as punishment, he withdrew from her the teaching that had given her a tantalising glimpse into another, brighter world, beyond her relentless toil. Yet, from this, as all else, Rebecca had broken free, finding her solace and salvation in the books about her, sole known survivors of his past.

Even during the months of his dying, when the cruelty of winter made her forays to the beach a harsher penance, and the cold wind from the sea cut through her, sharp and lacerating as a knife edge, and even the dried salt crystals upon the edges of rock pools gave way to a rime of frost and ice, she was not defeated. She tended him and her work with equal fierceness and devotion. At the end, when the little she earned deprived him of those few luxuries which would ease his sickness, she bartered, without his knowledge, the few saleable things which survived from his other life, for food and comforts. Yet his books she would not part with, even had there been a market for them among people as poor as themselves. They had no use for books, save as ornament, for few could read or write in their own tongue, much less in Latin or Greek.

After her father's death, the villagers had brought comfort to her grief and isolation. With the discovery of Mary Devereaux's poor body upon the sands, Jeremiah and Joshua had come into her life, bringing her the warmth of human friendship which had grown into love for them both. Jeremiah became the lovingly protective father she had never had; Joshua her true love, so dear to her that he seemed part of her blood and being.

Dr Peate, her tutor, seeing the pretty dark head bent low over her books, and the spring sunlight from the mullioned window turning her hair to that deep blue-blackness of a raven's breast, said gently, 'There is something in the text which troubles you, Rebecca? Some difficulty I might explain, perhaps?'

'No, sir.' The vivid eyes looked up into his, colour flaring into wide, high-boned cheeks. 'I believe that I comprehend it very well.'

Dr Peate smiled, then, aesthetic features gently amused. 'I am glad to hear it, for a true appreciation of poetry lends depth of elegance to living, and heightens awareness as nothing else. Perhaps you will read aloud what so absorbs you, that Elizabeth and I may share your pleasurable introspection.'

'If that is your wish, sir,' she replied, rising to her feet.

Dr Peate thought how absurdly young and vulnerable she looked in her gown of rose-pink silk, its colour subdued now by the warmer glow of her skin.

'It is from Arcadia, sir, by Sir Philip Sydney.'

'And written?'

'In the year fifteen hundred and ninety-eight.'

He nodded, motioning her to begin.

'My true love hath my heart, and I have his,/By just exchange – one for the other given . . .'

Dr Peate listened to the curiously poignant words of a poet long dead in the vibrancy of a living voice, so sure of feelings and emotions shared, undimmed by centuries.

'He loves my heart, for once it was his own./I cherish it because in me it bides . . .'

Looking from the radiance of her clear, unclouded eyes to Elizabeth's, gentle, reflective understanding as she listened, brown eyes intent, Dr Peate felt such a surge of affection and unexpected pain for his two young pupils, so hopefully and gloriously in love, that, for a moment, he was unable to speak. He found himself regretting that his own life had never known the consummation of such pure ecstacy or yearning – save, he corrected, guiltily, in that greater spiritual commitment of a priest to his faith. He was aware that Elizabeth's serene eyes were regarding him steadily with a compassion and understanding beyond her years. She had known so much hurt and despair in her brief living that she was acutely sensitive to the feelings of others.

'You may put away your books,' instructed Dr Peate, closing his own. Turning to Rebecca he said warmly, 'You read that quite beautifully, Rebecca, with true intelligence and understanding,' and was rewarded with a smile of such swift gratitude that he quite forgot the lessons he wished them to study for the morrow. It had pleased him beyond measure that Elizabeth had begged him to officiate as priest at her marriage to Captain Devereaux at the tiny chapel at Southerndown Court. She was a gentle, affectionate creature, and he was grateful that Roland Devereaux was aware of her loyalty and true worth. Dr Peate thanked God most devoutly that He had delivered her into the arms of a man who would cherish and care for her as she deserved. He straightened up from his books, a frail, almost desiccated, figure, face delicate-boned, skin stretched fragile as parchment under the fine thistledown hair. He paused before suggesting, 'Perhaps you would care to prepare for me an appreciation of Sydney's poetry, and explain its validity? You have some thoughts upon the matter, perhaps? Elizabeth?'

A slow flush seeped under her skin, and Elizabeth bit her underlip in sudden confusion, but when she spoke, it was calmly, and without hesitation.

'I believe, sir,' she said quietly, 'that his words are as relevant to lovers today as they were in his own century, and in centuries before his birth, and centuries yet to come. Times and mores may change, but people and emotions do not. They are constant, and the need for love, with its joy and pain, universal.'

Dr Peate nodded, his clear, perceptive eyes warm with encouragement.

'I only know, sir, that Sir Philip's words might have been written for me alone. They find an echo in my own heart and spirit. He uses the words I so long to say, but cannot, for I lack his skill, and courage.' Elizabeth broke off awkwardly, colour high, fearing that she sounded foolish, and had revealed too much of herself.

Dr Peate touched her shoulder with gentle reassurance. 'My dear,' he said, 'had the poet's words been seen by you, and none other, your understanding of them would be reward enough for his labours. Few of us achieve such harmony with another human soul, even in our own lifetime.' He turned away abruptly, pretending an absorption with gathering up his books, for he felt an indescribable sense of loss, and was strangely moved.

When he was sure that Elizabeth had left the schoolroom, he lifted his books and looked up, surprised to see Rebecca patiently awaiting him. He stared at her for a moment, vague, unseeing.

'Dr Peate,' she said, gravely, 'I would have you know that it is not only the poet's labours which bring us true joy and enlightenment. There are those, like you, who guide us and show us the way to a clear understanding . . . of others and ourselves.' She clasped his frail, dry-boned hand in her own warm and living flesh and, holding it tightly, bent and kissed him upon his gaunt cheek. 'I thank you for that, sir, from the bottom of my heart.'

Dr Peate nodded, and smiled, for he could not trust himself to speak. There were no words in all the world to describe his pleasure.

It was with a feeling of rare good humour and quite uncharacteristic self-satisfaction that the good cleric left the schoolroom to join his friend, Sir Matthew, in the library for a little pre-prandial talk and refreshment. Although Dr Peate's slight figure was bowed, and his complexion pallid through being closeted too long over his books, there was a jauntiness in his bearing as he entered the inner sanctum, which Sir Matthew was quick to observe.

Handel Peate was one of the very few people permitted to invade his library, for Sir Matthew counted his privacy a privilege which he was reluctant to share. In times of crisis, its very familiarity had soothed and calmed him, seeming, like his books, to offer him the wisdom and answers he sought. In times of despair, like the fearful void of his wife Emma's dying, he had buried himself within its walls; entombed, stripped of life and feeling, bound in his grief as securely as she in her grave-windings, until his slow reawakening. It was here that Edward, his son, had left him, swearing never to return, here that Rebecca, his granddaughter, crept in to him, waiting silently until his tasks were completed, to question and cajole, or to press an unexpected kiss upon his cold cheek. She was sunlight and springtime to him, he thought gratefully, after the bleakness of cold winter's dark, her warmth and brightness resurrecting feelings he had long thought dead.

Sir Matthew quickly recalled himself, aware that Dr Peate had made some observation and was expectantly awaiting the answer it demanded.

'I beg you will forgive me, my friend,' he apologised ruefully, 'for my mind was occupied elsewhere, upon concerns less worthy and rewarding than your company.'

Dr Peate smiled. 'It is plain to see, sir, from whom Rebecca inherits her generosity and pretty turn of speech.' He set his glass of Madeira upon a slender wine table and proceeded to relate to Sir Matthew the conversation in the schoolroom.

Sir Matthew nodded appreciatively, his fine perceptive eyes at first approving, then growing unusually troubled as he confessed, 'I am not sure, sir, if Rebecca's life with me here is the best preparation for what she must become, – a village constable's wife.'

'Surely,' demanded Dr Peate, 'you can have no reservations about young Stradling's suitability?'

'No. None!' Sir Matthew disclaimed at once. 'He is an excellent young man in every respect. I do not doubt that he loves her, and will do all in his power to make her happy. No, my doubts are about myself, whether I have acted selfishly in bringing her here, to be with me.'

'Nonsense!' dismissed Dr Peate brusquely. 'You did not bring her, sir! The decision was hers, and hers alone. What is it that you fear?'

Sir Matthew hesitated, then confessed truthfully, 'Not that Rebecca will be unable to adapt to a new and different life, for she has proved herself fitted to the demands both of poverty and plenty.'

'Your own loneliness, then?'

'No, that is of no account, and she will not be entirely lost to me. Besides,' he smiled warmly, 'I shall still have the familiar comfort of old friends such as you.'

'Well, then,' Dr Peate persisted, refusing to be deterred by Sir Matthew's compliment, much as he relished it. 'Well, then?' he repeated testily.

'I fear that others will not accept her, cannot. When my son's bitterness and rejection of his old life forced her to work as a cocklemaid, the cottagers accepted her as one of themselves – as, indeed, she believed herself to be. Here, at Southerndown Court, she is accepted by all as my granddaughter, a de Breos. Her ties of blood and birth have given her a new life, a new status and responsibilities. She will, one day, inherit my estates, and with them the duties and privileges owed to the tenants.'

Sir Matthew's lean, strong-boned face was so filled with confusion and hurt that Dr Peate put a hand to his shoulder in reassurance, saying gently, 'I believe Rebecca to have inherited not only your blood, Sir Matthew, but your courage and independence of spirit. She is a woman of intelligence and sympathy, not easily swayed by wealth, ambition, or the opinions of others.'

'But she is still only a child. I would have no hesitation, no reservations about her fitness to take my place, I swear, even were I to die tomorrow. But that is different. She is a de Breos, accepted and respected as such.'

'I confess,' said Dr Peate, bewildered, 'that I do not quite understand your dilemma.'

'Here, Rebecca's position is clear. But with her marriage to Joshua, the practical difficulties will be overwhelming. I fear Edward, my son, and I have a great deal to answer for. We have torn her between two worlds by our selfish cruelty.' As Dr Peate made to deny it, Sir Matthew held up a hand as if to brush his protests aside, declaring firmly, 'No, cruelty is not too harsh a word. Conscious or unconscious, it makes no matter. We denied her the life which was hers by right.'

'But she adapted to it . . .'

'Certainly, but not without grief, and physical and mental hurt,' said Sir Matthew regretfully. 'And now there will be another testing. How will she be accepted? As a gentlewoman or a cottager? She is neither fish nor fowl, my friend. Where will she live? How? She is alienated now, different. Too large a house and servants, and Joshua will lose the trust of those he serves, for they will feel neither kinship nor respect for him, and will not count him a friend. Yet she cannot return to a life of extreme poverty and need, for that would be mere affectation, and she would be despised and made a mockery. I tell you, Peate, I am deeply troubled, and can see no answer to it.' Sir Matthew's tall and spare frame, usually so confidently erect, seemed to have shrunk and become bowed under the burden of it. His eyes were uncertain, pleading for reassurance.

'I believe,' said Dr Peate stoutly, 'that Rebecca's life, although harsh, has strengthened and tempered her. I say this in all honesty, and not merely to comfort you. She has been deprived, but privileged, too, as few women of her birth and station. She can not only pity the poor and destitute, but feel their sorrow, for she has lived their lives. In the same way, she can mingle with gentlefolk upon their own terms, without reserve or intimidation. The cruelty she suffered has made her the woman she is, Matthew, and I beg you to believe that Rebecca cannot regret it, for it has brought her Joshua and you and so many true friends, and a compassion and understanding which will enrich the lives of others as well as her own.'

Sir Matthew nodded, unable to reply at once for the emotion which caught at his throat, thickening it with the threat of tears. He simply gripped his friend's shoulder in gratitude before turning away, struggling to compose himself.

Dr Peate, seeing the normally stern, autocratic old gentleman looking so vulnerable and old, reflected that Sir Matthew, like Rebecca, had been forced by circumstance into a life not of his own choosing. Unlike his granddaughter his whole education and life had been a conscious preparation for the privileges and responsibilities of his station. If he had rebelled or chafed at the chains of duty which so securely bound him, then none but he ever knew of it. He was a man of spirit and integrity who kept his own counsel, and was admired and respected by all he served, for, thought Dr Peate compassionately, his strength lay in the fact that he was more servant than master.

When he looked up, Sir Matthew was smiling quizzically, offering him a glass of Madeira, his spare frame erect, white head haloed by the light streaming through the tall windows. As he took another glass from Sir Matthew's outstretched hand, the light illumined the liquid within the glass and rendered his thin-boned fingers transparent, as if held at a candle flame. Dr Peate hesitated, seeing for a brief moment the skeleton beneath the flesh; the spectre of age and the approach of death, another's and his own. He took the glass thinking, this is how I will remember him, in this quiet, familiar room, among the books he loves, the celestial and terrestrial spheres, things treasured and touched with affection, and the smells of leather, polished wood and old, damp pages musty with print.

He raised his glass in acknowledgement, saying quietly, 'To what is past and shared.'

And, as if he echoed Dr Peate's thoughts, Sir Matthew responded gravely, 'Burdens and hopes; joys and sorrows; living and dying.' His fine, intelligent eyes looked steadily into Dr Peate's . 'All that is now over and what must inevitably come, made bearable, or joyous, by friendship.'

Dr Peate nodded, not pretending to misunderstand.

Chapter Fifteen

At the Crown Inn, Ossie had swiftly saddled a mount for Tom Butler, his usual gentle bantering crushed by the weight of raw anguish upon his employer's face. The ostler, who admired and respected the landlord deeply, and had experienced his warm generosity, would have told him he shared his grief over Bella and the babe and the absence of his son, but was unable to find the words. He could not even bring himself to ask if the child's condition had worsened, fearing that his voice would betray the closeness of tears and compound Tom Butler's sorrow. Yet he felt his pity constricting his throat and harsh within his breast as he bent to steady the landlord's boot heel with his clasped fingers to ease him into the stirrups.

Tom Butler looked into the ostler's eyes and, leaning low aside the horse's neck, briefly touched Ossie's bowed shoulder and nodded his gratitude. As he straightened in the saddle, Ossie saw that his cheeks were unnaturally flushed, as with fever, and his underlip trembling so much that he had to bite upon it to still it.

'I pray God that Dr Burrell or Dr Mansel will come,' he said quietly, 'for if they refuse, I do not know where I shall turn.'

'They will come,' promised Ossie, with conviction, 'have no fear.'

'But I *do* fear, Ossie,' said Butler, his eyes bright with

unshed tears under the heavy brows and shock of wiry, black hair. 'I fear that it is already too late. I go through the motions, for there is nothing else to do.' He shook his head helplessly, unable to continue, then closed his eyes tightly, his whole face ugly with hurt, and Ossie saw, with compassion, the tears squeeze between his lashes and run, unheeded, down his cheeks, splashing from his mouth and chin. Butler tightened the reins and rode out across the cobbled yard and under the arch, the horse's hooves striking forlornly upon the cobbles, clear and ringing as a knell.

Far and high above the Burrows, Ossie heard the sad forsaken cry of a curlew and shivered despite the warmth of the day. The cries of drowned sailors seeking their souls, the credulous villagers believed, but Ossie was the sanest and least superstitious of men, and thought it cowardly and irreligious to cross himself. Yet, now, he instinctively and shamefacedly did so, finding himself drawn towards the archway and the square, grey tower of the church beyond. Its constancy and solidity seemed the only thing unaltered in a swiftly-changing world. Yet it was stone, and inanimate, not living flesh and blood to quicken and decay . . . He turned away and walked slowly back to the stables and his beloved animals.

All we can ever hope to do is succour and love them while we may, he thought, laying his head gently against the mare's rough mane, and hope that they understand. Then relinquish them. Then comes the ending of their pain, and the beginning of our own.

John Burrell was at luncheon with Obadiah Mansel when Tom Butler arrived at the elegant house with its impressive façade atop the Clevis Hill. He urged the mare through the imposing wrought-iron gateway, his mind a seething maelstrom of nervous apprehension. Had he come in other circumstances, he would have taken note of all about him: the barbed and speared railings; the vast shrubberies and arbours; the neatly incised flower beds upon the sweeping, well-tended lawns; the classical statuary; the great conservatory with its superabundance of greenery, strange and lushly exotic in this orderly setting. Phoebe, his wife, would have demanded to know every detail twice over, so strange and splendid a place was it known to be. But today, the landlord's thoughts were only upon Bella, Joseph the babe, and his absent son, Reuben, and the ride he must later take to Tythegston to beg the rector come. He dismounted awkwardly, his boots crunching upon the fine crushed stones of the pathway, refusing the offer of stabling for his horse from a groom who had materialised quietly beside him.

'No, for I must ride out, at once, on a matter of the gravest urgency,' he declared. 'I beg you hold my mount until I return, for my business here will be brief.'

The groom nodded, and did as he was bade, knowing that only a matter of life or death could have brought a mere villager to seek assistance.

The housekeeper who answered Tom's swift tug upon the bell was an austere chatelaine, dignified, severe, yet unalarming, for despite her pursed lips and autocratic bearing, her manner was kindly.

'I cannot tell you whether it will be convenient for one of the doctors to see you, sir,' she began, 'but if you will wait awhile, I will enquire of them, for they are at their luncheon.'

But before she had turned upon her heel, Dr Burrell was beside her, dismissing her courteously, to demand, 'What brings you here, Tom? Is it the child? Has his condition worsened?' His voice was brusque, his saturnine face sharp with concern.

'No, Dr Burrell, sir. 'Tis Bella. I fear she is near to

death, and does not . . .' His voice broke, helplessly. 'I beg you come to her, sir, as soon as you are able.' The tears were coursing unchecked down his broad, florid face as he turned away to try and master his grief. 'We have money to pay, sir, for I have set it aside in the Friendly Society, and paid it regularly, never neglecting it, I swear.'

Burrell felt an ache of pity closing his throat, and put out a firm hand to clasp Butler's shoulder, saying, 'I will come with you at once. Have no fear.' He would have gone willingly, without payment, but knew that the few coppers the villagers set aside against sickness or death were a measure of their pride and frugality, and it would be cruelly insensitive to spurn their independence of spirit.

He gave orders to a servant to fetch his cloak and bag, and to bid a groom saddle a horse that he might accompany Butler to the Crown without delay.

'I beg you go alone, sir,' urged Butler, 'for I must ride out, at once, to summon the rector, if he will come.'

'The rector?' Burrell's voice was sharp, abrasive.

'A precaution, sir.' Tom Butler's hand was already upon his mount's bridle, and he swung himself heavily into the saddle, declaring, 'If, as I fear, it is too late and Bella dies, then the child must be christened over her coffin. It is the custom. We cannot deny her that last, poor comfort.'

Without another word he was upon his way, the horse's hooves scattering the small, chipped stones, his broad, slumped back evidence of his despair.

John Burrell, as he rode through the gateway of the house, was bitterly aware of what it had cost Tom Butler, in terms of anguish, to fetch him. He had no illusions about the standing of the medical profession in the eyes of the cottagers. Their services were accepted as a final resort, grudgingly, and with little hope of success, when all other treatment, by wise men and conjurors, had failed. Very often, it was true, there was a strange, inexplicable power for healing handed down to these people from generation to generation; a father passing on his charms, potions and, seemingly, the power within him to his eldest son or daughter, upon his death bed. Witchcraft? Superstition? Some unknown and atavistic sense which civilisation had failed to destroy? Some spiritual quality, even? Burrell had to admit that he did not know. Yet, he could not scorn or deride it, for had he not seen its cures, which he could only describe as 'supernatural' during his years of hellish incarceration in a common gaol? The power of suggestion upon ignorant, impressionable minds perhaps? Yet even if that could explain the success of those conjurors able to cure warts, shingles, toothache and whooping cough and other such maladies, how could it explain the banishing of infestations of snakes and rats upon the farms, or the recovery of sick animals, far removed from the wise man's touch or presence?

John Burrell thought uneasily, perhaps it is small wonder that we are held in such low esteem by those we choose to serve. We share neither their poverty nor the harshness of their lives. Were it not for my own misfortune, those years in prison, what would I know of the squalor and hopelessness of their lives? The endless treadmill of work, degradation, and owning nothing? The fear of sickness and the poorhouse? The vermin. The decay. The stench of their poor, ill-equipped, insanitary hovels.

No, the medical profession, physicians, surgeons and apothecaries, had little enough to be sanguine about! There was no answer to the killer diseases: scarlet fever, typhoid, typhus, tuberculosis, the scourge of cholera, or the diseases of childhood. Too many infants died at birth, often through gross neglect and incompetence upon the part of doctors and midwives themselves. Where hospitals existed, they would not willingly admit children, the dying, the infected, nor those 'fallen women', the unmarried who, when pregnant, were publicly ostracised, turned out of home and work place, reviled by the church, and all too often left to die, untended, or to take their own lives. He thought with pain of the girl whom he had so deeply and passionately loved, and who, bearing his child, had died, cruelly and bloodily, at the hands of some filthy, back-alley abortionist.

But the past was over and done with, and reliving its cruelty profitless. His fervent resolve had been to help the poor and disadvantaged upon his release from prison, and that was what he must now do, an expiation, a redress for a wrong he had been unable to right. He would not let Bella and the child die. He would fight for them with every nerve and fibre of his body and, if all else failed, give them the consolation of his compassion and care.

He rode under the archway to the Crown, and delivered his horse to Ossie, glancing only briefly at the coach loft where Emily Randall had made her home. He admired her and respected her, of that he was sure. Yet he had nothing left of himself to offer her. He was empty of love and could not bear the hurt of being responsible for another human being, for he knew the sadness of loss and its bitterness. With a word of thanks to the ostler, he made his way into the inn.

Ossie, glancing up at the small, deep-set window of the coach loft, saw Emily Randall's pale face staring down into the yard, and the eagerly raised hand which dropped awkwardly to her side as she had sought to acknowledge

Dr Burrell, only to see him turn away, occupied with his own concerns. She rebuked herself for her foolishness in hoping that his thoughts might have turned towards her when he was so obviously absorbed with the mortal sickness of Bella and the babe. Whether he had been summoned because the condition of mother and child gave immediate cause for concern, she did not know. She prayed, most devoutly, that the little family would recover, and Reuben soon be restored to them. In growing to love John Burrell, she had learnt how painfully and desperately one's happiness and wellbeing could be bound up with that of another. She had thought that there might be a future with him. Yet, perhaps, it was a misconception in her own mind, fostered by her need of him. There was nothing as pitiful and ridiculous as a spinster of questionable age harbouring romantic ideas about a man who had not the same regard for her. It was a joke and a humiliation. She must set her sights upon the new school which Rebecca was financing for her; turn her attention to the cottage children and their needs.

But what of my own? she cried silently. Once a life as a governness was all she had envisaged, or dared to hope for. It had been enough. But now? Well, she must make it so again. It was all she had.

Ossie had turned away that she might not see him witness her embarrassment and hurt. Fool! he thought of John Burrell. Can you not see that there is a warm, compassionate woman eager to cherish you? Someone who has suffered as you have, and survived because she has the strength and goodness to do so, and would bring those very gifts to your own life? 'Hell and damnation!' he exclaimed, leading Burrell's mount to a stall, grieving, 'Why are men so blindly insensitive? Why do they not accept with dignity the bounty offered to them, as animals do, grateful for the generosity of others?'

It was true that Burrell, more than most, had cause to be wary of hurt. Yet how eagerly Ossie would have embraced it, thinking it a small price to pay for a love he had never been offered. We all bear our own scars, he thought, for they are the proof of our living, and feeling. He stroked the horse's smoothly shining neck, feeling the ripple of life and warm flesh beneath the skin and flowing into his leathery palms and fingertips, and his own caring surging back; a fierce, unending flow, rhythmic and natural as a tide. He looked about his small domain. 'Ossie will care for you, my beauties,' he said aloud. 'Old Ossie will always be here. He will never let you down!'

Within the quiet sadness of the Crown, he could but hope that Bella and the babe felt the same comfortable certainty of love.

Tom Butler's thoughts upon the highway to the rector's house at Tythegston were bleak and comfortless enough. So real was his fear that he could believe it a vital, living thing; some ugly, hooded companion riding beside him upon the way, like death itself, and when its hood was cast aside, he would turn to gaze upon its hollow eyes and skeleton head, and know all hope had died.

Dear Lord! he could not bear to think how this might end. Bella, with no home or family of her own, had grown as dear to him as his own child. She was a kind, gentle creature, knowing neither envy nor malice and grateful for a home and comfort so long denied. 'In calmer waters,' she had once said, smiling and placing the child in his arms, and he had thought it strange that she spoke the words, her face bright with knowledge, and with tenderness. In calmer waters, but not that final awful calm, he prayed in silence, the unutterable stillness of the grave itself. And to lose the child, Joseph. How could they bear it? He was part of themselves, their flesh and their love, their hope for the future, as Reuben had once been. And how could they speak of it to Reuben, their son? Where could they find the words? How measure the depth and hollowness of their grief and his, or the pain of those years to come?

As he rode through the gateway to Robert Knight's house, Butler felt a lightening of his terror, a faith that within was a man in whom he could put his trust; someone who would share the awfulness of his burden, and so lighten the load that bore upon him so heavily that it must surely crush his soul itself.

He dismounted, clumsy in his haste, and battered fiercely upon the door with his clenched fists, fearful that the bell might not be heard.

Then, learning that Robert Knight was absent upon a journey and might not return for several days, he climbed back into the saddle, numbed and seeming not to comprehend the housekeeper's offer that he rest awhile, or ride on to some other place to seek the services of a priest.

'There is a message that you would have me deliver to Mr Knight?' she called after him, shocked by the desolation upon his face.

Tom Butler turned in the saddle, his eyes bewildered. 'Tell him that I am sorry,' he said, 'sorry . . .'

Bella, 'neath the clean, fresh linen of the familiar bed which she had shared with Reuben in the white-washed room of the Crown, was aware of the fierceness of the light. It appeared to have a radiance and intensity of its own, sharper than the whiteness of a flame, more dazzling than the sun. It seemed that it burned her eyes with its purity, yet for the first time there was no pain, only a feeling of loss, so great that nothing could ever assuage it. She would have arisen and walked through that long, dark tunnel that led to the light, but the languor pressed upon her, forcing her down. It was like no tiredness that she had ever known, seeping into her nerve and bone, weeping in her blood so hopelessly that, although she tried to speak, she could make no sound.

Yet there was weeping, she knew, but from whence it came, and who it was that wept, she could not see, for she was blind, save for that one fierce, impenetrable blaze of light. If she could reach beyond it, then she knew with certainty that there would never again be any pain or sorrow, but only the joy of the brightness.

The confusion had gone now. The hands had frightened her, reaching out, grasping pained flesh. Sometimes she believed they were her own, or Reuben's, or the child's, forcing her attention, but tiredness bore her down and when she reached out to them, they were the skinny bone-like paws of the little monkey, its pathetic eyes so filled with pain and despair that her heart ached with pity.

John Burrell, seeing Bella's flushed and ravaged face and her restless movements, felt a chill of fear, and when he pulled back the bedclothes which lay upon her, the stench of putrefaction from the suppurating flesh was so corrupt and overpowering that sickness and pity wrenched at his throat. In turning aside, his eyes revealed the horror of it to Phoebe Butler, clutching the babe Joseph to her, and rocking him so fiercely in her grief that he screamed aloud. For a moment the sound seemed to reach through to Bella, and some instinct made her raise a hand towards him, as in comfort or blessing.

Tom Butler, standing in the doorway, grieved and dishevelled, had scarce the time to take in the scene before a scream of such pain and rage ripped the air that it seemed to lacerate his very flesh. He thought, at first, it was Phoebe or the child who screamed, until he saw the pity for him upon John Burrell's face, and realised that the price for Bella's peace was the endless anguish of his own.

Chapter Sixteen

Dr John Burrell, upon leaving Bella's bedside at the Crown Inn, felt a sense of grief and desolation that silently echoed Tom Butler's wild, despairing cry. It recalled so painfully the anguish of learning of the cruel death of Ella Pearce, whom he had loved, and their unborn child, that, like Butler, his every instinct had been to flee that death-filled room, running he knew not where, as if he might escape the tragedy and pain of it. Yet he knew with certainty that grief was not some ugly, scavenging bird of death, bloody in beak and talons, tearing and ripping at still warm flesh. There was no shelter from the blackness of its wings, nor the relentless pursuit. Grief was within. The beating of its wings was no more than the beating of one's own heart, the pulsing of life and blood without hope or reason. The darkness was of the soul.

Burrell had forced himself to do and say what was necessary, giving to Phoebe Butler above the shrill, hopeless screams of the babe in her arms a reassurance and calmness he could not feel.

'It is kinder so, her suffering is at an end. You have nothing to reproach yourself with. There was nothing to be done.' The trite expected phrases had come easily to his tongue, and he damned himself for their uselessness and hypocrisy, unable to break the reserve and convention which demanded their utterance. Yet, would it have served better, he wondered bleakly, if he had been able to take her in his arms, holding her weeping head to his breast, cradling her as she cradled the child within her arms, and crying aloud, 'I know your pain. I have shared your grief. It will lessen, I swear . . . I beg you will believe me.' Yet how could he add, 'Forgetfulness is but a scab, a surface crust, to hide a wound which will ache and throb unseen, and in the winter cold, burn until you rub it raw and feel it bleed again.'

Burrell's footsteps upon the cobblestones without the Crown were slow and hesitant, and he would have turned towards the village and the house of a nursing aide and the shop of Evans, the obsequious little undertaker, yet he could not face their curious questioning, nor yet Dr Mansel's probing, clinical and detached. Almost without conscious thought he found himself within the stable courtyard of the Crown and his feet clumsily mounting the stone staircase to Emily Randall's loft. From the shadows of a stall Ossie watched him with concern, knowing by the droop of Burrell's thin shoulders and the hurt upon his dark, cadaverous face that Bella was already dead. Ossie laid his weathered face against the mare's smooth neck, his rough-skinned hands gripping the harshness of mane, and wept.

When Emily Randall opened her loft door upon her visitor, her delight was immediately subdued by the despair upon his ravaged features. She stepped aside, bidding him to enter with warmth and courtesy, and begging him to be seated while she brought him refreshment. She set aside the pitcher of shot, oatmeal crumbled into buttermilk, which she at first selected, and then poured instead a small beaker of carefully hoarded cognac which Ossie had pressed upon her for some such crisis. She did not know from whence he had acquired it, for he had mumbled only that it was payment for some churchyard fracas he had won, and she did not press the point. She was glad now of its warm, life-quickening properties, for even as John Burrell drank it, she saw the colour and vitality brighten his sallow skin.

He was silent and Emily made no effort to question him, seating herself at the small table which served her needs and waiting quietly for him to speak of what tortured his mind. When he at last looked up, the pain in his eyes was so all-consuming that she instinctively stretched out a hand to reach him, then jerked it back awkwardly to her lap, knowing that he was unaware of the gesture of comfort.

'Tom Butler's daughter-in-law . . . she is dead.'

'I am sorry.'

The pain in him told of some deeper, more personal, grief, and Emily, loving him, felt it as if it were her own.

'I will not say it is a release,' she said gently, 'for no death is that for those who remain. It binds them more tightly and painfully in regret and feeling. Reuben must add rage and guilt at his absence to the pain of loss.'

Burrell looked up at her in surprise, saying, his voice harshly abrasive, 'You speak as if from personal hurt, from experience.'

'Of course. There are few who go through life without a knowledge of death, its finality,' she said quietly, 'yet one's own tragedy is intensely personal. It cannot be lessened by sharing, or its cruelty diminished.' She broke off awkwardly, cheeks flushing under his scrutiny, but persisting, 'Yet perhaps it brings an understanding and compassion we would not otherwise know.'

Burrell said angrily, 'If it has brought me awareness of suffering, then it has not brought me the means to deal with it!'

Emily was aware that his anger was not for her, but himself. 'Your skill and your medical training?'

'They are more a curse than a blessing! They offer no solution!' he disclaimed fiercely. 'They merely remind me of how pitifully inadequate is my knowledge, and ability to help.'

'Yet people turn to you.'

'They turn to me when all other help has failed. When the conjurors and "wise women" have tried in vain to heal the rot. When charms and potions are useless and there is no other course open. They come to me when dying, that is the truth of it. Even then, it is with reluctance and no real hope, equating my presence with death.'

She could not argue with him, knowing it to be true.

'And if they came before,' he said wearily, 'what would it profit then? Even could they raise the shillings it costs, I can offer no solution to those diseases that afflict them – cholera, diphtheria, smallpox, tuberculosis . . . How can I advise or help, for I am as helpless and ignorant as they! It is no wonder they turn to opium to ease their ills, or religion to give them hope of some better life, for by all hell and damnation, they see little enough of it here!'

Fury and impotence brought his hand crashing hard into his fist, and Emily saw the gleam of tears upon his lashes as he rose unsteadily to his feet.

'You are wrong, sir,' she said, rising to face him. 'You offer them more than medicine or the forgetfulness of opium, which destroys even as it deadens pain. From your own suffering you offer them compassionate understanding and pity. There is no barrier between you, no obstacle of class or poverty. You give freely of yourself. They cannot ask for more.'

He bent towards her and touched her chin, lifting it gently so that he could look into her usually gravely serene eyes, now raw with anger and feeling.

'I could wish I shared your belief in me,' he said helplessly, 'but I know that what I can offer is not enough.'

He took Emily's hand and, turning the palm, impulsively set it to his lips before abruptly turning upon his heel and opening the door to the stable yard.

Emily moved to the small window of the loft and watched his descent of the stone staircase, then his gaunt, bowed figure moving slowly across the cobbled yard. At the archway, he hesitated uncertainly, as if reluctant to return to the world outside, then, with a conscious effort, straightened himself and resolutely strode away.

Ossie, entering the stable yard, glanced up and saw Emily's pale face at the window and raised a hand in acknowledgement, but she saw nothing of it, her eyes staring, unseeing, through the small breath-misted panes. Once, when first they met, John Burrell had told her that her calmness and serenity were a comfort to him; her simple room a haven of restfulness; a refuge from the demands of the world. That was why she must be always ready, waiting patiently, making no demands or conditions of her own. His words came back to her with such bitter clarity that he might still be standing beside her. 'I know that what I can offer is not enough.' To those who demanded his medical skills? Emily wondered, or had the words some deeper, more personal meaning? A warning that his past had used all his emotion and tenderness, and he would risk no more commitment or hurt? No, that could not be, or else why his grief for Bella and those sick and suffering, without hope of release save in death? She would offer him what help and solace she could, asking nothing in return. It would be enough that he was near.

The small panes of the window blurred and dissolved, giving the lie to her hopes as the tears seeped through her lashes and dropped, unheeded, from mouth and chin. She did not attempt to wipe them away. She had learnt to hide her emotions from others, but here could weep unseen. Even pain was better than feeling nothing. She would offer John Burrell the strength and comfort he needed, and would not think upon how dear it would be could he offer such tenderness to her.

Joshua, unaware of the tragedy at the Crown Inn, was filled with a gentle euphoria as his mare picked her way delicately along the sandy track, sensitive to the needs of the injured animal beside her. The air was sweet with warmth and the scent of growing things, and Joshua's encounter with the gypsies, and the unexpected return of Ruth's donkey, had served to lighten his spirits immeasurably. Even Job Abrahams, cantankerous and ungrateful though he be, seemed but a minor irritant, a blemish rather than a disfigurement upon the face of the earth.

The grey was an intelligent creature, and made no attempt to tax the small donkey beyond its strength, watching it anxiously for signs of distress, and slowing her pace, or halting altogether, when it seemed necessary. Joshua was heartened by such intuitive understanding between the pair, and by the thought of the pleasure Lucky's safe return would bring to Joe Priday's house, Tim, and the people of the hamlet.

As they travelled the familiar countryside leading to Maudlam, the donkey began to show signs of excitement and agitation, trembling, quickening its pace, and braying harshly, jerking so fiercely upon the bridle that it needed all Joshua's energy and wits to control it, and prevent it from trotting ahead.

Within sight of the forge, it let out such an ecstatic, discordant chorus of braying that it drowned even the clamour of Tim's blows upon the anvil. He came running out, all work abandoned, his young face so incredulous with joy and disbelief, that for a moment Joshua was not sure whether the lad would dissolve into laughter or tears. In the event, it made no matter, for the abandonment of kissing, hugging, honking and licking were so confused and intermingled, and the noise of the reunion so violent, that fur and flesh were inseparable. When that first frenzy of excitement and questioning had abated, and boy and animal were regarding each other with the quiet communion of friends too long set apart, Tim delved deep into the pocket of his leather apron and produced a titbit of carrot, and held it flat upon his calloused palm. The donkey lifted it delicately, its bony jaws chomping rhythmically, fat rump and tail twitching with pleasure. It looked long and hard at its benefactor, amber eyes bright, before kicking out skittishly with its hind legs. Then, with ears laid flat and head raised, its lips suddenly peeled back over yellowed teeth to let out a honk of such fierce, exquisite delight that it seemed to explode the bright air with its joyousness. Tim and Joshua could not help but laugh aloud, sharing its high spirits, and even the mare seemed to gaze upon it with the tolerance of an elder resolved to remain aloof, but amused despite herself.

When Joshua finally made to leave, the donkey was reluctant to budge, and stubbornly resisted all his efforts to tug it into obedience alongside the grey. Even when Joshua dismounted, it dug its hooves in determinedly and refused to move. Tim gave it an affectionate whack upon the rump with his vast hand outspread, ordering, 'Go, Lucky! You will come by again tomorrow. Joe and Ruth are waiting for you at the cottage. Go home now!'

The animal seemed to understand, and made no further demur, trotting along quietly beside Joshua and the mare. Tim nodded, and waved, brushing a fist across his mouth before re-entering the darkness of the forge. There was a new lightness in his step, as if some of the cares of early manhood had been lifted from his young shoulders. Tim had never once given up, Joshua thought. He had believed implicitly that Lucky would return, and had carried a sweetmeat for the donkey, as of old. A talisman? An amulet to strengthen his own belief? It was a sobering thought that Tim's confidence had rested in Joshua himself. Joshua was only grateful that he had not given him cause for disappointment.

Joshua's swift passage to Joe Priday's cottage was hampered less by the donkey's recalcitrance than by the scores of villagers of all ages who appeared, as if by magic, to impede their progress. Soon the welcoming band had grown into a vociferously excited throng, jostling, dancing and showering affectionate pats upon the bemused animal, hugging and kissing him until he seemed likely to expire under a surfeit of goodwill. The noise of jubilation had brought Joe Priday hurrying to his door, and the pauper hired to protect Ruth had taken up a belligerent stance beside him, cudgel at the ready. The concern upon their faces turned to bewilderment, then, with a cry of delighted recognition which seemed to reverberate from the hills themselves, Joe Priday ran towards the donkey, clasping its neck with his strong arms, burying his face against its rough hide. The children surged about, screaming, frolicking, scarce able to speak for excitement, but Joe Priday's ecstatic cries, and the donkey's, rose shrill above them all.

Joe Priday's cheeks were wet with cleansing tears as he took Joshua's hand in his roughened palms, gripping it fiercely, thanking him over and over, almost incoherent with surprise and gratitude. Then, suddenly aware, he glanced upwards to the window of Ruth's room under the eaves. Against the windowpane, her face showed white as the bandages which still bound her. She stood alone, unsupported, a hand raised in recognition, the smile upon her lips as brilliant and warm as Joshua's and her father's own.

'It is our own Lucky, my love! He is safe! The constable has brought him home.' Joe Priday's words carried to where Ruth stood, his voice triumphant. She nodded, and kept on smiling, although her mouth twisted wrily, as though she wept within. Joshua felt a coldness settle upon him as he wondered if he, alone, had observed that her lips had not tried to form the donkey's name, nor utter any sound.

John Burrell had done what little he could to help Tom and Phoebe Butler with the necessary sordid practicalities attending upon a death. There was little he could do to lessen the shock and grief they were experiencing at witnessing Bella's dying, save to give them the empty comfort of the trite phrases which sprang easily to the lips from training and long acquaintanceship with death itself; 'It was an end to suffering . . . They must be grateful that she knew nothing at the end, and that her death was peaceful . . . Their thoughts must now be for the baby who had need of all their love and caring.' Even as he spoke them, he knew the futility of the words, remembering the desolation of his own loss, the rage and rebellion of that pain, so overwhelming that he would have welcomed death to ease it.

He could, at least, remove from them the burden of finding a kind, reliable aide who would perform those final offices to the flesh with dignity and caring, and send notice to the undertaker. How cruel it was, that cold body and emptiness of flesh, a husk, an abandoned shell. Tragic reminder of all that was vital and pulsing, and so joyously alive.

He had closed Bella's eyelids gently over the wide, dark eyes, hiding their filmed emptiness, and giving the illusion of calm and peaceful sleep; and with that final gesture, he had shown them the reality of her passing. John Burrell had put an arm about Phoebe's and Tom's shoulders, Phoebe still clutching the babe, now asleep, his eyelids waxen and blue-veined as his mother's own, and led them quietly from the room and to their small parlour below.

It seemed to Tom Butler that it was a room that was strange to him, and that he had glimpsed once, long ago, in a dream, or through a lighted window as he hurried by. The ticking of the clock was familiar as a heartbeat, but without comfort, for time had no purpose or reason, save to take away all that was dearly loved. He would have put out a hand to Phoebe, or spoken some word of comfort, but his voice was a croak between dry lips, harsh and unrecognisable. He stared helplessly at Dr Burrell and then, without a word, walked out of the door, and out of the Crown itself, shirt sleeved, and with his apron tied about his waist. He walked slowly, and with the hesitant, purposeless shuffle of the old and poorly sighted, across the highway, the green, and on through the Burrows, leaving the rutted cart track for the dunes and plains. He was unaware of the cool wind from the sea upon his skin, or of his feet sinking into the pale-grained sand, legs raked by bramble and thorn. Neither did he recall falling upon the shifting, rolling barrier of pebbles upon the shore as they rubbed the skin to bare flesh, raw and excoriating. He felt no pain, not even of Bella's loss, for it was as if he, too, had died, and moved now without volition or feeling.

Then, suddenly, he was awakening upon the edge of the tide, the small ripples about his feet coldly and cruelly recalling him to life, with all its hurt. With a cry of despair which rang across the deserted bay, reverberating from dune and rock, and forcing the sea birds to rise into the air, echoing his cries of anguish, he turned to the land.

He huddled for a while in the shelter of a dune, arms clenched tight about his body, rocking himself for comfort, and weeping soundlessly. Then he arose unsteadily and, with a last look at the cleansing, restless sea, walked back to the Crown where there was need of him.

Chapter Seventeen

If Joshua's return to Maudlam with the donkey afforded him but mixed pleasure, then Robert Knight's expedition to Chepstow afforded the good cleric none at all. Apart from confounding the truism that, 'It is better to travel hopefully than to arrive,' it confirmed his long held opinion that, unless forced to it by circumstance, it is better never to travel at all!

The bishop's residence, at Chepstow in the county of Monmouthshire, whence he had inconveniently removed himself from a castle in the Vale of Glamorgan, was a most vexatious place to reach. Robert Knight, upon an impulse, had resolved to visit His Grace unannounced, persuading himself that it was merely a social call; the rare, unheralded visit of a valued friend who, unexpectedly finding himself upon the route past the other's house, would act as churlishly in passing by as would the friend in denying him hospitality. Should the bishop be unavoidably absent, however, Robert Knight had prudently taken the precaution of sending a servant ahead to secure chambers for him at the nearest habitable inn.

As he rattled uncomfortably along the ill-defined byways and the ill-maintained highways to His Grace's refuge, his thoughts about the turnpike trusts which administered the roads, and punitive tolls demanded at the toll houses, were less clerical than his garb. To add to his pique, his own coachman, Harris, had been irritatingly incapacitated by some gross inflammation of the bowels and intestines, which rendered a long drive upon the box quite untenable, since he would have survived for no more than ten minutes or so before halting the wheelers and leaders to climb down, agitatedly, from his perch. Consequently, the rector was obliged to call upon the services of a surrogate from Pyle, who came to him expensively but with the highest of testimonials, which Robert Knight was jaundiced enough to suspect might well have been forged, as there was obviously insufficient time for him to prove their authenticity.

However, the fellow seemed sober enough, civil, clean, and well-accustomed to horses, although Robert Knight did not immediately take a liking to him, believing his eyes to be set too close together, and noting a general air of shiftiness and unctuousness about him.

Leyshon, seated upon the box aside the coachman, with the footman/guard ensconced at the rear, suffered the cool morning air and the discomfort of his perch in stoical silence, his mind more upon the indignities visited upon his master's vintage port than upon his own person. The housekeeper, he knew, had prepared and packed enough victuals to provision a garrison till Michaelmas, with wine enough for Robert Knight to bathe in, should he feel so inclined. The servants must make do with rough ale, she had declared, and little enough of it, lest prodigality cause risk to their master's life, or provoke coarseness and irreverence. Leyshon sighed, and settled his fleshless bones and aching spine more easily upon the box, daring to hope that the fare might contain some softer, pappy offerings suited to his ruined, aching teeth. It gave him scant comfort that his old age fulfilled the biblical prophecy, 'And the grinders shall fail because they are few.'

He turned to the coachman, Barnes, saying, irritably, 'This confounded box is cold and hard as charity. There would be more comfort in sitting upon a tombstone or, indeed, lying beneath!'

Barnes, a moon-faced, well-fleshed fellow, and used to the jarring ruts and potholes along the way, declared jovially, 'It would be a drastic situation, sir, for a small inconvenience. Why, I mind travelling through a blizzard in deep snow, once, and the air so cold it froze the breath from the horses' nostrils. My own face was cased in ice, and we passed a stage upon the way which had fallen foul of a snowdrift, the passengers trying to heave it out as best they could, for the coachman was dead upon the box, frozen stiff as a board, and the horses too exhausted to stir.'

'Did you assist them?' asked Leyshon, distressed.

'Indeed, no! We would soon have been in the same sorry state.'

'So much for the companionship of the road!' declared Leyshon tartly.

'Less companionship for us had we been set upon by highwaymen, and stripped of all we possessed, and very likely shot!' said the coachman imperturbably.

'I thank you for that small comfort.' Leyshon's voice was wry.

Barnes smiled, unoffended, continuing, 'Since the other coach was so fortunately delayed, I was able to take its place at the very next inn, with my passengers so relieved and exhausted that they were grateful to bed upon the straw of the stables, men and women, giving no heed to propriety or acquaintanceship. Indeed, they were forced to huddle together for warmth.' He chuckled reminiscently, loosing a hand from the reins to slap his broad thigh and nudging Leyshon coarsely, 'What's more, they were eager to pay the landlord a guinea apiece for some stale pies and leftover porter.'

Leyshon regarded him with cold distaste, and remained silent.

'Come, cheer up!' said Barnes. 'You have a face longer than a fiddle! We will soon be coming to an inn where we, too, may refresh ourselves, though more cheaply, and see to our bodily comforts, for I confess, I am near enough to bursting and could make water enough to float a schooner!'

'Then you had best learn the virtue of continence,' replied Leyshon, stiffly, 'for we shall not be stopping upon the way.'

'Not stopping?' The coachman's face was a picture of comical dismay. 'Not stopping, you say?'

'No. Mr Robert Knight is insistent upon it. We pause only to eat our luncheon at some inn or tavern, called the Fox and Hounds, where a comfortable parlour is already reserved for us. Nor shall we be permitted to drink the landlord's ale, nor eat his victuals, for the master believes that many of the coaching inns are filthy, insalubrious dens where pox and consumption and other ills abound. He favours the miasma theory of sickness afloat upon the air!'

'Miasma be damned!' exploded the coachman, his florid face puffed with indignation. 'There will be more than that flying upon the air if I am not relieved upon the instant, I warrant!'

Leyshon, whose age and muscle weakness surpassed the coachman's own, but whose loyalty to Robert Knight was unswerving, cautioned philosophically, 'When all is said and done, perhaps 'tis for the best, for if you filled your belly too often upon ale, it would only serve to aggravate your condition all along the way.'

'All's not said and done,' declared the coachman, 'that is what I complain about, you garrulous old fool! Will you not take telling? It is all right for those enclosed in comfort within, who may relieve themselves in privacy!' He jerked his thumb disgustedly towards the body of the coach. 'Does he leap behind a hedge, a prey to weather, nettles and thorns, or vicious animals? No, I will not have it! I tell you straight, I will not have it!'

He whipped at the horses with quite unusual savagery, startling them so that Robert Knight was jerked most awkwardly, and flung about with such violence that he actually left the seat and had to thrust his head through the window to utter a caution and admonition, demanding, testily, 'What ails you, coachman?'

'It is not I, sir,' called down the coachman, drawing the horses to a halt and relinquishing the reins to Leyshon before stepping down from the box. 'I fear one of the horses has gone lame, and that one of the elliptical springs upon the coach has weakened, or come adrift. I know from my days upon the company coaches that there is a tavern upon the way where we may seek assistance.'

'Assistance?' Robert Knight's face grew irate and empurpled. 'You mean we shall be expected to loiter and waste time in some Godforsaken . . .' he recollected himself swiftly, 'in some devilishly outlandish backwater? Can you not repair it yourself?'

'No, sir.' The coachman's tone was unequivocal.

' 'Tis a fiendish inconvenience!' Robert Knight's plump jowls trembled irately, his protuberant eyes enraged behind his second-best lenses. 'I am not happy about it, not happy at all.'

'Nor I, sir,' said the coachman, bare-faced, and with such conviction that Leyshon all but believed him. 'I suggest, sir,' he continued, unperturbed, 'that you leave the guard to oversee the coach and the luggage while it is being attended to, and your manservant, Leyshon, and I will accompany you within, to protect you and see to your needs!'

'No!' declared Robert Knight, with asperity, his tone brooking no argument. 'The guard shall accompany me, with Leyshon, and you, sir, shall stay with the coach, for that is your province! You may take refreshment where and as you may, but first you will secure a clean private parlour for me where I may refresh myself, since I am forced to it by incompetence.'

The coachman stiffly remounted the box and drove into the cobbled yard of a nearby inn where a groom and ostler came forward to take the coach and unharness the horses.

Robert Knight dismounted in ill humour, spurning Leyshon's proffered hand, and as the coachman returned with the obsequious, thin-faced landlord of the place, entered within with poor grace, his corpulent figure as abristle with resistance as a hedgehog with spines. Indeed, his plump rear view was not entirely dissimilar. However, to his surprise and gratification, the premises were excellent in every respect, comfortable, clean and restful, and he was constrained to order a negus, a mixture of wine, eggs and spices, which set him in a rare good humour, then another. Leyshon, begging his pardon, excused himself from his master's presence, relieved in every particular. Upon his return, a glance into the stables and coachhouse revealed the rector's horses being lavishly refreshed and groomed.

'The lameness is severe?' asked the old servant hesitantly. 'We will need to replace the wheeler?'

'Lameness, sir?' replied the ostler, puzzled. 'Oh, you travel with Barnes, the coachman!' His honest face grew amused with sudden enlightenment. 'I'll wager he spun some yarn about a broken shaft or faulty springs?'

Leyshon nodded.

'It is but an old trick, learnt upon the road. There is money in it for the landlord and for him! A regular unearned income. He gets paid, too, for the food and drink consumed by those stranded here, although the pickings are fewer than upon the public stages. I fancy, sir, that he has set his snares all upon your way.'

'Indeed?' Leyshon's voice was mild, seemingly unconcerned. 'And where is he now?'

'Why, as he always is, eating his free victuals in the kitchen, and drinking enough porter to launch a ship of the line! Very likely he is making free with the serving maids! You would join him?'

'Indeed I will not!' Leyshon's lean, cadaverous face had grown so incensed that the ostler was afeared that the old servant would suffer an apoplexy, but set it down to plain envy of Barnes's undisputed nous and virility.

Leyshon slipped, unobserved, into the kitchen, and seized the miscreant bodily by the shoulder, roughly pushing aside the plump serving wench upon his lap, and demanded scathingly, 'So you think you have been clever, Barnes? Yet not clever enough! This time you have been hoist with your own petard!'

'Rubbish!' declared the coachman, not a whit abashed. 'What will you do about it? Inform Robert Knight? And if you do, you will not be able to proceed at all, nor even return, for my brother-in-law owns this inn, and others of my family man those upon the way! You will find that there is no coachman to be hired, not for love nor money! Besides, should you inform upon me, the justice will demand that we halt no more, and you will not fancy that, sir, for your old bones are not meant for scrambling over hedges and in and out of the mire!'

Nevertheless, he took leave of the hussy he had been embracing, pinching her backside with deliberately provoking lewdness, and resumed his position upon the box, with Leyshon sitting quietly beside him.

When they quitted the third inn upon their journey,

Barnes protesting convincingly about the ill-luck which had dogged their progress, Leyshon said obliquely, and with sly gravity, as Robert Knight climbed within, 'We must, nevertheless, give credit where it is due, sir.'

'Credit?' repeated the rector, testily. 'Credit?'

'Indeed, yes,' said Leyshon, with bland innocence. 'We have Barnes to thank.'

The coachman eyed him malevolently, shifting uncomfortably in his boots, awaiting betrayal.

'Barnes has begged me inform you, sir,' Leyshon hesitated, and saw the coachman's already florid skin burn with colour, 'since he is of a shy and retiring disposition, not willing to give offence . . .'

'Yes! Yes! Get on with it, Leyshon,' instructed Robert Knight irritably, 'else we will be here until sunrise!'

'He has taken a collection, sir.'

'A collection?'

'Yes, sir, at every inn where we have . . . rested upon the road.'

'What for?' demanded Robert Knight, perplexed.

'To give to the bishop, to aid the elderly and scrofulous poor of the diocese, so moved is he by their unfortunate plight.'

'Indeed?' The rector grew expansive, yet mortified that he had so misjudged a fellow human being, and merely upon an accidental closeness of the eyes. 'The bishop will be humbled and moved. He prides himself upon being a simple man.'

'As we all are,' said Leyshon virtuously, climbing cheerfully upon the box.

When the Reverend Robert Knight finally arrived at Bishop Edwin Copleston's gate at Hawick House, Chepstow, it was with some misgivings at the lateness of the hour, for dusk was already falling, and the poor, thin light of the whale-oil carriage lamps gave little illumination or comfort. Robert Knight consoled himself with the thought that these very qualities were precisely what His Grace, himself, could happily provide.

They had been friends over many tumultuous and exacting years, through war and peace, shared triumphs and notable failures, and this forged a closeness not easily put asunder by the passing of the years. It was true that the bishop was well advanced into his sixties now, but the intellect which had gained him a fellowship at Oriel in 1795, when but nineteen years of age, remained keenly incisive. Indeed, Robert Knight was inclined to think, without undue presumption, that there were quite striking similarities between them, apart from their calling. They were both acknowledged to be fine classical scholars, and Latinists, with a quite remarkably dry and pedantic wit, Tories, and with respectable antecedents who had ensured that they inherited estates of some distinction, and the wherewithal to uphold them. In addition, their annual, unearned incomes were commensurate with their refinement of taste, and the means to indulge it.

Eschewing modesty, Robert Knight might even have declared, with satisfaction, that were it not for his own contented nature and excellence of disposition, he might well be seated upon the bishop's throne. That was not to say that he saw Copleston's ambition and nervous energy as in any way to be deprecated. Rather the reverse. Such qualities were admirable. Perhaps, thought Robert Knight, kindly, his own views and expectations were nearer to true Christianity, while the bishop's leaned more to the aggressive orthodoxy of the Old Testament tradition. In any event, each perfectly complemented and enhanced the other, surely the basis for all enduring friendships.

The bishop greeted Robert Knight with flattering delight and warmth, declaring that he would not hear of his good friend removing himself to some miserable inn, where the prices would be exorbitant and the comforts few. He must stay overnight, there was to be no argument over the matter. It was a pleasure and a privilege to return a modicum of the hospitality which Knight had so graciously shown him in the past. Alas, there was one small impediment. The bishop must leave at six o' the clock next morning, to spend a long planned holiday in his beloved Offwell in Devonshire. But, at least, they would have the rare benison of an evening meal together and the assurance of excellent conversation.

Installed in his elegant sleeping chamber, with a spacious dressing room adjacent, and all his small comforts laid out most conveniently by the excellent Leyshon, the horrors of the long journey receded quite remarkably from Robert Knight's mind. Refreshed by a leisurely toilet, and a judicious measure of brandy, he arranged himself in his well-laundered finery and descended to a meal which offered all the ingredients he had so hopefully anticipated upon the highway.

Alas, it was not to be. The bishop awaited him, tall, elegantly clad, dark eyes lugubrious under the thickly overhanging brows and the high, shining dome of his intelligent forehead.

'You will see, Knight, that the fare is somewhat frugal, for I suffer, as you are aware, recurrent and most painfully disabling bouts of digestive collapse, which lead inevitably to nervous prostration. I am scarce able to eat at all, or, indeed, carry out the barest of duties or commitments.'

Robert Knight made suitably grave and sympathetic noises. 'Have you no remedy or advice from the doctors, sir?'

'Advice? Plenty. Remedy? None! Indeed, I spent a most distressingly uncomfortable stay at a fashionable watering place, to emerge thinner, poorer, and infinitely sadder in every way although, alas, no wiser, save to have learnt the villainy of charlatans!'

'I am sorry to hear it,' said Robert Knight, inadequately.

'You will see that I dine, of necessity, upon gruel, pap. Yet I beg of you, do not let that discountenance or discommode you. You have but to ask, and my housekeeper will supply any dish you have a fancy for. I regret my own abstemiousness, but would not have it affect your appetite.'

Robert Knight tentatively selected his fare from the somewhat sparse board, and was served it with much ceremony by a flunkeyed manservant.

'I believe,' declared Copleston, disconcertingly, 'that it ill behoves a man to indulge himself upon the luxuries of life, when so many are destitute and starving.'

'Indeed,' agreed Robert Knight, a forkful of capon to his lips, 'it is grossly immoderate. Your consideration for the poor has long been remarked upon, and admired; in particular, those poor benighted curates who have neither adequate stipends nor financial expectations.'

The bishop, happily launched upon his favourite topic, waxed eloquent, declaring, with some asperity when he saw Knight's gaze wander towards the wine, 'I beg you serve yourself with wine, sir, for my own poor constitution will not allow such free indulgence. You are fortunate indeed to be a man of such robust health and appetite. I fear my own sensitivity of body but reflects that of my mind and spirit . . .'

The conversation was not at all to Knight's liking, and he fidgeted uneasily, his protuberant brown eyes vexed and bewildered behind his lenses. He was grieved by the knowledge that Copleston had received his lavish gifts of food and drink with the barest civility and gratitude, yet had neither produced them for his visitor's benefit, nor offered their return.

'Now,' declared the bishop, 'there is a problem I would discuss with you, Knight. I should value your good sense and opinion being brought to bear upon the matter. It is upon the question of raising money for those poor clergy of whom you speak, to supplement their quite inadequate stipends, and to save their families from near starvation. A generous donation from the richer, more favoured brethren do you think? Or perhaps fund-raising in the parishes by the good ladies of the manors, upon whose goodwill we so depend, or the new industrialists, the coal owners and iron masters? Or even a continuation of the Lenten fast, to benefit the less fortunate?'

A pretty penance for those, like Copleston, unable to eat! thought Knight, with wry lack of charity. 'Why not all three, sir?' he suggested guiltily, salving his conscience with the promise of an absurdly large donation which uplifted the bishop's spirits rather more than his own.

'A most generous and acceptable sum, sir,' enthused Copleston, 'and quite in keeping with your known altruism. It is to be hoped that others, more parsimonious, will be spurred by your good example!'

Mindful of the bishop's restored humour and expansiveness, Knight was about to partake of the very fine port, bringing up the vexed subject of Abrahams's invasion of his church, when Copleston pushed his chair back abruptly, declaring, 'Let us now adjourn to the drawing room, sir, where coffee will be brought to us, for I am impatient to speak with you upon another and graver matter, which troubles me deeply.' He clapped his friend companionably upon the back as Knight arose, reluctantly, to accompany him. 'It partly devolves upon the excessive drinking habits of the poor, and the distress and misery it causes.'

To Robert Knight's credit, his face changed not a whit as he replied, 'Quite so. Over-indulgence is a foul curse among the labouring classes, who lack the education and self-discipline required for abstemiousness.'

'I can see, by your vehemence, that it is a subject upon which we are in full agreement!' declared the bishop approvingly. 'Your conviction does you credit, sir.'

There ensued a spirited and resolute discussion upon the afflictions of poverty, disease, and the need to counteract the pervasive influence of the Sunday schools of the dissenters and the ministers appointed to them from the working classes.

'That is their strength, Knight,' said Copleston earnestly. 'They are men of the people, bred of the people, speaking the same language with the same despair and aspirations to give them added fire. Can you honestly declare that we, with our estates, incomes and our "livings" within the gift of those equally privileged, can have the same Godly fervour or zeal?'

Knight thought drily that it might well be a specious argument for keeping their own curates poor! 'The zeal is sometimes misplaced, sir, ill-directed,' he replied cautiously, 'as with the Chartists, those who seek to secure parliamentary reform by rioting and violence, as at the Newport rising.'

'And grieviously it was answered!' declared Copleston. 'Soldiers of the forty-fifth regiment of foot brought in to shoot men down in cold blood. I'll vow the military had little stomach for the task! Twenty killed, and many more wounded, a bitter price for seeking independence and justice! They fight only to secure those privileges which are ours by birth.'

'Certainly enfranchisement must come,' agreed Knight, rebuked, 'but violence only breeds greater violence. You cannot countenance that?'

'What greater violence is there than living in hovels, with no hope? Knowing that there can be neither escape nor change? It is enough to destroy a man's reason and soul, as well as his spirit. He may labour unceasingly, from dawn to dusk, in some coal mine or iron works, in conditions which would defeat an animal, only to find, upon the morrow, that his work is ended by trade depression, or at the whim of another. It is small wonder that they band together, lawlessly, when their children feel the pains of hunger, and there is no refuge save the poorhouse, where the family will be wrenched apart, and forced to paupery and degradation in the name of charity.'

'It is not something of which I am completely unaware,' objected Knight stiffly.

'You have seen nothing of the new industrial towns, Knight. Your parish is rural, protected from the evils that these new works spawn, with their filth, Godlessness, degeneracy.' He brushed Knight's protests irritably aside. 'Yes, I know that there is poverty upon the farms and cottages, but the air is clean and unpolluted, and the spirit of neighbourliness and concern deeper, for they are all known, one to the other. These people are an influx of all types and persuasions, with neither common belief, custom, nor even language to bind them into a single homogenous whole. Vagrants, escaped prisoners, the rootless and dispossessed, those who would prey remorselessly upon others, as well as the hard core of good, honest folk. I have seen it, Knight! I cannot forget it! It is a foretaste of hell upon earth! All they share is the sordid hell of their working lives and conditions. I beg you to believe that I do not exaggerate, for I cannot tell you one half of the horror of it!'

He had spoken with rare fire and spirit for one so physically enervated, and Knight wondered, briefly, if this fury and helplessness could be the cause or aggravation of his bodily sickness.

'What will you do, sir?' asked Knight, helplessly. 'Send young and vigorous priests into the new parishes? Build schools and open more Sunday schools where the young may be educated and directed? Seek to establish clubs or buildings where they may relax?' Knight broke off, shamefacedly, aware of the impotence of his suggestions, even as he mouthed them.

'I swear, Knight, that I do not know where, or how, to begin, or even if there is a solution. It is a problem never before encountered, massive and festering corruption which, I fear, must burst, spilling its suppurating evil, contaminating all about.'

A manservant brought in the coffee, which Copleston declined, waving him aside silently, but Knight accepted a cup, drinking it with little enthusiasm or pleasure.

'I have heard the phrase, "My heart bleeds for them", and never before thought of it, save in context of the Cross,' the bishop continued quietly, 'but it is true that the heart can bleed with pain and pity, for I feel it, Knight. There is an actual, physical ache within me, real as their own suffering. I have entered their pathetic hovels, breathed the stench of them, seen their deprivation, their pitiful, verminous possessions. I have witnessed their hunger, their sickness and disease, the foulness of the places where they labour, for I have made it my God-given duty to do so. Yet I can offer no comfort, save words which they do not understand, for we do not speak the same language. Mine is of the pulpit and the academy. There is comfort in the resurrection and the life to come, yet when you suffer a daily crucifixion, the relief is cried out for now.'

Knight was silent.

'I have seen infants of four years of age carried, sleeping, upon their fathers' backs to the coal mines, awakened to work the air doors for twelve hours a day, that their fathers may claim a dram of coal in payment for their childish labour. Others, barely older, chained to the iron trams, pulling them like beasts along passages too small for men to drag their bodies through. Women labouring in darkness, below the earth. It is scarce civilised. Something must be done!'

Knight muttered agreement, laying down his coffee cup and saucer awkwardly, hearing its rattle and clatter as he blurted, 'There is a man who has forced his way into my church seeking sanctuary, fleeing some crime he claims he has not committed . . .'

Copleston stared at him, cold and unseeing, unimpressed by his outburst.

'I wondered what your opinion would be?' finished Knight lamely, removing his spectacles and polishing the lenses with unnecessary vigour.

'Be?' echoed the bishop. 'Opinion? It would scarcely be relevant, surely? It is a small parochial matter, needing no appeal to higher authority, or intellect. A matter for the autonomy of the parish priest, to test his intelligence, moral fibre, and his aptitude for the vocation to which he is privileged to have been called.'

'Quite so,' said Knight, abandoning all thought of propounding his theories on the virtues of fire-carts.

'Well,' declared the bishop, with satisfaction, 'my mind is made clear by the frankness of our discussion . . . a rare treat and privilege to be again in your company, Knight. I thank you for it. Now, I must beg that you excuse me, for I must be away early upon the morrow.' His eyes twinkled roguishly as he added, 'Needs must when the devil drives.'

'Indeed,' said Robert Knight, rising with him, and smiling thinly at the allusion, for he had not yet recovered from the rigours of the road.

His call upon Leyshon's services, when he returned to his sleeping chamber, was brusque and immediate.

'Bring me the remains of the feast which Mrs Parsloe prepared for my journey,' he commanded, 'and whatever is left of my wine.'

Leyshon's face took on a pinched quality, his expression concerned and lugubrious, as he confessed, 'Indeed, sir, you bade me eat the remains with the coachman and the servants of the house, since you would travel freshly provided with victuals from the bishop's kitchen tomorrow. Have you forgotten?'

'No!' His master's declaration was brisk and fierce. 'The wine, then.'

'The housekeeper appropriated it, sir, thinking it part of your gift for the bishop, deeming it suitable for his weak stomach and frail constitution upon his journey tomorrow.'

'Damnation and hell!' exclaimed Robert Knight, forgetting his occupation, and the roof under which he sheltered. 'Does no one think of *my* needs and constitution?'

'There is one small veal pie,' offered Leyshon, 'which I was saving . . .'

He did not confess that the pastry had proved too hard for his ruined teeth, and was therefore abandoned.

'Bring it!' commanded Robert Knight, remarking the irony of learning of hunger at his bishop's table.

Chapter Eighteen

Joshua rode back from Maudlam towards his cottage at Newton in a strangely confused and contradictory state of mind. He was little advanced with his enquiries, for his patient questioning of physicians, apothecaries and the few wisemen he could trace had yielded nothing to identify Ruth's attacker. Yet, at least she had lived. He must take comfort from that. The rapturous welcome given to Lucky had lightened his spirits, yet his pleasure was dimmed by the knowledge that Ruth Priday, who loved the animal best of all, had been unable to utter even his name. Was it some physical injury which prevented her? he wondered bleakly, or some deeper mental anguish which scarred her spirit as cruelly as her mind? Dr Mansel and Dr Burrell seemed as uncertain as he, and as helpless to solve the dilemma. It was true that she now stood, and even walked unaided, and her physical wounds had begun to mend, but trauma and loss of memory still bedevilled her. 'Time, the great healer,' Dr Mansel had said, but did it heal such hurt and degradation as she had suffered, the ripping away of that membrane of innocence? No, he could not think that Ruth would ever learn to trust again. The surface wounds might heal, but the scars would remain, livid and slow to fade. Had it been Rebecca who suffered such violation, he thought, his pain would have been deeper and more anguished than her own, for such evil would corrupt all of life and loving, and could never be expunged. Like Joe Priday, he would kill the man responsible, and glory in his dying.

As the mare approached the Crown Inn, Joshua's mood was so intense and introspective that he was reluctant to again inflict his company upon Ossie. He regretted his former churlishness over Abrahams. It had been puerile and ill-natured to take out his vexation upon his loyal friend, and when he was able, he would make suitable apology. Yet Joshua knew, even as he resolved to do so, that Ossie would merely dismiss it, his weathered face creased in embarrassment, as he protested, 'I swear to you, Joshua, that I have not dignified it with a single thought! Besides, my back is broad, though bent to suit my old legs, and will bear many rougher burdens ere I die!'

The grey had crossed the village green now, slowing with the force of old habit at the gateway to the church, but Joshua, with scant respect for Job Abrahams and his machinations, urged her along the pathway to the Burrows. Soon the crenellated church and the long, sinuous curves of its grey stone walls were behind him, with the small well ruled by the ebb and flow of the tide, and the multi-coloured brick of the brewhouse with its scattered messuages, its darkened stack soft with a cloud of vapour and pungent with warm yeastiness and bruised hops.

Across the sandy wastes of Pickett's Lease, he gave the mare her head, and she moved smoothly, effortlessly, mane and tail streaming in the warm spring air. All about was touched and scented by the westerly breeze. It drifted in with the tide, clotted with the sharpness of seaweed and wet sand, and settling a rhime of crusted salt upon lips and skin while, from under flailing hooves, rose the rich aroma of crushed thyme, early clover, and brittle decaying petals, long dead.

He turned her towards the bay and, swiftly obedient

and sure-footed, she left the hollowed plains to climb the dunes, the fine sand shifting as they climbed to cascade in fine grains, her hooves sinking and obliterating her traces. They breasted the last ridge of dunes between towering sandhills of marram tufted grass, its spears, silvery and rushlike, flowing and rippling in the wind like pale water. From his vantage point high upon the mare, Joshua, glancing back from whence he had come, then to the bay beneath, could almost believe that it was upon an island they stood, and all about the same soft tide swirled and eddied, ebbed and flowed.

He halted the mare for a moment, letting her drink in the coldness of the sea breeze, that gentle wind the old cottagers called, in their musical language, 'the breath from the ox's nostrils'. Then he dismounted, boots sinking into the fine bleached sand, and led her down to the sea. The bay curved before them, a pale golden sickle, a deeper, harsher gold upon its outer curve where the tide had receded, leaving a damp, metallic gleam. To the left, a barrier of black rocks, pitted and roughened by the sea and weather, ran like a jagged scar across the face of the bay to disappear into the foam's edge. To the right, the lower rocks, flatter and more deeply embedded, formed a smooth plateau, sea-washed and scoured by the tide until they were barely visible above the encroaching sand. Like mighty stepping stones, Joshua thought, and all about them massive sharp-hewn boulders, chiselled, and hurled at random, as if by some giant, petulant hand, bored with symmetry. Beyond them rose the gentler dunes, and then the tangled, sandy plain of Pickett's Lease, the Port, and common lands.

Joshua had seen, near the clear pools aside the Black Rocks, Jeremiah's cob and the unmistakable cart, brilliantly rainbow-coloured in the clean spring sunlight. Even had it been shrouded over, he would have known it, for, flying through the spray and spume, fleeter than the seagull it pursued, was Charity, leaping and dashing, feinting and threatening, high staccato barks drifting eerily upon the wind, thinned and diminished by distance, the rush of the waves, and the shrill, wild cries of the circling sea birds. Of Jeremiah there was no sign.

Joshua had to turn his full attention to steadying the mare and guiding her safely over the great humped barriers of pebbles thrown up from the sea bed. Of every shape and size, speckled and plain, grey, white or delicately pastel tinted, they lay piled haphazardly like the egg clutches of some forgetful bird in a nest of seaweed and bleached driftwood. Beneath the mare's hooves, they shifted and rang alarmingly, and it was only Joshua's firm hold upon the bridle, his soothing words, and her trust in him which brought her clear and on to the shore. Once or twice it had seemed that she must stumble and fall as the pebbles slithered perilously beneath her, and her eyes rolled in terror, showing the whites. She tossed her head, refusing to budge, teeth bared in warning, a cry breaking deep in her throat, but Joshua's voice, calm and resolute, urged her onwards, but she was still trembling and lathered with sweat as her hooves found firm sand.

In a moment Charity was beside them, barking an ecstatic welcome, whip of a tail thrashing as he danced about her heels and fetlocks. Composure restored, the mare unbent enough to bow her head, turning it towards him, her expression dignified and aloof; an aristocrat reproving an unruly street urchin. The bull terrier, unabashed, ran to the cicatrix of black rock and disappeared from sight, shrill barks still ripping the air, to reappear flanked by Jeremiah and young Dafydd Crocutt from Grove Farm. So burdened and festooned with lobster pots were they that they might have been some strange variety of hermit crab. The pair were talking earnestly together, heads bent, in such perfect accord and amity that at first they did not see Joshua and the mare, but when they did, their smiles of welcome were so spontaneous, and their delight so unfeigned, that Joshua's heart was warmed. Dafydd ran to his side, spilling his empty pots to the sand and crying out to Joshua that he must inspect Jeremiah's haul, for the lobsters caged within them were altogether, 'the fiercest, most vicious brutes in all the ocean, and could slice through a man's thumb as easy as a knife through butter! There was no man on earth to equal Mr Fleet as a fisherman, and that was a fact!'

'Indeed, I would not dare to argue,' said Joshua, smiling, 'for with you and Charity to champion him, and his lobsters as weaponry, it would be more than my miserable hide is worth!'

Jeremiah's handsome, weathered face was wreathed in smiles beneath the grizzled beard and shock of thick hair, his faded grey eyes amused as he bade Dafydd hold Joshua's mare, which the boy did with alacrity, his thin body rigid with pride at such rare honour.

'I am to go to school, Mr Stradling, sir,' he blurted. 'Mistress Randall is to teach me.' His cold hands, reddened with sea water, fidgeted with the mare's bridle as he kicked, half-heartedly, at a stone.

'I have told him what a rare opportunity it is,' said Jeremiah briskly, 'a chance to read and write and be a scholar. Yet he shows little enthusiasm.' He shook his head regretfully. 'I fear, Joshua, that youth is wasted upon the young! 'Twere better if the Good Lord had created us old, and simple as babes, to grow younger by the year, that when opportunity came, we would have both wisdom and strength to embrace it.'

'A young head on old shoulders!' exclaimed Joshua,

laughing. 'It is certainly an interesting proposition, Jeremiah.'

'I have tried to persuade the lad of the value of schooling,' declared Jeremiah earnestly, 'having none myself, and feeling the loss of it. Look to Constable Stradling, Dafydd,' he commanded. 'See what respect and obedience he commands. Learning has given him knowledge and authority. Would you not aspire to be a constable like him, were you given the chance?'

Dafydd hung his head and shuffled his bare feet in the dry sand, gazing at them as intently as if he might find an answer to Jeremiah's question in the grains of sand which clung to his flesh. His hand still held the mare's bridle, and it was at her he looked as he replied awkwardly, 'I do not know if I am clever enough . . .'

'And you never will,' declared Jeremiah testily, 'unless you try! If you are afraid of failure all your life, then you will do nothing, be nothing!'

Dafydd looked up at him, then, dark intelligent eyes clouded with hurt. 'I would choose to be a fisherman, like you, sir, or a farmer, as my father was. That would not be nothing. It would be something good and useful, for you are the finest man I know, Mr Fleet.'

There was a moment of silence as Jeremiah, moved near to tears, turned his attention upon a lobster pot, pretending absorption in his task.

'Then you must learn in order to be the best fisherman, or the best farmer God put breath into,' he said, his voice unsteady. 'Now you had best leave the mare with us and fetch the cob and cart that we might load our catch.'

Dafydd nodded and obediently relinquished the reins to Joshua, hesitating, and saying awkwardly, 'I did not mean offence to you, sir. I think you are a brave man, and clever, too. It is a fine thing to be a constable, work to be proud of . . .' He flushed uncomfortably under Joshua's scrutiny, continuing in a rush, 'But you are a gentleman born, sir, as I am not. James Ploughman, who helps upon the farm, says schooling is for the rich, with time to waste, for those who must work to live have none. He says it is foolish to aspire to what we are not, and can never be. You cannot make a silk purse out of a sow's ear!'

Jeremiah would have remonstrated indignantly, but Joshua's look warned him to silence as he said gravely, 'I am glad that James Ploughman thinks me a gentleman, Dafydd, and it is true that being a gentleman is born in one, but it has nothing to do with wealth, or parentage. It is a natural respect for others, a sensitivity for their feelings and dignity as human beings. You have shown it in your dealings with Jeremiah and others, and you are right to wish to emulate Jeremiah, for he would never wittingly, or unwittingly, hurt or degrade another, and that is the mark of a true gentleman. You understand?'

'Yes, sir.' Dafydd's voice was low, barely audible.

'But education is not just acquiring knowledge; it is learning how to use it, so that you may be a better man, whether you choose to be a fisherman, farmer, or whatever you aspire to.'

'Then I shall go to school, and gladly,' declared Dafydd, and having made the decision, paid no more heed, but sped swiftly across the sand, Charity leaping and cavorting at his bare heels. Suddenly the boy paused in his flight, feet sending up a shower of dry grains as Charity skidded to a perplexed halt beside him. 'I shall show James Ploughman that you *can* make a silk purse out of a sow's ear, sir!' he called back, laughing delightedly and racing the bull terrier to the sea's edge, their footprints patterning the wet sand as the gulls screamed overhead.

'A nice enough boy,' said Jeremiah with deliberate understatement, but unable to keep the pride from his voice.

'Indeed,' agreed Joshua solemnly. 'A credit to his teacher.'

Jeremiah's worn, weatherbeaten face was aglow with pleasure, which he did not attempt to disguise, as he said warmly, 'There is nothing so well becomes a man as the good opinion of his friends. I thank you for it, sir, but it is not to compliment me, I feel sure, that you are come.'

'No, for advice and information,' invented Joshua. 'I seek Job Abrahams's wife and the circus folk, to learn what I may of the alleged assault.'

'And to warn them?'

'Warn them?' echoed Joshua. 'Of what?'

'That they are laying themselves open to violence upon Job Abrahams's account. The men who attacked him are incensed beyond reason, and since he is safely out of their reach, they will turn, like a vicious pack of curs, upon any they suspect of having harboured him, whether Abrahams is guilty of the crime, or not. There are many hereabouts who would support them in their villainy, believing them to have just cause. It was a violent cruel assault, from all accounts, and the young maid innocent and well liked by all. 'Tis no wonder those men came seeking the culprit and did not hesitate to use force. I have a mind to join them, for they say the girl was pitifully beaten in her efforts to defend herself, and was scarce recognisable as human flesh. Indeed, her own father believed, at first, it was a bundle of old rags he had stumbled upon.' Jeremiah drove his great fist savagely into his palm, overcome with anger and distress. 'I have heard that they despaired, at first, of her living,' he continued harshly, 'and that now it is she who weeps, not for the wounds suffered, nor because she so nearly died, but because she lives.'

'I shall hunt down the culprit,' promised Joshua firmly, 'but I beg of you, Jeremiah, not to become involved in vengeance, however well deserved. It will do nothing save to inflame tempers and create more violence, even the deaths of innocent people. It might well be that Abrahams has no part in this affair, and if it proves so, what will it serve, save to add self-recrimination and regret to the bitterness already caused?'

Jeremiah hesitated, then said, 'I believe the circus people to be encamped at the great pool at Kenfig, for they have need of water for themselves and their animals, and a place to rest awhile. There must be villages where they may perform, for they have sore need of money to buy food . . . Yes, I know they are there, for but yesterday one of the farmers upon the vestry took a horse to be sold at auction and saw them clearly from the yard of the Prince of Wales tavern. But already, it seems, they suffer taunts and aggravation, and the landlord has fears that it will end in bloodshed.'

Dafydd was returning upon the pony and cart, harness ajingle, the wheels rutting the wet sand about the impressed crescents of the cob's small hooves. The dog stood beside him, trembling with pride until, unable to control its excitement, it leapt to the sand, running furiously in its wake.

'All is well at the farm with the Widow Crocutt?' asked Joshua, while Dafydd was still out of earshot.

'No, it is why I brought the boy today. It seems that there has been a fist fight between James Ploughman and Elwyn Morris, with acrimony and bad blood spilt, and the boy confused and distressed. It is sure that they owe a debt to James Ploughman, who has worked unstintingly and often without reward, to set the poor holding to rights since Jem's murder, for the land scarce pays its way in crops and animals are few, for they cannot afford to buy more, or pay paupers to labour.'

'Yes, it is true that he has worked selflessly,' said Joshua quietly, 'and loves those fatherless children as his own.'

'And the widow, too, I'll hazard,' Jeremiah's voice was low and troubled, 'but they are not his own, and we cannot learn to love to order, however deserving.'

'And what is Elwyn Morris's role in this?'

'He spends much time at the farm, but upon pleasure, merely. It seems he is much taken with Mistress Crocutt, and buys the little ones' affections with treats and sweetmeats.'

'But not Dafydd's perhaps?'

'No, the boy has a stubborn loyalty to his father, as is right and proper, and a debt of gratitude to Ploughman. He feels it keenly and, while admiring Elwyn Morris for his scholarship and his courage in the affair at the docks, is ill placed to arbitrate between them. It seems that Morris has invited the widow and her brood to attend the presentation of his reward for bravery by the directors of the horse-drawn tramroad, and she has accepted willingly.'

'And Dafydd?'

'For all his intelligence and sensitivity, he is but a boy, scarce nine years old, yet expected to take responsibility for the farm, such as it is, and the family. If the truth be told, I think he would resent whoever takes his father's place, feeling the farm to be a trust upon him, and Jem's memory sacred. It is a problem to tax Solomon himself, Joshua, much less a child, and I cannot see the ending of it without hurt.'

Joshua nodded, then, clasping Jeremiah's arm warmly, made to mount the grey.

The cob and cart drew up before the pebbled ridge and

Dafydd leapt down to ask, 'Shall I start loading the lobster pots, Mr Fleet?'

'Yes, but have a care for that monster in the far cage. Treat him with respect. Keep him well away from the others, lest he inflict some injury.'

Jeremiah's eyes met Joshua's in mutual understanding as the boy bent anxiously over his task of loading the woven pots on to the cart floor. When it was completed, Dafydd straightened up, saying to Joshua, with quiet dignity, 'I thank you, sir, for your company and for your advice upon the matter of the school. I would be glad to learn more and grow wise. There are so many things I do not know and cannot understand or make meaning of.'

'To admit it is a beginning,' said Joshua, reaching out warmly to clasp the child's tentatively offered hand in his own.

It was with regret that Joshua abandoned his fisherman friend and Jeremiah's coterie of willing acolytes, Dafydd, Charity and the plumply patient Welsh cob. There was a warm intimacy about the small group, set, as it was, against the wider, harsher landscape of rock and sand and the infinity of fused sea and sky, slate grey unbroken by horizon, so that the ships in full-bellied sail seemed to float, weightless and unfettered, amidst the clouds.

He set the grey back upon the familiar rough track edging Pickett's Lease, then carefully crossed the horse-drawn tramroad and skirted the mushroom growth of spawned sheds and workshops, chandlers, and company offices that had erupted haphazardly about the docks. He hesitated, briefly, considering whether to call upon his friend, Peter Rawlings, the exciseman, to seek his advice and the comfort of shared ale at the Ship Aground, but resolutely quelled the temptation, and dutifully rode, once again, towards Kenfig Pool and the circus supposedly encamped upon its shore. Jeremiah's information might well be right, although Joshua had caught no glimpse of them upon his earlier journey upon the highway. Encumbered as he had been by the donkey and its needs, it had scarcely been a time to stand and stare, and his return had been by the quieter track by Grove and Smoky Cot. If, as Jeremiah believed, the circus folk's reception had been cold, and violence threatened, then it would be politic to keep their animals and wagons well hid behind the shelter of the dunes.

When Jeremiah had spoken of Ruth's father finding her, and likened her bruised flesh to a pile of bloodied rags, the picture of it had returned so vividly to Joshua's mind that the gorge had risen within his throat, and he had turned away lest rage and sorrow betray him. Had he deceived Jeremiah into believing that such horrors were part of his work as constable and that he was able to remain aloof, pursuing his tasks objectively, as the law demanded? No, he decided, Jeremiah had not been deceived, but as a friend he had allowed Joshua the privilege of pretending that it was so, for to have done otherwise would have been a betrayal and compounded his hurt and impotence. Jeremiah was that rare creature, an honest and compassionate man. It was small wonder that Rebecca had grown to love the old fisherman as dearly as a father, and thought of him as her own flesh and blood. Yes, they were truly blessed in the loyalty of their friends.

Joshua turned the grey towards the bays beyond the common lands and cantered her across the miles of fine, golden sand at the sea's edge. He would ride her past the bleak house at Sker, and take a track through the dunes and scrubland, that he might come upon the circus people unobserved. It would not do to arouse interest and speculation in the villages surrounding the Pool, lest the cottagers be persuaded into some rashness upon Ruth's behalf. There were hotheads enough to provoke an attack and others willing and simple-minded enough to do their bidding.

The way now was wilder and less fertile, a tangle of scrub, thorn and fern. The track was poor and ill-used, pockmarked with holes, and scarred with sharp, rocky protrusions which made the mare cautious and uneasy, slowing her pace. Joshua made no attempt to urge her on, for she was a sensible creature, and he relied upon her instinct and intelligence. Besides, wild as it was, there was something savagely impressive in the view, blackthorn spiked and tortured into shapes by the sea winds, its barbs now massed with foamy, white petals, haphazardly flung, an echo of the sea birds above them. The tufted mounds of sulphur-flowered gorse gave off a pungent cloying scent, at their roots curled fronds of fern erupted through the dead brown leaves, clenched tight as little fists, or, sometimes, pale primroses set in crowns of silvery leaves. Urging the mare through a cleft in the dunes, Joshua's mind was upon those who could now be plainly seen, the inhabitants of that impoverished caravan, halted by the cold, bleak oasis of Kenfig Pool. He smiled, despite himself, as he approached the ugly, sprawled encampment of makeshift tents and wagons, for it was plain that whatever Job Abrahams's complaints, his deprivation scarcely bore relationship to the tribe's. He, at least, had food, warm shelter and the civilised refinements of life. They had nothing save this glacial watering hole and the harsh, unyielding land, arid and treeless, unwelcoming as those in the few cottages and holdings about, who had fought, and failed, to tame it.

He could not, Joshua thought wrily, have arrived at a

less auspicious time, for the circus was evidently marshalling to move upon its way, a ragged ill-assembled army, resentful and undisciplined, lacking Job Abrahams's leadership.

He traversed the length and breadth of it, bewildered by its unfamiliarity, the noise of upheaval and the confused shouts and cries of men, women, and their grizzling, hungry children, ill-disposed towards moving on, even from this inhospitable resting place. His presence was greeted with disinterest, but no hostility, although he feared that they held him responsible, with the justice, for their plight. The carts were haphazardly laden with the performers and their strangely esoteric properties and household goods, their performing and domestic animals settled beside them, or tethered to run behind. The air was clotted with subtly mingling smells: the sweat and ordure of the beasts, the smoke from dying, sand-quenched fires, the lingering aroma of stale food and unwashed clothing, and, over all, the insistent iodine sharpness of the sea and sand, borne upon the salt-laden wind.

It was Job Abrahams's wife who finally came to him, halting her damaged wagon beside him, its splintered door primitively repaired by bleached, sea-washed driftwood from the shore, the pretty, piebald pony scarcely higher than Illtyd's pony, Faith, trotting behind.

Mistress Abrahams stepped down to greet him, ludicrously dressed in her glittering circus clothes, their specious gaudiness revealed, and made touchingly crude, by the bright sunlight.

'You have news of Job, my husband?' she asked without preamble.

'None, save that he is well and cared for, ma'am.'

She nodded. 'You have not found the culprit, then?'

He hesitated, seeing that she sought his declared belief

in Abrahams's innocence, never doubting her own, then said firmly enough for those about to hear, 'No, ma'am, and I regret it. That is why I am come, to delve more deeply into the matter, and to interview those whom it concerns in the hamlets and isolated cottages.'

She nodded, and those listening murmured their approval.

'You will be returning hereabouts?' he asked. 'I ask, not because I wish to curtail your freedom, you understand, but simply because I would keep you informed of my progress.'

Mistress Abrahams's plump jowls trembled as she lowered her head, neck hunched into fleshy rings by the movement. Her eyes were bright in the ageing, over-painted face, yet its crudeness somehow served to give her an awkward dignity. 'I thank you for that, sir,' she said, 'and, yes, we will be returning here directly, for we would stay near Job, until his innocence is proved publicly. We have need of water for the animals, you see, and there are none hereabouts who will give us pasture or shelter, believing him guilty.'

'Where do you go now, ma'am?'

'To a village nearby, Maudlam 'tis called. The priest there, a kindly man, has told his flock neither to condemn us without just cause, nor to let our children and our animals suffer. It is the only kindness we have known, and I am grateful for his forbearance, although I cannot be sure that his words will be heeded.' She added with quiet resignation, 'We must brave the taunts and violence, should they arise, sir, and the stoning, if need be. We must perform, not merely to bring pleasure, but to survive.'

'I will ride alongside you, ma'am,' declared Joshua, to his own astonishment, 'it will give me delight, for I have a child's fondness for circuses, like all grown men.'

She smiled with real pleasure, and those upon the carts alongside nodded their appreciation, although none spoke of it, save she.

'We shall be grateful for your company, sir, and your protection, for I know that is what you are offering.'

Joshua said quickly, to hide his embarrassment, 'A moment, ma'am, I had almost forgotten.' He delved into his pocket and produced a gold sovereign, putting it into her palm. 'Your husband bids me give you this coin, that you may buy food for the children. I shall see that fodder is brought here from the farms about, and sent from the three hamlets, so that the animals will not suffer.'

The tears lay in individual drops upon her lashes even as Joshua spoke the words, and spilled over to make runnels through the painted garishness of her face. 'I accept it, sir, but as a loan only,' she said, 'for I know Job has no part in this. It is not in his character. You will be repaid. You have my promise upon it.'

Then, with a shouted command to the owners of the waiting carts and poor wagons, the ramshackle procession was upon its way, the faces of the entertainers graver and less filled with promise than the brash uniforms they wore. Joshua rode silently beside them.

Upon the rough track, Mistress Abrahams spoke only once. 'Will you tell Job, sir, that the little monkey is dead. I know it will grieve him sorely, and not for the money alone. It was a poor, frail thing, but without malice or hurt. Almost human, in its way.'

Chapter Nineteen

With Joshua as protector, the strangely ill-assorted procession of wagons, circus folk and bedraggled animals neared the little square-towered Norman church at Maudlam. If they had neither joy nor tawdry sparkle to enliven them it was small wonder, for the children hungered and cried incessantly, their parents were irritable and afeared, and the beasts scarce fitted to work. Their pace upon the way had been slow and tortuous, for the carts were crude and insubstantial and the way across the dunes rough. Joshua had often to pause and to help extricate wheels bogged down in shifting sand and once to right a cart when a pony stumbled upon a rabbit hole, its terror and distress overturning the cart and spewing its occupants and poor possessions all about. He chivvied and harried them relentlessly upon the way, unable to relax his guard lest sympathy for them unman him. It would serve no purpose to show his pity, save to deepen their apathy and sense of injustice. Yet, Joshua thought, he would not easily forget those dirty, anxious-faced urchins, fretful and ill-used, bumping uneasily upon their makeshift carts. Their cheeks wore the finger marks of earlier tears, eyes hostile in their clenched faces as they surveyed him, each clutching some small treasure or unkempt animal as talisman. To them he was but the harsh voice of authority, brutish and uncaring, herding and driving them towards some other place where they would be as unwelcome at the last. Their bellies were empty and their emotions raw. It was natural that, as they rounded the grey stone wall that marked the ragged boundary of graves half-buried in the wind-blown sand, they should falter and stop.

Joshua rode the grey alongside the straggling, twisting crocodile of halted carts, urging it on to no avail. Even Mistress Abrahams's abrupt descent from her wagon and rough demands could not set it upon its way, nor yet her tearful, anguished pleading. They were resolute upon it. They would not be moved. What could lie ahead of them but persecution and ill will? They were too dispirited even to perform. They no longer had heart or energy for it.

The sight of the large raw-boned figure of the priest who came loping awkwardly from the church did little to dispel their mutterings and threats of mutiny. One of the clowns had leapt upon his cart, foul-mouthed and sullen, whipping them to agitation, bidding them disband and move separately upon their way.

'We have suffered enough!' he cried, voice ugly with rage. 'Our children are hungry and our animals sick, some dying or already dead through starvation and neglect! Must we all die, too? Where is the sense in it? Does Job Abrahams think of us? Our sufferings? I tell you now, we owe him no allegiance! No gratitude! We are paying for his rapacity and greed! His sins!'

Joshua had climbed down from the grey and was about to manhandle the fellow from the cart, nerves so raw with anger and vexation that he might well have beaten him sorely. It was the priest, gangling and unprepossessing, who halted him, awkwardly raising a hand for silence, and saying, 'My friends, no violence, I beg of you. The people of this village are poor folk, as yourselves. They have barely food enough to live, for their land is poor and unproductive, rock and drifted sand.'

The clown's abuse and mutterings continued, growing ever louder and more blasphemous, but the priest, although he cut so poor and unimpressive a figure, would not be gainsaid. His voice grew stronger, more positive.

'What they have given, they have given freely and with goodwill, and could have wished it more. If you will but follow me to the barn beyond the church –' His sallow etiolated face jerked backwards in surprise and hurt as the stone struck his cheek, splitting the skin, raking it with drops of blood.

Joshua ran towards the cart from whence the stone had come and pulled the offender furiously from his perch, hurling him roughly to the ground where he lay muttering obscenities, his grotesque clown's mask of a face with its wide painted mouth grinning ludicrously, drops of painted tears frozen upon his cheeks. There was something unnatural and repellent about the spectacle, the spiteful animosity and the changeless smiling expression, and Joshua felt a shiver of distaste as he turned to hear the priest declare, 'I do not blame you that your tempers are raw, for you have been abused and suffered much for the crimes of others. I bid you follow me, for there is food and drink set out for you, and fodder for your beasts.'

He smiled at them abstractedly, including all in his gentle gaze. He had not put a hand to his cheek, and the drops had formed a runnel to his chin, and the wound was dark and crusted with congealing blood. Yet there was about his clumsy, awkward figure an innate dignity, a goodness of spirit which was unmistakable. Joshua found himself strangely moved and joined the jostling, thrusting crowd which pushed about him on the pathway to the barn, women with babes clasped in their arms and infants at their feet, men shuffling, awkward and subdued, leading their reluctant beasts upon the narrow rocky way.

Beneath the skeleton of an open-fronted barn there was fodder strewn for the ragged-coated donkeys and mules, and beyond, a grassy meadow where they might safely graze and drink their fill. A very paradise on earth. Nor were the other animals neglected or forgot, for the kindly villagers had heaped what few vegetables and hog-fat scrapings they could spare into a none-too-appetising heap, rotting and malodorous, which the hungry curs devoured with such speed and relish that they scarce had time to bicker and snarl lest their portions be lost to another. They ate until their jaws ached and their bellies swelled up and grew tight as bladders of lard. Yet there was food to spare. Some had been prudently set aside for those strange performing beasts, caged or free. Their evil-smelling mixture, set into an ancient pigs' trough, was a vast gruel, slimy and oleaginous, its contents mysteriously unappetising. The villagers knew nothing of exotic creatures, for few owned more than one or two scrawny hens, a bacon, or a donkey, winded and hollow-backed as the circus people's own. They reasoned, not without experience, that to a starving man or beast, prejudice is a useless vanity, and survival all. And so it proved, for from parrot to piebald cob, all were swiftly satisfied, and none complained.

To the circus folk, chastened, and some near to tears at such unexpected generosity, the strangers' welcome for them was the most heartening. Planks had been set upon rough-hewn blocks of wood to serve as crude tables, their surfaces bearing oatcakes and buttermilk and flat-baked loaves of cornbread, mashed cold vegetables spiced with bacon scrapings, and boiled puddings. Some jugs of ale for the men and home-made brews of elderberries, dandelion roots and herbs, and for the babes and infants precious wholemilk and small sweetmeats.

At first the villagers stood silently beside the tables, waiting to serve the visitors, suspicious and aloof, not sure if their parson's generosity was wise, or if it would be well received. The circus folk, too, were wary and uncomfortable, hanging back awkwardly, aware that the clergyman to whose charity they owed this feast had been abused and ill-treated by one of their kind. When he had led them, triumphantly, into this promised land and the richness it offered, his parishioners had angrily remarked the bloodied wound upon his face. Incensed by such ingratitude, and knowing their priest for a gentle, inoffensive soul, they would have turned their wrath upon the offender and leathered him soundly, then put his supporters to flight. Indeed, it seemed for a time from their resentful murmurings and the bristling discomfiture of the circus folk that a pitched battle might ensue. The priest, standing stiffly beside Joshua, simply held up his raw-boned hand, to confess unblushingly, 'I fear my clumsiness will be the death of me! I am as awkward as any mule, and 'tis certain I am less sure-footed, for I stumbled hard upon the way.' He fingered the crusted gash upon his cheek, saying with a rueful smile, 'I declare it can only serve to enhance my beauty, for I do not mind admitting that the mule also has a head start upon me there.'

Joshua and all about joined in his warm unaffected laughter as the priest took up a circus woman's infant in his arms and set her upon the grass that she might reach up a hand and take a sweetmeat from the table, which she did immediately, and with such innocent joyfulness that all surged forward, smiling and amused, resentment forgotten. Soon the visitors were indistinguishable from those who served them, their infants mingling with the village children, their laughter and warm enjoyment filling the air as the pile of victuals and refreshment vanished as effortlessly as snow upon a fire.

'It is hard to remain aloof when a child hungers,' observed the priest to Joshua, his ugly, large face warm with pleasure.

'Indeed,' agreed Joshua, gazing all about him, 'it is the happiest gathering, and with the most appreciative guests, I have ever encountered. I will long remember it, sir, as they indubitably will.'

The priest's deep-set brown eyes twinkled. 'I have always preached that it is more blessed to give than to receive,' he admitted, 'but I fancy this living example is worth a hundred sermons. Yes,' he said, intercepting Joshua's quizzical look, and laughing, 'even a hundred of mine! There is nothing that gladdens the heart and spirit so much as the gratitude and good opinion of others.'

'Then your parishioners are truly blessed, as they are in having you,' said Joshua truthfully.

The priest flushed with pleasure and shuffled his large feet, before saying, 'I have also preached that virtue is its own reward, Constable, and that one should do good by stealth, but that is a counsel of perfection. I believe the good Lord would excuse a little mild indulgence and self-satisfaction for the blessing of seeing his lambs fed. Do you not agree?'

'I do indeed, sir,' declared Joshua warmly, wondering how such a rare priest had come to serve God in such a wild, forsaken place, for he was plainly a man of scholarship and culture. Yet, even as he regarded him, Joshua noticed that his clothes were shabby and worn, his cuffs rubbed threadbare. Beneath his cassock hem the shoes he wore were, under their dusty layering of sand, misshapen, the uppers splitting with age.

In answer to Joshua's unspoken question, the priest smiled, remarking without self-consciousness, 'One cannot ask sacrifices of the poor and deprived unless one lives as they do. How could they accept my words and ask my understanding?'

He turned aside to Mistress Abrahams as she plucked at his sleeve, declaring, 'There is no way I can tell you, sir, of our gratitude for your kindness, save to give a performance of our acts. I swear that never will we have played with such joy and willingness. It will be small payment, but it is all we have.' She looked into the priest's eyes, her ludicrous painted face creased anxiously, biting her lower lip, fearful of a rebuff.

'You will do us honour, ma'am,' he said quietly, 'and bring us worthy enjoyment, I am sure.' He touched her plump arm reassuringly with his awkward hand.

Mistress Abrahams nodded, eyes bright. Crude white powder had settled upon her lashes and in the creases of her plump neck and face, yet she bore herself with dignity, assured of her worth. As she forcefully marshalled the circus folk into order and saw the tables cleared aside, and their properties set up, she declared loudly, that all might hear, 'We will accept no payment from you, now or at any time upon our return to this place. The debt we owe you is a debt that can never be repaid, for you have given us freely of the little you possess, and treated us not as outcasts, but as your own kith and kin.'

And the circus folk cheered and clapped and hugged those about them spontaneously and with real affection, and Joshua, taking the priest's brawny hand in acknowledgement, said quietly, as the performance began, 'Example, sir, is worth a hundred sermons.'

'Even of mine!' repeated the priest, his smile wider and more appealing than any upon the clowns.

There was a relaxed, festive atmosphere about the small gathering, a joyousness which lifted Joshua's spirits. It was as visible in the exuberant performances of the players as upon the countryfolks' faces, aglow with rapt excitement. Yet it was towards the young priest that Joshua's gaze turned most often, for he had never before seen such wholehearted enjoyment. It was as if the amity and goodwill surrounding him relieved him of some tiresome burden. His ugly, strong-boned face grew ever more childlike and carefree, and he clapped his large hands and stamped his feet with such fierce abandon that it was a miracle his misshapen shoes did not split apart altogether under the strain.

It was a pity that the young menfolk like Tim were about their labours, Joshua thought, and only the women, infants and ancients privileged to partake in this feast of entertainment set before them. A feast it assuredly was, as welcome and satisfying to those who shared in its bounty as the victuals had been to their hungry guests. Food for the mind was as necessary as food for the body, mused Joshua contentedly, and the circus folk had offered an honourable exchange for the fare provided by their hosts. None could reasonably doubt the warmth of their return of hospitality.

Alerted by a sudden quietness, followed by an immediate babble of excited exclamation, Joshua glanced up to see the towering thick-set figure of Joe Priday gingerly advancing. He carried Ruth within his strong-muscled arms, as gently and as effortlessly as if she were a babe. His shining face was wreathed in smiles beneath the thatch of black hair, and Ruth, too, looked comfortably relaxed, her eyes freed of all terror and strain, secure, at last, in the company of friends who wished her only well.

Everywhere, hands reached out reassuringly to greet her, and space was generously offered that she might be set down in comfort. In a moment the priest was kneeling down beside her, his comical face transfigured with delight, barely able to speak coherently for surprise and pleasure.

Priday had told Joshua how the curate had spent patient hours at Ruth's bedside, talking to her gently, urging her to life even when there had seemed no visible response. He had refused to be discouraged, telling her of the news of the village, reading aloud to her, willing her, always, to return from that dark void which imprisoned both body and mind. He took Ruth's hand now for a brief moment with surprising tenderness for so awkward and clumsy a man, and her smile was no less vivid and grateful than the priest's own. Then he scrambled to his feet, ungainly in movement, yet serenely unembarrassed, and with a kind of fierce dignity.

Joshua stayed at the priest's side, following the loping gangling figure as he moved from attraction to attraction, from one group of parishioners to the next, his large ingenuous face so alight with warmth and enthusiasm that it seemed to glow from his own flesh, lighting all about him. He shines, thought Joshua, amused, like a beacon flame or lantern in the dark, like a good deed in a naughty world.

For a moment the world impinged, and Joshua was sorely tempted to ask the priest what he had learnt of Ruth's brutal assault, and of Ruth, and Job Abrahams himself. Yet, following the priest abstractedly through the maze of clowns and fire-eaters, stiltwalkers, tumblers, jugglers, the animals and sideshows, he could not bring himself to sully the clergyman's rare contentment, nor return the harshness of cruel reality to so innocent a pleasure. Later, perhaps, Joshua would speak to him alone, demanding what he knew of the affair, for it was certain that he was deeply loved by those he served, and would be in their confidence. Yet, would he then betray their murmured fears, or desperate pleas for concealment, or forgiveness? Could he?

The question was answered with a drama and unexpectedness as bizarre as the happenings all about. There was a shouting and commotion from near the open barn, and a dangerous surging of the crowd which took Joshua by surprise, then an anguished screaming, as of some creature trapped in hideous pain, which numbed his senses with its desolation. Then he and the priest, after one brief, horrified glance, one to the other, ran as swiftly as their legs could bear them towards the sound.

The crowd instinctively parted at their priest's approach, their faces nervously bewildered, too terrified to act upon their own initiative. The womenfolk, grieved and stricken, were shielding their infants protectively to their skirts, the babes in their arms wailing and sobbing at they knew not what, with the old women confused and helpless and the old men clumsily rushing about wielding sticks or stones, or whatever they could seize for protection.

The onlookers had formed a small circle with their bodies, and upon the grass lay Ruth's frail figure, collapsed in some convulsion or swoon, an older woman cradling the girl's head fiercely in her arms, and weeping distractedly. Joe Priday stood helplessly beside them, upon his face that same look of tragic bewilderment and pain that Joshua had witnessed when he had come across him bearing Ruth's mutilated body at the Pool. Ruth lay pale and motionless as death itself, skin transparently tinged with blueness, eyes closed, showing no signs of breathing, or living, pale corn-coloured hair a softness about the stark delicacy of her features.

At once the priest scrambled awkwardly to his knees beside her, his unlovely face uglier yet with hurt, relieving the woman of her burden, and stroking the pale hair with affecting tenderness, touching the bruised cheeks with a gentleness which belied the clumsiness of his raw-boned hands.

'Oh, Ruth, Ruth,' he was crying despairingly. 'Oh, my dear, my dear . . .' His stricken eyes as he rocked her ceaselessly against his breast were so filled with pain and caring as they met Joshua's that Joshua felt the violence of his grief as surely as if it were his own.

A wild cry from the next field, and crashing of sticks and frantic shouts, took Joshua running through the open gateway in the hedgerow to the strange spectacle of a clown trying to tear his way through a thicket while fending off the blows of a group of enraged ancients, belabouring him mercilessly with sticks. Joshua dragged them aside, suffering not a few clouts and bruises for his efforts. The clown had abandoned his attempt to break free and had sunk to his knees, hatless, his orange wig slipping awry to reveal his dark hair. He was still protecting his head, hunched tight as a babe in the womb, unaware of his deliverance. When he looked up, Joshua saw the blood from his wounds seeping through the white mask of his face, pale as the unconscious girl's. The painted tears were still upon his cheeks, and now, some of his own. The blustering revolutionary upon the cart was now a cowed and pitiful creature, his ever smiling mouth a grotesque caricature, flecked with saliva.

' 'Tis the villain who assaulted her!' cried one old man, so enraged with fury that colour engorged his face and even the small veins of his eyes, a pulse throbbing hard at his temple. He had raised his stick, and would have beaten the clown unmercifully had not Joshua stayed his arm and calmed him.

'She saw his eyes,' declared a companion, 'and could not mistake them, sir, for I stood beside her as she cried aloud. Her screams fair froze my blood within me.'

'She knew her attacker?' Joshua asked. 'Said so . . . identified him?'

'Her words were, "That is the man! His eyes! I cannot forget, for they haunt me . . ." '

The wretch upon the grass had scrambled awkwardly to his feet, no man offering him support as he did so, but regarding him with such contempt and loathing that his blustering protests soon ceased, and he was pleased to surrender himself to Joshua's care, fearful to remain where he would have received a rough and more immediate justice.

When Joshua had led his prisoner back into the surging crowd amidst mutterings of violence and angry imprecations from the villagers and his own circus folk, a halter rope was fetched and the villain tied securely, and set upon a cart, with a mule to drag it, and an ancient with a stick set upon guard.

Ruth, who had fallen into a faint upon the sight of him, had recovered her senses, but trembled violently still, and could not gaze at him, her face buried hard against the young priest's black-clothed breast, his hand hovering awkwardly above her pale hair. When she briefly looked up into her protector's eyes, Joshua knew, without doubt, that her love for him was absolute, as his for her. He felt a raw compassion as the priest set her gently aside and delivered her to her father's care, saying gently, 'Best take her home, sir, for she has suffered grievously. I will go with the constable to see that her assailant is safely housed, but will return as soon as I am able.' He glanced about at his parishioners and the circus folk who were huddled shamefaced, and fearful of revenge. 'I ask you . . . No,' his voice grew stronger, 'I beg and command you that you will not vent your spleen upon these innocents. Their grief and fury are as deep as your own. Let there be no more violence, or hurt. There has been enough.'

There was no doubt in Joshua's mind that the priest's words would be obeyed, for his pain and sorrow were plain to all, and Joshua watched them disperse quietly and without hostility, allowing the circus folk freedom to take their horses and animals, and load their properties upon their wagons.

Joshua on his fine grey mare rode beside the priest, who took the reins of the mule and the cart, his etiolated face concerned and lugubrious. 'The mule has a head start upon me for beauty,' he had earlier said, smiling, and indeed, there was a certain similarity in the sad brown eyes and the over-long bones of forehead and jaw.

'You are fond of Ruth, sir,' said Joshua quietly, as the priest flicked clumsily at the mule's reins, his eyes upon the gently held burden in Joe Priday's arms.

He simply nodded, then confessed as if the words were torn painfully from him, 'She is so young, and so much has happened that is evil and cruel . . .' His gaze went involuntarily to the prisoner upon the cart. 'It would be wrong for her to remain where all is known. Pity can sometimes be harder than violence to bear. It is best that she goes to a safe place . . . but where?'

Joshua said quietly, 'I will find a safe place, where she will be loved and honoured for what she is, I promise, sir. When the evil of it is exorcised, she will return, cleansed of all hurt.'

The priest nodded gratefully, his strange eyes blurred with tears, as the mule stumbled upon the way.

'It is a rough road,' said the priest, 'but we have no other, and must go on . . .'

Chapter Twenty

The unlikely little procession had set out haltingly upon the way, the clown's mask of comi-tragedy cruelly reflecting the spectacle they had watched, and the strange spectacle they now presented. Could there ever have been such a confused, bedraggled troupe? Joshua wondered, or a sight so bizarre and unexpected to greet an unsuspecting traveller upon the road? A constable resplendent in his elegant uniform, upon the fine grey; the weeping clown; the fierce old man as vengeful guard; and the lugubrious young priest in his tattered raiment and toil-worn shoes. Indeed, they might have been the itinerant cast of some ancient miracle or morality play, quitting the arena of the church. Yet the audience remained, mute and unresponsive, the players lifeless mummers all. The only spirit and conviction had come from Job Abrahams's wife who, escaping from the crowd, had clutched the bridle of Joshua's mare, running for a time awkwardly beside her upon the stony track, stumbling upon the way, plump jowls trembling at every jerk and rut.

'You will bring Job home,' she begged, 'see that he is freed? We have need of him now.'

Joshua dropped a hand from the reins to cover her fingers reassuringly before gently unfastening her grip.

'I will go to him at once,' he declared, 'have no fear, ma'am.'

The tired eyes in the ludicrously painted face grew alive, animated for a moment, and Joshua was surprised and moved by the naked joy and compassion in them.

'Job is all I have,' she said helplessly, 'and his coming is all I have asked and prayed for.'

Joshua nodded his understanding.

'But you, sir!' she cried contemptuously as the makeshift cart rumbled and creaked by in Joshua's wake, with the clown huddled miserably upon it. 'I will not pray for you! Cannot!' Her words carried piercingly upon the still air. 'There will come another judgement, you may depend upon it! God's!' Her voice rose to angry shrillness as she shouted from the pathway, a forlorn, defiant figure in her grotesque clothes, 'Like that poor, defiled girl, you will pay, I swear, and none will raise a hand to help you!'

Joshua, looking back, saw that her own hand was raised in accusation of the cowed, snivelling creature upon the cart, who seemed to burrow deeper into the rough planks, as if he might escape or shelter from such relentless malediction. Then, surprisingly, Joshua saw the priest's large hand reach out and touch the clown's trembling shoulder in a gesture of solace and comfort, and as the priest's eyes, ravaged and pained, met the constable's, there was no doubting the effort of will it had cost him.

Mistress Abrahams's hand dropped to her side and she slowly retraced her steps along the pathway to the church. Joshua saw her pause and, with a visible effort, straighten her drooping shoulders, forcing herself back into the role of circus owner, a part in which she was so reluctantly miscast. Yet Joshua could find no mirth in the absurdity of her plump, ill-dressed figure, or in the mounted tableau pursuing him. The justice would be relieved of his uninvited guest, and the peace of the sanctuary restored as surely as Robert Knight's own. The wretch who had perpetrated the violence would be fairly tried, and brought to justice for his sins, and Job Abrahams freed. Yet, for the victim there might never again be freedom from hurt, or peace of mind. And for others? Joshua glanced back at the young priest, his long, cadaverous face grimly set, his hands gripping so tightly upon the mule's reins that his knuckles shone white as raw bone.

If it had been Rebecca, Joshua thought, I could neither forgive nor forget. I would have killed him gladly and with my own bare hands. Was that the struggle which made the young priest's face so grieved and intent? Good and Evil? Forgiveness or Retribution? Man of God, or simply man in love? That he was a good priest, Joshua could not doubt.

He turned his attention to the road before him. The way was indeed rough, but there was none other. One could not hope to pass unscathed, only to survive . . .

Along the lonely narrow track through hillocks of wind-drifted sand, bound with marram grass, and through plains of salt-washed turf, the party steadfastly made its way. Joshua, riding well ahead now, was deep in thought, with the occupants of the cart equally pensive and subdued, save for an occasional gulping sob from the prisoner, and a muttered oath and swiftly administered clout from his exasperated guardian. From beyond the far dunes came an occasional glimpse of the sea, the sun burning its surface into gold as molten and fiery as its own. None was aware of it, nor yet of the tufted gorse heavy with saffron buds, its pungent, musky odour lightened with the flower scents of thyme and clover and the cleansing tang of the sea.

Joshua, uncertain if the justice had returned from his journey to Chepstow to seek the bishop's advice, was trying to determine in his own mind whether he should house the prisoner in the Crown cell, or transport him in the gaol-coach to the security of the gaol-house at Pyle. It was certain that the wretch would need to be guarded well, for there were those who would willingly kill him for his crime.

The prisoner was dwelling less upon the location of his cell than his capture. The guard was regretting the roughness of the ride and the fleshlessness of his old bones. If the young priest's thoughts were upon more spiritual and emotional concerns, then it was certain, from his pained expression, that they brought him no more comfort. Flesh or spirit; freedom or incarceration; past, present, and what is yet to be – God-given choice or predestination? When the answers are known, it is already too late. The mule obligingly kicked up its hooves and trotted on; stubborn, unpredictable but undeniably content.

As they approached Nottage village, the blessed anonymity of the little group was no more. Thus far, they had encountered no traveller or workman upon the way, but now their progress aroused speculation and amusement at every turn. Like fire through a cornfield, the word of their coming spread, and the wilder and more inflammatory grew the rumours. Assuredly, apart from Joshua whom they admired and trusted, the rest were a weird and unprepossessing crew, and none could make sense of their purpose.

'Indeed!' declared Ben Clatworthy bemusedly to his apprentice as they hurried from his forge. 'I have scarce seen a meaner and more disreputable bunch of scallywags! 'Tis certain the mule is the best intentioned of the tribe.'

'And the best dressed!' countered his lad, grinning widely. 'But who, in heaven's name, are they?'

'Strolling players?' hazarded a bystander.

'Then, by the cut of that clown's jib, 'twill be a tragedy we may expect!' muttered a disgruntled voice. 'He has a face blacker than any thunder cloud, and eyes wet enough to match it!'

' 'Twas ever the same!' grunted Clatworthy. 'Every clown fancies himself a tragedien, 'tis some quirk of human nature.'

'You will admit he is convincing in the part,' ventured the potman from the Lamb Inn, in an effort to be fair, 'for his misery is quite affecting, indeed real, almost.'

'Nonsense!' declared an irascible old lady, tugging petulantly at her lace cap, then rubbing a gnarled fist across her nose. 'It is as plain as a pikestaff that it is some tantrum he is throwing, to gain attention. If he is a clown, then he should act like one! He should be clowning properly, making folk laugh. Instead he is trying to vex and confuse us. God knows, we have little enough to laugh at!'

Her anger was diverted by the sight of the mule's ordure dropping, steaming, upon the dusty highway and she fled to her cottage, to re-emerge with a wooden pail and scoop to gather up her unsolicited gift. By now, a vociferous crowd had gathered, and a gaggle of importunate urchins and sweeping boys were clinging to the sides of the cart, and being dislodged by the ancient's deftly wielded stick, an occupation which gave him a quite extraordinary sense of vigour and well-being which amply compensated for the discomfort of the ride.

Joshua, who had remained aloof and determinedly silent about the identity of those upon the cart, had the greatest difficulty in remaining straightfaced, for the crowd's guesses upon the subject were outrageously inventive. The strangers were definitely escaped convicts, apprehended by the constable on account of their ridiculous disguises. No, they were more likely to be lunatics, being transported to some safe asylum by a man of God! A man of God? Why, it was evident to anyone with a grain of sense that it was the priest who was the villain! It was there in his face, plain for all to see! The clown was but a distraction. No doubt the priest stood guard at the church door while the ancient entered, claiming a need to rest through faintness and hunger, then robbed the alms plate!

Joshua, having ridden out of earshot of the mystified and excited crowd, with only a few persistent and dauntless ragamuffins still clinging to the cart, or running half-heartedly behind, turned, in all the splendour of his uniform, to cry out with mock severity, 'Be gone, I say! Or risk the full consequences of the law!'

Shamefaced and aggrieved, the urchins fell back, their cries stilled. One, bolder than the rest, pretended to bluster and swagger, his cockiness so at odds with his childish face and rags that Joshua could not help but smile, and diverted the guttersnipe's embarrassment with a shower of halfpennies from his uniform pocket. Taking advantage of their mad scramble to retrieve the coins, Joshua directed the cart onwards, surprising a smile of amusement upon the young priest's face before he turned away from the urchins' noisy frolics, and gave his attention to the reins.

It was as well that he did so, for even as he tightened his grip, a noisy band of ruffians on horseback emerged from a leafy byway, galloping their mounts ahead, halting to make an impenetrable barrier across the highway. Joshua pulled the grey up sharply, undecided as to whether to ride on and confront them, threatening them with the full authority of his uniform and the law, or to return and protect his prisoner upon the cart.

He turned abruptly and galloped back to the cart where the priest was struggling vainly to quell the mule, face contorted with effort, palms skinned raw by the burn of leather. Joshua leapt from the grey and somehow clambered aboard the jolting cart to help him. For a moment he was tempted to give the mule its head, forcing the cart through the wall of horses and human flesh, but a glance at the implacable faces of the riders, and the vicious array of knives and cudgels they held ready, persuaded him to bring the mule to a reluctant stop.

The ancient who guarded the prisoner was blusteringly defiant, mouthing threats and wielding his stick courageously, and, surprisingly, the priest seemed more intrigued than fearful. Yet it was the clown whose reaction was the least expected, cowering and whimpering like a whipped cur, babbling, weeping, and all but bereft of his senses with terror.

Joshua remounted the grey without haste, and rode forward with deliberation to declare, 'I escort a prisoner to justice, with the authority invested in me as a constable. Allow me to pass without hindrance.'

The horsemen remained, obdurately blocking the way, unmovingly silent, their expressions unreadable.

'If you have business with me, state it, then be gone!'

'Our business is with the prisoner.' The man who had spoken was a glowering, ill-kempt fellow, sullen, and coarse-skinned, whom Joshua recognised as from the gypsy encampment.

'You will address yourself to me, since he is in my keeping, and the law's.'

The gypsy swung himself from the horse's back and walked forward arrogantly to stand beside Joshua's grey. In a swift movement he unsheathed the knife at his belt then held the naked blade-point to the mare's throat. The mare fidgeted and arched her neck high, eyes wild with apprehension.

'Harm my mare at your peril!' Joshua's voice was

harsh and incisive as a whip lash, and the gypsy instinctively stayed his hand.

Joshua was vividly aware of the hostile barrier of gypsies ahead, and the contemptuous rage of the man before him, hand briefly stilled upon the knife. His adversary's conceit made him a dangerous man, showy and unpredictable, and he would not hesitate to shed blood should he fear himself demeaned, or his position usurped in front of his followers. Yet Joshua, too, felt unable to relinquish the authority of the law. They faced each other as antagonists, neither willing to submit. Joshua's hand moved involuntarily to his pistol, strapped to the mare's girth, but was momentarily distracted by the sound of feverish activity behind him. Before he had opportunity to turn, the priest's words came quietly, but inexorably, 'Should you kill the constable, then you must needs kill me, too, but think hard upon it. I am not here in the law's name, but in the name of God. Kill me, and you risk God's vengeance, an eternity of damnation!'

The gypsy hesitated, face uncertain, and there was a muttering from the horsemen behind him. Then, swiftly and unobserved, another horseman emerged from the leafy shelter of the byway to command the gypsy to withdraw and sheathe his knife. The voice was curt, its tenor controlled, yet it held absolute authority, and Joshua would have recognised, even in darkness, that it was the Romany leader who spoke.

'The man you hold prisoner is one of us,' he said quietly to Joshua. 'He answers to a different law. You have no authority.'

'And you, sir,' the priest's voice was calm and certain as the Romany's own, 'are a man of authority over your own tribe and people, and I but a simple man with no power or authority of my own. Yet, in me and these poor garments, soiled and unimpressive as their wearer, lies all the authority of One who rules over both heaven and earth, and all therein. I beg you, turn your men away. I have nothing to fear from death. Yet, can you say the same of your living, should you kill a man of God?'

The gypsy leader stiffened, his strong-boned face tense and irresolute. Every muscle and nerve of his body seemed taut with unresolved conflict. All else was silent, save for the soft hiss and snort of the fidgeting beasts and the subdued, hopeless weeping of the clown upon the mule-cart.

Joshua did not know what the outcome would be, but, upon an impulse, he pulled from his pocket the carved beechwood figure of a horse, declaring with rash impetuosity, 'You gave me this, sir, as a token of good will, a symbol of your willingness to aid me. Will you not grant me that aid now, and allow me to proceed? Withdraw your men.'

The Romany reached over from his mount and plucked the carving from Joshua's hand. There was an arrogant lift to his head, an expression in his eyes akin to contempt as he replied with deliberation, 'A favour has been demanded, and given. A debt is paid. We part, not as friends, but as strangers, with nothing owed or left to honour. I will take my men, but I give you fair warning,' he stared contemptuously at the huddled wretch upon the cart, 'he will not escape our vengeance. It is our law he must face. If not now, then soon, and when the time is ripe.'

'Then we will meet as enemies,' said Joshua with equal resolve, 'for I am pledged to defend him with my life, and will not fail to do so.'

The Romany smiled wrily and nodded. His eyes met Joshua's inflexibly. 'It is understood. There is no more to be said.' He turned his mount to face his followers and silently they made a parting in their ranks to allow him through, then, hand raised in a swift signal of command, he led them away.

Joshua watched the band of horsemen pause, turn, then come thundering back past the mule and cart, their leader halting before the leafy byway to glance at him with a look as penetrating and regretful as his own. Then, with a sense of loss, Joshua marshalled his little company.

What would Ossie make of it all? Joshua wondered, as he skirted alongside the cart to ride ahead of it upon the wide highway to Newton village and the Crown Inn. The ostler had a sharp, incisive tongue and ready wit, but great compassion, too, and Joshua respected his understanding of animal and human nature. He glanced briefly towards the cart. The prisoner seemed calmer now, less wracked with grief. Whether his tears had been from fear for himself, and from guilt, or from remorse, Joshua could not tell. Ossie would certainly find humour in the sight of the cart's ill-matched cargo. Yet, like the clown's perpetual smile, he would know that the humour masked grave hurt, violence and depravity even, just as the priest's ugly elongated face masked a warmth and beauty of spirit. How often we take things at face value, Joshua reflected guiltily, equating beauty with goodness, a smiling face with purity of intent. Skin deep. Yet Ossie and the young priest saw clearly, their pity and protection for the ugly and the flawed, outcasts like themselves because they were different, set apart.

Joshua sighed, and stood aside before the archway of the Crown that the cart might enter and he might relinquish his burdens to Ossie's safe keeping.

Joshua's smile of welcome died upon his lips as the ostler emerged from the stables. It was clear from his hunched shoulders and general air of downcast listlessness that he was sorely grieved. When he raised his eyes to meet Joshua's, it was evident that Ossie had been weeping, for his eyes were raw-rimmed and his whole face ravaged with indescribable hurt.

'What is amiss, my friend?' asked Joshua in concern, hurriedly dismounting to take the ostler's arm. 'You are sick? One of your beasts is ailing?'

'Worse,' said Ossie simply, and for a moment he could not speak, but stared at Joshua, unable to form the words for the grief within him. He turned away, seeking to gain control of himself, then said baldly, 'Bella . . . she is dead.'

'Bella?' Joshua's mind, still upon his own affairs, was fuddled, slow-acting. 'Bella?' he repeated stupidly, before realisation came. 'How? When? I thought it was the babe who . . .' He broke off helplessly, flushing at his own clumsiness. 'And Tom Butler, and Phoebe?'

'Dr Burrell was here,' Ossie said quietly, 'for Tom had ridden to fetch him, but he could do nothing. It was already too late, do you see. Too late.'

The words hung bleakly between them, cold in their finality.

'The rector, Robert Knight, he is with them?' Joshua demanded.

'I do not know if he has returned.'

In an instant the young priest was beside them upon the cobblestones, his ugly, honest face concerned.

'If you will allow me to comfort them, sir, give them what little consolation I can offer, and God's greater compassion. For that is the only true healing of hurt.'

Ossie looked from the priest to Joshua in bewilderment, leathery face uncertain. 'Joshua?'

Joshua turned to the cleric in shame and embarrassment to confess, 'I regret, sir, that I showed the gravest discourtesy in not enquiring your name. I beg that you will forgive me, for my mind was greatly occupied.'

'As was my own,' said the priest, in gentle acknowledgement of Joshua's apology. 'It is of no great matter, but my name is Richard Turberville.' In reply to Joshua's incredulous look and unspoken question, he said wrily, 'Yes, my forebears have long been associated with the priory at Ewenny. Perhaps it is fitting that one of them now returns to its origins and root.'

The old man upon the cart had started shouting and shrieking furiously, his stick falling jarringly upon the edges of the cart as he swung at the prisoner who was already upon the cobbles and running towards the arch, desperate to escape. With a mighty blow which almost toppled the ancient from his perch, the stave cracked against the clown's backside, sending him first to his knees, then grovelling, face down upon the cold stones. Joshua rushed to drag him to his feet, fearful that the force of the blow had dislodged the victim's spine, but the fellow, although dazed and winded, seemed able to stand, and in possession of his voice and faculties, for he let fly with such a foul-mouthed tirade that the ancient had to be restrained by Ossie from attacking him again.

When order was restored, and two hefty lads from the stables sent first to warn Mistress Randall, then to escort the prisoner to the cell and stand guard over him, Ossie turned to the priest, studying him intently, as if seeking reassurance of his worth. The priest stayed calm and unspeaking under his harsh scrutiny.

'Yes,' said Ossie, satisfied. 'Tom Butler and his wife will be glad of your comfort, sir. I cannot doubt it.'

Joshua nodded as Ossie gently took Richard Turberville's arm and guided him, dust-stained and as shabbily clad as the least of the rector's poor flock, into Tom Butler's sad house.

'You will do me the honour, sir, of taking bread with

me at my cottage? Upon your return?' Joshua called out.

The priest hesitated, and turned.

'Ossie will show you the way.'

Richard Turberville nodded. 'I am grateful, sir.'

'And I to you,' said Joshua quietly, feeling an ache of pity and warmth as he turned abruptly away.

With the mule unharnessed and stabled by a willing lad, and the old man given a sixpence from Joshua's pocket to buy himself a jug of ale and a meat pie within the Crown, Joshua remounted the grey with the ancient's excessive gratitude still pursuing him. He bade the stable lad deliver the key of his cottage to Ossie, begging that the priest enter and await him there, since he must ride out at once to see if the justice had returned, that he might apprise him of the prisoner's capture and seek his consent for Job Abrahams's release. Joshua would return swiftly, he promised, and meanwhile the priest must use the cottage and all that lay therein, as freely as if it were his own.

Joshua was ill inclined to tire his grey further, for the mare had been ridden hard, and the day was warm. Yet he knew that it would grieve her were he to take another mount, for the rapport and affection between them was so great that Joshua sometimes found himself treating her as an equal, speaking to her as to a human and not a mere beast. However, she showed no signs of exhaustion, but cantered proudly upon her way, muscles rippling beneath her smooth hide, movement as rhythmic and effortless as the flowing of water. With her fine tail and mane streaming, and the elegantly clad young constable at ease in the saddle, they were a sight to gladden the most rheumy and jaundiced eyes. An old woman digging up dandelion roots from the hedgerow to brew root beer paused in her task, alerted by the mare's approaching hoofbeats. Her willow basket was half filled, as was the apron which she clutched to her flattened breasts, her gnarled fingers stained brown with the milky sap which oozed from the broken stems. She was misshapen of bone, sickle-backed through age and unremitting toil, yet, at the sight of Joshua and his mare, her eyes grew gentle in the withered face, and she held herself almost erect.

'A fine day, Constable, and a fine sight you are, sir, if I may make so bold.'

'It is a finer day for meeting you, ma'am, and for the warmth of your greeting,' called out Joshua cheerfully as he passed her by.

The old woman grinned toothlessly and touched a hand to the wisps of hair, grey as sheep's fleece, which escaped her shawled head. Her face was weathered as a russet skin and her joints stiff, yet she returned to her task with rare vigour. Then, with her basket filled, she wiped the broken blade of the knife, which had prised up the roots, upon a tussock of coarse grass before heaving basket and gleanings upon her awkward back. Strange, she thought dispassionately, that her fingers should be gnarled and twisted as the roots of some ancient tree, for within herself the flesh and sap was young, breaking into newness like the furled buds upon a springtime bough. She shifted the basket more securely against her hunched spine. When had she grown old? It must have come suddenly when she was unaware of it, spring into summer, autumn into winter . . . She sighed. Winter was a cruel time, and cold . . . and yet it held the promise of life to come. For the young constable, she thought wrily, but for me it brings only the Grim Reaper, with his scythe to cut me down. She cackled with dry amusement as she said the words aloud, 'It is to be hoped he has a mare as swift as the constable's, and a surer blade than mine!'

It was certain that Joshua's ride to Tythegston Court

was swift, but his reception there proved more wintry than he had hoped. The justice had indeed returned, Leyshon informed him as he took the constable's helmet and escorted him to the library, lowering his voice conspiratorially to confide, 'I fear, sir, that you will find Mr Knight discomfited and ill-disposed after his journey.'

Joshua, forewarned, entered upon the justice's command to the rare sight of the justice reclining testily in a winged-back chair, his feet resting upon an embroidered church hassock. Beneath his rolled breeches' leg, his foot was heavily bandaged, the toes erupting pallid and fleshy, save for the monstrous disfigurement of his big toe. Crimson and glowing as a sunset, it could scarce be missed, and Joshua, mindful of the justice's rising irritation, tried to control the wayward twitching of his lips and the mirth rising within him. In truth, it was the strangest toe he had ever beheld, swollen and shining as a bladder of lard, yet reddening as fiercely as Robert Knight's face.

'Gout,' said the justice, forestalling his enquiry. 'It came upon me suddenly.'

'It looks . . .' Joshua, at a loss to declare what it looked like without giving offence, finished lamely, 'painful, sir.'

'Of course it is painful! Damnably painful!' exclaimed Knight irritably. 'Any fool with half an eye could . . .' He collected himself with an effort. 'You will excuse my spleen, Stradling, for I admit that the anguish of it provokes my temper unfairly.'

Joshua nodded his understanding. 'And the physicians, sir, and the apothecary, what do they recommend?'

'Fools all!' declared Knight. 'They agree about nothing! Nothing, save that it is a disease of high living and excessive indulgence! Indulgent? I? It is a plain fact that

I am a man of pitifully moderate tastes. I neither drink nor take tobacco to excess, nor am I given to gluttony, abhorring it as one of the seven deadly sins. I cannot fathom why I should be so afflicted!'

'Perhaps, in view of your acknowledged frugality,' suggested Joshua, commendably straightfaced, 'the fare at His Grace the Bishop's table proved unpalatably rich, sir?'

'Rich!' thundered Knight, almost leaping from his chair in anguish, then subsiding after crying out in involuntary pain.

Joshua could almost see the justice's toe throbbing and engorging with his empurpled face in choler.

'It was a fast, Stradling! A self-imposed fast,' he amended, lest there be any doubt of his self-abnegation.

'Then, perhaps, sir,' suggested Joshua, blandly, 'this is an even greater test of your forbearance and resolution. It is said, is it not, that those who suffer the most grievous afflictions, and triumph over them, shall receive their reward in the afterlife?'

'Stuff and fiddlesticks!' said the justice tartly, his eyes glinting flintily from their pouches. He glanced down irritably at his disfigured toe, then his plump jowls began to shake, and he was laughing helplessly, unable to compose himself, a silk handkerchief clasped to his streaming eyes. Unable to speak, he simply pointed to the cause of his sudden mirth, raising his mummified foot with a groan of effort. Upon the exquisitely wrought tapestry of the hassock was stitched the text, 'A SOFT ANSWER TURNETH AWAY WRATH'.

Chapter Twenty-One

With the justice's humour and equilibrium restored, and Joshua invited to share the remains of a bottle of Canary conveniently to hand, the atmosphere grew decidedly more cordial than upon Joshua's arrival. If Joshua was concerned about the effects of the wine upon the justice's gout, Robert Knight had no such inhibitions or reservations. He drank copiously and with relish, his temper growing ever more placid.

'Now, what is the purpose of this visit, Stradling?' he demanded at last. 'For I feel sure that you have not come solely to enquire about my health.'

'Yet I have hopes that the news I bring you will serve to improve it, sir,' returned Joshua, smiling, 'for you need no longer suffer the imposition of Job Abrahams in your church.'

'Indeed?' The justice's glass had halted midway to his mouth which was frankly agape with astonishment. 'And the reason for this . . . unexpected reprieve?'

'The true culprit has been apprehended, sir.' Joshua's tone was modestly self-satisfied.

Not so the justice's as he asked querulously, 'Who? Where is he now?'

'It was the clown we first saw upon the village green, sir, and he is firmly secured within the gaol-cell at the Crown.'

The justice frowned in concentration. 'The Crown?

Then he must be transferred at once to Pyle, for his presence here will be provocative and inflammatory, in view of his crime. You will see to it, Stradling!'

'At once, sir,' said Joshua, rising obediently to his feet and replacing his glass.

'Not this instant, man!' declared Knight peevishly. 'There are more pressing matters to be discussed.' He waved Joshua irritably to be seated, saying unexpectedly, 'I knew at once that the clown's mask was but a clever disguise. Indeed, I thought his whole demeanour suspect. You will recall, sir, that I called your attention to it, most vehemently, at the time.'

Joshua, who recalled nothing of the sort, murmured non-committally.

'It is an instinct one develops,' declared the justice, 'a sixth sense, one might almost claim. I pride myself upon being a true judge of character, Stradling. It has frequently been remarked upon by those in authority. Indeed, my work as priest and justice depend upon such . . .' he searched for a suitable phrase, 'such inspired perspicacity. Insight,' he supplied triumphantly. 'You will remember that I spoke to him most sharply, Stradling. I realise now that I knew instinctively what corruption and villainy lay behind that painted mask. You did well to apprehend him,' he said magnanimously, draining his glass of Canary, and absent-mindedly refilling it as he spoke.

'You would have me release Abrahams, sir?' asked Joshua, amused in spite of himself.

'No,' declared the justice firmly. 'I will reserve that pleasure to myself. He had no legal right of sanctuary, Stradling, you are aware of that? No right at all, save the moral right to sanctuary within the church, which I granted unconditionally. As I explained to my friend and colleague, the bishop, it was my decision alone. I sought neither advice nor confirmation of the rightness of my action. A man must be unequivocal and self-reliant about such affairs.'

'He had no legal right to claim sanctuary, you say, sir? Abrahams, I mean?'

'Certainly not! It was a privilege abolished in 1624.' Robert Knight smiled deprecatingly. 'You were unaware of this, Stradling?'

'I confess, sir, that I was,' said Joshua, confused.

'It is true,' continued the justice, his smile broader now, 'that in ancient times he might claim sanctuary within a church, or churchyard even, and could not be removed to stand trial for his crime. Yet, even so, he was required to swear upon oath before a magistrate that he would quit the realm in forty days. During that time, any man might give him food and drink.'

'And after?' asked Joshua, intrigued.

'He would be charged with felony, unless he declared his avowed intent to leave the land, when he would be stripped to the barest clothing by the justice, and set upon the road to the sea, with naught but a crucifix to sustain him.'

'And then?'

'He walked into the sea till only his mouth rose above the waves, that he might utter his cry for a passage, a cry repeated until a ship could be found to take the felon aboard, and thence to safety, the cries of "God speed you!" a fading chorus from those upon the shore.'

'A harrowing enough experience, sir,' remarked Joshua solemnly, 'since the poor wretch risked drowning, or rejection by a ship's captain and crew.'

'As harrowing as the desecration of my own church, sir, by that vandal, Abrahams,' countered Knight abrasively, 'and with as little common justice. He has made free with the Communion wine, and disrupted my sermons with his incessant clattering. Worse, he has treated my personal possessions with contempt, and used the vestry as if it were some common lodging house!'

'But Abrahams, at least, was innocent, sir,' protested Joshua, determined to be fair.

'Innocent?' demanded the justice. 'Innocent, you say? Let me remind you, Stradling, that it is the court which decides a man's guilt or innocence. Do not take upon yourself those burdens and responsibilities which belong to others, better fitted for the task. Your part in the affair is ended, save to give impartial and accurate evidence at the hearing. I, sir, am the representative of the court, the arbiter of law. Pray, do not overreach yourself!'

Reproved, Joshua muttered an apology and the justice nodded curtly in acknowledgement, his dignity and arrogance somewhat diminished when he had to ask Joshua to tug the bell pull in order to summon Leyshon. His own attempts to do so had entailed so much involuntary groaning and cries of pain, and such contortions, that he had all but prostrated himself upon the floor.

'Leyshon, you will order the carriage,' Knight commanded, 'and bring my crutches, and that confounded invention of the apothecary.'

Within minutes, Leyshon had returned accompanied by a groom, and bearing a pair of crutches with armrests of hide padded with horsehair. The groom was carrying what looked suspiciously like a child's plaything: a wooden cart upon wheels and fitted with a soft velvet cushion. Joshua could scarce keep a straight face as Robert Knight was guided and manhandled by the two retainers through the wide doors of the library, his swathed foot supine upon the cushion, gouty toe fiercely erect, while he hopped and wheeled his way inelegantly through the long corridors and across the hallway.

Joshua followed circumspectly, bearing the justice's crutches. The journey to the Promised Land could hardly have proved more perilous or fraught with menace, thought Joshua, amused, as the justice's vituperation grew louder, and his complaints more fierce.

Finally, with assistance from all three, Robert Knight, panting only slightly less than his aides, was ensconced in the coach and his crutches hauled in beside him.

'Damned nuisance, Stradling!' he said gruffly. 'Most vexatious! Yet I will not allow myself to be beaten! You will await me at the church while the groom and coachman will assist me from the carriage. I shall speak to Abrahams most severely, and personally see him evicted!'

'Your . . . contraption, sir,' offered Leyshon, holding up the wheeled support. 'You had best not forget it, for you might have need –'

'Hell and damnation, Leyshon!' declared the justice, waving him furiously aside. 'Take that confounded farradiddle away! I cut a poor enough figure as it is. Would you have the parishioners see that . . . toy, and declare I had reached my second childhood!'

He turned irately upon Joshua, wincing as he did so. 'By the smirk and vacant expression upon your face, Stradling, it would appear that you have not outgrown your first! You would be more suitably employed mounting your horse and setting about your lawful business.'

With a swift glance at Leyshon, who raised his eyes expressively to the heavens, Joshua did as he was bade.

The justice's voice, bleak and petulant, floated back as the carriage creaked and grumbled upon its way: 'Why a man's affliction should be a cause of mirth is beyond my comprehension . . . some idiocy . . . a weakness of character . . .'

' 'Tis a fact,' agreed Leyshon, tucking the apothecary's contraption more securely under his arm, and smiling at

Joshua, to reveal the ruins of his teeth, 'that I cannot lay claim to any great learning.'

'It is not always a disadvantage,' said Joshua.

'True.' Leyshon's eyes creased about with humour. 'I have never yet seen a donkey with the gout!'

Joshua, having arrived at the gateway to the church of St John the Baptist well in advance of the justice's coach, tarried upon the green, undecided as to whether he should return his mare to Ossie at the Crown, or warn Job Abrahams first of Robert Knight's coming. Reasoning that Ossie might have already left the inn to escort Richard Turberville to his cottage, he fastened the grey to an iron ring in the churchyard wall, where she might crop in safety, and set his hand upon the gate into the churchyard. There was no doubting the justice's disquiet at Abrahams's occupation of the vestry, and his temper had undoubtedly been exacerbated by the pain of his gout. It was a pity that, although known now to be innocent, Abrahams was such an odious, selfish creature, with no care save for his own comfort and voracious appetite. He was supremely brash and unlovable, and did not deserve the loyalty of his wife and the circus troupe who had suffered abuse and deprivation rather than forsake him, believing always in his innocence.

Joshua's dilemma was solved by the emergence from the churchyard of an elderly cottager from Newton village, a thin whey-faced old fellow, with extreme lameness issuing from a leg wound received in battle against the French. He sought the constable's advice, he confessed, upon some boundary claim, for he was in dispute with a neighbour. So incensed did the poor fellow become in repeating the taunts and calumnies of his opponent that he could no longer speak coherently, and suffered such a fever of shivering and confusion that

Joshua seated him upon a mossy tombstone that he might recover his wits, fearful lest his rage bring on an apoplexy. When, finally calmed and reassured, the ancient was set upon his way, Joshua heard the jangle of harness and clopping of hooves which presaged the arrival of Robert Knight's coach. He moved reluctantly towards it as, with a creaking of springs and a rumble of wheels, it came to a bone-jerking halt beside him, setting up a cloud of dust, as the groom dismounted and set down the steps for the justice to descend. When Robert Knight emerged, his pale face and clenched jaw told of the punishment he had endured from the jolting and bumping along the way.

With set face, he allowed himself to be helped down ignominiously by his coachman and groom and, refusing all further offers of aid from them, or from Joshua, gathered his crutches beneath his armpits and, demanding only that the doors to the church be opened for him, made his limping, tortuous way within. Joshua followed warily in Knight's wake, sympathetic to his plight, yet not disposed to offer support which he knew would be irascibly rebuffed.

It was inevitable that Abrahams, alerted by the sound of the justice's crutch ends tapping unevenly upon the stoneflagged floor, should leave the vestry to investigate. The justice stood, swaying perilously upon his inadequate supports, face ashen, yet bathed in the sweat of exertion. He was deciding whether he might conceivably manage to hop and hurl himself into the safety of a pew, or whether the sudden movement might cause him too much pain, when Abrahams ran to stand beside him, unnervingly close.

His plump dark-grained jowls trembled, and his mouth twitched into foolish laughter as he surveyed the justice who stared at him in stony silence. Overcome by the humour of the spectacle, Abrahams erupted into such a paroxysm of mirth that he could scarcely stand, the tears rolling unchecked down his fat cheeks as he clutched his stomach, jerking about helplessly, making snorting, gulping noises which he was quite unable to check. Indeed, Joshua, despite the justice's wrath, was barely able to resist joining in, so compulsive was the man's laughter.

'I think, sir,' said Robert Knight, 'that you forget yourself, and where you are. Control yourself, I say, or I shall be forced to take my crutch to you!'

This served to redouble Abrahams's mirth, and, in truth, he was now so overcome that Joshua was afraid that he might fall into some kind of fit, and derange himself.

'We have come to tell you that you may leave, sir,' Joshua interjected quickly to calm the atmosphere. 'We know now that you are innocent of the crime. We have apprehended another.'

The justice's face was darker than a thundercloud at this interruption, but, lacking the dexterity to turn about and face Joshua, he vented his spleen upon his long-time oppressor.

'Are you deaf, sir, as well as simple-minded?' he demanded. 'You will leave this instant! Go, I say, for my temper grows shorter by the second, and I will not hold myself responsible for what might occur should you delay.'

Abrahams's hilarity was spent now, but he seemed bewildered, his laughter dwindling into staccato gulps which Joshua held to be more like sobs than mirth. The justice and Abrahams surveyed each other coldly, each cautiously assessing his adversary.

'Since I am innocent,' declared the circus owner inflexibly, 'and acknowledged to be so, I demand compensation.'

'Compensation?' The justice exploded in wrath. 'It is I,

sir, who should be claiming compensation for your villainous depredations. You have made a pigsty of this holy place! Begone, before I debase myself, and it, by striking you senseless. I would hesitate to spill blood upon these hallowed stones.'

'I will not go!' Abrahams's voice was as firm as the justice's. 'I would as soon stay here and await the money which is my due. Besides, I am comfortable here. I have shelter, warmth, and food better than I have known in all my life.'

'But your wife, sir?' Joshua pleaded helplessly. 'Have you no thought for her loyalty, and those who depend upon you for their livelihood?'

'None,' said Abrahams. 'Let them fend for themselves. I owe them naught, I am dependent upon no man!'

The justice was so incensed that he could barely speak the words that sprang to his lips, and had to pause to control his fury.

'You have been dependent upon the goodwill of myself, sir, and my long-suffering congregation,' he blurted, at last, 'who have housed and fed you, and emptied your slops, and borne with your selfishness and ignorance for too long. I will have no more of it!'

Joshua was not aware of what happened next, save that the justice raised his crutch as Abrahams stumbled forward, either by accident or stealth. Their bodies, each solid and unyielding as the other, clashed, and they were down in a tangle of limbs and flesh, screams of pain, and a flurry of oaths and imprecations which assuredly came from Abrahams.

There was no doubting Robert Knight's pain, for Abrahams had blundered upon his bandaged foot, and Joshua, seeing the justice's ravaged face and the excruciating hurt upon it, thought it best to let him lie there on the cold stones, undisturbed, until the agony of it had abated. He lay there, supine, unable to summon the strength of will to rise, his waxen pallor and stillness reminding Joshua, absurdly, of some marble effigy of a crusading knight upon a tomb, an irony and pun which would not have been lost upon the recumbent man in kinder times.

'Stradling, if you please . . .' The quiet humility in the rector's tone chastened Joshua, and he bent low to hear his murmured request. 'I beg that you will retrieve my crutches and help me to my feet, for I would not like my parishioners to see me so ludicrously cast down.'

Joshua retrieved Knight's crutches and, with difficulty, dragged him upright, and thence to his feet, supporting his heavy weight into the open air, upon his firm request. Then, with great gentleness, Joshua set him to rest upon a mossy bank.

'Yes, it is better here,' said Knight, beginning to regain a little of the colour which had drained from his cheeks, within the church, 'for I swear that my thoughts and lust for vengeance were ill-suited to a Christian place.' He thrust his hand into his pocket and produced the shagreen case from which he took his eyeglasses, snapping them across the bridge of his nose and over his fleshy ears. He peered myopically through the lenses, searching the churchyard, protuberant brown eyes intent.

'Abrahams?'

'Long gone, sir.'

Knight nodded, and smiled. 'Would it shock you, Stradling, should I confess that, towards that scheming wretch within, I felt a singular lack of charity. Indeed, were I the captain of a ship, and he a felon, I would most like have refused him passage. It does me little credit.'

'It is to your credit, sir, that you gave him sanctuary

when every man's hand was turned against him.'

Robert Knight considered for a moment before replying with a rueful smile, 'With hindsight, Stradling, I fear I might well have used my own, to push him under!'

When Robert Knight was sufficiently rested and had recovered himself enough to return to his waiting coach, Joshua assisted him awkwardly to his feet, and helped to position the crutches beneath his arms. Some of the fire and irritation seemed to have drained from the rector, and with them his energy, and he was unusually lifeless and spent. He made no complaint as Joshua manhandled him clumsily upright from his perch upon the grassy bank, although his lips were clenched tightly from pain and the effort not to cry out.

'I thank you for your aid, Stradling,' he said quietly. 'I am not unaware of the ludicrous and sorry figure I present. I admire your self-control in hiding your mirth, for the scene you witnessed within the church had all the elements of true farce.' As Joshua courteously strove to deny it, Knight continued, 'Gout has long been a cause for levity, perhaps because it is wrongly associated with excessive wining and dining. It is not surprising if those who have barely enough food to survive think of it as divine retribution for gluttony and over-indulgence, God's small shaft of humour.'

'It is true that the misfortunes of others are often a source of amusement,' agreed Joshua, pacing himself to Knight's clumsy hobbling, 'perhaps because they remind us of how easily we might be the victim. I think, sir, that it is less a conscious cruelty on the part of those who mock and jeer, than an expression of our own relief and embarrassment.'

Knight grunted audibly. 'Well, I am grateful that you, alone, witnessed my downfall – literal and moral!' he said gruffly. 'I would as soon not be toppled before my parishioners, who sometimes equate me with the cloth, or the church itself.' He smiled wrily. 'Although having survived for nigh on two thousand years, I daresay the church will survive the blunderings and ineptness of one insignificant, elderly priest.'

Joshua, uneasy about the way the conversation was going, and the rector's new-found humility, distracted him by referring to the events at Maudlam, and the quandary of the young priest who awaited him now at his cottage.

'Turberville?' the justice repeated sharply. 'You are sure that you have not mistaken the name, Stradling?'

'No, sir, I am not mistaken, for although I did not openly enquire as to his connection with the family at Ewenny Priory, he admitted it freely.'

'Richard Turberville, you say?' the justice persisted, pausing to rest upon his crutches with evident relief.

'You know of him, sir?'

'Indeed.' The justice's face grew bleak with remembrance and hurt.

Joshua knew that it was something long past which pained him.

Robert Knight hesitated, then continued in a voice which was barely audible, 'He was a friend from childhood of . . . Charles, my nephew who died.' He shook his head. 'No,' he said firmly, 'Charles, the nephew I killed. It is better to admit it openly, Stradling, for there is no disputing it, nor hiding it.'

Without waiting for Joshua's reply he steadied his crutches beneath his arms and moved awkwardly upon his way. As he approached the church gate, he turned, to ask abruptly, 'He is at your cottage, you say, awaiting you?'

'Yes, sir. If you would care to meet him, renew your acquaintanceship?'

'No.' The word was a long time unspoken, and Knight looked incredibly weary and old. 'It is better not. I am not ready.' He looked at Joshua in mute appeal before claiming awkwardly, 'My leg . . . I fear, Stradling, that it would make me clumsy, set me at a disadvantage. I would not wish to embarrass the boy, to be an object of his pity, you understand?'

Joshua was not deceived. 'Perhaps, sir, at some other time, and in some other place, you will be better prepared, or come upon him unawares.'

Knight nodded. 'It would be kinder so.' There was no mistaking the relief in his eyes. 'He was a good boy, I recall him well. There was a gentleness in him, then. A sensitivity.' His hand tightened its grip upon the leather support of his crutch. 'With hindsight, I see that it was a quality which my nephew lacked. He was all fire and fury, afraid of nothing and no one. He had always to prove himself the bravest and best. Yet, strangely, it was always Richard Turberville who won.' Knight's eyes, remorseful and filled with bewilderment, looked into Joshua's. 'It is something which I have not reflected upon before – the reason, I mean; why it should have been so. It is true that Charles could not recognise danger or the possibility of defeat. He was unaware of them. Turberville knew of their existence and yet conquered them. I suppose that is the difference between foolhardiness and true courage.'

'I believe that courage, sir, is what gives Turberville his will to be what he is,' said Joshua earnestly, 'an ordinary, labouring priest. The poor folk at Maudlam respect him deeply, and think of him as one of themselves.'

'I suppose that is what the bishop meant,' murmured Knight to himself, 'to abjure riches, and live as He did . . .'

'The bishop, sir?' Joshua was confused, thinking Knight's mind to be wandering.

Knight did not enlighten him.

'You have seen Tom Butler, sir, and his wife?' asked Joshua. 'Richard Turberville took it upon himself to bring them what comfort he could, in your absence.'

'Comfort?' Knight asked, puzzled. 'Why? What is amiss? I have heard nothing, seen no one.'

'Their daughter-in-law Bella, sir, Reuben's wife who lately gave birth to a child. She died when you were absent.'

'I will go at once,' said Robert Knight incisively, and with some of his old spirit. 'I have no doubt that my presence was not sought as I was believed to be remaining at the bishop's house still.'

As Joshua made to assist him, Knight motioned him away and continued with agonising slowness to make his way through the open gateway of the church and across the green to the Crown.

'Are you well enough to attend them, sir?'

Knight turned his head at Joshua's question and said, 'It is my duty, Stradling, and my privilege. These are my people, my flock. If I lack the common touch, I do not lack compassion or charity.' The words were an implied rebuke.

'I do not think your care for your parishioners has ever been in doubt, sir.'

Robert Knight looked at him keenly, then nodded, satisfied. 'I could wish I had young Turberville's gift of being at one with the people, touching their hearts and emotions,' he said quietly. 'You will give him my remembrance, and bid him visit me when my . . . my indisposition is past. He will understand, and know the way.'

'I will tell him, and gladly, sir.'

With exasperation and pity, Joshua watched Robert Knight make his slow, insecure way across the highway and into the doorway of the Crown, before he turned abruptly and unfastened his grey from the iron ring that tethered her to the church wall. As he led the mare under the archway to the cobbled yard, Robert Knight would have been surprised had he known what occupied his young constable's mind.

He is more like Richard Turberville than he knows, thought Joshua, with reluctant admiration. He, too, has a kind of courage, for he knows the meaning of fear, and his own limitations, and will not be denied . . .

Chapter Twenty-Two

'It has been a long day, Ossie,' said Joshua, delivering the mare into the ostler's willing hands.

Ossie nodded, one horny work-grimed palm soothing the animal's neck with his customary gentleness, while the other gripped the bridle so tensely that the knuckle bones rose hard and white as stone.

'A longer day for Tom Butler,' Ossie said quietly, 'and harder than any he has known.' Only the fierceness of his hold upon the leather showed the rage he felt at Bella's dying, for his voice was flat, emotionless. 'I swear, Joshua, I cannot make head nor tail of it. She was a kind girl, without cruelty or malice. I never recall hearing her saying an unkind word.'

Ossie's creased weather-beaten face was ugly in its bewilderment. Joshua put a comforting hand to his friend's shoulder, and Ossie nodded. His voice was thick with hurt as he confessed, 'I am not a clever man, do you see? But I have tried to make sense and reason of it . . . I have thought hard, but to no avail.' He wiped a hand tiredly across his eyes, and Joshua felt a surge of pity at seeing them sore-edged and raw, and the dirt of old tears smeared upon the grimy skin where Ossie had sought to wipe them roughly away. Joshua could think of no words to answer him.

'I keep asking myself, why?' Ossie muttered helplessly. 'What is the purpose in it? In life and in dying?

Yet there must be some, for if there is none, it is naught but a cruel, senseless joke. Yet surely the Almighty could not have planned it to be that? Could He have been so cruel?'

'No,' said Joshua soberly, 'I cannot believe it to be so.'

'And yet,' said Ossie, 'there is a young girl, scarce more than a child, dead within the inn. A babe, motherless, and a husband unbeknowing. Reuben must return to grief and a burden of guilt which will never leave him. Why, Joshua? In the name of God, why?'

With the sharpening of his voice, and the involuntary tug upon the reins, the mare grew restive, showing the whites of her eyes, and Ossie, immediately contrite, soothed and steadied her, his voice returning to gentleness.

'You had best ask someone more fitted to answer, my friend,' said Joshua gravely, 'for I am as confused and saddened as you, and must arm myself, directly, with pitifully useless words to add to Tom and Phoebe's pain, for that is what is required of me. It is a cruel, senseless practice, for even animals are allowed to grieve with dignity, and mourn their dead alone. I shall relish it as little as those I force my awkward pity upon.'

Ossie, glancing at Joshua's troubled face, saw that, for all his learning and being a gentleman, the young constable's doubts and impotence were as great as his own.

'The young priest, Mr Turberville, awaits you at your cottage, Joshua,' he reminded him gently. 'He will most assuredly welcome the comfort of your company, and a warm fire, and whatever victuals you provide. It was a generous act to invite him. I fear he denies himself even the barest necessities of life, for he is pitifully clothed and fed. He has less flesh than a dormouse in winter.'

'Then I shall hope he has its appetite upon awakening,' said Joshua, smiling, 'for it would give me pleasure to see him better fed, although I fancy his deprivation is deliberate and self-imposed, a chastisement of the flesh to feed the spirit. He will not live more prodigally than the poorest of those he ministers to.'

'I can but hope that his flock would do likewise,' declared Ossie tartly, 'but I beg leave to doubt it! Yet there is no denying that he is an honest and sincere man.'

'He gave comfort to Tom Butler and Phoebe, you think?'

Ossie's hands tightened upon the reins as he made to lead the mare away, and he turned his head so that Joshua was unable to see the expression upon his face.

'Comfort and pity, yes,' Ossie's voice was low, 'for there is no doubting his love for God, and his own kind, but reasons, no.' He looked back steadily at Joshua. 'He is a man sure in his own faith. Accepts. Does not doubt. A saint amongst the sinners. Yet it is the sinners who must be convinced, and pardoned, in the end, or what is a life for?'

Joshua watched him lead the grey away, Ossie's boot soles and the horse's hooves clattering bleakly upon the cobblestones. The little ostler's back was awkwardly bent, his misshapen legs bearing cruel evidence of rickets and past deprivation. Joshua watched them enter the stable, then walked out under the arch. 'What is a life for?' Ossie's words echoed in his mind. It was a question philosophers and sages had sought an answer to throughout the ages, with as little certainty. A trial? A testing time of endurance and triumph over painful adversity? Joshua wondered. Then Ossie had already suffered a burden that would have crushed a man of lesser spirit.

Joshua's own spirit was cheered by Richard Turberville's transparent pleasure at his return to the cottage. The priest's long, cadaverous face was aglow with animation as he arose to greet the constable. With his awkward, gangling limbs, he reminded Joshua irresistibly of a boisterous puppy, all warmth and eagerness to please, his clumsy enthusiasm a hazard to all about him.

He observed that Turberville had taken neither food nor drink, as he had been urged to do, nor had he borrowed a book from the shelves to while away the tedium of the waiting. Indeed, from the intensity of his stillness and concentration when Joshua had disturbed him, he had been intent upon his own thoughts, or deep in prayer.

When Joshua had delivered the message from Robert Knight, the young priest simply nodded gravely, his dark, intelligent eyes filled with compassion.

'He begs that you will excuse him,' added Joshua, 'for his indisposition makes him awkward, a figure of fun, or so he feels.'

'Then he must take comfort from the fact that his indisposition is but temporary,' said Turberville, with a ready smile, 'unlike mine, which is immutable.' Joshua smiled with him, for there was no resentment in the observation; it was stated as simple fact. 'Yet my clumsiness and droll appearance are sometimes an asset,' said Turberville, 'for there is none who, seeing me, and remarking my ugliness and inferior cast, would hesitate to seek my help.'

Joshua could not deny it.

'If you are poor, you pity a man who is poorer; if you are ugly, you have an immediate affinity with a man who is even less elegantly endowed, just as, if you are inadequate, you understand and warm to a man no better favoured.' His eyes twinkled mischievously. 'And yet you rejoice, too, that at least your lot is better than the poor wretch's whose advice you sought. It is human nature, and what cannot be changed must be put to use. Do you not agree, sir?'

'Most certainly,' said Joshua lightly, to hide the embarrassment and pity which the priest's words had raised in him. 'And since my mother has been clear-sighted enough to send me a surfeit of victuals from the farm, then we must not let them go to waste. It would be charitable if you would help me in their disposal, else I shall be eating them until Michaelmas.'

Confounding Ossie's predictions and Joshua's fears, the priest ate a good meal after reciting a simple grace of thanksgiving for the bounty which Joshua had so lately accepted as a right. How strange it was, he thought, that the man before him had been nurtured in wealth and privilege, and had willingly abandoned it for the poverty and deprivation he now embraced. Would his fortune not have brought prosperity to the whole of the community he now served, indeed to the entire parishes of Newton, Nottage and Port, and countless others besides? He was loath to broach the subject with his guest, feeling it to be rude and impertinent. Yet, almost as if he had spoken his thoughts aloud, Turberville said, without preamble, 'I daresay you have wondered why I have chosen so austere a life? Why I do not use the money and advantages I possess to better purpose?'

'Yes. I admit my puzzlement.'

'It would not be to better purpose,' said Turberville simply. There was no denying his absolute conviction as he continued earnestly, 'The money would be quickly spent, and to no purpose, save to make a return to poverty harder to bear. As a priest, my duty is to support, and not to carry, to inspire men to strive towards a betterment of flesh and spirit.'

'Is it not hard when there is no work, and their bellies lie empty?' asked Joshua practically.

'Indeed. I have found it so myself, and often faltered, and prayed that it was otherwise,' confessed the priest honestly.

'But you have never sought your family's help, for they would undoubtedly give it freely?'

'No.' The answer was unequivocal. 'If I live as my parishioners, and with them, it would invalidate all I do, or am. I cannot renounce my past, nor would I wish to, for it is what has made me. Yet the present and future are in my command. I have made my choice.'

'And your family?' Joshua asked quietly. 'Do they understand?'

Turberville looked at him consideringly, as if trying to resolve the question in his own mind before speaking the words, 'It is hard for them to understand that I do not reject them for others with no ties of kinship or blood, I reject only their way of life, the inessential trappings of wealth, but do not condemn them that they are fortunate. I regret only the harshness the accumulation of such fortune has brought to others who have laboured, or died vicariously, to secure it.'

'Yet without such work, would they not have been destitute?'

'Perhaps, yet it should not be thus. No man should own another as if he were a slave, to be bartered or sold. Making him dependent upon another's charity for a home, food and warmth for his family, life even. It is this I reject. I do it because there is no other way to ease the injustice of it save by living as one of them, trying to salve their poverty and hurt, sharing it. I bring them nothing but love, God's and my own. That is why I cannot lessen my purpose by giving love to another, for the love of a man for a woman would be so deep, and demanding more than I can give, gratifying my own selfish needs. Such a commitment would weaken what I offer to so many whose need is unending.'

Joshua knew that it was Ruth Priday of whom he spoke, but could not bring himself to speak her name.

Turberville was regarding him intently, eyes watchful and anxious.

'I am scarce in a position to comment,' responded Joshua with deliberate lightness, 'being so recently betrothed.'

They laughed good-naturedly, the tension and seriousness between them broken.

'You are to be congratulated, sir.'

'Yet not emulated,' responded Joshua, unthinking. Then, seeing Turberville's awkwardly tentative smile, and the effort it cost him, damned himself for a stupid, insensitive fool, declaring, 'I do not belittle the personal sacrifice you make, sir, in your efforts to do what is best for the greater good.'

'But you do not agree with it?' observed Turberville shrewdly.

'I do not think that love for one person must be at the expense of another. Love is not a finite thing, to be weighed and measured. It is infinite, unending . . .' He broke off, embarrassed and ill at ease under Turberville's scrutiny. Then self-consciousness rendering him unnaturally abrasive, he persisted, 'A stream is not diminished when water flows out of it or is taken away. It is replenished at its source, the well spring . . .' He flushed, stammering into silence.

'That is precisely what I try to preach,' Turberville's eyes were bright with affectionate understanding as he placed a hand upon Joshua's shoulder, 'that the love of

God, as His mercy, is infinite. A never-ending source, but I, alas, am human, Stradling . . . Joshua,' he amended. His ugly, wide mouth curved into a rueful smile. 'I am merely a well, commonplace and unreliable. In days of drought, or when too much is required of me, I have a propensity to run dry. Then all must suffer.' His grip upon Joshua's shoulder tightened briefly, then fell away.

They regarded each other silently for a moment, caught in rare understanding.

'Tomorrow I will ride to Southerndown Court,' promised Joshua, 'and ask Rebecca to take the young woman who was so cruelly attacked into her household. We are to be married at midsummer, and will make our home here. Then, perhaps, she will be recovered enough to return with us.'

Turberville nodded, his bony face warm with gratitude.

'I will send word to you, by messenger, or come myself if I am able, to take the young woman to Southerndown Court. She will be safe there, and none will hurt her, or remind her of what she has suffered, I promise.'

'Ruth . . .' Turberville hesitated over the name as if it were strange to him, and he could recall it only with difficulty, 'Ruth, as I, sir, would be grateful for that.' He stood indecisively for a moment, then said, 'I will go now to the Crown, where my mule and cart await me.'

'Then I will come with you,' offered Joshua immediately, 'and return you by the innkeeper's coach.'

Turberville smiled, but shook his head. 'I thank you for what you have given me in warmth and comfort this night, and for your friendship.' His strangely ugly face was unreadable as he took Joshua's hand and bowed his head in conventional leavetaking. 'We will meet again in kinder times, God willing.'

'You are sure,' insisted Joshua, 'that you will not take a mount from the stables of the inn, or have use of the coach? The night is dark and the way uncertain.'

Turberville's generous mouth grew wider with his radiant smile. 'A mule and cart is luxury enough,' he said, 'and the way is certain, for I follow the steps of one who rode triumphantly upon an ass.' He strode into the night, ill-clad and poorly shod, a pitifully unprepossessing figure with his loose shambling gait. Yet Joshua felt a sense of loss, a regret at his leaving.

As he turned wearily to enter the house, he was alerted by the sound of a horseman riding near, and paused, surprised when the animal halted without the cottage and the rider hurriedly dismounted. By the light of the lantern above the doorway, he recognised the flushed, perspiring face of Rawlings, the exciseman from the Port, and warmly bade him enter and take refreshment, for they were friends of long standing, and had survived many a battle against common foes and their arbiter, the justice.

'I am uncommonly glad to see you, Peter,' exclaimed Joshua truthfully. 'It has been a strange, confusing day, and I will relish your cheerful company.'

'I bring no cheer, Joshua,' said Rawlings sombrely, 'and my news will but add to your confusion and hurt. *The Stormy Venturer* is reported overdue, lost in a storm, it is feared, off Valparaiso. Her sister ship has returned safe, although crippled by the same gales and tempest. They watched the *Venturer* flounder, and drift into the eye of the storm and were powerless to help her.'

'Dear God!' cried Joshua, seized with such terrifying weakness of limb that he had to steady himself upon the doorjamb, and would have stumbled and fallen had not Rawlings come to his support.

'I have ridden at once to tell you, knowing that

your friend, Devereaux, is master of the vessel.'

'You have informed the justice?'

'No. I ride now to Tythegston. And you?'

'I will go at once to Southerndown Court and give Sir Matthew the news, for Elizabeth must not hear it from another. It would be too cruel.'

'I will give Tom Butler the news at the Crown, for his son, Reuben, was one of the crew,' Rawlings said tonelessly. 'It is not a task I relish, yet it must be told.'

Joshua, feeling shame and remorse that in his grief for Elizabeth he had forgotten Butler's son, declared penitently, 'Then I must come too, as a duty, and a mark of friendship to him, although I have as little heart for the breaking of it as you.'

'And Reuben's wife, and the child?'

'Bella is dead.' The words were bleak and cold as the hurt in Joshua's breast, but, like the duty before them, there was no way to soften the truth of it.

Neither Rawlings nor Joshua spoke again until they reached the inn. Yet their thoughts were as clear as if the words had been cried aloud: how will Tom Butler survive?

When Joshua arrived at Southerndown Court upon a mount hired from the Crown stables, it was daybreak, the sky already lightening from its pewter greyness, and slashed with vermilion, pink and gold. He was as little aware of it as of the sharp wind from the sea that scythed through his tiered coat, for his own mood was darker than the night had been, and the bleakness within him colder than any wind.

His mind had been upon Tom and Phoebe Butler at the Crown, and the controlled dignity of their grief. It seemed to him that they had sought to ease the clumsy baldness of his telling of it, for although he had rehearsed the words in his head, they came out crudely disordered, as though it were a stranger who read them aloud in some foreign tongue, without sense or understanding. As he spoke of the loss of Reuben's ship, he had been surprised and ashamed to find the tears coursing down his cheeks and running into his mouth, so that he could taste the salt of them in his throat, choking him, thickening his voice. Tom Butler and Phoebe had shed no tears. Perhaps, Joshua thought, because they were already drained of grief, with Bella's dying. There was an emptiness about them, in their eyes and movements, as if sorrow and pain had been sucked away and, with them, all flesh and feeling, leaving only a brittle carapace, a useless shell.

'There is hope, sir,' Peter Rawlings had blurted awkwardly, seeing how Joshua's grief had unmanned him. 'There is no word of a wrecking, only the storm. It has blown them off course, perhaps.'

'Perhaps.' Tom Butler's voice was polite, without inflection.

'It might be that they have sought shelter somewhere,' Rawlings suggested, 'or the vessel has sustained some damage and awaits repairs.'

'Yes, that is true.' Tom Butler nodded, but his voice lacked conviction.

'Their sister ship weathered the storm and has returned to port, sir, crippled but seaworthy, and none is missing of her crew,' Rawlings persisted clumsily before falling silent.

Phoebe Butler, who had been nursing the sleeping child, her head bent low, had looked up, face flushed, eyes bright with unshed tears, to say quietly, 'Reuben is safe. I am sure of it. It must be so, else I would know and feel it. I bore him within me, as Bella bore the babe within my arms. Living or dead, I would know . . . I would feel his loss as if he were, again, torn from my own flesh.'

There was a silence in the room so profound that Joshua was aware of the child's soft breathing and his own heartbeats. Phoebe Butler surveyed them calmly, her eyes bright, but filled with certainty, as she continued to rock the sleeping babe. 'I would feel grief and pain if Reuben were dead,' she said, 'but I feel none, you understand. I feel nothing. Nothing at all.'

It seemed that she suddenly became aware of the disbelief and hurt upon Joshua's face, for she stretched out a hand to him, the other clutching the infant the more securely to her breast.

'Your grief is for Captain Devereaux, too, and Miss Crandle,' she said.

'Yes, ma'am. I ride there, now . . . to Southerndown.'

'Then I beg you will give her my kind remembrance.'

'Yes, ma'am, that I will gladly do.'

Joshua's eyes met Tom Butler's, and by the fleeting, barely perceptible expression of fear in them, he knew, without doubt, that Butler shared his thoughts. Perhaps Phoebe felt no pain, not because their son lived but because, with Reuben, she felt only the empty ease of death.

Joshua sighed, and glanced below him to the jagged rocks and the crumpled dark sea, the rays of the dawn sun striking the surface with a wound of red, as if a stream of bright blood flowed through it.

No, not Devereaux, please God, he thought, or Reuben who so lately and without thought for himself had struggled into another storm-tossed sea to save Tom and Phoebe, Jeremiah and the boy, Dafydd, from certain death upon the rocks. But that craft had been so small, drifting rudderless and helpless, for they were none of them sailors. Surely a schooner was built to withstand the fiercest gales, sturdy and resolute as the men who sailed her, and as unlikely to be cast down. And yet . . . the worry gnawed at his mind relentlessly . . . could anything made by man, or man himself, withstand the destructive rage of the elements, and survive?'

Joshua deliberately turned his horse towards the North Lodge, unwilling to pass the converted lodge where Elizabeth and her mother lived. It would not do if either was awake, or had arisen, for the unusual sound of a rider, arriving so early, would arouse curiosity and alarm.

It was a measure of Joshua's own alarm and unhappiness that his thoughts were not upon Rebecca, but the news he must bring to Elizabeth and Sir Matthew. He dismounted with haste and, as quietly as possible, not to alarm those within the Court, rapped upon the door of the lodge to summon the gatekeeper. The servant, confused, and wiping the sleep from his eyes, rasped back the bolts and peered out tentatively, a stout stave clutched in his hand. His workaday clothes were disordered from sleep, and his face puffy and reddened as he scratched himself, then stretched his sluggish limbs, swallowing a yawn quickly as he recognised the constable. At Joshua's instruction, and still clutching the forgotten stave, he sped along the dew-soaked lawn, his unshod feet making silvery prints in the grass, to stir a footman without awakening the household. Then, with Joshua's mount taken and stabled by the lodge-keeper, and Joshua waiting with restless impatience in the library, the servant went, discreetly, to arouse his master.

Sir Matthew entered almost at once, perturbed by Joshua's unheralded arrival at such an inopportune hour. He had made some effort to dress suitably, upon discarding his nightwear, but it was plain that his valet had not been in attendance, for his clothing had been haphazardly selected and matched, and his usually immaculate hair and necktie were awry.

'Joshua?' His voice was sharp and the fine eyes watchfully alert. 'What brings you here at this hour?'

'I fear I am the bearer of bad news, sir. Perhaps, Sir Matthew, it would be better if you were seated.'

Sir Matthew brushed the suggestion aside and remained standing in the doorway, purposefully erect and assured, as if to brace himself against the news he feared that Joshua must impart.

'It is Captain Devereaux, sir. There is news that his ship is missing, believed sunk, off Valparaiso.'

'You are sure of this?' Despite his commanding height and presence, Sir Matthew seemed suddenly older and more frail, as he walked, unseeing, to the desk, supporting himself upon a corner of it before seating himself, heavily, in a chair. 'Elizabeth,' he said, helplessly. 'Elizabeth . . .' For a moment he seemed bewildered, lost, then, with a conscious effort of will, he regained control of himself. 'You are sure of this, Joshua?' he repeated abruptly. 'It is not some rumour, speculative, groundless?'

'No, sir. I was informed by Rawlings, the chief exciseman at the Port. There can be little doubt, since its sister ship was caught in the same violent storm, and limped home, battered, yet miraculously under its own sail. It seems Captain Devereaux's vessel was sucked into the vortex of the storm, and was seen no more.'

'It is long overdue?' Sir Matthew's voice was sharp with anxiety.

'I fear so. It seems that the schooner which survived and reached port was herself delayed a month or more, listing, and making painfully slow progress. Her master was fearful that she would sink, and all aboard be lost.'

Sir Matthew rose reluctantly to his feet, as if overcome by a great heaviness of flesh and spirit. 'I will tell Elizabeth,' he said, 'for the truth is owed to her. It would be more cruel to keep the news of it from her, lest she inadvertently hear it from some other source. Oh, but it will grieve her more deeply than all that has gone before! She has survived so much in her young life, Joshua, but this is the cruellest wound of all, and I do not know if she can bear it, physically or emotionally. Captain Devereaux was the one source of happiness and security granted to her, someone who would cherish and love her for the woman she is, loyal, and with as brave endurance as his own. I pray, most earnestly, Joshua, that his endurance and Elizabeth's will not be tested too far.'

The possibility of death seemed alien and far removed from the quiet orderliness of the room in which they talked, yet each felt the threat of its presence.

'It is a deeper grief to me that I must tell Elizabeth now, at this time,' confessed Sir Matthew, helplessly, 'for the wedding plans are made, and the small Dower House so lovingly furnished. It was to be her own haven of peace and security, the first she had ever planned, or known.'

'And that was . . .' Joshua corrected himself quickly, 'that is true of Roland Devereaux, too, Sir Matthew, for since his parents' death, he had no home, and no family, save Mary.'

'Oh, what a hellish, futile mess it all is, Joshua! I would give all I am, and more, could I but undo the wrongs and tragedies Elizabeth has suffered, for she is as dear as my own grandchild to me, and I cannot bear to inflict greater pain upon her than she has already known.'

'Would you have me speak to her, Sir Matthew?'

'No. I thank you that you are prepared to take it upon

yourself,' Sir Matthew's eyes were bleak, 'but it is a burden which is mine by right, and I cannot shed it, nor pass it to another. It is a measure of my love for her that I refuse you.'

Joshua watched in silence as Sir Matthew looked about him, his gaze wandering over loved, familiar objects, as if seeking strength and purpose from their permanence. Then he turned and walked out, resolutely, through the open doorway.

Chapter Twenty-Three

Neither Joshua nor Rebecca was ever told of the meeting between Sir Matthew and Elizabeth. They could only guess at what transpired and the words exchanged between them, for Elizabeth thereafter refused to speak of Roland Devereaux, or hear mention of his name. Sir Matthew seemed older and less in command of himself afterwards, as if pity and helplessness had diminished him more cruelly than the passing of years.

No one saw Elizabeth cry, and it is likely that she did not shed a tear, for she steadfastly refused to believe that Devereaux was dead. Louisa Crandle tried to approach her daughter that first day, and many times afterwards, to offer her affection and consolation, but her awkward efforts had been gently but nonetheless positively rebuffed. To add to her bewilderment, Elizabeth went unerringly on with the plans for her wedding to Captain Devereaux, insisting that her trousseau be completed as ordered, and herself supervising the arrangement of furnishings within the Dower House. She no longer discussed her plans or displayed her acquisitions to Rebecca, who tried in vain to broach the subject of Devereaux, and what the future held. She parried all questions with silence, ignoring them as if they had never been spoken, and diverting attention skilfully to other matters. She was often closeted with Sir Matthew in the library, or to be seen walking with him in the grounds, their heads bent in earnest conversation. Yet, what they spoke of no one knew, and neither volunteered the gist of their talks to others.

At first, Elizabeth had begged the use of that small room at the Court where she had dressed herself for Rebecca's birthday ball, when she had danced so heedlessly with Devereaux's protective arms about her. For days she ate and drank little, but sat alone, writing perhaps, or quietly reliving their short time together. Her mother and Rebecca attempted to seek her out to force her back into the mainstream of living, but Sir Matthew bade them leave her in solitude, for it held, like nature, the power of healing, and had served him well in the days of his wife Emma's death, when grief was his only companion.

When Joshua had told Rebecca the purpose of his early-morning visit to Southerndown Court, her pleasure and excitement at seeing him so unexpectedly were immediately stilled, and the warm colour which had flooded her cheeks drained away, leaving her curiously pale and sick at heart. So shocked and enervated was she that Joshua grew afraid and ran to support her lest she stumble and fall. With Rebecca barely conscious in his arms and demanding his full attention, he was unable to reach out to the bell pull to summon aid and was forced to call aloud until his cries were heard by a passing servant, who helped lift her on to a sofa, then hurried to seek the help of the housekeeper. The good woman, all starched capability and dourly practical, entered with a reviving draught in hand, and wasted no time in administering it, with additional relief from the pierced silver vinaigrette suspended upon the chatelaine about her waist. The potion and the acid pungency of the vinegar-soaked sponge having restored Rebecca's colour and senses, the housekeeper would have sent at once for the physician, but Rebecca would not hear of it, declaring that his services would be better directed towards Elizabeth and Mrs Crandle, and that she was fully recovered.

'It was naught but a ridiculous maidenly swoon,' she insisted; she was ashamed at her weakness, and humiliated by the furore she had unwittingly caused.

The housekeeper was not convinced, for Rebecca's vitality was sadly subdued, and her pretty animation had deserted her. Yet Miss de Breos was adamant, and not even young Mr Stradling's earnest pleas could persuade her to relent.

With a crackle of starch which, Joshua suspected, came as much from the rigidity of her backbone as her skirts, the doughty lady retired, defeated, leaving Rebecca to Joshua's milder ministrations with a stern injunction that should her services be needed, he must brook no delay.

'I suspect,' declared Joshua with a frail attempt at humour, 'that she fears it is my nearness which set you in such a flux, and that I am altogether too forward and importunate in my advances.'

He had brought up a chair to be beside her, and Rebecca put out a cold hand to his, which he enclosed between his own large palms, rubbing it gently to warmth from his flesh.

'I am glad that you are here, Joshua.' Rebecca's voice was so thin and forlorn as to be barely recognisable, but there was no mistaking her sincerity. 'Should I go to Elizabeth, do you think? To try and bring her comfort?'

'No.' Joshua's grip tightened upon her hand, restraining her from rising. 'It is better not, Rebecca. Your own grief will serve to distress her further, and you will scarce be able to bear the unhappiness of it all. Elizabeth is a very private person, and would not wish her grief to be shared, even by someone she loves as dearly as you.' He gently released her hand, then knelt upon the floor beside her couch, watching her with concern and affection. 'Elizabeth will come to seek you out when she is ready.'

'Oh, Joshua,' Rebecca buried her face in Joshua's waistcoat, weeping helplessly, 'we were so happy. I do not think that I can bear the tragedy of it, truly. Yet what is my grief to Elizabeth's?'

She raised her tear-stained face to his, and he gently brushed the tears from her wide cheekbones and the curve of her mouth with his fingertips, as she said despairingly, 'Roland was all that Elizabeth ever loved or wanted. He was all of her life. I do not think she will be able to go on living.'

'Hush now.' Joshua cradled her to him, kissing her dark hair and rocking her in comfort as if she were a child. 'We do not know if Roland is . . . if he survives,' he said firmly. 'It will serve no purpose save to crush what little hope Elizabeth has, if you think in that fashion. You will have to be strong and positive, Rebecca, for Elizabeth will have need of your strength.'

Even as he spoke the words, he regretted them, thinking himself cold and unfeeling, and damned his churlishness. Yet, they had their effect upon Rebecca, for she searched his pocket for a handkerchief, and he helped her wipe away the last traces of grief, only to see her eyes shimmer and fill again with unshed tears behind the thick dark-fringed lashes. She forced her eyes to open wide in an attempt to stop them spilling, and Joshua was so filled with love and pity that he turned his head aside, roughly, lest he betray himself, and add his own despair to hers.

'I do not see,' admitted Rebecca tonelessly, 'how we can proceed with our wedding plans.'

'I do not understand you, Rebecca,' Joshua protested

sharply. 'How will that help Elizabeth? It will only serve to be a more cruel reminder if you add the extra burden of guilt to her loss. She would feel nothing save anguish, I am sure, if she believed herself the architect of such useless self-denial.'

'I cannot enjoy my own selfish happiness when Elizabeth has so little!' Rebecca cried out vehemently. 'It is unfair! She has neither hope nor comfort, Joshua, and I have so much, in you and grandfather, and all that is to come.'

'Do you think Elizabeth would grudge you such happiness?' demanded Joshua quietly. 'It is as little in her nature as it is in yours. As for having no hope, I believe that she has that, and the cruellest thing of all would be to destroy it. Do not force doubt upon her, for if it is true that Roland is indeed dead, then it is surely kinder that the realisation comes gently, and with the passing of time. It is too violent and terrible a loss to be thrust upon her needlessly.'

'Oh, Joshua, I truly love you, my dear.' The tears which she had tried so vainly to check flowed over now, unhindered, splashing from cheek and chin, and wetting his shirt front as she burrowed her head against him, like some frightened creature seeking warmth and protection. 'If I lost you,' the words were muffled, thickened with tears, 'then life, and all I hold dear, would have no joy or meaning.'

Joshua put his fingers to her chin and raised Rebecca's face to his, gazing earnestly into the vivid blue eyes, softened and washed with hurt. 'You cannot doubt my love for you, Rebecca,' he said, 'any more than you can doubt that the sun will rise and set each day, or springtime follows the bleakest of winter days. It is as true and inevitable as my love for you.'

'Yes, Joshua. I have never doubted that,' she said, her voice low.

He smiled, then, at her seriousness, seeking to dispel it. 'It is an immutable fact of life,' he said lightly, 'like your beauty and your vanity and your devious scheming wiles . . .'

'And the riches which ensnared you,' she finished, smiling tremulously in return.

'Indeed,' agreed Joshua, heartened, 'for even as a cocklemaid, Rebecca, you were all the riches I desired, or hoped for in my wildest dreams.' He lifted her hand to his lips, kissing the fingers one by one. 'The soft hands of a gentlewoman are no more dear to me, I swear, than those poor, work-roughened ones I first beheld, when you drove with Jeremiah from the shore, and brought your cob and cart to rest beneath my bedroom window.' For a moment he saw her again, pale-skinned in the early morning light, her hair a blue-black cloud about her face. He was remembering, too, the paler face of Roland Devereaux's dead sister upon the sacking apron that lay upon the cart floor, the dampness of the sea settled upon her, soft as dew upon a morning flower . . . but he would not think of that same sea closing upon Roland's and Reuben's living flesh.

Rebecca felt the shudder which trembled through him, and said, remorsefully, 'It has been a long journey for you, Joshua, and sad, with only the grief of others at its end. I beg you come with me and seek refreshment, for you must be tired and hungry.'

'I have been hungry only for sight of you, my dearest love,' said Joshua with a broad and all-embracing smile, 'and would as soon remain here and sup my fill upon your kisses.'

'You forget yourself, sir,' declared Rebecca with chilling hauteur, 'and will dine like other less favoured mortals upon the victuals that the kitchen will provide, or grandfather will know the reason why.'

'Then I must be satisfied with that,' he said with mock humility, 'at least until we are wed.' His tone was humorous, his lips curved into a smile, but there was a look of gravity and questioning in his eyes.

'I will marry you, Joshua,' said Rebecca quietly, 'as and when we planned, and with gratitude in my heart, and joy that it is to be.'

Joshua nodded, satisfied. Then, assisting her gently from her couch, could not resist adding, with admirable foppishness, and flourishing his handkerchief, 'I declare, Miss de Breos, your excessive pleas have quite worn me down, and I will consent to marry you, since you are determined upon it. I had best pen it in my diary, ma'am, lest other, more importunate, maidens turn my head with their fawning flattery, and seduce me from my promise. You are sure, ma'am, that you can offer me nothing more tempting than breakfast?'

'Nothing, sir,' said Rebecca, smiling properly for the first time, 'since I am sure that, having already tasted the wine of my lips, you will have no appetite for pale imitations . . .'

It was not surprising that, despite the comfort of being in one another's company, breakfast proved to be a sombre and unsatisfactory meal. Joshua ate little, and that only to satisfy Rebecca and not his appetite, which had deserted him. Rebecca ate nothing at all, her pallor and listlessness preventing Joshua from taking her to task for the omission, since he was sure that the effort of swallowing the smallest morsel would have defeated her, and resulted in another outburst of distressed tears. The dishes of delectable food left for them upon the serving board, therefore, were left barely touched, or with covers unopened.

The servants had been dismissed that they might serve themselves, but even the unusual intimacy of being so long alone together, without Mrs Crandle's austere presence as chaperone, did little to raise their spirits, since their thoughts lay too heavily upon the reason for her absence. Joshua tried to divert Rebecca with news of their friends in the three hamlets, and ludicrously embroidered tales of the 'Fiery Archer', the justice's gout, and even Job Abrahams's triumphant eviction from the church vestry, but she could not be distracted, although she tried as hard as he to find humour in absurdity, which would normally have seen her laughing and clapping her hands in unfeigned glee. When Joshua told her of Richard Turberville, and his promise to the priest about Ruth Priday, she listened gravely, face intent.

'Of course, she must come here to the Court,' she offered impulsively, 'and I will find occupation for her, at sewing, or as a laundress, maid, or at whatever task she will be best suited. You need have no fears about her safety, or peace of mind, Joshua, you may depend upon it.'

'I am grateful, Rebecca,' he said honestly, 'for Turberville is deeply distressed about the whole affair, and its effect upon her.'

'You say he is kin to those at Ewenny Priory?' Rebecca's voice was puzzled, 'Why then, Joshua, does he not send her there to be cared for, or found work? Would it not be kinder?'

'I believe that he is in love with the girl,' Joshua muttered.

'Indeed? Then what is the obstacle? I confess I do not understand, Joshua. Surely he cannot be ashamed to admit his affection. Is it because of her poverty? Her lowly station? Fear of his family's disapproval?' Rebecca's mind was clearly upon her own rejection in the past.

'No. It is none of those things!' Joshua was swift and emphatic in defence of Turberville. 'He is an extraordinarily gentle and humble man, Rebecca. A gentleman in the true sense, devout, loving and self-sacrificing . . .'

'It seems to me that he is sacrificing her,' said Rebecca tartly.

'No. You misunderstand,' declared Joshua earnestly, unhappy that Rebecca should think badly of someone he admired. 'He really believes that his dedication to God, and the poor, will be lessened if he loves and marries her, for then he must give her too much of that love and care.' As Rebecca made no reply, he continued quickly, 'It is her well-being he has in mind, her happiness and future.' Even in his own ears it sounded weak and unconvincing. 'I fear I do not explain it very well, Rebecca.'

'On the contrary, Joshua, you explain it very well indeed!' she said obliquely. She regarded him carefully. 'He is really in love with her, you believe?'

'I have no doubt of it! I have seen him tend to her, speak her name. There could be no mistake.'

'And she loves him?'

'Certainly,' said Joshua, confused.

'Then she must come here at once,' declared Rebecca, 'for I must do what is necessary to speed her recovery, to make her life happy and fulfilled. Oh, and Richard Turberville's, of course.'

Rebecca smiled with all her old animation and charm, and Joshua was uncommonly grateful that in allowing Turberville to tread the lonely path he had chosen, Rebecca would find diversion and satisfaction of her own.

When Joshua finally took his leave of Rebecca, he did so with the promise that he would soon return, that they might be together when constraint did not lie so heavily between them. He would take her to his parents' farm, he promised, and to see her old friends of the three hamlets, and gave her news of their progress and the warm wishes they bade him deliver. He was scrupulous in giving her Phoebe Butler's remembrance, but made no mention of Bella's death, feeling that it would serve no purpose, save to add to her sadness, and to Elizabeth's too. To his relief, Rebecca enquired only about the babe and his progress, and he was able to reassure with honesty that Dr Burrell considered the child vastly improved. Then, having paid his respects to the grieving Sir Matthew and Dr Peate, he made his way to the stables to claim the mount which Ossie had selected for him from the stables at the Crown, for Joshua's mare had been over-ridden, and he would not add to her discomfort, although she would willingly have carried him.

He paused for a moment beneath the porte-cochere, gazing about him at the well-clipped lawns and shrubberies, and the flower-filled borders, their colours richly burgeoning against the muted greyness of the sheltering stone walls. He must return by the carriageway which led past the lodge where Mrs Crandle and Elizabeth dwelt. From affection and common courtesy, he could not pass it by with no word spoken between them.

As he reached the stables, it was to see, with astonishment, that Elizabeth awaited him there, coming from the shadows of a stall to greet him, her face gravely composed.

'I had not thought to see you here,' he said, 'and would have paused at the lodge, Elizabeth.'

'That is why I have chosen to come, Joshua, to spare both you and my mother embarrassment and hurt.'

Joshua nodded his understanding, boots fidgeting awkwardly upon the stones of the path, hands clenching and unclenching in his distress.

'There is so little to be said, Elizabeth,' he blurted.

'Save that I thank you for coming, Joshua. It could not have been easy.' Her voice was low, controlled. 'I have brought you a letter for Phoebe and Tom Butler at the Crown.'

He looked at her in concern, unsure of what to say, but stretching out his hand tentatively to take it and place it within the pocket of his tiered coat.

'It is but a brief note, an assurance that Roland will take care of all those in his company, the crewmen, like Reuben. We are not yet wed, but it is what he would wish me to do.'

'I do not know if Tom and Phoebe are able to read . . .' Affection for her made him clumsy, unhelpful.

'It makes no matter. Mistress Randall will tell them what it says.'

There had always been a quietness about Elizabeth, a serenity which Joshua found calming and restful. It came, he supposed, from some inner strength, forced upon her, too soon, by circumstance. Elizabeth would need every small part of that strength now.

'You do not doubt that he is safe, that he will return, Joshua.' It was a statement rather than a question. 'Like me, you have no doubts.'

'No.' The word was wrung out of him, but once said, he could not regret it, for it brought Elizabeth peace of mind, he believed. Yet, when he looked into her eyes, he could see that Elizabeth's fear and uncertainty were as great as his own.

'To confess a doubt, Joshua, would be a betrayal,' she said quietly, 'of him and all that has been promised between us. You understand what I am saying?'

The pretty reticule of chestnut silk which so perfectly matched her gown and her warm brown eyes was secured by a cord at her slender waist and she prised it open with her free hand, taking out the small silver model of a ship in full sail which had long ago belonged to Mary Devereaux.

'It was a gift from Roland,' she said, resting it upon her palm, 'first to his sister, then to me, for he promised that while it was safely in my keeping, then he would surely return. You think it superstitious nonsense, perhaps, Joshua?'

'I think it a perfect gift from a man who travels the world and sails the oceans to the woman he loves,' said Joshua truthfully, 'and it expresses a hope that every man cherishes deep in his heart, that he will return to the one person, and the one place, which mean more to him than any other.'

Elizabeth nodded. 'I am glad that you understand, Joshua,' she said, 'for I cannot explain to any other that I hold it as a talisman for Roland's safe return.'

She moved impulsively towards him, reached up and gently kissed his cheek before turning and walking silently away across the wide sweep of lawn. Joshua watched her until she was hidden from view by the curve of the carriageway and the thick dark foliage of the shrubbery, then he set his foot into the stirrup and swung himself into the saddle, feeling an ache of pity and regret as he set his mount along the path to the highway. How long ago it seemed, that first time he had set eyes upon Elizabeth, when she had helped him search her brother Creighton's room, above the stables at Dan-y-Graig House, for the evidence which would brand him inexorably as Mary's killer. Joshua had thought then how gentle and dignified she was, how honest in all her actions. At some other time and place, and in kinder circumstances, he had told himself, he would have sought the warmth of her friendship. And now Elizabeth sought his, and he was unable to bring her any real comfort.

* * *

Elizabeth was seated in the small gazebo alone, not feeling the coldness of the day although she wore no cloak or warm bonnet. Her mind was upon Roland Devereaux and a distant sea in some climate she could but hope would be kind. In her hand was the silver ship, its delicately wrought sails and rigging cutting remorselessly into her clenched palm, as if the physical pain of holding it might serve to deaden that greater pain of anguish and of loss.

She did not know what long-forgotten memories stirred within her mind; some echoes, perhaps, from an ancient time when she had no existence save through others of her kind; a continuation of blood, a stirring of some inherited belief, deep and atavistic, with shadows of atonement and sacrifice.

'Dear God,' she said the words aloud, 'do not let Roland die, I beg You, most humbly. If someone must die, then let it be me, for without him I would be dead in all but flesh.' She felt neither guilt nor shame at the blasphemy, for she knew it to be but the simple truth. She could not know that there had already been expiation, and had she learnt of Bella's death, it could have brought her no deeper sorrow than she already knew, only the saving grace of vicarious, healing tears.

The journey from Southerndown to Newton barely made impression upon Joshua, so physically tired was he from the ravages of his rides to Maudlam and to the Court. His mind, deprived of sleep, grew not sluggish but overactive, his thoughts a restless, swift-changing pattern of colour and shape, unpredictable as the pieces in a child's toy kaleidoscope. He supposed that he must have given the horse he rode instruction, turned her in the right direction, for she bore him safely home. Yet he had no knowledge of doing so, and his only recollection was of hearing the animal's hoofbeats, ringing out clear and lonely as the tocsin, as they crossed the hump-backed dipping bridge crouched over the Ewenny river. Above its curved sides and through its dipping holes he had glimpsed a torn-off tree branch, swirling and eddying in the river's flood, rootless and helpless as he, but it was of Devereaux he thought, and *The Stormy Venturer*, sucked and spewed out in a maelstrom without beginning or end.

He had little heart for meeting Tom Butler and Phoebe, and burdening them with Elizabeth's kindly meant letter, for he felt that each reminder would be to them as the tearing away of a slowly forming scar, an exposure of the flesh beneath, raw and unhealed. With a word of hurried explanation to Ossie, who, seeing his exhaustion, forbore from questioning and simply led the horse away, Joshua slowly mounted the stone steps to Emily's loft. Emily was distressed by the weariness upon the young constable's face, and the air of defeat about him, but, like Ossie, she wisely forbore from questioning, begging him to be seated, and to partake of some refreshment, which he courteously refused, saying that he must be about his business and make report to the justice. Emily would dearly have loved to urge him to rest awhile, but waited instead to learn the purpose of his visit.

'Elizabeth has given me a letter for Tom and Phoebe,' he said without preamble, 'and begs that you will read it to them. I fear that I would stumble over the words.'

'Have no fear, I will take it to them when the moment is opportune.'

Joshua nodded and passed a hand wearily across his eyes, saying, 'Elizabeth will not accept that Roland is dead.'

'Then her letter will be a comfort to Phoebe, for she is

of the same mind about Reuben.' At seeing Joshua's involuntary movement of disquiet, she stilled the words he was about to utter by saying swiftly, 'It is what we all hope, and it is kinder so, for what the mind cannot bear, it rejects in order that a person may survive. Whether it is steadfast faith or self-deceit, it serves the same purpose. How cruel it would be to take away that solace, and how harmful. If Roland and poor Reuben and the crew survive, then those like Elizabeth and Phoebe who refused to acknowledge even the possibility of their deaths will have no cause for regret, or self-recrimination.'

'You speak as if from experience,' said Joshua quietly.

Emily did not answer for a moment, but when she did, her self-composure had not faltered, although two circles of colour showed high in her cheeks, raw as new burns.

'I speak from my experience of Mary's death, and my time in the poorhouse,' she replied, without self-pity, 'and from my knowledge of another whose suffering, and loss, was greater than my own.'

Joshua knew that it was of John Burrell she spoke.

Emily's gentle mouth twisted in wry amusement as she confessed, 'If Littlepage, the workmaster at the poorhouse, could not entirely vanquish all hope within me, then the future can hold no terrors for me. Do you not agree, Joshua?'

Joshua, remembering the quiet dignity of the woman before him when he had told her of Mary Devereaux's violent death, and Emily's composure in the face of Littlepage's studied rudeness and contempt for her, a valueless pauper, was filled with admiration for her spirit, as he had been then.

'I believe, ma'am, that the future must be kind to you, as reparation for the past,' he promised gently.

'People have been kind, sir,' she said, 'as you yourself, in bringing me here. I count myself fortunate in my friends, for there was a time when I had none. Whatever the future may hold, it will be the warmer for such friendship, as Elizabeth and the Butlers will surely find.'

Joshua nodded acceptance of the fact. He hoped that John Burrell would prove such a friend, and one who would grow to appreciate Emily's true worth, whether through pity, need, or caring. It was hard to know where one emotion ended and the other began, for love was all of them.

Chapter Twenty-Four

It was with little enthusiasm that Joshua rode out from the Crown Inn upon his own mare for a meeting with the justice. The grey was absurdly pleased to see him, and Joshua's spirits could not fail to be lifted by the mare's show of affection. It was, he knew, unfeigned, although he had taken her a titbit, a piece of raw carrot, concealed in his clenched palm, and smiled to feel the moistness of her softly enquiring nose and tongue as she sought to nuzzle his fist open that she might retrieve her prize. The night's rest had plainly refreshed and enlivened her, and Joshua would have been grateful for a modicum of the energy and anticipation she displayed at the prospect of their outing.

After leaving Emily, he had walked back to his cottage, stripped himself naked in the concealed yard, and showered upon himself cold water from the well, scrubbing himself with rough flannel to scour away his fatigue. Then, with a light meal of oatcakes and ale, he dressed himself in his uniform, leaving his elegant gentleman's clothing upon his wooden butler, and walked back to the Crown stables. Although the meal he had taken was deliberately light, lest he fall asleep over his victuals, he had abjured the inviting welcome of his bed, reasoning that once settled, he would undoubtedly slumber like a hibernating squirrel until recalled to life.

Leyshon greeted Joshua with warmth when a groom

had led his grey away, and relieved him of his helmet as respectfully as if it were a coronet he offered.

'The justice's gout?' Joshua's voice was deliberately low and muted.

'As little improved, sir, as his temper,' confided Leyshon, straightfaced, 'although I have hopes that the new physician and apothecary will serve him better.'

'He has disdained to send for Dr Mansel or Dr Burrell?' asked Joshua, surprised. 'How so? I thought he was –'

The justice's voice, raw-edged with impatience, interrupted from the library, 'Confound it, Stradling, you are an unconscionable time loitering upon your way! Leyshon's work, as my own, is pressing, if yours is not, sir!'

Leyshon grimaced expressively and discreetly retreated, while Joshua advanced reluctantly.

Robert Knight was sitting in the depths of his wing chair, his engorged toe propped uncomfortably upon its embroidered hassock, a bottle of Madeira upon a galleried wine table at his side, his half-empty glass giving evidence of the work which had so pressingly engaged him. If Joshua's glance strayed involuntarily to the offending glass at the justice's elbow, his host showed not the smallest sign of guilt or irritation at this flagrant discourtesy. To the contrary, he grew surprisingly expansive, saying, 'Be so good as to tug upon the bell pull, Stradling. I am too incommoded to do so.'

When Joshua did as he was bade, Leyshon appeared in swift response, and was instructed, testily, 'Bring another bottle of Canary, there is scarce enough left in this bottle to offer my guest. Stradling and I have much to discuss, and I would not have him silenced or offended by my parsimony.'

Waving Joshua's hesitant protests aside, Robert Knight sent the old manservant upon his errand, his resigned but barely audible sigh and rigid back showing clear disapproval of his master's over-indulgence.

'You recall it is the court hearing tomorrow, Stradling,' he began brusquely, then, sensing Joshua's evident bewilderment, 'come, man! It cannot have slipped your mind that the Fiery Archer comes to justice before me? You will be expected to give evidence.'

Joshua murmured something noncommittal, asking, in turn, 'Will you be wise to attend, sir?'

'Wise?' repeated the justice. 'What has the law to do with wisdom?' Then, glimpsing Joshua's hastily suppressed smile, he corrected himself by declaring abrasively, 'The wisdom of ruining my health must be balanced, as is justice herself, in the scales of service.' He seemed pleased with his impromptu analogy and poured himself a glass of Madeira, apologising that there was no glass for Joshua, as Leyshon reappeared with another bottle upon a tray.

'You will partake of a glass, Stradling?'

Joshua declined the offer gracefully, and Robert Knight appeared well pleased, though whether at his refusal or his good manners was not clear.

'The Fiery Archer is to be charged with what offence, sir?' asked Joshua.

'Assault,' declared the justice implacably, 'fire-raising, vagrancy, the destruction of property, creating a disturbance of the peace, assault upon the person, and, of course, theft – of my personal property!'

Joshua's expression must have betrayed his surprise and disapproval, for the justice said censoriously, 'Such villains cannot be handled with a show of weakness, Stradling, as you should be aware! They must be used as salutary examples to deter others of that kind. Clemency is wasted upon them for they are fools and ingrates all.'

By the justice's expression of acute anguish and uneasy fidgeting, Joshua gathered that his toe throbbed as painfully as that poor wretch the prisoner's hide might well do upon the morrow.

'How will you be transported, sir?' He regretted the words even as they were spoken, aware that transportation, public lashings, burial up to the neck in a hole, or public execution seemed excessive punishment for what were all too often venial and ill-proven offences.

'I shall be transported in my private coach, how else? And you, sir, shall ride with me, since I shall have need of your support, physical and moral.'

'Of course, I shall be privileged to assist.'

'Now,' declared Robert Knight sharply, 'to that other prisoner, he who is guilty of the assault at Maudlam . . . well, he who is charged with the assault,' he amended, recalling his past castigation of Joshua for presuming guilt, 'that circus fellow taken in Abrahams's stead . . .'

'He will be taken to the cells at Pyle by gaol-coach as you requested, sir, with a vestry man as driver and Cavan Doonan as guard.'

'Good! I fancy that any urge to escape justice will be outweighed by the urge to escape the Irishman's fist!'

'Tom Butler usually accompanies the prisoners, sir, but . . .' He broke off awkwardly.

'Yes, I am aware of the circumstances, Stradling. It is a grief and torment to those poor people, as to Miss Crandle.' The justice's florid face was grave, the unusually alert eyes sombre within their fleshy pouches. 'I would not consent to give the child of the young woman who died a coffin Christening. Could not. I know that they are sometimes requested by a dying woman who believes that, otherwise, the child's Christening would be forsworn, and his spiritual good neglected, but that is not so in this case.'

'No,' Joshua agreed warily, unsure where the conversation was leading.

'I find it a barbarous custom, harrowing for all, and with little to commend it, unless unavoidable. In truth, Stradling, I think the association of a Christening over the body of a dying woman, or a corpse, is morbidly repugnant. It speaks of superstition. I believe a Christening is a new birth and beginning, and the child has a need and Christian right to an independent existence; a celebration of joyousness among family and friends, not a macabre expediency.' Robert Knight's plump jowls trembled and his brow was creased in indecision as he looked at Joshua in mute appeal, begging his support.

'I believe that you are right, sir, and I am certain that Tom and Phoebe Butler are aware of your dilemma and agree with your decision. She will not believe that her son is lost to her, and awaits his return. Will you not hold the Christening then?'

'The burial will take place at once,' said the justice, 'for it cannot be delayed. As for the Christening, the child improves, and a delay is not crucial. Yet I believe that Tom Butler, like me, believes that it is better that the child is named soon, and baptised into the church, for the longer the wait until Reuben's return, the harder it will be for Phoebe Butler to bear, and to admit that perhaps he is already dead. You understand? To do so will seem a betrayal of faith, and a finality she will not be able to endure. Oh, I grieve for these people, Stradling. I truly try to reach out to them and help, but unlike Richard Turberville, I am not one of them, and will not be accepted wholeheartedly, with love, and without reservations.'

Joshua said carefully, 'I am sure, sir, that you are deeply respected and admired in all three hamlets.'

'Perhaps, yet I would give all I possess to be accepted as he is.' He smiled wrily. 'Perhaps that is why he is loved, because he actually gave all he possessed, while men such as I merely give lip service.'

Robert Knight and Joshua stared at each other awkwardly, the justice fearing that he had revealed too much of himself, and the constable seeking some way to divert him from embarrassment, for it was plain that no one could deny the truth of his observation.

'About the presentation, sir, to Elwyn Morris for his bravery over the affair of the Dyffryn–Llynfi tramroad?'

'It is to be held on Thursday of next week, Stradling. You will be there, of course, in your official capacity as constable to the three hamlets, as will the port officials, surveyors to the highways, the exciseman, the hayward Cleat, Bevan the relieving officer to the poor, the workhouse manager . . .'

Remembering Morris's unenviable past as a pauper in the poorhouse at Bridgend, and Littlepage's antipathy towards him, indeed his contempt for all those under his 'care', Joshua doubted if the workmaster's presence would raise the tenor of the occasion as much as Morris's righteous indignation.

'I had thought a meal for the principals and guests might be appropriate,' declared the justice, 'since the company has empowered me to spend a not inconsiderable sum upon entertainment, and the purchase of a suitable gift.'

'Who is to make the presentation, sir?' asked Joshua. 'It has been rumoured that the prime minister himself, Mr Disraeli, will do so.'

'Indeed?' Robert Knight's voice was coolly dismissive. 'It is true that he is the largest single shareholder in the new Dyffryn–Llynfi Railway Company, Stradling –

three thousand pounds or so, I believe.' He grunted loudly, and Joshua could not be sure whether it was gout or disdain for the project which occasioned it.

'Surely, increased prosperity for the three hamlets is to be encouraged, sir?'

'Certainly, Stradling, I admire your perspicacity. Indeed, so firmly am I of the opinion that I admit to being a modest shareholder myself. In fact,' he declared with a self-denigrating smile, 'I have been pressed, almost against my will, into serving upon the committee responsible for the management of the undertaking.' There was no doubting his satisfaction.

'I am sure, sir, that your knowledge of the locality and the people, and your . . . business acumen, will make you admirably suited for such responsibility,' declared Joshua, urbanely.

'Quite. Quite,' returned the justice, 'and responsibility for my parishioners and others of the three hamlets is my main reason for acceptance, Stradling, that I may safeguard their interests as well as my own.' He groped in his pocket for the shagreen case which held his eyeglasses, and settled them over his nose and well-fleshed ears, to regard Joshua the better. 'Already plans have been approved for a second dock and an increase in wharves and loading bays, which will mean more work for the able-bodied men of the area and paupers from the workhouse at Bridgend. There is no denying that it is needed, for the iron works and spelter works grow apace, with others being built, and new furnaces at Tondu, also increased quantities of coal from the collieries lately opened upon the line of the tramroad. Yes, life here must change, Stradling, but I would prefer that change to be gradual, for otherwise the destruction of a way of life is poor exchange for prosperity. That is why I cannot wholeheartedly agree with propositions by mere outsiders to build a steam railway, to link with the proposed South Wales Railway, should it ever come to fruition.'

He lifted his glasses, irritably, from his nose, then let them settle again, his protuberant brown eyes earnest and magnified behind the gold-rimmed lenses as he declared, unequivocally, 'No, Mr Disraeli will not be coming, sir. And I cannot pretend that I am entirely sorry, for it would have set too heavy a burden upon us to protect and entertain him. Indeed, my gout would indubitably have marred his stay here at Tythegston Court, for that was what was intended.'

He poured two glasses of Canary, and handed one solemnly to Joshua.

'It seems, Stradling, that affairs of state take precedence over affairs of the nation and its people – the common people!' He sniffed derisively. 'We are the nation, sir, its flesh and backbone! I am a poor alternative to so eminent a gentleman, no doubt, but I am only too eager to deputise for Mr Disraeli, since he evidently does not consider the occasion to be worthy of his patronage. I feel it is my privilege and duty, despite my . . . my troublesome affliction.' He raised his glass gravely to Joshua, although his eyes twinkled mischieviously as he promised, 'There will be games and prizes for the children of the hamlets, but I have most definitely stipulated no circuses, Stradling.'

Joshua smiled, but then asked, with real concern, 'You think it wise, sir, to attend the celebration and be forced to partake extravagantly of food and wine which might aggravate your condition?'

'Fiddlesticks!' replied Robert Knight. 'I have sought the services of a physician from Pyle, since Dr Mansel and Dr Burrell have such rigidly authoritarian views upon the subject, and indeed frequently disagree about its causes and cures. I find it irritating and confusing, and it does no service to my state of health!'

'He is a reliable physician, sir?' asked Joshua innocently.

'Excellent, sir! I cannot commend him too highly. He believes that gout is a disorder of the blood itself, and is inherited, which is why it attacks the upper classes, since the genealogy is purer and the blood more concentrated and refined, as with members of foreign royalty with haemophilia. He most firmly declares that it owes nothing to over-indulgence of food and drink, and it would be valueless to curb my natural appetites, or indeed positively harmful.'

'You are fortunate, sir. How did you chance upon such a paragon?' asked Joshua straightfaced.

'Not without searching,' admitted the justice.

Joshua had barely returned to his cottage after leaving his mare at the Crown, and was tiredly levering off his riding boots, which appeared to have become attached, limpet-like, to his flesh by virtue of long association, when he was disturbed by a peremptory knocking upon the door. Cursing the misfortune which kept him from his bed, which was growing ever more inviting, he stumped awkwardly to the door in the boot which resolutely refused to be dislodged. To his amazement it was one of the justice's grooms who stood there, clutching his horse's reins, the other hand holding a letter bearing Robert Knight's unmistakably florid handwriting. He took it with the barest civility, swiftly breaking the justice's seal, to read:

> Stradling. I have received news of the gravest import. It came to me by the man, Doonan, who has returned from his mission to Pyle, to deliver

the prisoner to the cells. Owing to monumental stupidity and dereliction of duty on the part of the gaolers, which you can be sure will be most strenuously and fully investigated, the wretch who styles himself the 'Fiery Archer' has been allowed to escape. It seems that a man disguising himself most impertinently in a monk's habit was in possession of a dancing bear. It so distracted the gaolers with its confounded antics that they blatantly neglected their duties, leaving their prisoners unattended, against all regulations. As a result of the false monk's deception, and the collusion of some others whose identities are unknown, the prisoner made good his escape. Your presence will therefore not be required at court tomorrow, as planned, in order to give evidence. I have no doubt that you will be as grieved and incensed at this fiasco as I, sir, and will do all that you can to rectify it.

Robert Knight
Priest and Justice

I can help you no further, save to say that when the putative monk's cowl slipped, he was seen to be most hideously scarred. Make of that what you may, sir.

Joshua thanked the messenger, trying desperately to keep a solemn face as he told him that there was no reply, for he would attend the justice to discuss the matter as soon as he was able. Then, when the horseman had ridden away, Joshua's mirth so overcame him that he had to hold on to the walls of the narrow stone stairway as he limped determinedly to bed. He lay upon it, not even attempting to take off his remaining boot, the tears of laughter and weakness running down his cheeks, washing away the pain of the day; the tragedy and the farce; the ineffable weariness. Then he slept.

Young Dafydd Crocutt was returning with Jeremiah Fleet and Charity, the bull terrier, upon the cart track that led to the small and isolated farm at Grove. It was a fine day, and the cob and cart upon which they were seated was a gay and colourful sight, with its painted sides. The jangle of harness and the clip-clop of the sturdy little pony's hooves were quite soporific upon the springtime air, and the sounds of birdsong and the rustling and stirring of spring were all about them. It had been a good day for fishing and Dafydd was richer by a lobster and a crab which he had caught for himself, and a fine pouting, a present from Jeremiah. The boy was sated too with spice cakes and shot, that delectable mixture of crumbled oatcakes and buttermilk which Sophie Fleet had pressed upon him, brooking no refusal, although, to be fair, he had made none. Sophie was fond of the boy, and since Illtyd, her son, was grown in years, and often absent upon his work as hayward, Jeremiah claimed, without rancour, that she was apt to spoil the child.

'Cosset, yes. Spoil, no,' Sophie had disclaimed with spirit. 'He is a kind, intelligent and good-natured boy, Jeremiah, and it would be impossible to make him otherwise, for there is not a mean bone in his body.'

'Or a lazy one,' agreed Jeremiah, pleased that she had taken so kindly to the lad. 'He works upon that impoverished earth with the fierceness of a grown man, for, since his father's death, there is none but the boy and James Ploughman to tend it.' Jeremiah was silent, thinking of the horror of Jem Crocutt's death as he was murdered by the wrecker, brutally skewered to a cross beam in the great barn by the tines of his own hayfork . . . and of the child's discovery of his death.

'No, my love,' said Jeremiah, putting an affectionate arm about Sophie's pretty waist, and dropping a kiss upon the nape of her neck beneath the fall of her dark hair. 'You do not spoil him, any more than you spoil me, or Illtyd, or Charity there.' He smiled at her pretended indignation, kissing her again, declaring, 'And if you treat him with kindness, it is only what he deserves, for his life is hard, and he is already breadwinner to that poor widow and her fatherless brood. When you are but nine years old, it is sometimes hard to be a man.'

'Then, my dear,' said Sophie gently, but with perfect truthfulness, 'he can have no better example than you. You are an excellent man in every particular, and he would do well to emulate you. I thank God every day for the privilege of being wed to you, and for your loving goodness.'

Jeremiah was so moved and pleased by her declaration that, for a moment, he was unable to speak, for his throat muscles were gripped with hurt, as if they were being squeezed hard, and there was a curious pricking behind his eyes.

'I fear, my love,' he said at last, his voice embarrassed, 'that all your geese are swans, for I am the most ordinary man alive, with neither skills nor scholarship to commend me. I am but a simple fisherman, no more.'

'No more?' demanded Sophie briskly. 'But Jeremiah, it is the finest occupation upon God's earth. There is none more blessed or better.' She searched her memory for some proof of her claim. 'Why, my dear, did not Christ Himself choose such men to follow Him?' she asked triumphantly. 'The salt of the earth and sea, men to be trusted and admired. I daresay He would have been proud to pick upon you.'

Jeremiah rose and, with the dog at his heels, smiled and went out, without a word, to make ready the cob and cart. Perhaps, he thought with satisfaction, as he climbed aboard, every poor goose long past its prime has it in him to blossom into a swan when seen through the eyes of love.

Jeremiah was dwelling upon the remembrance of it now with pleasure, and thinking how blessed he had been in gaining Sophie for a wife and Illtyd for a son, when a small subdued gulp from Dafydd from the floor of the cart, and the disorderly nail-scrabbling of the dog in its rush to comfort the boy, alerted him.

'Dafydd?' His voice was concerned as he turned his head, easing the pony into a slower pace. 'What ails you, lad? Are you sick? Too many spice cakes, I'll be bound.'

The abject misery upon Dafydd's face chilled him, and he brought the cob and cart to a halt. The boy was now lying face down upon the wooden boards, the bull terrier snuffling and slobbering at his exposed neck, frantic in its efforts to rouse him, or bring him cheer.

'Dafydd,' said Jeremiah tentatively, descending from his perch and, with the reins clutched awkwardly in his hands, going to stand at the side of the cart beside the weeping child. 'Come, my boy, there is nothing on God's earth so terrible that it cannot be put to rights.' His hand hovered above the boy's shuddering back, then dropped to his side. 'Perhaps you had best tell me,' he said with careful lightness, 'before your lobster and crab revive in all those salt tears and are swept out to sea again, and Charity, the cob and cart, and me with them.'

A gulp and dying away of the anguish followed as Dafydd, smiling shamefacedly, wiped away the traces of tears from his cheeks with his clenched knuckles.

'Well?' Jeremiah asked briskly, although his every impulse was to gather the boy to him and soothe his hurt. 'What slight, or duty forgot, or undone, has brought such an end to our day?'

'I do not want to go home, Mr Fleet, sir.'

'Not go home?' Jeremiah was astounded. 'Why, you love the farm, and the animals, and your mother and kin,' he said, vexed. 'I swear, I do not understand you.'

Dafydd's mouth trembled, the wide dark eyes grieved at his idol's condemnation, and Jeremiah thought with pain that perhaps it was the memory of his father's brutal death which so haunted his mind that he could not bear to relive the scene, in entering the barn.

Ashamed of his harshness and lack of understanding, Jeremiah asked quietly, 'Is it your father you mourn for, my boy? Are you missing him, but cannot weep before your mother and the infants? Is that it?'

'No, sir. It is not that, for I can weep unheard at night, when in my bed in the inglenook aside the fire, or in the fields.'

Jeremiah knew, without doubt, that it was from harsh experience that Dafydd spoke.

'Is the work upon the farm too demanding, then? Are you unable to do all that is required of you? Do not be afraid to confess it.'

'No, sir.' Dafydd's face was bleak. 'There is James Ploughman to help. He is kindness itself to my mother and the babes, and does the work of two men without bidding, or complaint. He has never a harsh word for me, or our few remaining beasts. He will turn his hand to house or field, sir, and will work until he drops for the few shillings we can pay him.' Even as he spoke, his face crumpled with anguish; Jeremiah knew that here, somewhere, the fear lay.

'Yes, James Ploughman is an honest man,' he said, 'respected and liked by all, despite his poverty and misfortune. He was a good friend to your father, my lad, and will be a good friend to you.'

'I fear he is thinking of leaving, sir,' Dafydd blurted, 'and soon.'

'He has said so? Mentioned why?' Jeremiah asked in concern. 'I cannot see reason for it, for he is not afraid of hard work, and built his own small hut in a night and a day, labouring unceasingly that he might claim it and the poor land upon which it stands as his own. It is all he has, and you the nearest kin to family.' He shook his head, perplexed.

'He does not visit us now, within the house,' Dafydd's voice was low, troubled, 'and has not spoken to my mother for many weeks. If he should bring a hare or pigeon, it is left upon the doorstep, sir, with never a word, and the little ones fret, and ask for him, for he carved them small playthings, and brought sweetmeats from the market at times. Although, it is not for that that they miss him,' he said defensively, 'it is for himself.'

Jeremiah laid a reassuring hand upon Dafydd's arm. 'You would have me speak with him? Find out the truth of it?'

'No, sir. I beg that you will not.' Dafydd's voice was firm, his self-possession restored. 'It is a kindness, and I thank you for it. But such questions are for the man of the house to set, Mr Fleet, sir, and must be resolved between those involved, lest they bring anger or hurt.'

'That is true,' said Jeremiah gravely, climbing back on to the cart, 'and a mark of your good sense and maturity. Now I shall drive you home, for you are resolved in your mind, and will have no further reservations about returning.'

Dafydd put an arm about Charity who was regarding him from slit, pink-rimmed eyes, blunt head cocked enquiringly. Then, reassured, it thumped its whip of a tail upon the cart floor, scattering lobster pots and Dafydd's treasured catch, so that the boy protested, laughing, and setting the fish astraight.

'If you will set me down at the farm gate, sir,' said Dafydd politely, 'I shall be obliged, as I am for all the pleasures of the day, and your kindness.'

Jeremiah looked at him, but said nothing.

'Elwyn Morris is within the house with my mother, sir,' said Dafydd, 'and Haulwen. He comes to make arrangements for the presentation. He has asked that she stand beside him as his guest, and we are to go, too. My mother is firm about it. She will brook no argument.'

'It will be a splendid occasion,' said Jeremiah carefully, as he studied Dafydd's set, mutinous face.

'Haulwen should stand beside her father,' declared Dafydd, 'and she alone. We are not kin, sir,' his chin lifted stubbornly, 'nor like to be. My mother should stand beside me, and proudly, for I am the head of the family now. It is a woman's place to stand behind her husband or nearest kin. 'Tis fitting. Were my father alive, sir, it would be beside him she would stand, and with pride, for he was a good man, and should not so easily be forgot.'

As the cart halted at the farm gate upon the stony track, Dafydd struggled to take his lobster and crab and the fine pouting in his grasp, then set them reluctantly down again upon the floor of the cart, saying, 'I would ask you to give them to Mrs Butler at the Crown, sir, if you will. They would bring her some comfort perhaps, and I do not wish them to be discussed and admired by others, or eaten by them.'

Jeremiah nodded, trying to hide a smile, and yet his heart was filled with pity.

'A kind thought, Dafydd, and one which will be appreciated by Mrs Butler, I am sure.'

Dafydd's feet shifted in the wooden clogs which had been a gift from Joshua, and so prized that they were worn only upon special outings, such as today's.

'You are welcome to share a meal with us, sir. It is not through rudeness that I did not press you to stay, for you are always a welcome visitor to my house, as I to yours.' His eyes met Jeremiah's in embarrassment, pleading, begging him silently to reject the invitation.

'No,' said Jeremiah with understanding, 'I beg that this once you will excuse me, for already it grows late, and I must return to set my night lines before dark.'

Dafydd nodded his gratitude and steadied himself upon the cart edge to hug the bull terrier, which licked his face voraciously, loose jowls aslobber.

'I will deliver your fish to the Crown,' said Jeremiah.

Wiping his mouth, Dafydd turned away, then, opening the gate, walked into the yard, wooden soles striking upon the cobbles, head bent.

'It was the biggest crab I ever caught . . .'

'There will be other crabs, other days,' Jeremiah called after him, but he did not answer.

Chapter Twenty-Five

James Ploughman, in the poor hovel that housed and sheltered him, looked about him dispiritedly. What had seemed so secure and admirable when he had laboured so hard to build it between the hours of sunset and sunrise, as decreed, he now saw for what it was, a crude hut and nothing more. Its rough stone walls and turf roof were little better than those which housed the beasts upon the farms; even the farrowing sows and their litters fared no worse, for their value was higher than a pauper dispossessed. His gaze took in the floor of compacted earth, the bare stone walls sprouting wind-blown grass and ochre lichen, the crude furniture of rough, unfinished wood. Without lay the small vegetable plot he had wrested from the stony soil, its boundaries, by custom, the distance he had been able to throw his axe to the north, south, east and west, that he might claim it for his own.

He smiled wistfully, amused against his will; 'morning surprises' such one-day dwellings were sometimes called, perhaps because it was a surprise that they survived the first gale, or, indeed, that any man was sore-pressed enough to live in one, for it must be done secretly in some God-forsaken spot, where none would wander by choice.

He was a fool to choose this isolated place, and more of a fool to believe that he could take Jem Crocutt's place, either upon the farm or in his wife's heart. There was no denying that he had worked hard and with good grace to save the farm and its bereaved family from ruin, but he had done so from affection, and not the hope of gain. Eira was a beautiful woman, there was no doubting it, for there was a warmth and sweetness about her, fresh as springtime blossom upon a bough, and he, James Ploughman, as rough and unprepossessing as the house he had built, and with as little appeal for any woman. No, he had lost the little sense the good Lord had given him in thinking that one day she might see his worth. Worth? He was naught but a worthless pauper, and would best take to the road and be upon his way. There were no possessions or ties to hinder him, save those he yearned for and could never hope to claim. It was clear that Elwyn Morris was to fill Jem Crocutt's vacant chair. He was a man of courage, much acclaimed by all. 'Twas no wonder he was welcomed at the farm, and treated as a man of substance, a guest to be deferred to and respected. His bravery had earned him a company presentation and work for which he was well fitted, for he could read and write, and speak to others who had been schooled as an equal and better. There was no doubting that he would make an excellent husband in every way. His wife and family would be looked up to and admired, and all their needs provided.

But what of James Ploughman's needs? he thought wrily. Was not he, too, a man? A human being, of flesh and blood? Had he not given all that was within his gift, freely and with joy, to Eira Crocutt and her children? He had slaved from dawn to dusk in the foulest of weathers, making, mending, and tending the soil and the beasts, taking upon himself the meanest and most physically degrading of tasks that the lad, Dafydd, might be spared? Yet it had availed him nothing. He was truly sorry for the boy, for in addition to the horror of his father's death, he was forced to relinquish his childhood and take upon himself a man's harsh burdens, when scarcely more than a child himself. James Ploughman sighed. What kind of a world was it where a man was of less worth than the animals he tended? Where a woman could be sold in the market place by her husband like a beast of the field, harangued, and held up to ridicule before all? Where children were sold into every sort of vileness and persecution by unscrupulous men? From the meagre pittance that he earned at his pauper's labours, had he not rescued that poor, broken-down and winded carriage horse from its owner, so incensed at his violence to an animal, near blind? Yet, who had raised a finger to help? He remembered no home, no word of affection through all his childhood days, farmed out from earliest memory to one and another, beaten or ignored, hungry enough sometimes to share the animals' food, grateful even for shelter. Yet there was kindness, too, and in unexpected places, for Ossie had taken his poor mare into the Crown stables, when she was no more fitted for work, and he could no longer earn the few pence needed to feed her. Well, at least the mare would notice he had left, for he visited her whenever he might walk to Newton upon some errand. She was better housed and tended than in all of her life before.

No, there was none on earth to shed a tear, even if he should die upon the morrow. A poor epitaph, and there would be none upon a pauper's grave. He would be as unremarked in death as in life. And even should he live, the future, wherever it lay, promised to be as barren as the past.

With a shrug and a smile which did not quite reach his eyes, James Ploughman roused himself from his introspection and went out to secure the animals and see to their needs.

Dafydd, within the farmhouse, knew that his curt replies to Elwyn Morris's questions about the day spent upon the shore with Jeremiah Fleet did not go unremarked. The absence of a catch of fish meant that he had to endure Haulwen's mocking taunts and her father's commiseration and, worse, his sympathetic babbling about the state of the tide and weather.

'Such things are beyond our control,' Elwyn Morris had rebuked his daughter, 'and no reflection upon a fisherman's prowess. Is that not so, Dafydd?'

And Dafydd, irritated and rawly shamed, had been forced, from politeness, to agree.

He knew that his whole manner had been discourteous and his conversation brusque to the point of rudeness, yet he could not help himself. He was aware of his mother's puzzlement, and then annoyance, for she scarcely spoke to him directly, and then only to bid him see that their guests' needs were filled.

Dafydd could eat little, and what he did manage stuck fast in his throat, as if there was some swelling or growth which impeded his swallowing. It was a pity, because his mother had taken much care and time over the meal, making bakestone cakes, and flat bread with honey, to which Haulwen, his sister Marged, and the babes did full justice. Perhaps it was because he had eaten so well at Mistress Fleet's table, he thought, that he lacked an appetite. Yet he could not honestly think it so. Even the long living room with its smoke-darkened beams, from which hung flitches of yellow-crusted salted bacon, pearly and pink within, and the bright fire in the huge inglenook grate gave him no pleasure, nor even the thought that his box bed beside it would be warm and comforting in the darkness to come.

At first Elwyn Morris persevered in his attempts to win the boy's interest, talking of the sailing ships of the Port and their strange exotic cargoes, and of his work upon the horse-drawn tramroad which, he promised, Dafydd should inspect upon the day of the presentation, for he would be 'my special guest'. As Dafydd's replies grew ever less enthusiastic and more laconic, Elwyn Morris's attempts to draw him into the conversation faltered, and finally died. Eira Crocutt's expression grew gradually more tense, her lips more compressed, and when Elwyn Morris and Haulwen arose, earlier than expected, to depart, for the silence and atmosphere had grown embarrassingly awkward, she said coldly, 'Dafydd, you will harness Mr Morris's donkey and cart, and bring it to the door.'

'No, ma'am.' The refusal hung heavily between them. 'I regret that there is work to be done upon the farm; it cannot wait. I am the farmer here, the breadwinner,' he said the words distinctly, and to Elwyn Morris, so that there should be no mistaking their meaning, 'and I must be about my duties, as my father would.'

Without another word he opened the door to the yard. Even as he walked, he knew that had his father been present, he would have taken him without and chastised him soundly for such discourtesy, reducing him to shamefaced tears and penitence that he had grieved him so, and yet he would not have beaten him, for he had never taken a stick to him at any time.

Tears pricked Dafydd's eyes, but he blinked them back, daring them to fall, and set about his work with less joy than usual, for his small victory brought him no pleasure.

When he returned, staying out longer than was needed for his tasks, Marged and the smaller children were already abed, and Elwyn Morris and Haulwen gone. His mother turned from the fire where she had been bending low, her face flushed with heat or anger, her eyes reddened.

'You humiliated me before a good man!' she rounded upon him furiously.

'No, ma'am,' he said stubbornly, 'I did what needed to be done.'

'You will apologise to him the next time he visits.' It was a command.

'No, ma'am.' His mouth was as firm as her own. 'I recollect my father's . . .' his voice stumbled and slurred over the word, 'death, and take upon me his responsibilities.'

'Damn you!' she cried, goaded beyond all restraint. 'Do you think I forget? Are you all not a constant reminder? A measure of what I must suffer and endure?'

'I am sorry, ma'am, that we are a burden to you,' his voice cracked childishly, 'but we are kin, we belong. He, Elwyn Morris, and Haulwen are nothing! We have no need of them here.'

'Need? Need! What do you know of a woman's needs? Of anything? You are but a child.' Her hands were clenched in helpless fury.

'I am almost a man –' Before the words were said, a swift blow to his cheek sent him reeling awkwardly, to steady himself upon the great beam above the fire, for otherwise he would have fallen into the flames.

Eira Crocutt looked at him helplessly, eyes stricken, seeing in the firelight the livid red weal across his cheek, and stretched out a hand to him, but he turned away.

'If you have no more need of me, ma'am, I beg that you will retire, that I may go to my bed at the fireside,' his voice came back, muffled but resolute, 'for I am almost a man, and should be treated with that much respect.'

Eira Crocutt reached for the cruse oil lamp upon the dresser, her tears flowing remorselessly and dropping from her mouth and chin, so that all she saw was a rainbow of coloured light as she made her way up the stairway and to her room.

If the prospect of Elwyn Morris's presentation, and the frolics and entertainment to follow, were not greeted with the usual exuberant anticipation by the folk of the three hamlets, it in no way reflected upon Morris's personal standing, or their respect for his bravery. He was greatly admired by all the cottagers, who thought there was none more worthy of recognition and reward. They were as any united family, loyal in adversity, happy in shared fortune, involved in any grief. Their grief was for Tom and Phoebe at the Crown, the loss of Reuben and Captain Devereaux, and Bella's death. Indeed, the tragedy set such a pall upon them that there was little heart for merry-making, save with the children who did not understand. Even the escape of the Fiery Archer, which would normally have been a source of much hilarity and dry humour, was almost unremarked.

Bella's funeral was the largest and best attended of any within living memory, for even the lowliest had sacrificed an hour from their labours, and a few coppers of their frugal earnings to 'pay their last respects'. Indeed, there was not an employer in all the three hamlets, however avaricious, or any bully of a master, who would have dared forbid it, for the wrath of all would have been turned upon him, and his position made untenable.

It was but a walk across the village green to the graveside from the Crown, and no funeral hearse was needed, although the rector had willingly offered his own fine carriage with his matched horses and their nodding funeral plumes, should Tom Butler so wish.

Tom Butler had thanked him gravely, declaring, 'I know, sir, 'tis kindly meant, and we are grateful, but Bella was a simple working girl, and such trappings, while being fitting for gentlefolk, would have fazed her sorely. I mean no disrespect, sir, and I hope you will take none. We will bear her coffin upon our shoulders, for it is what she would have wished. She was a slight delicate thing at the end, sir, and it will be no great burden . . . saving our loss, and none can lighten that.'

Robert Knight had replied awkwardly, for he was moved by Butler's quiet honesty. 'You will see, by my clumsiness, that I am painfully indisposed, lame. I would not wish to make the funeral . . . to render the service less dignified than it deserves. If you would prefer that I ask another priest, the young curate, Mr Turberville, perhaps, whom you know and respect?'

'No, sir.' Butler's reply was firm. 'You are our own, one of us. How can any man's affliction render him less dignified? There is little enough dignity in death itself, and we must believe that what lies ahead for Bella will be recompense for that. As for respecting a priest, 'tis of no great matter. He must be respected for what is God's nature, and what is his own. You are respected, sir, by all your parishioners, on both counts. I would have you take the service, if you will.'

Robert Knight had simply nodded, and clasped Tom Butler's shoulder, for, despite his clever way with words, there was nothing to be said.

'I will have no sin-eater, sir,' Tom Butler promised, 'to eat bread and drink beer over Bella's coffin, and take away her sins for payment. 'Tis barbarous and unchristian, and besides, Bella had no sins, although I know 'tis said we are all born into sin, and you could argue the matter, since you are a scholar bred.'

Robert Knight shook his head.

'I will go and arrange the vigil now,' Tom Butler said, 'for there are those who would wish to sit overnight with the coffin, from respect, for Bella was an honest girl, and much admired. I believe there will be almost too many anxious to do so, but each must have his turn, however brief. None must be belittled or hurt by rejection.'

'That is true,' agreed Robert Knight, as he was helped, limping awkwardly, into his carriage.

As the coach moved away with a noisy creaking and a jangling of harness and hoof, he was as unmindful of his surroundings as of the jarring of wheels in the cart ruts, or the pain of his throbbing limb. He heard only Tom Butler's earnest words, 'None must be belittled or hurt by rejection.'

Was this, then, the secret that he had so long struggled to comprehend? The message that Richard Turberville taught, and that Christ Himself had preached? Was all that analysing, probing, and questioning of other men's ideas and rhetoric mere pedantry? Nothing but a superfoetation of discarded shell, pretty as a coral reef, yet as empty and dangerously useless? No, it would not do to think of that, for it would invalidate all the work of the scholars, saints, and devout and holy men throughout the ages. No, it could not be so artless and simple, else why would God have given men brains to reason and reject? The throbbing in his head grew unbearable, deadening all thought, and with it came a resurgence of the pain and throbbing in his swollen limb. At least he was sure of one thing. It was not true that pain honed and sharpened the intellect. It numbed the senses. He smiled, drily, as he reflected, 'Yet not as pleasantly as a glass or two of the best Canary wine.'

If Bella's youthful death grieved the minds and hearts of all in the parish, from Robert Knight to the humblest of paupers, they did not forget the wider tragedy of the loss of *The Stormy Venturer*. They were fisherfolk, sailors, and farmers, whose lives were bounded and shaped by the sea as surely as the land itself. If it brought them trade and prosperity, it also brought them hardship and death, for there was not a family in the three hamlets which had not known the loss of a husband, father or son through its depredations. They were dependent upon it for their livelihoods, but could not love it. Like a rough taskmaster, they gave it servitude, and even a grudging respect, yet they were ever mindful of its unpredictable rages, the sudden violence of its nature. Its one redeeming virtue was its impartiality. It was devoid of all pettiness and meanness of spirit. Like the wrath of God, its vengeance was universal and desolate. None could escape it.

While all the villagers sincerely mourned Reuben, and the horror that had befallen his family, they did not forget Captain Devereaux. Although he had come to Newton but lately, to make his home at the Crown, his warmth and gentleness of nature had endeared him to all. He was a gentleman in every particular, for he treated high-born and low with the same respect, counting them all equal. Nor had he let the tragic murder of his sister, Mary, embitter him, or make him suspicious of the cottagers' actions or intent, but thanking them most gratefully that they set flowers upon her grave in his absence, and tended it as if she were one of their own.

Joshua's burden was heavy, for he missed Devereaux sorely as a friend, and carried the added weight of Elizabeth's grief and the sorrow of all those at Southerndown Court. Emily Randall wept, too, often and long, for she had grown to admire him, and then to love him dearly, as if he were her son. He was her sole remaining link with Mary, whom she had taught and cherished, and she could not believe that all was so cruelly and abruptly ended. Yet, it was Illtyd who felt Roland Devereaux's absence most keenly. His friendship with the master of *The Stormy Venturer* had given him an insight into a new world beyond the limits of the crippling affliction of his deformity which had imprisoned him for so long. His life as hayward had immeasurably increased his horizons and confidence, and gave him a reassurance of his own worth, yet he valued his friendship with Captain Devereaux even more. It was born of natural affection, asking and demanding nothing, and taking no account of Illtyd's infirmity, or Roland Devereaux's status as master of a sailing ship. There was neither pity nor envy between them, simply that tie of friendship which could be lessened, tightened or broken at will. Yet the break had not been at will, but arbitrary and cruelly abrupt. Illtyd's meticulously inscribed letters, and the journal which Devereaux had been keeping for him, and the 'treasure chest' of spices, fabrics and evocative mementoes of his voyages would cease to be – as Devereaux himself.

Illtyd could not bear the thought of such a loss to his life, yet his only tears had been for Elizabeth when he was alone upon his piebald and scouring the windswept remoteness of Stormy Downs. Elizabeth had been friend and companion to him in those darkly remembered days when, beaten near to death by the sheep stealers, she had sat by his bedside, willing him to life. If she could but set the same passionate resolve to Devereaux's life, Illtyd thought, then surely his friend must survive. He prayed that it should be so, but, like Elizabeth, without demur or reservations he would have given his life to save another's.

It was a measure of the hayward's loyalty and clear-sightedness that he had never grudged Devereaux his adventure; and neither his physical strength, nor Elizabeth's love, although painfully aware of his own imperfection. It would never have entered his thoughts.

Illtyd's immediate urge had been to go to Elizabeth at Southerndown Court, and to bring her the friendship and comfort she had given to him. Yet he knew he must not, for it would tell her, too clearly, that he felt Devereaux to be dead. He would simply write her a letter to raise her spirits and remind her of her special place in his thoughts and prayers. It would be a hard task. Not the words, for they were already crowding into his mind, but the writing of it. He had but lately learnt to form the letters, and his penmanship was slow and painstaking, and his hands clumsy. He would endeavour to keep the page clean and free from ink stains and blots, for the quill was apt to grate and spatter the words. Nor would it serve him, or Elizabeth, should she trace upon it the washings of his intractable and uselessly falling tears.

Elizabeth Crandle had returned from a visit to her father at the private asylum where Sir Matthew had found him refuge, after Hugo Crandle's escape on to the moors from the foetid, vermin-infested gaol where he had been incarcerated. Elizabeth had never failed to visit him, although it is doubtful whether he ever knew she came, or even recognised her, for his mind had mercifully blotted out all remembrance of the past: of his crime, and his son's savage death-leap from the cliffs at Dunraven. Elizabeth might well have ceased her journeying to the place where he was now immured, for, despite the beauty of its gardens and surroundings, and the care of the medical and custodial staff, it was a sad, depressing place. All detained there were pitifully disordered in mind, and either violently aggressive, unpredictable, or sadly passive as her father now was; an empty husk without response or emotion, feeling no joy, pain, or the anguish of those who remembered them as once they were. Yet it was a small comfort to her that he at least suffered no more. The guilt and retribution for his crimes, and Creighton's death, were Elizabeth's to bear, and she bore them as all else, even the burden of Roland Devereaux's absence, for she would not acknowledge his loss.

Her father, led by his attendant as meekly as an obedient child, had stared at her without curiosity, eyes vacant, as she had pressed the small comforts she had brought him into his unreceptive arms. She sat with him in his own small room, furnished with the familiar ornaments and books which were all that she had saved when she and her mother had been dispossessed of all else. Now they stirred her to pity and regret for the past, and a father who was as lost to her in mind as Creighton and Mary Devereaux in flesh. She sat there silently holding his large, unresponsive hand, feeling his fingers lie limp within her own. Then, without warning, his fingers had tightened on hers, his grip not menacing but filled with comfort, as of old in all her childhood fears and hurts.

'My dear,' his voice was compassionate, 'I cannot bear to see the sadness upon your face, for you are all I love upon this earth. I beg you, do not grieve, for it breaks my heart, Elizabeth, my sweet child, and all my joy.' His tears fell, harsh and cleansing, bathing his cheeks, and that pitifully misshapen flesh of his nose and lips, rendering him uglier and more absurd, so that Elizabeth's tears mingled with his own. Then, as suddenly, his expression grew empty again, his eyes unseeing, as though the mask which protected him had been mercifully restored.

At a sign from his watchful keeper, Elizabeth rose to her feet and saw her father being led away, docile as a tired child, his only thought to ease his weariness in sleep.

At Southerndown Court, she was assisted from the

carriage, but did not make her way into the house. She was unable to face her mother's carefree prattling, or the kindness of Sir Matthew and Rebecca, for she feared that it would cripple her brave resolve and make her weep. She had need to be alone.

She went at once, and instinctively, to the small cottage of the old coachman, Edwards, and begged a favour of him, that he might convey her to the quiet shore beyond the dunes at Newton, for it was to Newton that he had taken her when she and Captain Devereaux had first met. Edwards showed no surprise, and did not demur, despite his age and the gunshot wound that had forced his retirement from Sir Matthew's service. The flesh of his leg was slow to heal, and his movements awkward and crippled, so that he could not, with comfort, sit upon the box. Yet his admiration and affection for Miss Elizabeth were so profound that he felt it a rare honour to accompany her.

'You are sure, Edwards, that it will not cause you pain, discommode you?'

'My only pain, Mistress, would be if you were minded to ask another,' he said hoarsely.

Elizabeth nodded, and touched his bent shoulder in acknowledgement as Edwards resolutely placed his long-forsaken tricorne upon his straggling grey locks, and limped towards the coach house.

Illtyd had abandoned his watch on the cottagers' flocks at Stormy Downs, and had ridden hard across the common lands that edged the rocky shore at the far end of the parish, towards Sker. He was scarcely aware of the bushes of gorse, heavy with sulphurous blossom, or the salt-washed turf, cropped by sheep and westerly gales into a springy greenness beneath the pony's hooves. Its surface was misted with creeping thyme, violets and slender harebells, while the pitted grey outcrops of stone beyond gave unexpected succour to the plump cushions of sea-pinks and fleshy-leaved samphire which defied its barren lack of hospitality.

Illtyd's checking of the flocks was perfunctory, and without heart, although it is certain that he would have protected them fiercely from attack by marauders or predatory bird or beast. Yet it was without his usual enthusiasm and lightness of spirit that he turned the piebald towards the wasteland of Pickett's Lease and the Burrows, to see if any ewes were lambing upon the plains within the dunes, or had gone astray.

Elizabeth, walking at the sea's edge, felt the fierce tug of the west wind upon her shawl and the hem of her gown, and let loose her bonnet strings. The wind, smelling of salt and iodine and the wetness of sand, burned in her nostrils, and disordered her dark hair, but she felt it not as a menace but a friend, its presence spiriting away the confusion within her. The lines of the poem Rebecca had read for Dr Peate came to her now, poignant and clear, their rhythm soft and insistent as the ebb and flow of the wavelets at her feet:

My true love hath my heart and I have his
He loves my heart, for once it was his own
My heart was wounded with his wounded heart . . .

Is it his wound I feel so deeply, or my own? Elizabeth asked herself impassionedly. If Roland were dead, would I not know it and feel it in my blood and being? Would I not feel the languor and numbness of death instead of this cruelly lacerating hurt, for I, too, would be nothing, feel nothing. Was this the same tide that lapped that other distant shore, and if she bent and set her hand into its coldness, would it not reach out to him and touch him with love, wherever he had strayed? Yet not, she prayed silently, beneath these dark, grey waters, silent and deep, where sunlight and human love could never reach.

The harsh screaming of a gull overhead, anguished and forlorn, found an echo in her soul, and she felt as if he cried aloud for all who wept, and suffered loss; the grieving cry of all mankind.

It was thus that Illtyd saw her as he breasted the dune upon his pony, Faith, and halted, unseen. Elizabeth's dark hair streamed in the wind from the sea, and every line of her body was etched with unbearable hurt. He could not, at first, bring himself to intrude upon such a private and terrible rawness of feeling, nor could he turn away from her need. With a swift pressure upon the reins, he urged the pony forward to stand beside her.

When Elizabeth turned to face him, he said gently, 'I came here but by chance, Elizabeth, and if you wish it, I will go away.'

'No, not by chance, but by God's good grace,' returned Elizabeth, reaching out a hand to take his. 'Stay, I beg of you, for I have need of a friend, and I have no dearer friend than you, Illtyd.'

Illtyd nodded, saying with a wry smile as he looked down at her from the saddle upon the little piebald, 'For the first time, we are upon a level, Elizabeth. You do not look down upon me.'

She knew there was hurt as well as humour in his lightly said words. 'No one could look upon you with anything but affection, and admiration for your courage.' There was no doubting Elizabeth's sincerity. 'You are the bravest man I know, and the most loyal and understanding friend. I would have none other beside me at this moment.'

Illtyd's intelligent and expressive eyes were warm with

gratitude as he dismounted awkwardly to stand beside her, his ungainly head twisting upon the wry neck as he said, 'Perhaps the harshness of the past has not been wasted, then, for we have both known disappointment and the censure and cruelty of others.' He smiled briefly. 'Perhaps ours is an affinity of outcasts, Elizabeth.'

She put out a companionable hand to touch the ugly curve of bone at his spine, as he continued earnestly, 'Yet I cannot wholly regret the . . . imperfection, being as God made me, if it brings me the understanding to be of comfort.'

Elizabeth turned aside, that he might not see the tears scalding her eyes, for she had not cried throughout Devereaux's long absence.

'I should hate the sea!' she exclaimed passionately. 'And yet I cannot, for all its wildness and raging, for I see it, now, through Roland's eyes, for he loves it so, its moods and savagery, its beauty and calmness. It is a woman, he says, tempestuous, unpredictable, sometimes coming in hatred, sometimes in love, but never stale nor cloying. I shall have a fierce and jealous mistress always as a threat, Illtyd, do you not think?'

'I do not think, Elizabeth, that you will have anything to fear.'

She read into the words Illtyd's certainty of Devereaux's safe return, and was gladdened by it.

'Before you came, there was a seagull crying. Its voice was so sad and forlorn, as if all hope was gone.'

'It is the cry which heartens all those upon the sea,' said Illtyd, 'wherever they are bound, for it tells them that land is near, and home – those they love.'

Elizabeth watched him as he put a foot awkwardly into the stirrup and swung himself into the saddle. No more was said between them as he raised a hand in salute and rode back the long way he had come.

Chapter Twenty-Six

Bella's funeral was upon a morn so bright and clear that the air itself seemed to sparkle crisply, as if with crystals of hoar frost, although the day was warm, lacking even the faintest breeze to ruffle the grass or the newly leafing trees. The sky was a clean washed blue, the few small feathers of cloud thinning early into wisps of vapour, and disappearing altogether.

Phoebe and Tom Butler had arisen before dawn after a night filled with sorrowful regret for things done or left undone, as is the burden of those who mourn, and each dreaded the day which lay ahead. Even the babe whom they loved so dearly could not distract them from their grief, for he only served to remind them of Bella and Reuben's happiness, and the death of that bright promise which heralded his birth.

At the timid, then more forceful knocking upon the door of the Crown, they stared at one another anxiously, the half-formed hope of Reuben's coming struggling, then dying away, unspoken.

'You had best go, Tom,' said Phoebe, instinctively tidying her disordered hair beneath the lace-edged cap, 'although I daresay 'tis only some stranger who has lost his way, or begging a room.'

But it was Illtyd who stood upon the doorstep, the small piebald fidgeting restlessly beside him. The hayward's face was flushed with awkwardness as he handed over the small parcel, wrapped in thick Bristol paper, pressing it carefully into Tom Butler's unresisting hands.

'It is a gift from the people of the hamlets. All have given of their own free will, even the poorest of us, for Bella was much loved, and will long be remembered.' His beautiful, unusual eyes grew dark with hurt. 'It is not that we feel she needs remembrance, but because we hope it will bring you, and the child, comfort when all is . . .' He left the words unspoken.

Tom Butler thanked him numbly, much affected by the hayward's kindness, and that of the cottagers.

'I rode to fetch it this morning, early, from Ewenny,' said Illtyd quietly, 'that you might have it by you today.' He set his foot into the stirrup and rode swiftly across the highway and on to the green, then took the path to the Burrows.

Phoebe came and stood beside Tom, and for a moment they stared at the gift, unwilling to open it, until he set it upon the scrubbed table and tore off the covering paper.

It was a pretty mourning jug, a memorial piece of shining white glaze, with the words upon it written in bright pink lustre: Bella's name, her age, nineteen years, and the dates of her birth and death. In a small banner with scrolled ends were the words: 'Bella, lovingly remembered by all in Newton, Nottage and Port.'

Phoebe wiped her eyes upon her apron, then took a chair to stand upon and lifted the jug carefully to the top of the dresser, where none could dislodge it or brush it by accident. Then she said briskly, 'You had best take some breakfast, Tom, to line your stomach, and give you strength for the day ahead. I have set your clothes upon the bed, for you will want to do Bella justice.'

He nodded, leaning heavily upon a chair, and admitted, 'It was a kind thought of the cottagers,' his voice grew rough, 'and it is true that she was a good little maid, with sweet and loving ways, ever smiling, and slow to take offence. We will not see her like again, Phoebe.'

There was a great weariness in him as he turned from the chair, his breakfast untasted, for the thickness in his throat was choking him.

'I am glad, my dear, that you set it safe, where it cannot be broken.' The words came out with the greatest difficulty. 'It was a kind enough thought of the cottagers . . .'

'Yes, Tom, and our Reuben will be pleased by it when he comes.'

Joshua, stiff in his best uniform, stood beside Jeremiah, Sophie and Illtyd at the graveside, thinking not only of Bella, but that other grave beneath the sycamore tree's dappled shade where Mary Devereaux lay. And now, in some alien soil, he thought, perhaps Roland Devereaux lay dead, or was his grave the quiet depths of the sea he so fiercely loved? Yes, they were undeniably true, those words the rector spoke now, with such regret and feeling: 'They are cut down as the flowers . . . in their youth, and colour, and beauty, and the dew of the morning still fresh upon their petals. Fragile, delicate blossoms all, never to be bruised or discoloured by the harsh winds of life . . . perfect in memory . . .'

The small posies of fresh flowers were thrown upon the coffin lid, and the earth spattered, and the void filled. But the void within the flesh of those who mourned, how could that be filled?

Joshua's eyes strayed to Tom and Phoebe Butler, she supported upon his arm, he as pale as the white rosebuds he still held, forgotten, in his fist. The voices of those at the graveside and beyond arose in a hymn, softly as a whisper at first, but swelling in sound and sorrow, until it soared in mighty resurrection, and died away. Tears burned his eyes, for the sound had arisen swift and effortless as the flight of a bird, and as natural, and beautiful. He felt a soft hand slip gently into his, and turned to see Rebecca beside him, her eyes as bright with tears as his own.

There could seldom have been a more poignant committal to earth, Joshua thought with sadness, save, perhaps, that of Mary Devereaux, who, young and unknown, had come trustingly to an alien place to find a new life. Instead, she had found the violence of death by a stranger's hand. At least the mourners at Bella's graveside were known to her; friends and family all, and they came in gentle sorrow to grieve for one of their own. Yet the one who had held her close in his arms, sharing the warmth of her living flesh, creating a child from his own blood and bone, was absent, cold and silent, perhaps, as Bella and the grave itself. Perhaps it was kinder so, for how could Reuben have borne the anguish of it, the extinguishing of that bright hope and all of light?

Rebecca kept her hand forlornly in his as they left the graveside and mourners behind and walked, in silence, across the green and to the Crown yard where her coach was waiting. Ossie was with the mourners still, and deeply as Rebecca held him in affection, she could not but be glad, for she had little heart to speak, even to Joshua whom she loved.

'You think Reuben will return? Is safe?' Her voice was low, near to tears.

'I think that every day makes it less likely to be so.'

'Yes, I fear you are right.' Her face under her soft grey bonnet was gravely troubled. 'It is something I have been afraid to admit, even to myself, Joshua, lest Elizabeth lose heart altogether. I think that if she had no hope, she might die, too.' She bent her head, her face hidden by her bonnet brim, as she confessed, so quietly that he was not sure if he had really heard the words, 'As I would die, my dear, without you . . .'

He put a gentle hand to her chin and drew her face upwards, so that her eyes met his. Their vivid blueness was blurred with tears and pain, and small teardrops lay upon her dark lashes. He wiped them away tenderly with his fingertips before drawing her close to his breast, and saying firmly, 'No, Rebecca. It is wrong to speak in that way, and it grieves me to hear it. Like Elizabeth, you have the courage and honesty to survive, whatever hurts life inflicts upon you. It is what first drew me to you, and made me love you. I would not have all that brave spirit broken.'

'But *I* would be broken,' she declared passionately, her cheek still pressed hard against his breast, his arm about her, 'and if it is my honesty you seek, then you have found it, for I speak only the truth.' She wrenched herself away from his grasp. 'I could not, like Jeremiah, survive for thirty years, and more, his wife and child dead, for I would have no joy in living!'

'And you believe it was easier for him?' asked Joshua quietly. 'Do you not recall how it was when you first met him? Jeremiah was a man without hope or spirit of joy, his very existence a burden and punishment. Yet now, after all those years, he has Sophie, who loves him tenderly, and Illtyd for a son. Would you grudge him that, Rebecca? Or his last poor chance of happiness?'

'You know I would not, for I love him as dearly as a father!' Rebecca's voice was raw with hurt. 'I say simply that were you to die, Joshua, I would never take another . . . love no other man.'

'You speak now, Rebecca, with all the passion and rage of your youth and loving,' observed Joshua compassionately, 'and my own love for you is as deep and all-devouring, I swear. How could it be otherwise, for you are all I desire and hold dear? Believe that my need for you, Rebecca, is an ache within me, a rawness, which nothing can ease or assuage, save to be with you in flesh, as in spirit, always. I would share your flesh and warm blood, my dear, your thoughts and emotions, your sorrow as your joy, as if we were truly one, indissoluble, indivisible.' He bent low and set his mouth to hers, kissing her long and hard, and with the utmost conviction, before holding her gently at arm's length to say, 'Yet I would hope that even such love as this might grow and deepen with the years, Rebecca, and its changing serve only to draw us closer together, for there are many kinds of loving, like Jeremiah's and Sophie's, Bella's for her husband and her child, mine for you. And who is to pass judgement upon them, save to say that each is different, and perfect of its kind.'

Rebecca threw her arms impulsively around his neck, saying penitently, 'Oh, I do love you, Joshua! And we shall be wed in June, I vow, whatever comes, for naught must stand between us. Jeremiah and Sophie are truly deserving of love, and poor Bella's life was short and filled with hurt, yet she knew the joy of Reuben's loving, and would not have foregone that, or his son's birth, even for the promise of life itself.' Rebecca's pretty, earnest face grew intent as she asked quietly, 'You think she and Reuben will meet again, Joshua, in . . . some other place, should he be dead? For all eternity, I mean?'

'I am sure of it,' he said gravely. 'Else what purpose is in life?'

'Yes,' she nodded, satisfied that he had answered honestly, 'it would be too cruel if this was all.' She dropped a soft kiss upon his cheek. 'I will go, now, Joshua, and beg that you will tell Jeremiah and Sophie and the rest that I will return upon a kinder day, when our spirits are less sorrowful.'

Joshua opened the door of the de Breos coach and helped Rebecca within. 'Where do you go now, Rebecca? You return to Southerndown Court?'

'Yes, to be with Elizabeth, for she knows of Bella's death, but could not bring herself to come. I have made my apologies to Phoebe and Tom Butler, for they bade me stay for the funeral meats, yet I could no longer bear to witness their pain. It is a cruel custom, Joshua, that demands they share their grief and board with others, when they would nurse their sorrow alone.'

'Yet necessary,' Joshua reminded her without rancour, 'for there are many who have walked long miles over rough tracks, and will return by the same way, in darkness. It is but a simple courtesy.'

'You will attend, Joshua?'

'Yes. It is expected of me, though I will relish it as little as you.'

She nodded. 'I am to take luncheon with Robert Knight at Tythegston,' she confessed. 'I could not refuse, for he is plagued with sickness and the hurt of his nephew's death. I think it would not serve him kindly to dine alone. His thoughts and emotions would be bitter company.'

'Then he could not ask for greater privilege than yours,' said Joshua gallantly. 'I would that I were in his shoes.'

'Shoe!' corrected Rebecca, smiling for the first time. 'And if you were, sir, then my forthcoming nuptials might not bring me such unbounded joy.'

At a sign from Rebecca to the coachman, the coach and four moved off, the paired chestnuts prancing arrogantly with manes tossing. Joshua watched the elegant plum and gold carriage with its liveried coachman and footman and proud escutcheon until it was out of sight, and only the rumble of its wheels and the clopping of hooves could be heard as it took the Clevis Hill. It was a far cry from his first sight of Rebecca upon her simple cob-drawn cart. He thanked God, most fervently, that Rebecca herself had not changed, then turned, and resolutely entered the Crown Inn.

The funeral of Tom and Phoebe's daughter-in-law would long be recalled in the three hamlets as a 'warm' funeral, in contrast to the cold committal to a pauper's grave. There was no call to pay the inmates of the poorhouse a few pence to act as mourners, lest there be none to follow the coffin; nor was she denied headstone or marking. She was returned to the anonymous earth from whence she had sprung that she might, at the end, enrich it more usefully in death than in living. No, the tears for Bella were warm and cleansing as summer rain, and perhaps as swiftly passing, for life goes on whether we want it to or not.

The gravedigger's shovel, meticulously polished, and left without the church porch, had been so heaped with copper coin that its brightness had been eclipsed. Within the church, too, the 'priest's collection' grew heavy with its hoard of small silver and a few coins of gold. None saw who placed them, for the dish was discreetly covered with a linen cloth, that none might feel his offering insignificant, or, through pride, be tempted to give more than could be reasonably afforded. It was the rector's way, being a man of substance, to pass the collection, unobserved, to the bereaved, for the cost of a burial could be a crippling burden upon a family, and place them into debt, despite the few pence frugally paid each week to a funeral society. It was a matter of honour that death deserved a lavish celebration. It was, after all, a public avowal of the departed's worth, and the sacrifice and loss of those surviving. If, in life, the deceased had been poor and hard-working, then surely he deserved better in death? There was no doubting that he would receive his just reward in heaven and dwell in glory, but here upon earth, those who toiled and wept could give him no less. It was their final service to him; a testimony and expiation, a release. The pity was that he could not be there to share it . . .

Robert Knight did not offer the priest's collection to Tom and Phoebe, for he knew that their circumstances and pride would not allow them to accept it, but he did tell them that it would please him to give it, in Bella's name, to the fund for the aged and impotent poor of the parish, and so it was arranged. There were many who grieved for Bella, and thought of her with regret, and none, perhaps, more than Rosa Doonan, who was not a cruel girl, but heedless and unthinking, and reviled herself sorely that she had not seen that Bella was sick and troubled upon the day of the circus fete. Cavan, seeing her distress, tried to reassure her that it was but the way of the world and Bella's death could in no wise have been altered, for it was meant to be. Yet Rosa was not convinced, and learnt a bitter lesson that was long remembered.

Tom and Phoebe, when all the mourners had left, knew the emptiness of heart and the cheerlessness of hearth of all those who recognise, with a pang, that there are places which will never again be filled. If their grandchild brought them joy, he also brought Tom the pain of knowing that they might never see him grow to manhood, for they were already old and set firm in their ways, and as the boy grew, their obstinacy and lack of understanding might alienate the lad rather than draw him close. Whatever the cost to them, they must not spoil him with over-indulgence, nor curb him because of Reuben's loss. He must be allowed the freedom to choose his own way, for none can walk in the footsteps of another, but must make his own tracks through life, else he will be but another man's shadow, without worth or substance.

'You had best come to bed, my dear,' said Tom, 'for you have been anxiously fretting since before dawn, and there is nothing which will not keep until the morrow.'

'No, my love,' replied Phoebe, striving to keep the weariness from her voice, 'there are a few small tasks to occupy me yet. I had rather see them done, for that is my way. But take yourself to bed, for you are all but asleep upon your feet.'

He nodded, then turned to lay a hand upon her shoulders.

'We have walked a long road together, Phoebe,' he said quietly, 'and some of it, as today, hard to travel.' His eyes were bright with unshed tears, and she could hear them thickening his voice. 'But there have been good times, and quiet places.' He bent and kissed her cheek. 'I would not change a step of the way, nor walk with any other.'

'No, my dear, no more would I.'

He stood beside her, awkward for a moment, and she saw that his lips trembled, and his face was no longer young, but that of a man borne down by responsibilities and fear for the future, and wondered how he could have grown so old unnoticed by her.

'I will bring you a warm negus, my dear,' she promised, 'for I know that you have neither eaten nor drunk a drop this day.'

He nodded and, shoulders bent as though beneath a great burden, went slowly upon his way.

'Tom?'

He turned, startled, to look at her.

'You have been a strength and rare comfort to me

today. Without you, I could not have borne it.' Their eyes met in sorrowful understanding. 'You are the greatest blessing of my life.'

'And you, mine, my dear, for I am a man slow with words, not given to a show of affection, and I am truly sorry that I cannot speak what I feel, for the words will not come to me.'

'You have shown your love in your care for me, Tom, every hour of every day,' insisted Phoebe truthfully. 'It is actions which best prove a man, for words are cheap enough, and easily spent.'

He shuffled, awkward with surprise and embarrassment, but there was no denying his pleasure.

'It was a good funeral,' he said at last, 'dignified and fitting for the little maid, from start to finish. Bella could not have wished for a better. You are a good woman, Phoebe, for you gave her the only real affection she knew in her whole life, save for Reuben's.' He turned blindly and blundered through the doorway, and she heard his footsteps upon the stone stairway, halting and painfully slow.

'She was kin,' Phoebe said quietly, 'the only daughter I ever knew. How could it be otherwise?'

She forced herself to set about making the negus for her husband. When it was finished and set upon a wicker tray, she took Tom's chair and carried it to the dresser. Then, lifting a cruse oil lamp from the table, she climbed upon the chair and, in the poor, flickering light, set her lips gently to Bella's memorial jug. One day, she would ask Tom to read the words to her again, for, although his reading was hesitant, and he sometimes had to admit defeat, she could not read at all. Yet, did it really matter? The jug showed that Bella was dearly loved by all in the three hamlets, but, for today, the date of Bella's burial, as for the day of her dying, there was no real need for words. They were already written deep in her heart, and for as long as she lived, they would stay with her.

On the eve before Elwyn Morris's presentation, a wind had sprung up with unexpected violence; not the westerly wind from the sea that was a gentle harbinger of rain, but an alien wind, bleak and destructive. It seemed to arise without warning, wrenching the blossoms from the trees and strewing the bruised petals upon the grass, as if it found some capricious delight in destroying such fleeting, fragile beauty. It came from all directions and none, gusting through the tops of trees, tugging roots of grass, whirling sand and dust from the highway into brisk storms that stung the eyes and clogged the nostrils and throats of men and beasts alike. The squalls were swift and excoriating, and as swiftly as they had risen they died away to an airlessness and oppressive warmth which told of a thunderstorm to come. Everywhere, infants grew hot and fretful and the older children unnaturally loud and high-spirited, their screams and noisy restlessness mimicking the elements. Even the animals were agitated, their behaviour strangely unpredictable, so that the docile wide-eyed cows seemed no less irritable than the gadflies which tormented them.

When the storm finally broke, it was with a savagery that was primaeval in its force. Lightning ripped the bruised sky, forking above the sea in vivid blue-white flashes, swift and sharp as a sword blade. Thunder rattled all about, its violence bouncing and echoing from the hills and cliffs, magnified and distorted, until it seemed to emanate from every wall and roof, every chimney and crack, even from the bones and hollows of the skull itself, so that a thundercrack overhead came, not as a threat, but as a relief from the relentless monotony of sound. But the greatest relief came from the rain, slanting and inescapable, its coolness bringing a clean freshness, so that the cottagers opened their windows wide to welcome it, and ran outside, turning their faces as eagerly to the sky as the green shoots and leaves.

In his simple lodgings at Port, Elwyn Morris opened the skylight to his attic room, grateful that the storm had broken. Tomorrow, he thought with satisfaction, will be a special day. He turned to the poor iron-framed bed in the corner, where Haulwen slept, thumb thrust into her mouth, black hair spread upon the straw-filled pillow. No day could ever again be as special as the day when he had finally found her at Hawksreach, after so many years of searching without hope. Yet, with Eira Crocutt beside him, there might be warmth and love and the promise of brighter days ahead.

In the bedroom of the farm at Grove, Eira Crocutt sat, restless and uncertain, her clothes for the morrow set out upon the wheel-backed chair near the window. The bed she rested upon had been hers and Jem's from the day of their marriage, and had known their loving. It had witnessed their joys and sorrows, the birth of their children, and of Jem, himself, and the deaths of others who had, like him, tried to wrest a living from the barren inhospitable soil. Now, some other, more fertile, earth set them apart, as cruelly as it set young Dafydd against her. But she could not let him break the future which was hers by right. He was a child, and did not know the way of things. Soon he would be grown, and away from this God-forsaken place, which offered neither comfort nor living, although he stubbornly clung to it, as he clung to the memory of his father, trying to find in them a substance which had already fled. The memory of the boy, tight-lipped and defiant, at the height of the storm, filled her with anger and hurt, for she tried, as he well knew, to do what was best for them all.

'I have set your new breeches and coat upon the chair,' she had said. 'I shall be proud of you, for you will look a gentleman.'

'I am not a gentleman, ma'am,' he had replied, standing stiffly erect, 'but a farmer, as my father was. I will wear the coat and breeches cut down from his, and wear them proudly, for they will not disgrace me, or you.' His eyes rebuked her silently. 'I would feel more comfortable and honest, for a man's clothes are no measure of his worth. I am not a gentleman,' he said coldly, 'nor like to be.'

She felt anger rising swiftly as the storm without. 'No. Nor like to be,' she said contemptuously, 'unless you leave this place. You will go to Mistress Randall's school and learn to read and write, and make your way. I will see to it! I will brook no argument or tantrums, I tell you straight, for I am tired of your insolence, and your rudeness to those who would help you, and wish you nothing but good. You understand?'

'Yes, ma'am.'

'Then you will behave, tomorrow, with courtesy. You will not spoil my day, or that of the babes and Marged. No, nor Elwyn Morris's and Haulwen's either. You are selfish and undisciplined, and if you do not mend your manners, then . . .' she paused, lost for a suitably harrowing punishment, but ending triumphantly, 'I shall box your ears before all present, including the constable and Mr Fleet. Yes, and the justice, himself!'

'How will we travel, ma'am?' His voice was restrained, polite, yet it did not match his expression. 'Upon the donkey and cart? You would have me prepare it tomorrow, early?'

'No! Mr Morris will hire the carriage from the Crown, and will, very likely, drive it himself, for we are to be his guests.'

'Then I shall bid James Ploughman to be ready.'

'James Ploughman?' She stared at him incredulously. 'What has he to do with it? He will tend to the animals, for it is no affair of his, and to ride with us would not be fitting.'

'Then it is fitting that I work beside him on the farm, and when our work is done, we will walk together to the Port, or take the donkey cart, for without him, there would be no farm, no bread for any one of us. We would be paupers, ma'am, and sent to the poorhouse, our family split.' His voice faltered, but his gaze was firm. 'I will wear the suit you have set out for me, if it brings you pleasure, for it cannot alter what I feel within, but I shall walk or ride with James Ploughman beside me, and naught will change my mind. It is owed to him.'

Two spots of bright colour burned in her cheeks, but she said nothing, simply nodded and, taking a chamber-stick from the dresser, set light to the candle within it with a taper and the flame from a cruse oil lamp, and made her way up the stairway to her room. Her rage and resentment at his stubbornness flickered with the candle flame's fitful light. She would not let him spoil the day! He was wilful. Heedless. Needing a man's firm hand. Elwyn Morris would curb him. When the school was opened, Dafydd's name would be the first upon the roll! He could not know the humiliating grind of poverty she had endured, the misery of filling empty mouths and bellies when there was no money and too little food. She would be glad to flee this lonely, miserable place if Elwyn Morris would but ask her.

The candle trembled with the agitation of her thoughts, throwing out longer, brighter flames that merely served to deepen the shadows about her. She saw, again, Dafydd's set face, childishly defensive and vulnerable, and felt a pang of shame and remorse that he had been forced to a man's responsibilities with childhood scarce begun. It only served to sharpen her resolve. He must leave this place. She would not let any of the others drudge and labour as he, even if she lost him.

In his single-roomed hut at the end of the rough track to the farm, James Ploughman settled himself upon the straw heaped on the earthen floor. The only light was the square of sky seen through the solitary window, an opening left in the dry stone-wall. The air was fresh now, for the storm had abated, yet the turf outside remained too wet for sleeping in the open air, as he would have wished. There were few enough comforts here, in this poor forsaken place, yet he had built it with his own hands, grateful for rough shelter and a place to lay his head.

He smiled wrily. He would get used to the wetness of earth, and to vagrancy, and there would be no ties, and none to command him. Tomorrow he would be upon his way, and beholden to no one. He wondered why he felt so little joy.

Chapter Twenty-Seven

As morning broke, sunrise stretched the sky with fingers of saffron, pink and red, and that wider canvas beyond which had been muted and dark grew light. The change was gradual, imperceptible almost, like the rising of a mist, so that the colours bled and ran together, merging in a blurred wash of lavender, rose and palest gold, before fading altogether. What remained was a sky of clearest speedwell blue, cloudless, and without blemish. Elwyn Morris would, indeed, have a memorable day.

All was clean-scrubbed after the rain, and the children and their elders no less so as they made their way expectantly to the village green where joy and entertainment awaited them. Ossie, nut-brown and perky as a sparrow, had taken charge of the nose-to-tail donkey races, at which art he had become a master. Indeed, he bumped and swerved the beasts with such fierce abandon that the plump farmers' wives, clutching their tails, shook and wobbled alarmingly, jaws rigidly clenched, as they strove to retain both hold and dignity, and very often retaining neither. Illtyd, who was a great favourite with all, gave gentler rides upon his pony, Faith, to the infants and babes-in-arms, while the Morris men clashed their sticks, and shook their wrist and anklet bells joyously in celebration of the ale and veal pies which awaited them at the Crown and Ancient Briton.

' 'Tis certain,' said Doonan, surveying their antics with

wry amusement, 'that it is hunger which drives them to cavort so. With a brace of veal pies lining their bellies, 'twould feel more like church bells they lifted!'

'Then learn from it,' replied Rosa with mock tartness, 'and take your ale and victuals at home in future.'

'I would, my love,' said Doonan, gallantly offering her his arm, 'should I have an urge to join them, but I fancy my efforts would not be much applauded at the quarry face.' His massive face creased into a grin, the missing front tooth lending him a curiously rakish air as he lumbered beside her, shock of red hair unruly as he. 'Oh, but Rosa, my own sweet love, I would sing and dance for you, for ever if need be, for you are prettier than a rose, in that bonnet and gown of pink, as soft to touch and as sweet-scented . . .'

'Get on with you, you great silly loon,' said Rosa, colouring with pleasure and embarrassment as he mimicked the Morris dancers, and minced along beside her. 'Everyone is looking this way!'

'And if they were not,' he said, 'they would be blind, or fools, for you are the most beautiful thing in all of creation.'

About them, the crowds smiled, ebbing and flowing in a warm tide, and the stalls and sideshows and games flourished, and the infants grew sated on sweetmeats. And if the thoughts of a few strayed to the freshly piled earth beyond the churchyard wall, then sadness was swift and fleeting. There was little enough joy in the world, and Bella would have been the last to grudge them this small, unexpected fragment.

At Port, the civic dignitaries and august shareholders of the Dyffryn-Llynfi Railway Company were assembled. Assembled they indisputably were, for 'gathered', with its echoes of common flower plucking, was altogether too mundane a word for such an illustrious throng. However, it must be said that they were not unlike flowers in the glory of their raiment, although, perhaps, less like the flowers of the field and hedgerow than hothouse blooms, exotic, rare, and ill-at-ease in their alien surroundings.

All the folk of the three hamlets who knew Elwyn Morris were there to witness his triumph, and they came without envy, for his good fortune was well deserved, and he was much admired for his courage, and the way he had triumphed over the poorhouse. Indeed, even the workmaster, Littlepage, was disposed to unbend, his elderly cherub face pinched into a prim smile, the curls upon his forehead piled high to hide the hairs stretched sparsely across his pink scalp.

'Well, Morris?' he ventured as he alighted from his carriage, with two paupers, cowed and apprehensive, to serve as coachman and footman. 'You will concede, I fancy, that your present good fortune owes much to your days in the workhouse?'

'Indeed, sir, all,' said Morris, straightfaced, 'for your very presence gave me the spur and incentive to better myself.' Then, leaving Littlepage unsure as to whether he had offered a compliment or an insult, Elwyn Morris guided the paupers to an honoured place, promising them victuals and refreshment when all was done.

'You are looking uncommonly spry, sir,' exclaimed Joshua as Rawlings, the exciseman, came and sat beside him, 'and uncommonly pleased with yourself, too! Perhaps you are expecting some commendation from the justice for your small part in this affair.'

Rawlings's broad intelligent face wore a sly, self-satisfied smile as he declared enigmatically, 'I expect no more than you, sir; yet I confess that I know more. With that you must be content.'

Puzzled, Joshua said nothing, glancing about him with interest, nodding courteously to those who acknowledged him, and seeing, with curiosity, that Eira Crocutt and Haulwen sat beside Morris, her young brood beside her, Dafydd stiff and uncomfortable in his new clothes, and with the precious clogs he had insisted upon wearing. Despite his protestations to James Ploughman that he would finish his work, then walk to Port with him, or ride upon the cart, Ploughman had been adamant in his refusal.

'Your place is beside your mother, Dafydd,' he insisted, 'and it is what your father would have wished. I beg you go, and I will follow after.'

'You promise, sir, that you will come?' Dafydd's face was anxious, pleading.

'I promise.' It was a vow that Ploughman had been reluctant to make, for he was set upon leaving before the boy's return, yet he would not go dishonestly. He watched the family leave in the carriage with its fine horses, and Elwyn Morris at the reins, and if it grieved his spirit to greet Morris courteously, and with a smile, he did not show it. Ploughman continued waving cheerfully until they were out of sight, laughing indulgently at the babes' antics and Marged's vanity as she paraded her new dress before him, and giving Dafydd a reassuring pat on the shoulder as he climbed aboard. Then, having fed the hens and pigs, and watered and made safe the beasts, he returned to his dwelling, tied his few belongings within a cloth, and picked up his shotgun.

'So,' declared Robert Knight, beaming upon the company which overflowed on to the quayside and wharf, spilling like the mounds of coal, the pit props, minerals and iron ore on to the dockside, 'we are here upon a fine and noble occasion, to honour one of our own citizens.' Before him, upon a polished table, lay the shining, silver cup to be presented to Elwyn Morris with the inscribed parchment scroll, and pouch of gold coins, a reward from the grateful Railway Company.

There was a ripple of delighted anticipation and applause, but the justice had scarcely got into his stride, which seemed not a whit hampered by the painful inconvenience of his gout. He praised the exciseman and constable for their parts in the affair, although with reserve, for it was clearly their duty to assist and, with more warmth, the help of the people of the three hamlets.

'Before I make the presentation,' he declared, protuberant brown eyes alert behind the gold-rimmed lenses of his glasses, 'I have some small pieces of pleasurable information to impart. First, thanks to the generosity of a donor who begs to remain anonymous, we shall have a free school before the summer's end. A house has already been purchased in Newton village, and Mistress Randall will preside, aided by a second teacher; a gentleman by the name of Captain Edward Power, a distinguished soldier and scholar, who will settle here, in our midst.' Dr Burrell who was seated near Emily stared at her questioningly, his mouth drawn into an uncharacteristically disapproving line, his lean saturnine face distinctly troubled. Emily smiled at him ingenuously, her fine eyes serene 'neath her distinguished bonnet edged with lace, and he dropped his gaze awkwardly.

'Next,' declared Robert Knight, mercifully unaware of the undercurrents that flowed through his audience, 'we come to the celebration of the nuptials of our constable, Mr Joshua Stradling. To celebrate this auspicious occasion, there will be the usual festivities, as one would expect . . .' This, then, thought Joshua in embarrassment, is what Rawlings thought better hid. He kicked him hard with the toecap of his riding boot, but Rawlings neither responded nor flinched. '. . . So,' continued the justice, with growing excitement, 'my own contribution to the hamlets, on behalf of Mr Stradling and his bride-to-be, Miss Rebecca de Breos, will be to have repaired the church bells, and provide Newton, Nottage and Port each with a fire-cart.' He beamed benignly, all about, and Joshua heard Rawlings's ill-concealed and spluttered laughter from the seat beside him, quickly subdued in the burst of clapping and approval by the bemused villagers.

To the justice's irritation, he was rudely interrupted in the midst of this generous applause by a rustling whisper from the dignitary seated beside him. After an inaudible and acrimonious exchange between the two, the harbour master, Captain Ayde-Buchan, RN, pushed his way forcefully to Robert Knight's side. With a gaze dark as a thundercloud, the justice listened, his face growing ever more relaxed and delighted, until he burst out, without ceremony; '*The Stormy Venturer* has been sighted, and returns to port this very day. Captain Devereaux and Reuben Butler are safe! Thanks be to God!'

The noise and uproar were so fierce, with all the hugging and weeping, laughter and kissing and relief, that none but Jeremiah Fleet, whose eyes were fixed accidentally upon the boy, Dafydd, saw the child's face grow pale, and the terror of realisation upon it, as he struggled through the seething mass of bodies towards the fringe of the crowd. Jeremiah, with dread, and a sickness rising in his throat, bitter as gall, saw upon a donkey cart, newly halted, the ill-clad, wild-eyed figure of James Ploughman, a poacher's rifle in his hand, his aim set upon Elwyn Morris.

Dafydd had somehow reached him now and with his face torn with bewilderment and pain as fierce as Ploughman's own had leapt upon the cart, throwing his arms about the man, more in a gesture of pity than restraint, shielding the gun against his own flesh. In a swift movement, Ploughman had hurled the boy away, and Dafydd and shotgun went hurtling to the ground as Ploughman, face streaming with tears, urged the donkey and cart upon its way. Jeremiah, waiting for the explosion from the gun, felt his heart beating so loudly in his breast that he thought he must die, and his limbs could scarcely bear him for weakness, but he pushed his way to the boy's side. Dafydd had scrambled to his feet, the gun held limply before him, and Jeremiah took it gently from his unresisting hands, and cradled the boy's tear-stained face to him. Jeremiah's eyes met Sophie's above the heads of the crowd, and she stared at him with helpless pity, motioning silently that he take the child away.

'I want to go home, Mr Fleet.' Dafydd's voice was low.

'Then you shall, my lovely,' said Jeremiah, taking the boy's cold hand and leading him to the cob and gaily painted cart.

'My mother will box my ears in front of all,' said Dafydd, trying not to weep, 'for Mr Morris is a hero, sir, and I am to watch his presentation or she will know the reason why.'

'It is because you are a hero, my boy. Every whit as brave as he,' said Jeremiah gruffly. 'Now climb upon the cart and let us be gone.'

When they reached the farm at Grove, the donkey and cart stood unattended in the yard. Of James Ploughman there was no sign. Dafydd scrambled from the cart and, with a cry which rent Jeremiah's heart, he ran across the cobbles, his clogs clattering noisily, and on to the track to Ploughman's hut.

Jeremiah followed on foot, for the way was too narrow for his cart, and he did not hurry, for his heart still beat uncomfortably in his breast, and he did not want the boy to feel himself harassed or spied upon, but given the privacy of a man.

Dafydd ran to the cottage and flung open the door. It swung clumsily on its hinges to reveal the room bare of James Ploughman and all else, save for a small box upon the floor. When he prised off the wooden lid, he saw within a small carved rattle for the babe, a wooden likeness of a Tamworth pig for his brother, and for Marged, a string of wooden beads. In its corner, wrapped in sacking, James Ploughman's knife, the only treasure he possessed. Dafydd hurled it in fury to the farthest part of the room, and it clatterd against the stone wall and on to the earth floor. In a moment he was scrabbling beside it, wiping it tenderly upon his new coat, rocking himself to and fro upon his heels.

Jeremiah, who had witnessed it from the doorway, turned away and took the pathway back and waited awhile. Then he made a commotion with the bushes, seeming to have trouble in finding his way upon the overgrown, brambled, track. Dafydd came to the door, his face pale but composed.

'He has gone away, Mr Fleet, and left some presents for the others. If he could write, he would have left me some word . . .'

Jeremiah said, 'Yes. I am sure of it.'

Dafydd's face twisted in terrible grief as he burst out despairingly, 'He did not love me enough to stay, Mr Fleet!'

'No,' said Jeremiah. 'He loved you too much.'

* * *

All the cottagers in the three hamlets, save Dafydd Crocutt perhaps, were agreed that it had been that rare and splendid thing: a perfect day. Everything had conspired to make it so, the weather, the coming of the new school, the fun and festivities, the presentation itself; but, most of all, the safe return of the voyagers. Yet, to their credit, they did not let this God-given miracle overshadow or dim the glory that rightfully belonged to Elwyn Morris. Even if they had done so, he would not have cavilled or resented it, for his own rejoicing at the homecoming of *The Stormy Venturer* was truly greater than in his own achievement. To his immense credit, the justice was only mildly piqued that his promise to restore the cracked church bells and provide fire-carts was swamped by the greater news of Captain Devereaux's and Reuben's safety. Perhaps the bishop's strictures had not been entirely wasted, or his gout had improved. In any event, his enthusiasm for the project was undiminished, and he consoled himself with the thought that to a good parish priest, the safety and physical welfare of his flock is only marginally less crucial than their spiritual care. Besides, he told himself, it is man's nature always to choose circuses before bread, an aphorism which, for some reason, brought him scant comfort.

Joshua had received the news with such incredulous relief and pleasure that, for a time, he had been unaware of anything save that Rawlings was gripping his hand tightly, and shaking it with such vigour that he seemed set upon crushing its bones. As soon as the furore and excitement had died down to manageable level, and the presentation made, Joshua made his warm congratulations to Morris and sought Robert Knight. He had thought, fleetingly, that it was strange that Dafydd was nowhere to be seen, and his chair beside Eira Crocutt empty, but since Jeremiah, too, appeared to be absent, and Sophie deep in conversation with Emily Randall, he dwelt no more upon it, believing that they had escaped to the shore. It would account, he believed, for Mistress Crocutt's evident vexation and Sophie's distress, for she was unusually pale and discomposed.

With the justice's agreement, indeed at his command, Joshua was now, despite the lateness of the afternoon, on his way to Southerndown Court to share in their thanksgiving. He chose to go by the quickest route, for the tide was right, and he could gallop the grey across the bays to the estuary of the Ogmore, which would be drained to firm, green mudflats and damp sand by the ebb of the sea. The mare seemed to feel the same fierce exhilaration as he, for she galloped across the wet sand of the bays with a sense of freedom and release, mane and tail streaming, muscles rippling smoothly as the wavelets that fell in showers of spray about her hooves. Looking back across the rocky shore, Joshua saw that her glancing hoofprints had left crescents in the sand at the tide's edge, and already the clear ripples flowed over them, softening and blurring their tracks, and, soon, all traces would have disappeared as if they had never been. He had a sudden vision of that same gentle sea closing inexorably upon the dead faces of Devereaux and Reuben Butler, washing away all imprints of their lives, and he shuddered despite the warmth of the day, as he urged the mare across the raised green islands of the river's mouth, setting the wading birds and the gulls to noisy flight.

At Southerndown Court, there was little joy in anyone's heart, for it was upon the morrow that Elizabeth and Roland Devereaux were to have been wed, and none could convince her that it was unlikely that he would now return. Sir Matthew was deeply troubled, for he loved Elizabeth as his own flesh and blood, having witnessed her courage and loyalty in so many ways; to that poor, demented husk, her father, and her efforts to make amends for her brother Creighton's crimes. Roland Devereaux, he had thought, would, by his deep love and steadfastness, have made up for all the hurts and betrayals of her past. His calm protectiveness would have shielded her from all future ills, and, with Devereaux at her side, she would have surely found the security her young life had lacked.

Now he had sent an urgent letter, by messenger, to Dr Handel Peate, Elizabeth's tutor and his long-valued friend, begging him to talk to her and, with his usual gentle persuasion, to reason with her. He was sorely afraid that upon the morrow Elizabeth would insist upon dressing in her bridal finery and awaiting Captain Devereaux at the altar of the small church at the court, as planned. When she finally construed his absence as death, believing that naught else could separate them, then Sir Matthew feared for her sanity. It would be a further tragedy which he doubted Elizabeth could survive.

Sir Matthew, who had begged to be allowed to be present at the interview between Elizabeth and Dr Peate, awaited anxiously in the library of the Court for the scholarly priest's coming. For once, Sir Matthew's air of dignified control had deserted him, and although none could have faulted his sartorial elegance, his usually erect figure was slumped low over his desk, his face buried helplessly in his hands. The strong bones of his face now seemed drawn and old, the shadowed planes beneath gaunt and hollow, as hollow as the feeling of helplessness and inertia within him. Rebecca, who was Elizabeth's dearest friend and confidante, had been grieved to see her friend's wedding gown and all the pretty extravagances of her trousseau set out in the room placed at her disposal within the Court, perfectly arranged for the ceremony. Louisa Crandle was so distraught that Sir Matthew's physician had been summoned to her bedside, and had pronounced himself to be extremely worried by her nervous, debilitated state and her extreme agitation. He had prescribed complete rest and the blandest of invalid diets, declaring that he feared that she might suffer complete nervous collapse and prostration.

Despite her inability to accept her husband's villainy, and the burden her failure to visit him had placed upon Elizabeth's young shoulders, Sir Matthew still had a real concern for Mrs Crandle's wellbeing. There was no doubting that she loved Elizabeth, and had been a most generous and willing mentor to Rebecca in her new life. Despite a regrettable tendency towards social striving, and a certain rigidity of manner, she was never deliberately cruel or malicious. If her slavishness to the minor dictates of etiquette and fashion sometimes irritated, perhaps she merely sought to restore the secure structure of a life style which had once been hers by right, and which her husband's frailty had destroyed. No, he thought, Louisa Crandle was merely what life had prepared her for and made her, an ornament in the drawing rooms of society, pretty and useless, meant only to be admired. She was no more vain and empty-headed than thousands of other women of her station. She had not been equipped for the realities of life, and so withdrew from them, ignoring their existence. But Rebecca and Elizabeth were set into a different mould, strengthened and refined by misfortune.

The furious noise and clatter of footsteps in the hall outside, and the heightened exchange of voices, shocked him from his reverie, and he was already upon his feet when the library doors burst open without ceremony, an unheard of intrusion, to admit the excited, travel-stained figure of Captain Roland Devereaux, bearded, dishevelled, and altogether unexpected.

Sir Matthew, forgetting the natural courtesies for the only time in his life, sat down, amazement and disbelief rendering him speechless.

'I beg you will forgive me,' Roland Devereaux began, 'but I took a post chaise from Cardiff, and came, sir, the moment I set my feet ashore. There was no more urgent way to tell of my return.'

Sir Matthew's face was still pale and bloodless, and there was a noticeable tremor in his hands as he arose and walked around the desk to where Devereaux stood, clasping his arms about the young man impulsively, unable to speak for a moment any word of welcome or relief.

None ever knew what conversation passed between the two men in that brief incarceration, for it was never repeated. Roland Devereaux was forced to unburden the full horror of all that had occurred in that hellish, ungovernable storm, with the ship helpless in the violence of those towering, crashing waves that crushed and mutilated all in their path, splintering and laying bare. The wind was barely audible above the ceaseless roar, yet its savagery was perhaps the greater, for it twisted and slewed the vessel as if it swirled in some maelstrom which would suck it remorselessly below, and even as it swept them, it shredded canvas and snapped rope and cable, and plucked two of the crewmen to their deaths in the sea.

When, finally, battered and sick of soul, they had drifted to land in the storm's lull, the long tedious work of setting *The Stormy Venturer* to rights had begun. There were few on shore in that remote, inaccessible place to aid them, and none with skill, and many of the crew were physically hurt and incapable, with little ease for their wounds. As for the rest, they were exhausted and demoralised, and did not believe that they would ever return to their homes.

Yet, return they had, but not without some dying upon the voyage from their corrupted wounds, and the food and water which they had taken aboard from the shore was too soon exhausted, or rotted. There were tears in Roland Devereaux's eyes and he wiped them away roughly, begging Sir Matthew to forgive his unmanliness in burdening him with such a report, yet it eased his mind for the telling.

Sir Matthew arose and set a hand upon Captain Devereaux's shoulder, gripping it tight.

'There are some things better shared, sir,' he said quietly, 'lest they corrode the mind and spirit and can never be forgot. Yes, it is better so. I will seek out Elizabeth and tell her of your return, which she has never doubted. You will rest here at the Court until tomorrow, and all that you need will be brought to you. Yet I fancy your greatest need is to see Elizabeth. I will see that you are not disturbed, and inform Mrs Crandle and Dr Peate of your safe return, for their despair at your absence has been as deep as my own.'

Elizabeth, as was her wont, came quietly into the room, and only by the trembling of her lips and the brightness of her dark eyes did she betray the love and joy she felt at Devereaux's safe return.

'Elizabeth . . .' Devereaux held out his arms and she moved into them as easily and naturally as if they had never been apart. 'Oh, my sweet love, my dear, I am home. I have come home,' he said, his lips touching her dark hair.

She raised her head and looked at him, and he saw that the tears she had so long restrained were running down her cheeks with the joyfulness of his coming. 'I never doubted it . . .'

He had to bend low, for her voice was so gentle and at peace. He lifted her fingers to kiss their soft tips, and saw clenched tight in her hand the little silver sailing ship that he had bidden her to keep against his safe return. He knew that he should tell her that there would be no more voyaging, no more fear that she must bear alone, but he could not speak the words.

'I shall keep it always,' she said gently, 'for there will be other voyages, and other ships for you, yet none that will so happily await your coming.'

If he kissed Elizabeth tenderly, and with increasing passion, it was for her own dear sake, and not because she understood.

Despite all that had gone before, it was not surprising that Elizabeth's and Roland Devereaux's wedding eve should have been one of joyful thanksgiving and reunion with their closest friends. Sir Matthew, knowing the full history of the young sea captain's ordeal, and not wishing to place too great a strain upon him, since he was plainly emotionally and physically spent, ordered that the small dinner party, prepared to honour his return and the forthcoming nuptials, be informal and unelaborate. Mrs Crandle appeared quite miraculously recovered from her decline of spirits, yet fearing that the morrow's excitement might tax her strength too greatly, begged to be excused from the evening's revelry.

So great was the good lady's delight at Captain

Devereaux's safe return, and the prospect of Elizabeth's wedding him, that she forbore from mentioning the impropriety of the betrothed pair spending the night under the same roof – even one so large and prestigious as that of Southerndown Court. If she regretted that Elizabeth's trousseau was ludicrously modest, and not the conventionally decreed dozen of everything, she kept her reservations admirably well hidden. Rebecca's wedding was still in preparation, and Mrs Crandle reflected, not without satisfaction, that her acknowledged flair for design and organisation could then be given full rein, her tasteful extravagances unbridled. Yes, she decided, as she dined delicately but expensively, as befitted an invalid, from the exquisitely prepared tray at her bedside, it was all most satisfactory. There would be the bride's cards to be sent, of course, giving the names of bride and groom, and their future address. 'The Dower House, Southerndown Court'. It was a pity that Elizabeth's former friends were now so distantly placed, but, doubtless, they would be suitably impressed by her deserved good fortune. Yes, all was admirably ordered, and as it should be, nothing had been omitted. Why, then, this depth of sadness and hurt? It was but a weakness, a legacy of the sickness which had come upon her. She would dwell upon it no more.

The party of guests which gathered at Sir Matthew's table was, to all intents, unusually strange and varied, yet all were drawn together by affection for the betrothed pair. Sir Matthew had invited his closest and most respected friend, Dr Handel Peate, who was, at Elizabeth's request, to officiate as priest at the ceremony upon the morrow, at the private chapel within the grounds. Joshua had arrived late in the afternoon, and was prevailed upon to spend the night at the Court, for the wedding was to be at half past the hour of eight upon the morrow, and as bride-man, or groomsman, as the duty was being increasingly called, he needed to be at hand early. Rebecca, of course, took her place as hostess, and to the delight of them all, Sir Matthew had sent the smaller de Breos coach to fetch Illtyd and Emily Randall from Newton to be honoured guests.

Those present were, without exception, intelligent and warm-hearted, and found delight in the company of equals. Neither Illtyd nor Mistress Randall felt in any wise intimidated by the occasion, for both Joshua and Rebecca had previously shared in the bleakness of their lives and daily toil; Elizabeth and Captain Devereaux were their staunch friends; while Sir Matthew, a gentleman by birth and nature, judged others upon their merit, and not their fortunes, and held both hayward and governess in proud esteem. As for Dr Peate, he would have been gravely offended had anyone remarked upon the differences in station of those invited, because he was a man not given to triviality, and thereby intolerant of it in others.

The conversation between the company was companionable and wide-ranging, with much discussion about Mistress Randall's role as teacher at the new school, events in the three hamlets, and Elwyn Morris's presentation at the Port. Captain Devereaux's accounts of his voyage were carefully turned towards the excitement and colour of foreign ports, and the lure of strange, exotic places, with their people and customs. He did not speak of the storm, nor of those who had died ashore, or at sea, and none was tempted to ask him. By tacit consent, no word was said of Bella's death and Reuben Butler's cruel homecoming, yet it indubitably lay raw in the minds of them all.

When all was regretfully ended, and the time almost

come to retire for the night, Illtyd hesitantly begged a few moments of Elizabeth's and Roland Devereaux's time. Sir Matthew, having bade his guests a warm good-night, had mounted the staircase with Dr Peate beside him, the pair conversing companionably as they made their way to their respective rooms. Rebecca had taken Emily to the room which had been carefully prepared for her comfort, and had shown Joshua to his, and the three remaining friends stayed together below.

'It is but a small gift I have chosen for you,' said Illtyd, cheeks flushed, as he produced it from a pocket, clumsily wrapped in brown paper. He pressed it into Elizabeth's hand, his awkward head twisting upon the wry neck as he watched her open it. His extraordinarily beautiful eyes were anxious as he studied her expression.

In Elizabeth's palm lay a seagull of carved beechwood, outstretched as if eager to take wing. One delicately slender leg was poised upon a rock, the other raised as though it had already forced itself towards the sky, the membrane of its feet spread taut between the scaly claws. Its curved beak was opened wide in a cry of triumphant release. It was so vibrant with life that it seemed fashioned, not of wood, but flesh and bone, infused with warm blood.

Elizabeth said gently, 'It is the most perfect and lovely thing I have ever seen, Illtyd. It breathes life and movement.' Her grave brown eyes met Illtyd's in compassionate understanding, for she knew that he, too, was seeing that quiet shore, and the sea birds whose forsaken cries guided returning mariners home. Elizabeth bent low and kissed Illtyd's cheek, her eyes bright with pleasure and warm affection, and Roland Devereaux gripped the hayward's hand, and touched his misshapen shoulder in a gesture of true friendship.

Elizabeth's voice was gentle as she promised, 'It will bring me remembrance of sunshine and springtime's hope in many a dark winter.' Then turning towards Devereaux, she said impulsively, 'You understand, Roland, that Illtyd was as certain of your return as I.'

Devereaux's questioning eyes met Illtyd's, and knew the strength and depth of his loyalty, for he saw the knowledge that, in truth, the hayward's faith had been as faltering and unsure as his own.

Chapter Twenty-Eight

That Reuben Butler's homecoming brought him less comfort than Captain Devereaux's was in no wise due to any lack of affection towards him by the cottagers. Indeed, so deeply did they feel for him in his loss that they were unable to approach him to speak of their sorrow, fearful to intrude upon so private a grief. So it was that his arrival at Newton was greeted not with bunting and celebration, or with children and well-wishers jostling upon the streets, but a cold palpable silence. Captain Devereaux had begged that Butler accompany him in the post chaise to Southerndown Court, that when he had alighted, the carriage might convey Reuben to the Crown Inn, but Reuben would have none of it, declaring that he would waste no time, but leave at once upon the cheaper stage-coach for Bridgend, and beg a lift thence by carrier or farm wagon. Bella would be frantic for news of him, and the babe already born, and he could brook no delay.

When the carter from Sker House set him down at the foot of the Clevis Hill, Reuben, with his heavy canvas bag of gifts and small treasures, took the highway to the inn. It was a warm day and the bag heavy upon his shoulder, but his stride was swift, for in his mind was the certainty of Bella's joy at seeing him, and her pride in their child, and the excited exclamations and gentle rebukes the extravagance of his purchases would bring.

Yet, as he walked, he was aware of some strangeness all about him, an unusual quietness, with none rushing from cottage or garden to bid him welcome home. He thought, once, that he glimpsed a face at a casement window, pale and ethereal as a wraith, and as swiftly gone. After a while, the silence grew more oppressive than the afternoon heat, and the weight of it more burdensome than the pack he carried upon his shoulder. Something was wrong, unnatural, and instead of the joy he had felt, a cold fear touched him. His every instinct was to hesitate and drag his feet, or halt altogether. He felt an overpowering urge to flee, but forced himself onwards, almost running the last few yards into the doorway of the Crown, and then through the passage beyond.

His father's face as he beheld him was a mask of mingled shock and pain as tears struggled with joy. Then he came forward to enfold him in his arms, as if he were not a man returning, but a child again, needing reassurance in some dark and alien place.

Reuben Butler thought afterwards that hell itself and the darkness of Bella's grave could have been no more deep and impenetrable than the darkness which enshrouded him. It had no beginning and no end, and was the loss of all meaning and hope. He was as wracked with tears as with guilt, and the pretty gifts of cloth and colourful trinkets seemed to mock him with their cheap tawdriness, and in his blind fury and impotence he would have ground them underfoot, that none might see or touch them if she could not. The child he would not visit, despite Phoebe's urgent and distressing pleas, until, finally, like Tom Butler before him, he blundered unseeingly across the sands of the Burrows and to the rocky shore. There he railed at the sea like a man possessed, raging at it as the cause and architect of all his misfortunes, heaping back upon it the anguish it had brought to him.

When he returned to the Crown, Phoebe's heart bled at the ravaged knowledge upon his young face, and she would have gone to him, but Tom motioned her silently to let him be. Reuben went to the cot where his son was lying, a hard knot of coldness and resentment twisting his breast, and looked down at the sleeping child. He felt nothing but dislike for him, there was no love, no protectiveness at all. With a sigh, Reuben tucked the blanket about the sleeping figure, seeing the thick lashes lying separate and fine as silk threads upon the curved flesh of his son's cheek. The child's fist curled itself about Reuben's outstretched finger as he awoke to regard the stranger with neither fear nor surprise, but gentle curiosity. The child's eyes were so like Bella's that Reuben felt the knot of coldness within him dissolve and find release in healing tears. Bella was here to lead him home.

Upon the morrow, almost from early dawn, there was an air of excitement and cheerful expectation about the Court, for the servants were in a fever of delight that Miss Elizabeth, whom they so liked and respected, was to be wed, after all, to young Captain Devereaux.

Sir Matthew had insisted that Elizabeth's new household must have a lady's maid, a cook and attendant kitchen acolyte, and a housemaid, all of whom had been trained 'neath Mrs Crandle's exacting and ever observant eye to near perfection. Now, Elizabeth's personal maid and coiffeuse confidently prepared the bride-to-be's toilette, cleansing, anointing, dressing, scenting and teasing her long brown hair into an elegant topknot, with curls falling prettily about her slender neck, as fashion, and Mrs Crandle, decreed.

Rebecca, her bride-maid, should, by custom, have sat

with her late into the night, reassuring her as to the virtue of being wed. Elizabeth needed no such reassurance, and was immodest enough to admit the fact, a breach of etiquette which would undoubtedly have vexed her mother.

'You had best remember not to gaze in the mirror after you are dressed, and have a final thread stitched into your dress ere you leave,' reminded Rebecca, 'and take care not to peep, should Devereaux pass, else you will have no luck.'

Elizabeth, standing prettily in her swirl of petticoats, said, smiling but with truth, 'I have no need of luck, or charms, Rebecca, for I have all of good fortune in Roland's return.'

'You will be the most beautiful bride in all the world!' cried Rebecca extravagantly, kissing her friend with affection.

'No,' said Elizabeth, without rancour or envy, 'that distinction is reserved for you, for your beauty is startling, and arrests all. But I swear, Rebecca, that I shall be the happiest bride in all the world,' and with that no one seeing her shining loveliness, least of all Roland Devereaux, could disagree.

The men were equally set upon making themselves an elegant foil for their fashionable ladies of quality. Joshua had shown his foresight in sending a message by the coachman who had driven Emily and Illtyd to Southerndown, to be delivered to Mistress Randall immediately upon the carriage's arrival at the Crown. Taking the key which the constable had prudently dispatched, Emily packed both Devereaux's gentleman's clothing and Joshua's own, from inn and cottage, with Ossie as her willing adviser and chaperone. She was, after all, an unmarried lady with no experience of gentlemen's more intimate apparel, and a visit, alone, would seriously have compromised her. Emily did not remind the ostler of her days in the workhouse laundry, although it was a part of her life not easy to forget, but thanked him ciyilly for his aid as the trunks were placed upon the carriage, and she and Illtyd were waved admiringly upon their way.

So, upon this wedding morn, Devereaux, expertly valeted, and Joshua, no less fastidiously groomed, stood together within the tiny private chapel of Southerndown Court, awaiting Elizabeth's arrival. They were, thought Emily, amused, like two emergent dragonflies, newly released from drabness, gaudily iridescent yet shyly conscious of their colourful finery. From the tops of their shining heads to their gleaming boots, they were looking-glass images, one of the other – proportioned, matching in height, sharing that same sun-warmed fairness of complexion and corn-coloured exuberance of hair. Their white shirts were immaculately frilled, their dove-coloured unmentionables of doeskin sleekly moulded and wrinkle-free, their frock coats impeccable. Here lay the only disparity, for the bridegroom's, as befitted his superior role, was of warm claret colour, piped with silk, and Joshua's of a deep inky blue. Both wore toning weskits and ties which somehow managed to appear distinctive, but modestly elegant. In fact, they were the very models of sartorial splendour, without excess.

Sir Matthew was, as always, superbly presented, but in a gentler fashion, for he had the gift of subduing all he wore to a muted elegance, natural and unselfconscious as his own quiet charm. Dr Peate, in clerical garb suited to the occasion, looked precisely what he was, an aesthete, scholar and priest. Small and frail-boned as a child, with the gentle unworldliness of a dreamer, he yet commanded immediate respect and attention. It was hard to say why this should be, for his thin frame was stooped through being bent too long over his books, and his features were delicate under the white hair which hung long and innocently dishevelled about him. Yet his eyes were shrewd and intelligent, filled with a knowledge of life which his appearance belied. They were at once old and young, clear-sighted but compassionate, and there was none who came to him, despairingly, to seek comfort or advice, who left without knowing himself for what he truly was, and the course he must follow.

Dr Peate surveyed his modest congregation, observing them with benign and affectionate eye, yet missing nothing at all, from Roland Devereaux's nervousness, and the strain and fatigue about his eyes, to Emily Randall's serene face under the pretty lace-trimmed bonnet, softly coloured as a pigeon's breast. He noted Mrs Crandle's tensely anxious expression and her undeniably modish gown and bonnet of eau-de-nil silk, which seemed to reflect pleasing colour into her translucent skin and brighten the faded copper of her hair. Illtyd looked uncommonly well in trousers of lavender with a coat of lilac blue, and Dr Peate, remarking the beauty of the hayward's clear, incredibly arresting eyes, thought with compassion of the intelligence and affection trapped so cruelly within Illtyd's grotesquely twisted frame, and marvelled at his kindness and lack of envy.

There was a simplicity and warmth in the tiny church which permeated the nuptial service and the hearts of the few close friends gathered within. Elizabeth, in a gown of white silk, fitted and flowing to the curves of her slender young body, and with a small veil of Valencienne lace falling from a circlet of fresh orange blossoms, looked affectingly beautiful, and as Devereaux turned fleetingly to gaze upon her, his face was so radiantly transfigured with love that Dr Peate heard in his mind, as if they had been spoken aloud, the half-forgotten words, 'My true love hath my heart, and I have his,' and knew them to be true and irrevocable, for this was no mere marriage by arrangement, but a meeting of minds and hearts, and a fusing of spirit itself.

'With my body I thee worship . . .'

'And forsaking all others, cleave only unto him . . .'

'From this day forward, for ever and ever . . . until death do us part.'

The promises were made, and the rings exchanged, and Rebecca, in her gown of softest aquamarine, turned instinctively to Joshua, as if the words had been on her lips as well as in her heart. Mrs Crandle, as mothers always will, wept for what was ended and what was begun in her child's life, and Emily's gentle hand stole out to console her, fearing that it was of her own long-murmured vows that she thought, and the poor unhappy creature no longer by her side.

Louisa Crandle, gripping Emily's hand in gratitude, pressed a dainty lace-edged handkerchief to her eyes, for her tears were not for him, or Elizabeth, who had no need of her grief. She wept for a red-haired fox, arrogant and restless, who would never know love, or stand beside her upon such a day.

When the wedding breakfast had been cheerfully consumed, and the toasts and speeches, laughter and tears, come to an end, Roland and Elizabeth Devereaux wholeheartedly thanked and praised those who had made it so perfect a day. All were aware that they had been witness to, and part of, a celebration they would long remember, all the more poignant for having been so nearly sacrificed to tragedy. The servants were as wreathed in smiles and delighted as the guests at the espousal, wearing special favours of silk and lace, and heartened by the promise of a hogshead of ale, and their own feasting below stairs when their duties were over.

Rebecca was richer by two pairs of fine gloves of

kidskin: one pair which she had claimed from Elizabeth as her right for relieving her of them, together with her flower posy, and vinaigrette, during the nuptial service, and another pair from Roland, as was the custom. Roland's personal gift to her had been an exquisite miniature ship, carved in green jade, sails and rigging so delicately fashioned that they were almost transparent. To Elizabeth he had given a gold bracelet, its links interspersed with small, but perfectly formed, seed pearls, to match the necklace which had been Sir Matthew's gift to her upon Rebecca's birthday.

Before the wedded pair climbed into the carriage that would take them to their home in the Dower House, Elizabeth had tenderly embraced her mother and all about, and Devereaux had clasped hands with their friends in true gratitude, then, with satin slippers tied upon the carriage, and in a shower of flower petals, they had been driven upon the short journey to their home.

Roland Devereaux descended first, and, swinging Elizabeth from the carriage steps and into his arms, carried her over the threshold and within. The smell of the orange blossom that circled her hair, and the softer perfume of her skin and flesh, and the scent she wore mingled and surrounded him with fragrance.

'I love you, Elizabeth,' he said quietly as he set her down, 'and now, and always, wherever I go, you will never be out of my thoughts and my heart, I swear.'

'Then I am glad,' said Elizabeth demurely, 'but since you are here beside me, will you not take me to our bed, for I will not always be within your arms, and that is where, at this moment, I would most dearly wish to be.'

Gradually, almost imperceptibly, life returned to normal in the three hamlets, and many were relieved that it was so, not least Joshua.

'It was,' he confided to Jeremiah, 'like that welcome calm after a furious storm, when all the elements have clashed in discord, and their spleen and violence are finally spent.'

Jeremiah nodded sympathetically, but he was an older hand at the game, and did not remind Joshua that, as a fisherman, he was only too mindful of the squalls and tempests which blew up suddenly and without warning from the sea. 'Sufficient unto the day is the evil thereof,' he said to himself as he flicked the reins upon the cob, and with Charity cavorting and barking upon the cart, made his way gratefully to the shore.

Elizabeth had pressed her bridal posy into Emily's hands as Roland had assisted her into the carriage that would take them to their new home, begging Emily to lay it upon Mary's grave. Emily had been touched and pleased by the gesture, and kissed Elizabeth with warmth and affection for her remembrance of another upon such a special day. Devereaux had gravely shaken Illtyd's hand, bidding him tell Reuben that he would visit the Crown as soon as he was able, with Elizabeth at his side, for Tom and Phoebe Butler had been kindness itself to him, and treated him as warmly as a son. There was no doubting that both Emily and Illtyd would dine out for many a week upon the distinction of their stay as guests at Southerndown Court, and their memories squeezed for the smallest morsel of gossip, description, or new information by the avidly curious cottagers. Emily had not even shown Illtyd the tiny sliver of bride cake, set into a minute silver box and tied with white ribbon, which Elizabeth had slipped into her reticule, with a gentle kiss upon her cheek. To Rebecca, as bride-maid, had fallen the honour of cutting it, thinly enough to pass through Elizabeth's wedding ring, and then to present it only to the nubile maidens attending. Since she and

Emily were the only ones unwed, Rebecca's task had been made easy.

'You must sleep with it under your pillow,' Elizabeth had advised, 'and then you will see a vision of the man you will wed.'

Rebecca had smilingly claimed that her future was already set, and Emily had protested that she was too old for such pretty superstitions. Yet neither had refused the gift, but put it most tenderly and carefully away.

Neither ever confided if she had slept with her head pillowed above the bride-cake, as custom decreed, but Emily was not slow to observe that Dr Burrell's visits were more frequent and his manner altogether more relaxed and charming in her company. His interest in the proposed new school, which had always been perfunctory, grew deeper, and his enquiries about the handsome young gentleman who was to share Emily's task most anxious and explicit.

It was, as Emily remarked to him, blandly, a measure of his rare humanity and kindliness that, despite his own harsh workload, he was as concerned for the intellectual wellbeing of the children as their physical care. If Emily saw the flush which suffused his sallow, cadaverous cheeks at this praise, she gave no sign, for which he was grateful.

The justice's gout was vastly improved, to his immense satisfaction and to the confusion of Dr Burrell and his partner, Dr Mansel, who had prophesied suitably harrowing results from his over-indulgence. Nemesis would undoubtedly overtake him, but for the moment he waxed plumper and more cheerful, as his cellar and pantry grew proportionately leaner. Gluttony, Robert Knight consoled himself, was certainly a deadly sin, but eating and drinking as a prescribed cure could only be counted as a virtue. This moral dilemma solved to his satisfaction, he was able to turn his full attention to the provision of the fire-carts for the three hamlets, and a way to recruit volunteers to man them, should need arise. Meanwhile, his judicial duties must not be neglected, a fact he demonstrated by disciplining the wretch who had so cravenly assaulted Ruth Priday at Maudlam, then sheltered behind both his disguise as clown, and the innocent, if odious, Abrahams. His sentence was imprisonment for ten years at a house of correction, the initial three weeks to be spent upon the treadmill, but first he would be publicly whipped around the Brideswell, to deter others.

Rebecca had willingly taken his victim, Ruth Priday, into her care and service, and declared her to be a gentle-natured, intelligent girl, and eager to learn. Rebecca would, she vowed to Joshua, take the girl with her as her personal maid when they were wed and settled in the hamlets. What she did not confide to him, for reasons of her own, was that she had plans to address Emily upon the subject of taking her into her school, and teaching her to read and write, that later she might, perhaps, assist in the work of teaching. In any event, the girl was eager to study, and Rebecca would guide and help her in this ambition. There would be ample time allowed from her duties to visit her home at Maudlam, when all was forgot, and she felt such need. Meanwhile, Joshua must cultivate the young curate, Richard Turberville, and see him fed at his table, for the priest would welcome both victuals and company, and doubtless neglected himself sorely, a proposition with which Joshua gladly concurred, thinking that Rebecca was, indeed, the dearest, most generous girl in all the world, as well as the most beautiful, and he the most fortunate of men.

Of the Fiery Archer, and James Ploughman, there was neither sight nor sound, and Joshua, who was absorbed with the day-to-day misdemeanours of the hamlets – vagrancy, drunkenness, assault and feuding – did not exert himself unduly in the quest for missing persons.

From gleanings over tankards of ale at the inns, it was garnered that Elwyn Morris and Mistress Crocutt were to be wed when the time was appropriate. All were agreed that it was a most suitable match, and none could blame her for seeking the protection of a good man, with every prospect of advancement, for she had laboured cruelly and to no avail upon that barren holding where her husband had met his death.

But Jeremiah came to Joshua in some distress, declaring that Dafydd laboured feverishly, and for all the hours the good Lord gave, to do the work that James Ploughman's absence thrust upon him. He would take no help from Morris, or any other, not even from Jeremiah himself, nor travel with him upon the cart to the shore. The boy grieved and grew thin, for his mother had told him that Grove Farm must be sold, and none could alter it.

Joshua mounted his grey and began the long ride over Dan-y-Graig Hill and across the byways of Stormy Downs, to the farm. The late spring hedges were thickly leaved, and the warm air clotted with the sounds of insects and the songs of birds. The sun was warm and the sky blue, and empty of cloud, the larks rising from the pastures and hovering high, with frail sweetness of song. All about, sheep and lambs were plumply grazing and cows paused in their soft-lipped chewing and lumbered to the hedges to regard him with gentle surprise, for all the world, Joshua thought, amused, like chaperones at a grand ball, assessing the manners and eligibility of a dancing partner for the young ladies in their charge. The hedgerows were thick with greenery, small, curled fists of honeysuckle and a frothy icing of elderflower, and the grassy verges bright with delicate pink flowers of ragged robin and campion. There was a rich verdancy in the growth of all things, a lush abundance pitifully absent from the aridness of the farm he visited, dismounting and leading the mare within, carefully securing the gate, his boots clattering with the grey's hooves upon the cobbles of the yard.

Dafydd, who had been feeding the squawking, greedy hens in the yard, emptied the bowl in their midst as, in a blur of feathers, they pecked each other and the corn with relentless selfishness.

'Constable Stradling, sir.' Dafydd came forward hesitantly to take Joshua's mare. 'I shall tell my mother you are here.' He seemed to Joshua unusually listless and sharp-boned, his eyes bruised around with dark shadows.

'No,' Joshua stayed his arm, 'it is you I have come to visit.'

Dafydd studied Joshua's face and nodded. 'Perhaps we had best take your mare to the barn, sir. We shall not be disturbed there.'

Joshua followed him, seeing with pity the frailness of the boy's neck, and the bony wrists that held the mare's reins. His bare feet were grimy with the dirt of soil and yard, and the cut-down suit of his father's which he wore, too large, and threadbare with use.

Silently the boy tethered the horse and, turning, gestured awkwardly to Joshua to be seated upon a bale of hay.

'I am to leave the farm, sir,' said Dafydd, standing stiff and defiant before him, 'but I will not go! If you have come to persuade me to change my mind, then I fear your journey is wasted.' Then feeling that he had been uncivil to a friend who had only shown him kindness, he said, defensively, 'I cannot go, for it is mine by right, and a charge upon me from my father.'

'He would only have wanted what is best for you,' reminded Joshua, gently.

Dafydd shook his head, standing rigid with pride and despair. 'My mother will marry Mr Morris, and I am to go to school . . . to be a scholar! I have begged that she leave me here, and send two paupers to help me, for I am old enough to live alone, but she will not!'

There was such hopelessness in the boy's voice and bearing that Joshua would have reached out his hand to draw him close and comfort him, but knew he must not betray the pity he felt, for it would be a betrayal of the boy himself, and his proud independence of spirit.

'It would be a hard task, even for three men,' said Joshua carefully, 'and no woman to cook, and clean, and make life comfortable as your mother does.'

'The farm would be comfort enough!' Dafydd burst out. 'And how can I leave the animals? They know me and love me, and what will happen to my red-haired Tamworth pigs? They are all that comes to me from my father's death. All of payment, save the few gold coins from the wrecker's wife, and I want none of them! They are the price of his blood.' He began to weep, silently at first, burying his face against the large down beam of the barn, then sobbing aloud, his frail shoulders trembling beneath the ragged cloth of his coat.

Joshua let him weep until he could weep no more, and, finally, Dafydd turned to face him, awkward with shame and embarrassment, tearstains streaking the dirt of his face. He sniffed, then rubbed his nose and eyes with his closed fist. The memory of Jem Crocutt transfixed upon the beam in the barn by the tines of a hayfork, like some monstrous insect, lay unspoken between them.

'Now,' said Joshua firmly, 'if your weeping is done

sir, we will discuss this dilemma as men should, sensibly, and as equals, open to ideas and suggestion, you agree?'

Dafydd nodded.

'First, I have come here to make an offer for this farm, you understand?'

Dafydd, eyes wide and bewildered, said nothing.

'It is a poor place, the soil arid.' As Dafydd made to deny it, Joshua raised a silencing hand and continued relentlessly, 'I am a farmer, and know it to be so. However, I shall buy it upon one condition only.'

Dafydd's eyes were intent upon Joshua's face, and his body so still that he might have stopped breathing, as he waited in an agony of suspense.

'The condition is that, when you are a scholar and a grown man, you may agree to buy it back from me, if that is your wish. Meanwhile, I shall make enquiries all about, and find a man capable of running it until you return, with the help of some willing paupers from the poorhouse, men with wives who will be as anxious as they to secure a roof of their own, and help with all that is needed.'

Joshua rose to his feet, eyes questioning, awaiting the boy's answer.

Dafydd's face was so transfigured with hope, and his gratitude so fierce that, forgetting for a moment the proper conduct of a man, he flung his arms about Joshua's waist, almost unbalancing him with the force of his enthusiasm for the plan.

'Steady, sir!' reproved Joshua. 'Let us shake hands upon the bargain in a sensible fashion, like the business partners we are.'

Dafydd solemnly set his small fist about Joshua's, eyes bright.

'I have no doubt,' said Joshua conversationally, 'that the labourer who cared for the Tamworth pigs at Sker

House will be pleased to attend to them, for he is without work since the imprisonment of the wreckers. I think we may safely trust him to see to their welfare, rather than his own. He has undoubtedly learnt his lesson.'

Dafydd said, in an effort to be fair, 'I daresay, sir, that if I, too, learn my lessons well, I may put them to good account upon the farm. I shall work at them until I drop from exhaustion, if need be.'

Joshua tried to hide a smile as he replied, 'I am sure that you will distinguish yourself at your books, sir, as you have at your work upon the land. I will ask the notary in Newton village to draw up a suitable contract for the transaction, if you will trust my goodwill.'

'You are an honest man, sir, and a just one,' declared Dafydd solemnly, 'and I would trust you with my life.'

Were the words an echo of what his father had once said to James Ploughman, Joshua wondered, or to Elwyn Morris? The next words assuredly were.

'Pray come inside, sir, that we may celebrate with fitting refreshment,' invited Dafydd, 'since we do business together.'

'Nothing,' declared Joshua truthfully, 'would entertain me more.'

Chapter Twenty-Nine

Joshua, who had forsworn life at university, and upon his father's lands and well-ordered farms, for his work as constable, had never considered that he might, one day, be the owner of as poor and arid an apology for a holding as Grove. He did not know what mental aberration had persuaded him to take it off Dafydd's shoulders, for it was more of a burden than a prize. However, he could not regret the impulse which had prompted him, and his father, dour and hard-headed as he professed to be in all his dealings, was the first to offer assistance and knowledge to set the crippled place to right. His mother, extravagant and frivolous as she sometimes appeared, had a strong core of practical sense, and with the greatest goodwill offered curtains, bedding and napery that the pauper wives might be fittingly housed upon their arrival at the farm when the widow Crocutt and her young brood had removed to Newton village. That Charlotte Stradling's elegant gowns and bonnets were unsuitable wear for pauper women, labouring long hours at scrubbing and laundry work, seemed not to have occurred to her; Joshua would certainly have been a churlish and ungrateful son to rebuff such graceful charity. Even had he done so, she would merely have rebuked him with the gentle reminder, 'All women have a love and need for pretty things, and those who have been denied them have the greatest need of all.'

It was a truth which Rebecca, had she been asked, would undoubtedly have affirmed. Yet, for the moment, the incessant designing, measuring and fitting of her wedding gown and a trousseau for the Grand Tour, which was Sir Matthew's wedding gift to them, filled her with irritation and boredom. Rebecca was missing the companionship of Elizabeth, both at lessons and play, and Dr Peate tried hard to divert her and stimulate her interest, although he had to admit that she was not always the most attentive and rewarding of pupils. Her music master, and tutors at drawing, were scarcely better favoured, although Rebecca's devotion to the sick and scrofulous poor of the neighbouring hamlets never faltered, and her visits to newborn babes with appropriate gifts of warm clothing and pretty gew-gaws, or with nourishing soup and tempting victuals for the nursing mamas, or aged infirm, continued to give her pleasure.

With Mrs Crandle as duenna and social arbiter, Rebecca dutifully repaid calls and sat through excruciatingly boring and trivial conversations as though entranced by the wit of the participants. She continued to play the part of the gracious hostess at her grandfather's small dinner parties, and accompanied him upon visits concerning the estate, which interested her more than the empty affectations and ceaseless prattling and tittle-tattle of the drawing rooms. As her visits to Joshua's parents at their farm in the Vale increased, so the new understanding between her and Charlotte Stradling deepened into real and mutual affection. In the absence of a mother, and of Elizabeth's friendship, Rebecca turned increasingly to her for advice, and to share those minor triumphs and small anxieties which womankind is heir to, and which men entirely fail to comprehend or dismiss as frivolous.

' 'Tis their nature, my dear,' declared Mrs Stradling

equably, 'to pretend that their minds are set upon a more rarified and elevated plain. They purport to be pondering upon affairs of state or the spirit, when 'tis clear, even to the simple-minded, that all they are pondering upon is their cellar, or the nearness of their next meal. It is a fact of life, and there is no altering or denying it.' At Rebecca's delighted laughter, she added irrepressibly, 'Yet I fancy that Joshua will, for some time, be more concerned with affairs of the heart than the stomach, for you will make a beautiful, proud and independent bride, my dear, and he will find you irresistible.' She embraced Rebecca impulsively, declaring, 'You have it in your power to make yourself always so, for you are as intelligent and compassionate as you are pretty.' She coloured as she offered, with charming diffidence, 'If there are . . . certain things which, being denied a mother, or confidante, you wish to ask of me, my dear . . .?'

'I thank you, ma'am,' returned Rebecca gently, 'and there is none I would rather instruct me upon so delicate a matter, but my observations in my past life, and my knowledge of Joshua, lead me to believe that I have nothing to fear, and, in fact, might welcome whatever . . . intimacies our union might provide.'

Charlotte Stradling's relief at a duty so honourably offered, and skilfully parried, plus the tribute to her son's excellence, put her in a most expansive mood.

'My dearest girl,' she exclaimed, embracing Rebecca again, 'Joshua is the most fortunate young man in all of the world, and I the most appreciative of mamas.'

Her elegantly regal manner softened further as she confessed with a conspiratorial smile, 'I have always found that, like an untutored horse, a man responds more readily to a treat than a goad, you understand? I am not one to offer advice, but I have invariably found that to defer with good grace in matters of small import makes a man more ready to accept those vital decisions upon which a woman is determined, and will not be swayed. If the man can then be persuaded that the idea was entirely his own . . .' She broke off, raising her pretty hands expressively, and they both smiled in agreement. Rebecca did not doubt that it was the most pertinent advice she would ever receive, concerning all men, and Joshua in particular. Who could know a man better than his own mother? Except, of course, his wife?

Charlotte Stradling had been delighted when asked to accompany Rebecca to the London house, overlooking the park, for there were many visits they could make together, shopping expeditions and excursions by carriage, accompanied by Mrs Stradling's unmarried brother, Henry, who, fortuitously, lived close by. He held a most prestigious position in the City, which none the less allowed him to place himself at the two ladies' disposal. He was a quite charming, avuncular gentleman, with all of his sister's sartorial elegance, and proved an amusing and distinguished escort. He was as captivated by Rebecca as his nephew, declaring gallantly that were he but thirty years younger, he would give the young blade a race for his prize, enchantment lending wings to his feet, like Mercury, messenger of the gods. Mrs Stradling cautioned him severely for his nonsense, but, in truth, she was as diverted as Rebecca by his company, and her final parting from her brother was only moderately lightened by the success of their London visit, and his firm promise to be at the wedding and at her side.

Mrs Crandle had begged to be allowed to remain at Southerndown Court, for she must direct all her energies to preparing the forthcoming nuptials. Besides, Elizabeth would be receiving calls as soon as was decently suitable. It was true that there had been no bridal tour, but the exigencies of Captain Devereaux's duties and his recent experiences had precluded it. She was only grateful that the dear good man had survived, and none would cavil over a trifling breach of etiquette when a life, itself, was at stake.

Meanwhile, there were a million and one arrangements to be made for the comfort and housing of the distinguished guests expected, their servants, and their carriages. There were the caterers to interview yet again, and instruct, the florists, the dressmakers, the household servants, the service to be arranged with its rehearsals, and strict protocol, for there was a stern, immutable etiquette demanded, that none might feel slighted or unfairly placed. Then there were the usual day-to-day household affairs to order and supervise. She grew ever more animated, and more voluble, always finding some new difficulty to vex and confound her, and then solve most gratifyingly, occasionally, only very occasionally, with Sir Matthew's gentle guidance and unstinted praise for her capability. He would, he promised, put in hand all the necessary preparations for the bride tour, setting up carriages and suitable hotels upon the way, informing his friends at the Consulates and the merchant banks of the newlyweds' proposed route, that they might be suitably provided for in all eventualities.

Thus reassured, Mrs Crandle was able to return her attention to details more directly affecting the ceremony itself, the preparation and allocation of the bedchambers, the selection of the silver for the table, the choice of epergnes and crystal, the flowers, the fruit, the swags for the decoration of the Great Hall, the conservatory, the proper conveying of ice for the desserts and ice creams from the ice house in the grounds, which would certainly be at their best, in particular the rose gardens and arbours. Her mind was in a whirl with excitement and plans, and she would not have foregone or abdicated a single one of them, no, not at peril of being removed to the stake.

Her fervour was heightened, rather than diminished, when Sir Matthew summoned her to the library to confide that, although he had wracked his mind to decide upon a suitable gift to mark his appreciation, he had thought of nothing appropriate. However, a chance remark from his friend, Dr Peate, had given him inspiration. It seemed that the good cleric had longed to set out upon a tour of the principal cities of Europe, visiting their art galleries, museums, cathedrals and cultural shrines. Would it not be a fitting tribute then, to both Dr Peate's endeavours and her own, were he to arrange such a visit for them? Mrs Crandle might take any lady companion of her choice, and Dr Peate had already stated his willingness, indeed delight, at providing respectable escort, for surely none could be more suitable? He was a gentleman of the utmost scholarship and refinement and, in addition, a man of the cloth. There was no more to be said, save for Mrs Crandle's gratitude, which was mercifully stifled by the magnificence of the gift. An observation which did not escape Sir Matthew any more than the thought of the tranquillity which would undoubtedly descend upon the Court and the dower house. He would regret Handel Peate's absence and probably even Mrs Crandle's, for she was good-natured enough, yet it is a poor friend who puts his own selfish concerns before the unfulfilled ambitions of another, and Elizabeth and Captain Devereaux, and, later, Rebecca and Joshua, would prove excellent dinner companions and surely not desert him.

To Rebecca he casually let fall the observation that Mrs Crandle appeared to be uncommonly pale of late, perhaps she was regretting Elizabeth's leaving, or too much was being placed upon her shoulders, for she had, after all, survived many griefs and hardships. Rebecca, who was a kindly and sympathetic girl, thought that Louisa Crandle did indeed look anxious and strained, although her energy and enthusiasm appeared undiminished.

'Perhaps,' Sir Matthew ventured 'you might care to suggest and organise some celebration for your friends of the three hamlets, who will not be attending the church ceremony and wedding feast? Or possibly there are arrangements you would make for the out-paupers of whom you told me, for you mentioned that they were aged and impotent? Would it not be a kind gesture to make them some gift, and so include them in your celebrations? Then there are the children, and adult in-paupers at the poorhouse at Bridgend, and, of course, our own tenants to consider. It would be a pity were they to feel displaced or rejected.'

So, subtly guided, but not led, Rebecca set her energies to the task of ensuring that her own good fortune spilled over into the lives of others whose poverty she had so lately shared. It was a salutary lesson that her grandfather, who had never known deprivation or hunger, should have been more concerned with their misfortunes than she, and Rebecca duly profited from it. That she was also relieved of her restless boredom and lack of purpose was a blessing that she had not anticipated. With his usual honesty, Sir Matthew would have admitted that it did not surprise him a whit.

Joshua, meanwhile, was involved in the more mundane matter of his work as constable, for the human condition continues to offend, despite the example of those punished for their frailty, or the exhortations of those, like the rector, who would have us aspire to perfection. It was, Joshua thought, a curious anomaly, that should Robert Knight perform this miracle, as clergyman, then his role as justice and, indeed, Joshua's own, would be superfluous. If the constable had cravenly handed over all matters of sartorial nicety to his mother, then Charlotte Stradling did not demur. She had, in any event, to arrange suitable clothing for her husband, and for Aled, Joshua's brother, who, as an unmarried kinsman, was to be his bride-man, or groomsman, as he insisted upon being called. Mrs Stradling had scant respect for her menfolk's predilection for bizarre and totally unsuitable weskits and neckties, and so ensured that they would appear respectfully dressed at the wedding, and not disgrace themselves, or her. It was, she thought wrily, not one of the minor questions upon which she readily deferred, but a grave matter of principle, from which she could not be swayed, and a splendid example to Rebecca.

Roland Devereaux and Elizabeth, setting aside convention and their natural reserve, visited Reuben Butler at the Crown Inn. They arrived quietly and without ceremony in a small gig, with Captain Devereaux at the reins, unremarked by any, save Ossie and Emily Randall, and both ensured the newlyweds the privacy they desired. Elizabeth, whose gentle-heartedness made her take upon herself the burdens of others as if they were her own, but with compassion, not sentiment, embraced Phoebe Butler warmly, and begged to be allowed to see the child, declaring that Emily had assured her he was all that was handsome and good. She admired him without reserve and, despite the tears Phoebe shed upon Elizabeth's pretty blue gown, her face pressed to Elizabeth's shoulder as the new Mrs Devereaux comfortingly stroked her hair, there was no denying that the generous praise of her grandson cheered and uplifted her.

He was, indeed, a most handsome child, with Bella's

wide eyes and Reuben's russet hair paled to a soft coppery gold, fine as silk. When Elizabeth remarked upon it, Phoebe said with mingled pride and awkwardness, 'There is no fear that young Joseph is a changeling, ma'am, for he is as like our Reuben as . . . two peas in a pod. 'Tis only superstitious fancy, I know, talk of fairies and such, but the older folk hold store by such tales, so I have fastened some red ribbon upon the cradle, and put a sprig of mountain ash in a jug nearby.'

It was a custom which was new to Elizabeth, and she found it strangely disturbing, but gave no sign that it was so, lest Phoebe be offended. She reached into her reticule for a coin to place in Joseph's hand, but Phoebe stilled her hand, saying quietly, 'It is the first piece of gold, Mistress Devereaux, that has ever been given to him. I beg that you will allow me to offer him bread and salt, and a Bible, too, that he may show the direction his life will take.'

Elizabeth felt that such a strange pagan ritual would scarcely please the rector of the parish, nor the use to which the Bible was placed, but could not object without seeming churlish or cold. It could do no harm, she persuaded herself, as Phoebe hurried away to gather the necessary objects, for surely no one could really believe such puerile nonsense. Phoebe came back red-faced through hurrying, with salt, bread, and a Bible upon a wooden tray, to which Elizabeth solemnly added the gold coin.

' 'Tis naught but superstition, ma'am,' confessed Phoebe, shamefaced, 'but it is the custom hereabouts, you understand? A diversion, merely to amuse. None believes in it . . .' She hesitated before blurting awkwardly, 'The coin is for riches. The salt for journeying. The bread is for never hungering. The Bible for all that is good.'

Joseph was crying and flinging his fists haphazardly,

and as Elizabeth bent closer to see him the better, a hand fastened upon the pearl necklace at her throat, and the other, in brushing away the tray, settled upon the salt.

'No!' cried Phoebe, abruptly snatching away the tray. 'It is nothing, stupid nonsense, without sense or meaning! An accident, that is all!'

Yet, even as her eyes met Elizabeth's, and Elizabeth retrieved the coin and set it into his fist, it rolled away, and his small fist groped again to encircle the pearls at her throat.

'He will never go to sea,' declared Phoebe, 'not while there is breath in my body! There has been enough grief in this house.' She looked at Elizabeth despairingly. 'It makes no matter that he was born with a caul covering his face, which says that he will never drown. It is but superstitious rubbish, and of no account. A foolishness, to be forgotten, and never repeated.'

Devereaux's talk with Reuben was reasoned, and more direct, as befitted men who had faced danger and survived death, for it is a link not easily broken. Tom stood by, saying nothing, as Reuben confessed that it was his one desire to be back at sea, for the feel of it was in his blood, and he had a hankering, now, to be under sail. Perhaps, if the child were older, or Bella were here, it might be different, but it would serve no great purpose to remain, save to intensify his longing and grief. When Captain Devereaux put to sea, he would be proud and privileged to serve with his crew. Neither Tom Butler nor Captain Devereaux sought to dissuade him, for his mind was plainly made up, and he was firm upon it. Yet, as he drove away beside his young bride, with Emily, Ossie, and the Butlers waving them across the cobbled yard and out through the arch, Roland Devereaux's face was unusually sad as he thought of the task Reuben must face in telling Phoebe Butler of his plans.

'Reuben will return to sea,' Roland said, face expressionless, when he had safely turned the carriage and they were mounting the Clevis Hill.

Elizabeth's hand came to rest gently upon his arm on the reins. 'I have never doubted it,' she said, 'for the sea is a mistress which always lures a man away. She will not be denied.'

'Yet it is to his wife he returns,' reminded Devereaux, quietly.

'Yes,' said Elizabeth, voice low, 'that is why Reuben must go.'

If all those at Southerndown Court, the tenants upon the estate and the surrounding villages, were deep in their preparation for the de Breos-Stradling wedding, then the folk of the three hamlets were altogether immersed in them. Rebecca de Breos was, after all, one of them. Had she not lived among them, worked with them? Had she not shared their poverty, their small triumphs, and their greater griefs? Was not Constable Stradling their very own protector, appointed by the vestry? It was sad, they agreed, that the wedding ceremony was not to be held at the parish church of St John the Baptist, for then all might have seen the bride in her finery, and their constable in his. Still, it was but common sense to use a church in the Vale, for many of the gentry would be travelling long distances by coach, some, it was said, from as far afield as London, and by law, the service must end by noon. It was only proper that they should be made welcome at Southerndown Court, for they were people of importance and altogether more sensitive to discomfort than common folk. Even the Crown and the Ancient Briton, luxurious as they were, would strike them as rough and homespun, lacking the refinements they considered necessary. There was no denying that those with blue blood were bound to be different from those of common stock, whose blood flowed red. It was nature, and could not be altered. The church at Llantwit Major was said to be bigger, too, although that did not make it any holier or prettier, even if none had seen it to compare. Well, it was here that Mr and Mrs Joshua Stradling would be living, for work had already begun upon a thatched cottage in Newton village, making a coach house and a small outhouse where the constable could see folk in private, lest their business be overheard. It was a modest place for people of rank and station, but those who are true gentry, or nobility, have no need to proclaim their superiority. It is there in the breeding, for all to observe.

Rebecca's and Joshua's closest friends were to return to Southerndown Court for the wedding breakfast, and the dancing and entertainment in the evening. Yet, it would certainly not outshine the frolics promised upon the green and in the taverns of Newton, Nottage and Port. From the youngest to the oldest, the least to the greatest, none would be forgotten or denied a part.

The dances were already being rehearsed upon the village green by the more nubile of the village maidens and their obedient swains, and many a romance blossomed or died in that rough wooden pavilion aside the green where they stored their costumes and sedulously 'practised their movements', not all of them planned, or strictly traditional. Walter Bevan, the relieving officer for the poor, was, at Rebecca's instruction, to take to each of his male out-paupers, too aged and impotent to work, a clay pipe, an ounce of tobacco, a jug of ale, and a shilling. Those women or men who did not indulge in the habit of smoking, or chewing tobacco, were to receive an extra sixpence. The children were to have sweetmeats and nettle beer, or oatcakes crushed in buttermilk, at her expense, and a wooden plaything, to be dipped for as a surprise in a tub of bran. There would be barrels of ale provided for the working folk at the inns, and all would wear favours and great rosettes in plum and gold de Breos colours, and receive a commemorative tankard of Ewenny pottery, celebrating the nuptials of the happy pair. For the in-paupers at the workhouse, a special meal and ale were ordered, and each child was to be allowed to choose a new dress, or jacket and breeches from samples of cloth brought to them, in bright and varied colours, as unlike those drab and coarse-textured uniforms as it was possible to be.

Rosa Doonan was to attend the bride, a rare honour, and her dress was to be stitched in London, no less, for her measurements had already been taken, and a canvas-covered 'body' made to resemble her own exactly, and the gown fashioned upon it. Mistress Devereaux, Captain Devereaux's new bride, was also to act as matron of honour and chief bride-maid, for they were the closest of friends. Above all wonders, Jeremiah Fleet was to lead Miss de Breos down the church aisle, her hand resting upon his arm, and was to deliver her publicly into the safe-keeping of the bride-groom, in the absence of a father. She had begged him most particularly, Sophie Fleet confided, for he was as good as a father to her, and as dearly loved.

As the wedding day drew inevitably closer, perhaps it was not surprising that Rebecca felt the restrictions and responsibilities cast upon her as irksome. She had no qualms about her love for Joshua, or her desire to marry him, but wished that, like Elizabeth, she might be wed quietly, and without pomp and ceremony, in the chapel in the grounds. Yet she owed it to her grandfather, the estate tenants and her friends of the three hamlets and beyond to make the day memorable for them. It was not hard to recall how vividly, and with what pleasure, a happy event would be relived in a life of unremitting toil and deprivation. Yet she felt restless and ill-at-ease, unable to concentrate upon plans for the feasting and the firework celebrations planned for the staff and tenantry.

Without a word to Mrs Crandle, who would have dismissed the expedition out of hand or worse, insisted upon accompanying her, Rebecca took a light travelling cloak and bade the coachman drive her to Newton village in the smaller de Breos coach.

When she arrived at Joshua's cottage and dismounted with a footman's help, the young constable was stepping briskly on to his doorstep, in order to attend the justice at Tythegston Court.

'Rebecca?' His voice was anxious, perturbed. 'What brings you here? Something is amiss?' His eyes searched the interior of the coach. 'Where is Mrs Crandle? She is not unwell?'

'No. I came upon an impulse. I told no one.'

'An impulse, Rebecca?' He took her elbow fiercely. 'Have you no thought of what a stir it will cause? They will think you have eloped, ma'am, or been abducted, and will have half the militia in Glamorgan searching for you!' His grip tightened upon her arm. 'It was a stupid, irresponsible thing to do, and you will return this minute, else you will be sorely compromised.'

Normally she would have stamped her foot and defied him, and made some sharply barbed response, but so great were her fatigue and disappointment, and her humiliation before the servants that she burst into uncontrollable sobs and, despite Joshua's efforts, could not be comforted.

'You are making a scene, ma'am!' he declared helplessly, then, dispatching the coachman and footman to the Crown, bidding them seek refreshment and await his return, he bundled her inside the coach, and drove her, at once, to Jeremiah's cottage for Sophie's comfort, and that she might be properly chaperoned. There, with her woes spilled out to Mrs Fleet, and a strong reviving dish of tea, well-strengthened with medicinal brandy, she became more coherent and calmer as her hostess, upon some hastily devised pretext, left the betrothed pair together.

The protestations that Joshua no longer loved her being immediately and most convincingly stilled by a series of satisfactory kisses, Joshua declared that did he not love her so selflessly, he would have recklessly driven away with her the instant she set foot upon his doorstep! Yet only a blackguard and a rake would treat a respectable gentlewoman so, ruining her reputation and future.

'But I would gladly drive away with you, Joshua.'

'And I with you, my love, for the preparations, as the wait, grow tedious, and, above all things, I would be with you always. I beg you will not doubt it.'

Rebecca wept again and grew penitent, and they kissed and made promises and avowals of enduring love, as all lovers do, before Sophie diplomatically returned, with unusual noise and bustle preceding her coming.

'I will escort you as far as the justice's house at Tythegston, Rebecca, my love,' he promised, 'for that is where I am expected, but first I must return to the Crown and saddle my mare, and bid the coachman and footman accompany me here, that they may vouch for Sophie's role as duenna. You are rested now, more composed?' he asked anxiously. 'For you were so pale and tearful that my heart bled within me.'

'Yes, Joshua, I am restored now, and most humbly beg your pardon, and Sophie's, too.' Sophie pretended an absorption with a loose thread upon the sofa as the pair embraced most tenderly, her presence forgotten.

'Why do you go to the justice's house?' asked Rebecca when her bonnet and cloak were fastened, and her equanimity restored.

'He has a wedding gift he wishes me to inspect, and approve.'

'You know what he intends, Joshua?'

'I believe a *garniture de cheminée*, of Sèvres porcelain, or so he has hinted.'

Rebecca clapped her hands together with real excitement, saying, 'Oh, what a delight! It will be most acceptable and treasured. Oh, what a dear man he is, Joshua. He is generous to a fault, do you not agree?'

'I would scarce phrase it so,' said Joshua, smiling indulgently, 'but I admit that it is a relief and pleasure. I had fears that it might be a fire-cart!'

Chapter Thirty

Upon her wedding morn, Rebecca arose unusually early, dressed herself with haste, and made her way secretly to the little octagonal gazebo in the garden. The midsummer sky was already luminous and clear, with small wisps of cloud, thin and gauzy as veils, already dissolving. The grass was wet with early-morning dew, and the scent of the roses heavy and full-blown, and the mingled odours of summer jasmine, honeysuckle and lemon thyme were both sweet and astringent. She looked back across the wide lawns and saw that her footprints were mistily silvered as with a frost, and every spider's web exquisite and delicately wrought, its filigree threads strung with transparent drops of moisture, ephemeral as tears.

She could not say why she felt so deep a sadness when all about was beautiful and virginal in its innocence, pristine, untouched. Perhaps because, like the drops of dew that beaded the spider's thread, and this solitary perfect moment, it would swiftly pass and never come again. Her mind returned to Jeremiah and the cottage, the bays and rock pools, her friends of the three hamlets, her grandfather, and all that had befallen her in her brief life. In a few swift hours, all would be changed. She would never again be as free and unfettered as now, but bound to another by flesh and blood, by caring, by her marriage vows. If the bonds were of her own choosing, and soft and fine as spider's thread, so that they seemed barely visible, she would know, and sometimes resent them and struggle ineffectually to be free, for ever bound by a society and convention from which she could not escape. Yet the bonds which secured her to Joshua, she would not try to escape, for they were bonds of loving and sharing, of spirit as of warm flesh and bone. All that she was, and would become, was in his keeping. There must be no more yearnings for the past, no regrets for the present, no fears for the future. She would go to him willingly, and with joy, because, without him, there would be nothing in life that had meaning.

She arose from the small bench where she had sat reflecting for too long, seeing as she did so that, already, the dew was fading from the lawns, sucked by the heat of the sun, and her footprints dying from the grass as if they had never been. A new day. An ending and a beginning.

Sir Matthew, too, had arisen early, for he had been unable to sleep, his mind not upon the rigours of the ceremony and the day ahead, or the guests already beneath his roof and those still to greet, but of his parting from Rebecca. He watched her, now, from the window of his library, as she returned across the lawns to the house from the rose garden. She was not unlike a rose, herself, in her gown of shaded pink, the matching slippers darkened with the wetness of dew. She glanced towards the library window, unexpectedly; seeing him, she raised a hand, her face alight with pleasure, her remarkable blue eyes so disturbingly like those of Edward, the son he had lost, that he felt the prick of tears behind his own eyelids.

Weakness and age, inevitable and inseparable, he thought, returning to his chair to await her coming. How cruel they are, and yet so gentle a preparation for death, perhaps, that we drift, gradual and unresisting, to the grave's edge and final ease from hurt. He thought of Emma, the wife whom he had so deeply loved, and Edward. Would they be old and wearied as he, he wondered, or had time ceased, and age, so that they would remain as Rebecca was now, beautiful in their youthful flesh and spirit? He hoped that all the ugliness of age and the misunderstandings upon earth which kept them apart would simply fall away, and they would be united again, as Rebecca and Joshua Stradling this day.

Rebecca did not knock upon the door, but entered smilingly to run to his side and fling her arms about his neck, kissing him with eager affection, before declaring impulsively, 'Oh, Grandfather, I love you so, and I shall miss you most desperately, for you are the dearest, kindest man I know, and the wisest.'

Sir Matthew smiled. 'I hope, my dear, that you will not tell Joshua so, for it is a distinction which should rightly be his!' He squeezed her hand reassuringly. 'You will be the most beautiful bride Southerndown Court has ever seen, my dearest girl.' His voice faltered and grew thin as the hand which held Rebecca's. He would have said, 'I shall miss you more than I can ever say,' but knew that the words would grieve them both, and sadden Rebecca's heart, as his own. 'I have a gift for you, my dear.' His hand reached out to the drawer of his desk as he brought out a jewel case of dark blue leather, tooled with gold leaf.

'But you have given me so much, Grandfather!' exclaimed Rebecca, truthfully. 'A home, your loving, a new life. All that I now am, and own, springs from you, even this wedding day, with all its kindnesses to recall and treasure.'

'You, my dear, are my living treasure,' declared the old gentleman, his eyes bright, 'for without you, my life was bereft.'

Rebecca knew the depth of pain her loss would bring him, for they had never before spoken with such rawness of feeling. She gently kissed his white hair, as his fingers, thin and fine-boned, prised open the lid of the jewel case. The diamond necklace and bracelet which lay upon the dark velvet gleamed bright and iridescent as the dew upon the shimmering strands of web, as the tears upon her lashes.

'I have never, in all my life, seen anything so beautiful!' she exclaimed, hesitating to put out a hand to touch them.

Sir Matthew fastened them gently about her throat and wrist, saying, 'Nor I, my dear, for even they cannot do you justice. You are a de Breos born, and will remain so, although, today, you take another's name. You told me, once, a long time ago, when first we met, that it was the people who bore it who made a name proud and respected. You recall?'

'Yes,' Rebecca's voice was low, 'I recall it, Grandfather.'

'You told me that you had always tried to be honest, and to do what was right, and asked if that were not enough.'

'And you replied, sir, that it was all that is required.'

He nodded. 'I knew, then, that all I had worked for, and all that I inherited and owned would be safe in your keeping, for you valued people above all else, as I value you. Be happy, my dear, for it is all in life which I now wish for.'

'How could I not be, Grandfather,' asked Rebecca, 'with you and Joshua to love and guide me?'

There was ceaseless bustle and feverish preparation by the servants at Southerndown Court, although the guests' carriages had long since borne them to the church in a flurry of elegance and aristocratic gaiety. Sir Matthew, too, had departed, dignified and handsome, Mrs Crandle, and even the bridesmaids, Elizabeth and Rosa, in their rustling gowns of rose-pink silk with matching circlets of gently opening rosebuds upon their prettily ringleted hair. Sir Matthew had gallantly declared that 'matrons of honour' was altogether too dowdy and austere a phrase for such charming young ladies, one so delicately fair and one so radiantly dark, and it would be a rare privilege and honour to escort them to their carriage 'neath the porte-cochere.

Now Rebecca and Jeremiah descended the curving sweep of staircase into the hall, her hand lightly resting upon his eloquently distinguished sleeve. Rebecca wore a gown of rich Macclesfield silk, cut low at the neckline to reveal the necklace of de Breos diamonds. The bodice was softly sculpted to the gentle curves of her breasts and body, tightly gathered at the waist, and falling into a long full skirt, unhooped, and subtly flowing with every gentle movement. Upon her dark hair, swept into a chignon from which fell a cascade of soft black ringlets, was a ring of fresh white orange blossom and myrtle, with rosemary for remembrance. Its fragrance, subtle and haunting, filled Jeremiah's senses as pleasingly as love and pride for her filled his heart.

His work-roughened hand fastened over Rebecca's gloved one, as he said, so quietly that it scarce seemed he had spoken, 'You are the dearest little maid who ever lived, Rebecca, and I shall treasure this moment, and the fragrance of it, until I die.'

Ruth and the servants gathered together in the hall below marvelled at Miss de Breos's loveliness, and the quiet serenity that touched her mouth and eyes, and they did not miss the look of love and happiness which she cast at Jeremiah Fleet before kissing him gently upon his grey-bearded cheek. He was a fine figure of a man, there was no doubting it, tall and splendid as an Old Testament prophet in his strength and vigour and, save for Sir Matthew himself, there was not a man amongst all the guests to match his natural dignity. With infinite tenderness, Jeremiah touched the delicate veil of Honiton lace that clouded to the floor.

As they rode by in the glass-sided carriage to the church, the lanes were spanned with beribboned archways of flowers, the pauper children as bright in their vivid new clothes, and scattering rose petals as they passed by. At every house and hedgerow upon the byway, and on the highway itself, people stood and cheered, the menfolk bowing formally and the women dropping swift curtseys, the progress of the carriage marked by a celebratory hail of gunshot which had Jeremiah declaring that had the battle with the French been fought with half such fervour, they would surely have surrendered upon the very first day!

At the church, Joshua and his brother, Aled, awaited Rebecca's coming, their height, handsome bearing and extreme elegance bringing self-satisfaction and a modest tear to Charlotte Stradling's eye, and admiration from every woman present, married or unwed.

The Bishop of Llandaff, Dr Peate, and the Reverend Robert Knight looked scarcely more sartorially splendid than the bride-groom and guests although, with most unclerical lack of charity, the rector had observed that, although his own gout still lingered, Bishop Copleston's indisposition seemed miraculously cured, and His Grace had unashamedly declared himself eager to enjoy the fruits of the marriage feast, and the vine, to the full.

When the music of Handel's Processional March signalled the arrival of the bride at the church door, Joshua felt a raw pulsing of his heartbeats, and such a quickening of nervousness that it all but stifled him.

He would not turn towards Rebecca, could not, and when at last he forced himself to glance at her, as she stood beside him, what he glimpsed was a stranger: beautiful, remote and with the cold untouchability of sculpted marble.

'With my body I thee worship . . . With all my worldly goods I thee endow . . . And forsaking all others cleave only unto thee . . .'

The words he repeated seemed alien upon his lips, the responses halting and unreal. He turned and looked into the face of the woman beside him. Her eyes gazed back steadily into his own, vividly blue, dark-lashed, filled with love and understanding. Below the glitter of diamonds at her throat he saw, pinned at her bodice, Jeremiah's simple brooch. She smiled gently, the Rebecca of old, honest and unchanged, pure in the constancy of her loving.

'From this day forward and for evermore.' The words were a promise and a hymn of praise. Joshua Stradling stretched out a hand to Rebecca, his wife.